DEATH ON CROMER BEACH

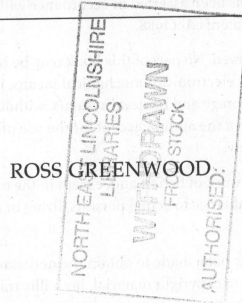
ROSS GREENWOOD

B

Boldwood

First published in Great Britain in 2023 by Boldwood Books Ltd.

Copyright © Ross Greenwood, 2023

Cover Design by Head Design

Cover Photography: Alamy

A CIP catalogue record for this book is available from the British Library.

Paperback ISBN 978-1-80415-693-3

Large Print ISBN 978-1-80415-692-6

Hardback ISBN 978-1-80415-691-9

Ebook ISBN 978-1-80415-694-0

Kindle ISBN 978-1-80415-695-7

Audio CD ISBN 978-1-80415-686-5

MP3 CD ISBN 978-1-80415-687-2

Digital audio download ISBN 978-1-80415-689-6

Boldwood Books Ltd
23 Bowerdean Street
London SW6 3TN
www.boldwoodbooks.com

Dedicated to the RNLI.
The crew, the volunteers, and those who donate.

For Catriona Woods
A right Royal mystery.

Only when there are seven
Can they rest in heaven
For nobody can deny
The Hungry Sea

— ANON.

NORFOLK MAJOR INVESTIGATION TEAM STRUCTURE

Detective Superintendent
Zara Grave

Detective Chief Inspector
Vince Kettle

Detective Inspector
Peter Ibson

Detective Sergeants
Ashley Knight – Bhavini Kotecha

Detective Constables

Hector Fade – Barry Hooper – Salvador Freitas –
Emma Stones – Jan Pederson

Family Liaison Officer
Scott Gorton

**Care Coordinator, Community Mental
Health Team**
Dylan Crabb

Forensic pathologist
Michelle Ma Yun

1

EARLY APRIL

Dora Thorne rested the basket on the concrete promenade, stared past the fishing boats out to sea, and hauled the salty air deep into her lungs. The sky was still a dark grey, but the soft glow on the far horizon hinted at the coming sunrise. A gust of wind brought tears to her eyes and a smile to her lips. There was nowhere quite like the east coast at that time of the morning.

After checking she could see well enough to pick her way through the stones, she lifted the basket again. Her chihuahua, Happy, looked up adoringly. He loved the dawn, too, but his feet were delicate, and he often whimpered on the sharp shingle.

She carried him past the high-tide line, through

the last of the shifting surface, and he jumped out. The scamp chased after three sandpipers as he headed for the nearby water's edge, making high-pitched 'ruff' sounds as they took to flight. Away from the shelter of the buildings, it was much windier than she'd thought, and the black waves sounded as if they were roaring in.

If the sea was calm during the summer, they'd both paddle, but the water was freezing at the start of April, so Happy splashed in the shallows and Dora kept to the sand.

This was the only time of day she came here now. Out of season, it was rare to see another soul while it was still dark. A few lurked on the cliff tops to catch the rising sun, but they were too far away to interrupt her special time. Nowadays, standing on the shore with her dog was the only place she felt truly at peace.

Dora turned right as always and headed south. Years ago, she and her husband used to walk the two miles along the beach to Overstrand. They'd head up the slope to the Cliff Top Café and order Norfolk smoked-bacon sandwiches with doorstop slices of crusty bread. Ketchup, butter, and contentment oozed between their fingers. She paused as the familiar lurching jolt hit her once more. Seven years now, and still the same response.

Joe had retired on his sixty-fifth birthday, and they'd sold up straight away in Oundle and moved into a bungalow close to Cromer seafront. He'd kidded that they were eloping to escape from their two kids, but their children both had busy lives in London. Joe also joked they were coming here to die. It was an unwelcome surprise when, a year later, he did just that. A good death, she supposed, warm in his bed, but the abrupt shock of waking up next to his stiff body had never left her.

Nothing had been the same since. Her existence had become a curling photograph slowly drying out in the sun. She'd only known one man intimately and had no interest in getting to know another.

A year later, she'd trudged alone along the shore, up the steep path once more to the café they'd loved, and ordered their usual. She wept when it arrived. The kind owner, Karen, tried to calm her, but Dora fled down the slope to the beach and collapsed in the sand. She had never gone back.

For months afterwards, she walked to the end of Cromer pier and stared at the wild North Sea. The swirling water below was called the Devil's Throat by locals, with its unforgiving rip tides and hidden depths. Dora dreamed of oblivion in those moments, and she prayed for the strength to embrace it.

But life still had a surprise for her. Three years back, her neighbour, Malcolm, had a litter of five to sell from his chihuahua. Four had been found homes. He brought the last one round, shivering on the flat of his hand.

'No charge,' he said. 'This one's the runt.'

'I don't want a dog.'

'Nobody wants him. All he needs is a happy home.'

Dora smiled at the Norfolk pronunciation of happy, which sounded as if he'd said harpy. She looked at the shivering creature and something long dormant stirred inside her.

'You look like you might need the company,' said Malcolm, who then pushed the animal into her arms on the doorstep and ambled away.

How had he known? Norfolk people seemed to understand such things.

Dora had called him Happy, because by the end of the first day of sitting on her lap he was, and that was how he made her feel. He'd been a weak puppy, but they'd grown stronger together through beach walks, rich tea biscuits and tuna steak. Dora loved that he was quiet and respectful, like herself. He rarely barked loudly and never made a mess. She'd saved him, and he'd saved her.

With a friend to live for, she rejoined society, even taking a part-time job in one of the town's many charity shops. Once a month, she had her hair styled and coloured, and most days she popped into the Doggie Diner café with Happy for a latte and a nice paw-shaped cookie for him. It was a special place for them.

Dora wiped her eyes, although this time the breeze wasn't to blame, and couldn't help grinning at Happy's joy as he raced up the beach ahead of her, scattering seabirds by the dozen. The narrow strip of wet sand that remained, which stretched into the distance, glistened like a mirror under his little feet as he scurried along it.

As the growing golden fingers of sunlight lit up what she always felt was never-ending sky, a rush of water almost caught her out. The wind, which was luckily an easterly, bullied her towards the flotsam and jetsam that had been deposited by the previous high tide. She jerked her head to her left. With the quickening dawn, she could now make out the size-able white-tipped waves as the rising gusts ripped the tops from them.

Dora pulled her woolly hat down and inhaled

deeply, dragging the cold air deep inside her chest, then strode after the dog, feeling alive. The orange sun edged into view ahead of her and lit up the towering cloud bank with such an array of yellows and gold that she put a hand to her mouth. Dora ruefully wished she and Joe had made the move decades before they had, while his heart was still healthy.

After twenty minutes had passed, she'd made more progress than she expected, and they reached the steep steps that rose towards the lighthouse. It was time to go back. The clouds had won their eternal duel and vanquished the ball of fire. With it beaten back, the light dwindled. Once again, the lonely shore was a bleak and barren place. Dark clouds boiled and swirled above. A sea mist speckled her glasses. She'd need to head home now or the flat sand would be covered, and she'd have to carry Happy over the shingle.

Dora had a good whistle on her. In fact, Joe always said it was the first thing he'd fallen in love with when they'd met at college and were cheering on the same rugby team. She put two fingers in her mouth to call Happy back, but stopped when he barked. It was a deep, rasping sound she'd never heard him make before.

A screeching howl of the wind wrenched the hat

off her head and blew it up into the air and away, but she paid it no heed. She stared ahead. A tension crept into her shoulders. Happy was standing next to two black shapes much further up the beach. Dora moved as quickly as she could, misjudging a deep puddle in front of a groyne. Her boots instantly filled with freezing water, but she staggered onwards to her beloved pet.

To her surprise, Happy then let out a noise that could only be described as a snarl.

An icy hand with bony fingers encircled Dora's heart. He'd never made that sound before, either. She slowed as she neared him. The dark shapes were two big black builders' buckets, upside down, with boulders balanced on them. They appeared wedged into a slight incline on an isolated patch of less packed, drier sand, but still below the line of plastic rubbish and old nets that indicated the last high tide.

Dora looked to her left at the incoming sea. From this slightly higher elevation, she could see big rollers rising and dumping closer than she'd imagined. The threatening, crowded clouds had descended now and churned overhead. Weather turned on a sixpence down this coastline. They really had to leave the beach.

Another wave hurtled towards her, died, then vanished into the sand less than a metre from the buckets, leaving fizzing foam around Dora's feet. Her knees trembled. Behind the bucket on the right of the two, a spade had been driven into the stones like a marker, or, she realised, a tombstone.

Happy growled again. It was a low, continuous sound that brought the hairs up on the back of her neck, even under her warm scarf.

All she wanted to do was grab him, stick him in his basket, and flee, but Dora knew she had to take a peek. The gathering gale billowed her clothing, lifting her thin hair in a mad dance. She stepped towards the bucket on the left. After a deep breath, she moistened her dry lips, bent down and removed what she now saw was a large building block, worn smooth by the relentless elements.

She dropped the brick, then glanced back at the bucket. Her heart hammered in her chest. She could feel a vein pounding on the side of her head. Dora slowly reached down and rested her hands on the sides of the plastic. She took a deep breath, and another, then quickly yanked the bucket high in the air, while stepping back, as if she expected a creature underneath to leap up at her throat.

Happy's growl stopped.

It was hard to see what was there through her

blurred glasses, so, with a nervous hand, Dora removed them.

On the sand in front of her, with long grey hair slicked down in a centre parting and buried up to his neck, was a man's head.

2

Dora stared down in utter disbelief. His eyes were
closed. A blast of wind buffeted the head, causing
something to emerge from the gaping mouth. Dora
was half-expecting a small crab to scuttle out, so she
was relieved when it was a thin trail of watery
blood.

It wasn't until a rush of sea water knocked the
head over, causing it to roll down the sand past her
into the choppy surf, that she shrieked. It was a high
soprano note, which tailed off. The only time she'd
made it before was the morning she'd woken next to
her husband's stiff body.

She turned and watched the receding wave pull
the head away with it. Another enormous wave rose

like a yawning mouth, and the head disappeared as though devoured.

As her attention slowly returned to the other bucket, she noticed a movement fifty metres away up near the cliff steps. Without her glasses on, she couldn't make out what it was, but it seemed human-sized.

'Help!' she yelled, but her cry dwindled as she realised it might be the person responsible.

Dora's gaze dropped to the second bucket, which Happy was now staring at, looking anything but worthy of his name. His keening sound tore at her weakening resolve, but she managed to control her bladder. She made a step to the right, then another. She should just leave.

Dora pulled her mobile out of her pocket, but there was never any signal on Vodafone down here, so she put it away. She removed the moisture from the lens of her glasses with a finger, then put them back on and peered to the right towards Cromer. She could make out the pier, but that was it. Would tractors be dragging the boats to the water's edge in weather like this? The fishermen and women would help her if they were there, but they were nearly half a mile down the beach.

Dora staggered in that direction, boots splashing

in the shallow surf, but Happy didn't follow. She twisted around to see he'd sat on his haunches next to the other bucket with his back to her. He tipped his head and whimpered. The seagulls above joined in. The haunting dawn chorus wrenched at her, and rising panic threatened to override her fragile control.

She took a deep breath. Then another. The dead can't hurt you, she reminded herself. Dora returned to her loyal companion, crouched, and placed a hand on his head. He glanced up with white showing around his eyes. She stood, undid her coat, and pulled the bottom of her shirt out from her jeans to properly clean her glasses. She frantically stared across at the wooden cliff steps, scanning the surrounding area, but the dog and she were alone. Then she noticed a tent fifty metres or so along the cliff, half hidden by tall grass.

Dora's eyes narrowed at what might be inside that, and decided she was going nowhere near it.

Instead, she lifted the worn piece of concrete off the second bucket and dropped it to the side. Another wave crashed behind her. The eager water encircled the bucket before retreating. Dora had to force herself to reach down. Her hands felt weak and slid up the wet plastic instead of lifting it. She gritted her teeth, seized it hard, and raised it up. Underneath was another head.

This one appeared to be a female with short grey hair. Dora didn't make a sound. At least not until the woman's eyes opened. Then they screamed together.

seized it hard, and raised it up. Underneath was another head.

3

Dora pulled in a deep breath, tipped her head back,
then screeched again. When she looked down, she
half expected the sand in front of her to be empty.
Perhaps she'd mixed her pills up somehow, but when
she focused, the woman's eyes were burning into hers,
vividly aware of the inevitable progress of the relentless tide.

Happy yelped loudly next to the head, and the
seagulls kept up a cacophony of screams to reinforce
her sensation of having descended into hell. The
woman tried to shout over the dawn chorus, but her
speech was slurred as though she was drunk, and, despite having good hearing, Dora only made out the
last two words by lip-reading them.

Help me.

Dora dropped to her knees, the arthritis in them sending shooting pains up her thighs and into her back. Dora's weak and rheumatic hands clawed at the sand in desperation. She managed to reveal the grey, pallid skin of the woman's neck and the top of a red coat. Dora glanced up into frantic eyes.

'Can you help dig yourself out?' she bellowed.

The woman shook her head as best she could, eyes rolling in their sockets. Her reply was a gasp. Dora realised she must have shouted herself hoarse.

'Tied,' the victim mouthed.

Before Dora had chance to respond, a much bigger thumping sound came from behind her. This time the sea submerged her walking shoes, drenched her jeans, and streamed past the woman's head up to her mouth, leaving it like an island with eyes above a vast lake. Happy, who'd been barking at the sea, was bowled over. He bayed when he got to his feet. The water subsided, and the woman's head tipped back to rest on the wet sand as she silently cried.

Dora knew enough from playfully burying her children on the beach when they were young that there was no way at her age she had the strength to dig this woman out of the wet sand, even with the spade that had been left next to the buckets. Dora glanced back towards the pier. Her mind slowed, and she found herself thinking rationally. If she jogged, she might make it to the fishing boats in five minutes. There would be someone younger there.

Dora looked down at the woman, who was spitting out seawater. She seemed to realise what Dora planned to do. Dora heard the woman's shout clearly this time.

'No! Don't leave me.'

Dora grabbed the two stones that had been on the buckets and put them in front of the lady's face to make a small barrier.

'I'll fetch help.'

'No, pull me out!'

Dora looked where she'd dug at the woman's shoulders. The tide had filled the hole.

'I'm so sorry. I'll be back.'

Dora rose, face a grimace, then, for the first time in decades, she ran. Further along, the sea had covered the packed sand, forcing her to stagger into the treacherous and unforgiving shingle. Her chest tightened as she lurched and slipped in the loose pebbles.

She stumbled and almost fell. Her breath rattled and wheezed in her throat. Tired legs pleaded with her, but she picked herself up and pushed herself forwards. She and Happy had walked all around Cromer and the surrounding villages for mile upon mile. Dora considered herself fit, and not just for her age. She gritted her teeth and drove herself faster.

Dora heard another cry, or maybe a caw, and peered up. The sky echoed with the screams of circling gulls. Happy raced past her like a greyhound, seemingly now untroubled by the shifting surface.

Behind him, a thick wave crashed down. The seething mass of the cruel sea surged forward, and swept over the woman's head.

4

Detective Sergeant Knight was already awake when the call came. The ringing tone was distant and muffled due to the phone being in the pocket of a pair of hastily discarded jeans downstairs on the lounge floor. Bethany, the other occupant of the bed, waved her hand around as though waving for a taxi.

'Answer it, or Marnie will wake up,' she hissed.

There was no need to worry about waking Bethany's daughter because it'd gone to voicemail, but even though the sergeant wasn't on call, it was time to get up, anyway. Ashley Knight slid from the covers and left the room. There was an attempt to stay quiet on the stairs, but it was an impossible task. Each step on the thin carpet was like treading on a mouse.

Downstairs, Ashley found the phone. The display revealed the call was from work. Ashley concluded they could wait a few minutes, seeing as it was a rest day, and pulled on underwear and the crumpled pair of jeans. It took a few seconds to sort through the pile of clothes that had been abandoned on the sofa the night before.

The clock on the mantelpiece chimed for 7 a.m. Ashley decided there was still time, so nipped back up the stairs and said goodbye to Bethany.

'Hey, that was work, so I'm going to head off.'

'That's for the best.'

Ashley detected a tightening around Bethany's eyes and tried to lighten the moment.

'I know. I don't want to outstay my welcome.'

Bethany didn't reply. A shadow crossed her face, which reminded Ashley that the purpose of last night's visit wasn't for the normal arrangement of booze and sex. Bethany tugged the duvet over her head and rolled towards the wall.

Ashley's cheeks rose into a grin at the expanse of dimpled bottom that was now exposed, but the smile gradually distorted into a frown. Bethany's obvious decision, when she delivered it, would hurt.

After a pocket rummage, Ashley slipped three twenty-pound notes onto the chest of drawers near the door, then, after a final rueful glance, returned downstairs.

The number for Control appeared twice on the phone's recent calls, so they'd both slept through the first ring after all. Ashley hit redial, stepped out of Bethany's front door, then began the fifteen-minute walk home. A young female voice answered.

'Control room, Jenny Groves.'

'Hi, this is DS Knight.'

'Morning, Sergeant. Thanks for calling back. There's been a deadly incident.'

The phrase brought a smile. Jenny Groves had visited them all at the Major Investigation Team's office at Wymondham near Norwich as part of her training and sat with the team for an entire day. She'd been very professional and that came across over the phone, but when it came to serious issues, she sometimes sounded dramatic.

'Okay, what is it and where?'

'It's a double homicide on Cromer beach.'

Ashley's eyes widened as Jenny rattled through the scant information she had.

'So, there's no immediate danger at the scene,' stated Ashley.

'Correct. Are you able to attend?' asked Jenny.

'I'm walking by the pitch-and-putt green towards

the town centre now. Which part of the beach did it happen on?'

'DI Ibson said to tell you it was two or three hundred metres past the Banksy, heading to Overstrand. He reckoned you'd know where that is.'

'Ah, so that's why you rang me.'

'Yes, DS Kotecha was on call, but she had to attend a violent domestic in Felbrigg. The inspector said you live in Cromer.'

'I do. Is the incident in Felbrigg connected to the Cromer one?'

'It doesn't appear to be.'

'Okay, I'll be at the beach in fifteen minutes or so.'

'Excellent. DI Ibson and DC Fade will meet you there.'

After cutting the call and sliding the phone into a back pocket, Ashley pulled the fleece zip up to chin level and crossed the road. It had been mild last night, and a coat hadn't been necessary, but it was noticeably colder with spots of rain in the air this morning, and there was a gusting breeze, which hurried the dark clouds above.

Uniform would control the scene, so there wasn't a mad rush, but a swift pace would help with the windchill. Besides, jogging and keeping fit had slipped off the agenda a long time ago, amongst many other things.

Christ, thought Ashley. Murders happened now and again in Norfolk, but it was years since there'd been a double one. The gruesome revelations from Control meant there might well be a fugitive hunt that morning.

It would be Easter soon and the crowds would come, but, right now, there wasn't another person about as Ashley hastened down New Street, past Golden Sands amusement arcade, towards The Wellington pub. Cromer was an interesting place to be a detective. Four months of the year, it was a ghost town, but the rest of the time it had a busy seaside vibe.

That rhythm added an enjoyable extra challenge because the seasons brought a variety of police work and that was what made it preferable to a big city for Ashley.

Even if you did manage to leave, Cromer had a habit of pulling you back, and Ashley had been no different.

It was a lively town, but it could be a dangerous one as well, and that, when it came down to it, was the real reason she stayed.

5

The tall seaside buildings sheltered Ashley from the elements, but she could already hear the rumble of the sea as she passed Windows ice-cream shop. The wind howled around what used to be her favourite pub, The Dolphin, and was now Lily-Mai's Bar and Grill. There were ghosts in Cromer, both people and places.

It was hard to believe that soon the streets would bustle with tourists, but at that moment, she was surrounded only by memories.

When she reached the Hotel de Paris, a stunning Regency period hotel that dominated the seafront, Ashley realised the threat of the coming storm. Low black and grey clouds stretched off into the distance.

It wasn't fully raining yet, but the air was damp and salty. There were two police estate cars, blue lights flashing, at the bottom of the gangway, but she carried on along the cliff top, knowing it was easier than walking along the beach.

She raced past the bust of Henry Blogg, which looked out to sea, then took the sloped path downwards in front of the pavilions. She peered at an ambulance below, which was parked up with flashing lights. Other emergency blues flickered in the gloom on the shore much further along.

The fishing boats were pulled close to the wall, so she almost missed the uniformed policewoman sheltering in the lea of one.

When the other woman spotted Ashley, she snapped straight, stepped forward and held out her hand in a stop motion.

'Sorry, madam. This area is closed.'

Ashley nodded as she pulled her warrant card from her pocket.

'DS Knight. MIT.'

'Sorry, Sarge. My partner's gone to get more tape, but we've cordoned off further up the beach.'

'Good. I take it the ambulance wasn't urgently needed.'

'It's hard to say. The woman who discovered the

bodies is inside being given oxygen. She was exhausted after running back from the incident.'

'But she still rang 999?'

'No, she managed to explain to a fisherman what happened. He had a signal, so he called it in. He left her propped up against a groyne, then went down to the scene.'

'Any survivors?'

'It doesn't sound like it.'

Ashley strode around the back of the ambulance, and knocked on the closed doors. The familiar lined face of a paramedic appeared along with a gust of warmth.

'Hey, Ash, long time,' the woman said, with a thick Scottish accent.

'Good to see you, Joan. How's your patient?'

'Tough, she's had quite a shock. She says she'll be okay if I take her home. They'll send another bus later.'

Joan didn't need to state what the other ambulance would be picking up. Joan had been doing the job for nearly forty years. She was well aware the deceased wouldn't be taken to the morgue for a while.

Ashley looked back again at the lady who was lying on the bed staring at a basket on the other side of the ambulance. Ashley could see what she was interested in: two trembling furry ears were sticking out of it.

Ashley raised an eyebrow at Joan, knowing the paramedic would probably have asked the questions Ashley needed the answers to.

'Dora says her dog will want his breakfast,' said Joan. 'Her house is opposite The Grove, number five, if you want to talk to her in a bit. She told the fisherman everything, but it wasn't much. She just found the victims. Geoffrey's still at the scene. You know him.'

Ashley nodded with appreciation. Joan had saved her time by already asking for that information. It was always easier chatting with a paramedic than a detective, and it was a good way of seeing if the patient was on the ball.

Ashley froze.

'Mad Geoffrey?'

'Aye, the fisherman who used to drink with us in The Cottage. Only he'd be crazy enough to come here on a morning like this. Talking of which, I haven't seen you or him down The White Horse or The Welly for a while.'

Ashley had stopped going to pubs, what with all the drama of the last few years. She used to drink most regularly at The Cottage public house, but that had now been converted into flats. Ashley had heard the story, that it was in there many years ago that Joan had given Geoffrey the nickname. She'd told him off for swearing too loudly at a football match on the big plasma screen, and he'd memorably called her Joan of Arse. She'd screeched at him, 'Geoffrey, you're fucking mad.' Both nicknames had stuck, but only Geoffrey had his used in earshot.

'Geoffrey and I haven't eloped together,' said Ashley. 'To be honest, I've been trying to keep a lid on pub visits, if you get my drift.'

Joan nodded.

'Aye, of course. There are a few others gone as well. The world's getting expensive.' Joan glanced down at Ashley's fleece, then handed her a hi-vis yellow soft-shell jacket that was hanging up in the ambulance. 'Here, take this. It's gonna hammer down in a minute.'

Ashley put it on, shut Joan back in, then strode along the concrete promenade, already missing the warmth from the ambulance's heaters. As always, she experienced a twinge of guilt as the adrenaline kicked in and her pace quickened. She was almost trotting as she reached the multicoloured beach huts. Each gust from the wind felt like a shove from an invisible hand, and the first big blobs of rain fell on her face.

She dropped onto the stones where the Banksy had been painted on the sea wall and cursed her choice of footwear last night. She took ten paces to the right, then her loafers tapped along the top of an old concrete sea defence to delay her having to work through the shingle.

Up ahead, she could see a group of people milling around, most in uniform, others in long coats. She recognised Detective Inspector Peter Ibson's lean frame leaning into the breeze at the water's edge. As usual, he was sporting his undone light-grey raincoat. It flapped with each gust like a western gunfighter waiting for the stagecoach. Either he'd had the same one since she'd known him, or he kept buying the same style and colour.

It took a few minutes for her to reach the flickering police tape that had been secured along a groyne and up to a bush on the cliff. The cliff, which towered a hundred metres above her on the right, seemed to be alive as the stubby trees that grew there swayed and bucked like tethered stallions.

Ashley recognised the uniformed officer at the tape but couldn't recall his name. He lifted it up for her without comment, and she trudged through the stones to Peter. Mad Geoffrey was next to him in a filthy-looking dark-blue donkey jacket. Another taller, much younger man was beside him in an expensive-looking black trench coat. They all appeared to be staring out to sea.

A wave crashed down in front of them, causing the police to scamper back, but Geoffrey had wellies on and held his ground. Ashley stood beside him when the water had retreated. The wind whipped her bobbed hair around, which was now wet, and stung her face as she followed his gaze. She reached into her pocket, hoping to find a hairband, then froze mid-movement.

As another wave built, the sea level dropped, and the top of a person's head appeared.

6

Ashley looked across at Mad Geoffrey.

'Was she buried alive?'

'Yep, for the sea to eat.' His eyes squinted. 'It's just about high tide, so whoever did it knew what they were doing. If she was buried any nearer the cliffs, she might have survived.'

Ashley watched the water until the swirling sea shallowed and the head was exposed again. There was something terribly surreal about it. For a moment, she let herself wonder where the part of her that should be struck dumb by such horror had vanished to, and whether it would ever reappear.

All Control had told her was that a woman had drowned, and a man had been decapitated. She found herself glancing right and left up the shoreline for the other body. Geoffrey commented, but the wind tore his words away. He leaned into her, close enough for her to see the thread veins spidering his ruddy cheeks. She had no idea how old he was. Working on the sea did that to a complexion. She got a blast of stale smoke as he bellowed in her direction.

'I picked the head up because the surf was rolling it onto the rocks.'

Geoffrey mimed a digger-claw action, then raised a grey eyebrow on his impassive face. Geoffrey and she had drunk together on the odd occasion when she was having her struggles. He was also in a bad place at the time after a boat in dry dock had fallen over and crushed his brother. They had attempted to work through their demons pint by pint.

'Not a sentence you imagined saying when you got up this morning,' she shouted back.

'No. Not one I ever thought I'd say. I knew the head would get battered rolling around on the stones, but I didn't know where to put it. So, I stuck it in the tent with the body. I held it by his long hair. Felt like I was in *Jason and the Argonauts*, or something.'

He jerked a thumb behind him towards a zipped-up green tent next to the cliff that was rocking with each gust. Two uniformed officers were at each end, holding on to the upright poles. Ashley was pleased there hadn't been time for breakfast. Looking inside wouldn't be easy on a full stomach. What made it worse was that working and living in Cromer meant she could guess who the two victims were. Apart from the young man in the expensive clothes, she suspected they all could.

'Ashley.'

Detective Inspector Peter Ibson had walked the few paces towards her.

'Sir,' she replied.

She called him Sir and Peter, but never Pete. Nine years she'd known him, and she knew very little about his life out of work. He lived a little more than a mile from Cromer in Overstrand, close to the Sea Marge Hotel, in a big imposing building set back from the road. A partner or children had never been mentioned or seen, nor a call taken from them.

Peter was a good boss though, or at least he used to be. He was teetotal and fit. If he worked at the weekend, he occasionally cycled there even though it was about thirty miles each way. That had all stopped this year, and Ashley couldn't help thinking that even on *this* beach, he would still be the most deathly looking.

'Detective Superintendent Zara Grave is at OCC

co-ordinating with the respective uniform inspectors,' he said. 'They've opened a command suite up for the initial stage of the investigation. Let's hope we catch whoever did this swiftly, because it will be our case. The media have been informed, and the usual steps are in motion. A roadblock has gone up on Over-strand Road, checking vehicles and pedestrians, but this happened more than an hour ago. Even walking, the perpetrator could be close to Sheringham.'

Ashley wondered where the DCI was if he wasn't at the OCC, which stood for the Operations and Communications Centre.

'How long for the body to be uncovered?' she asked Geoffrey.

'Tide's just turning. Maybe an hour.'

'Okay. Right, Geoffrey, you saw a head rolling in the waves and this woman under the water. Was there anybody else about?'

'Nope. The old woman told me nothing more, nei-ther. Said there might have been someone on the steps, but she couldn't be sure.' Geoffrey shook his head. 'I was only talking to Ron a few days ago. He oc-casionally came out on the boat with me. Liked a crab every now and again.'

'And it was definitely Ruby who was buried?'

'Yes. By the time I got here, the water was up to

her eyes. She was gone, thank fuck. No way I could've dug her out when the sea was past her, anyway. I'd have had to watch her die. I've seen grisly stuff in my years, but nothing like this.' He scowled. 'Ron and Ruby had no enemies. Doesn't make sense.' He rubbed a knuckle across his stubbled chin while shaking his head. 'I'm going to get going. My boat isn't secure enough for how bad this storm's gonna be.'

'Sorry, mate,' said Ashley. 'I'll need a statement from you this morning.'

Geoffrey's face hardened. Ashley had seen him fight many times over the years, but he was a straight-up guy, and the brain behind his weather-beaten visage was sharp enough for him to be unlikely to torment anyone five hundred metres from where his boat was kept.

'Were any other boats out? RNLI?' she asked him.

'Nope.'

Control would have put a call in to the coast-guard, but they or the RNLI would have been un-likely to appear. It was a beach incident and there had been no lives to save.

She glanced at Peter, who was again staring out to sea. The young man with him looked confused and uncomfortable.

Ashley called a PC over to escort Geoffrey to his

boat, saying she'd join them within the hour. Then she recalled where Geoffrey had been.

'Hang on, show me the sole on those wellies,' she asked him. 'What's your shoe size. I'm about to look at the scene and I'll be able to eliminate them.'

'Twelve,' he growled.

Ashley pulled out her phone while Geoffrey raised a foot. She took numerous pictures, then nodded at him. He turned and trudged away.

Ashley glanced around, analysing the area. There was drifting sand and rubbish up and down the beach. Geoffrey would have also trampled over the vicinity of the tent with Ron's head in his hands. Peter came and stood next to her and gave her a millisecond of eye contact.

'Yeah,' said Peter. 'We won't get much from here.' He pointed at the man a few metres away. 'This is Hector Fade. He's the one I told you was coming to join us for a while. Hector was the only person to pick up the phone first thing. Kindly said he'd come here, even though he was only supposed to be looking around the office today. Sal just texted to say he'd head straight to the office and help set up the incident room. The others haven't responded.'

Hector walked over and shook Ashley's hand,

while she pondered where the rest of her team would be.

'Nice to meet you, Hector.' She turned back to Peter. 'Barry hasn't got any friends and doesn't live far from here,' she said. 'I'll give him a try when I've got a signal. Who was on the domestic?'

'Bhavini, and she did a full night,' replied Peter. 'It sounds like a messy GBH with mental health complications, so she's out of the equation. You live here in Cromer, so you're going to be point for this. Come and look at the body.'

Peter and Hector walked towards the tent, and she followed. Hector passed her a pair of plastic gloves and shoe covers from his coat pocket, having correctly assumed she didn't have any. As she pulled them on, she observed two uniforms making their way down the steep cliff steps behind the tent, and another two police 4x4s were trundling in their direction next to the high-tide line.

She was pleased to find stepping plates down to make one path towards the tent. Ashley tested the balance of the first plate, then carefully walked along them. She stopped at the last one and realised the others hadn't followed.

'We've seen inside,' shouted Peter.

She nodded to the two constables at either end of

the green tent, then paused at the entrance. It seemed decent quality material with double layers, but one of the guy ropes appeared to have been cut, which was why the constables were holding it down.

She looked around the front of the tent at the sand. There were a lot of marks and imprints, but they were already blurred by the effects of the breeze. She had a glimpse at her phone at Geoffrey's soles. He was a heavy man, and she could only pick out a couple of his footprints.

Ashley crouched, which gave her a bit of shelter from the wind, unzipped the tent door, held her breath, then poked her head in. She released a slow breath as she surveyed the scene.

The inside was two metres square. It was a mess in there, with sleeping bags and clothing covering the floor. Toilet paper and newspapers, books, and food items were scattered around. The stench of death was strong even with the wind finding its way in via a rip that she noticed at one of the corners.

Ron's body lay in the centre of the tent, socked feet towards the entrance, arms by his sides. His khaki shirt and trousers were damp and dark, soaked in his own blood. There were squirts of it on the sides of the tent and the apex, suggesting it was arterial blood. This indicated the solid-looking hacksaw, which rested on his legs, had been used to remove the head while Ron's heart was still beating.

Ashley was forced to take shallow breaths as she took her time analysing the interior. She spotted a slit in the fabric at the bottom of the deceased's shirt near the last two buttons. She lifted the end of the shirt up. There appeared to be a stab wound in the stomach.

Ashley backed out and pulled the tent zip down, blowing hard to expel the smell of human waste and blood from her lungs. She noticed two pairs of well-used sturdy walking boots next to the tent, which had been almost covered by the shifting sand, but her mind was still on the head that had been placed on the victim's chest.

It was another image to add to the others that she kept in her mind. They would all be with her until her dying day.

7

Peter and Hector were talking to three people in light-blue PPE suits when Ashley stood back from the tent and glanced around. They must have arrived in one of the 4x4s. She recognised the short, thin frame of Michelle Ma Yun, the forensic pathologist for the area. She had a habit of listening with her chin raised and an ear cocked even when it wasn't blowing a hooley.

The other two were crime scene investigators. The man looked like Dracula, even from forty metres away, which was the nickname Barry had given him, but he was a relatively new manager, and Ashley couldn't remember his name. Peter was showing them photographs on his phone.

Their CSI van wouldn't have coped with the shingle, but in a few hours hard sand would be exposed and more vehicles could get closer. Difficult access was the worst part of incidents on a beach. It slowed the initial investigation down when speed was of the essence.

That said, this wasn't the movies. It would take CSI all day, maybe two, to process the scene. For a start, the area would need to be photographed and videoed. That would include all the possible exits, entrances, and routes between, which was going to be tricky when the murderer could have come either way up the beach, down from either of two directions from the cliff top, or even made their arrival and exit on a boat.

Then every footprint, partial footprint, trace of footprint had to be measured, diagrammed, and photographed with scales besides them. Blood spills would be assessed. Were they drops, smears, or splatters? They'd need recording in the same way as the footprints. Blood samples would need to be taken from all areas and their location recorded in diagrams and photographs.

For crimes of this magnitude, often those who weren't on call would attend to help. Careers were defined by cases like these. The sooner the body was back at the hospital mortuary for a thorough examination, the quicker they would know an exact cause of death, but the scene itself couldn't be rushed.

The pathologist, Michelle, left Peter and made her way to Ashley. She grinned widely.

'Ash, we have to stop meeting like this.'

'It's the only way I can be sure to see you,' replied Ashley.

They shared another smile. Michelle lived about twenty minutes away in Mundesley, but she often came to Cromer to see her parents. For years, Ashley and Michelle had been saying, 'Let's get a coffee or a drink out of work,' but it had never happened. They occasionally joked that they were busy, but Ashley suspected that, outside their careers, neither of their lives were.

Even though Michelle was an attractive bubbly woman in her mid-thirties, she had a quirky intelligence that men struggled to deal with. She absolutely loved post-mortems, which even Ashley found a little weird.

'Peter's given me a rundown and shown me a photograph of the deceased in the tent, but he seems distracted. Is he okay?' asked Michelle.

'He's struggling a bit at the mo.'

'Who's the film star he's with?'

'My new partner.'

Michelle raised an eyebrow. They stopped talking as Dracula joined them.

'It's Ashley, isn't it?' he said. 'I'm Gerald Buckley, if you've forgotten. Terrible scene conditions. What do you want to know asap?'

'The usual. Someone's come down here and attacked Ron and Ruby. There's a stab wound. I'd guess Ron was knifed in the stomach to incapacitate him, then the perp's sawn his head off. Most likely while he was still breathing, so Ruby was probably also wounded to stop her escaping. Then she's been buried alive in the sand at the water's edge as the tide came in.'

'Were those their names? Ron and Ruby,' said Michelle. 'I'm not much of a beach person, but I think I've seen him walking in town with another similar type, hand in hand.'

'Yes, it's got to be them,' said Ashley. 'This type of crime where a statement is made makes me suspect a gang angle, drugs, that sort of thing, but that doesn't fit at all with these two victims. Most people would call them hippies. I can't see it being an argument that got out of hand either, so that has me thinking it's a psychopath. I suppose it's also possible there were multiple offenders, but it's too gruesome for kids.'

'You'd need to be strong to dig in this sand, so whoever it was would be fit,' said Gerald.

'Agreed,' said Michelle. 'You wouldn't believe the amount of folk that end up in a pathology department after digging. It's hard work.'

'So, Gerald,' said Ashley. 'At this point, I'm most interested in the danger to the public. Is the bladed article that caused the stomach wound in the tent? Are there any other weapons in there?'

'Understood,' he replied.

'The fisherman who placed the head back in the tent and some of the police have thoroughly stomped the surrounding sand,' said Ashley. 'With this wind and rain, we won't get much outside the tent full stop, but a guess on the number of attackers would help.'

'No problem,' said Gerald. 'If I see anything obvious, I'll ring in straight away. I'll specifically look for anything unexpected, but I tend to do that first anyway. Judging by the clouds, this scene will worsen as the morning progresses, so we'll prioritise.'

'I'll let you guys crack on,' said Ashley.

The misty rain and the big isolated spots that had alternately fallen seemed to have combined and were now being swept horizontally across the beach. Out to sea, the sky was almost black.

Ashley returned to Peter and Hector. Hector was

again staring at Ruby's head as the retreating tide lifted her hair up and down in a way that reminded Ashley of a jellyfish. Peter was looking at her with a nonplussed expression on his face.

'What's the plan, Peter?' shouted Ashley a bit too loudly.

He blinked three times. Ashley had seen what was happening to her boss before during her two-decade career. Slow breakdowns were common in the police. Peter hadn't been the same since they pulled the bodies of two young students out of the sea a year ago at Happisburgh. He took a month off afterwards, which had been called accrued holiday, but Ashley had her suspicions.

When he returned, he was capable, but he'd changed. Weight dropped off him, and the bags under his eyes became heavy. He'd always been reserved, so perhaps it wasn't too obvious to others. But only a few weeks ago, Ashley suspected he'd been crying in his office.

Sometimes it was just one incident that finished a career, other times it was an accumulation. It was only a few months back that a young PC on probation had resigned after being first on the scene to a cot death.

Peter had been in the job for nearly thirty years. If

his career was Jenga, then this day's horror might well be the brick that would bring it all down.

'Erm, er, what do you think?' he asked.

Ashley was in a dilemma. She felt for him, but if he was incapable of taking control of the situation, he should go home.

'You look a bit rough. Are you sure you're all right?'

'Yes, it's okay. I'll be fine,' he replied, seeming anything but.

She blew out her cheeks.

'Okay, there's no point in us hanging around here. If you return to OCC, I'll take Hector with me and have a proper talk with Geoffrey. Then I can do the same with Dora, who only lives down the road. Geoffrey knows this beach like the back of his hand, and he'll give me the backstory on the victims. He's a volatile bloke. If I tell him now that we need his clothes, he might explode.'

'Especially if he did it,' said Hector.

It was the first time she'd focused on Hector's speech. His accent was quite posh, but not from anywhere near Cromer. Seeing as Ashley knew what his father did, she guessed it was from south London.

'Yes, all things are possible,' she replied. 'Although I suspect he'd be covered in blood if he did it. I'll ring

Barry to make him aware we'll need to analyse Geoffrey's clothing.'

She hated to second-guess her line manager, but what did or didn't happen at that moment would have consequences further down the line. Then she spotted Peter's boss striding up the beach. DCI Kettle was one of those people who put others on edge. He was brusque to the point of rudeness, but he'd gone through the ranks and knew how to get the best out of his team.

'Come on, you,' she said to Hector, leaving Peter standing alone.

She walked towards Kettle and updated him on the morning's events. He glanced at Hector.

'Tough first day, son, but you'll cope,' he said. 'Could you give us a moment?'

When Hector had moved away, Kettle clenched and unclenched his jaw.

'Is Peter in control?'

Ashley almost smiled. It wasn't surprising that he'd noticed Peter's decline. Kettle missed little. Ashley knew the answer. Police rarely pulled the rug from their colleagues, but things had gone too far.

A solid rain fell as she looked him in the eye.

'No, sir, he's not.'

8

Kettle stared hard at her from under his thick black eyebrows. He was short, bald, round, and had hunched shoulders with no neck. Kind of like a cannonball. That description suited his temperament, too, but he was fair, and he had a quality that Ashley believed came above all others: common sense.

'Okay, Ashley. Take your statements. Find next of kins. There'll be a meeting at OCC at midday. Be there. This is your hometown, isn't it?'

Ashley nodded.

'Excellent. Ready for acting DI?'

'No, sir.'

'You're still not interested in progression?'

'Nope. I'm no desk jockey.'

'Understood, but I'll need your guidance on this. I'll be SIO, but you're going to be my number one.'

Ashley shrugged as he stamped away through the shingle towards the tent. Her being busy as deputy senior investigating officer was probably good, seeing as the Bethany thing was coming to an end. She walked past Hector and gestured for him to follow her as she trudged to the ambulance and Geoffrey's boat, feeling bedraggled. Her jeans hung heavy from the knees down where Joan's coat hadn't reached, and her socks were already sodden from her feet sinking into the wet sand.

Back near the pier, a large red vehicle had arrived at the bottom of the gangway, which was a hundred-metre concrete ramp at the bottom of the town giving access to the beach for boats and vehicles alike. She didn't envy the fire crew their job of digging Ruby out of the sand.

The wind had shifted and pushed at their backs, meaning she and Hector received a little appreciated assistance as they strode along the promenade back to Dora and Geoffrey. The paramedic, Joan, was about to close the rear of her ambulance when they arrived.

'How's the patient?' asked Ashley.

'Dora is doing well. She's in great nick. Pulse

good, BP great. I reckon she'll live to a hundred and fifty.'

Inside the ambulance, Dora gave Ashley a tight grin, indicating that living for so long might not be the greatest news, but she did look remarkably calm, if a little tired.

'I'll take her and the pooch home and make her a cup of tea if I'm not called elsewhere,' said Joan. 'It's on my way back to Norwich. She'll be fine for a chat with you later.'

'Okay, thanks for your help,' said Ashley, beginning to take off the jacket Joan had given her.

'Give it me back later. We've got plenty of coats. It's the people to put inside of them that we're short of.'

Ashley nodded and walked towards the fishing boats. She found Geoffrey and the PC who'd gone with him out of the rain in the wheelhouse of Geoffrey's boat. She could hear them laughing.

Geoffrey had been a crazed individual when he was younger, which had led to him having a lengthy criminal record in his youth, but he'd mellowed with time. At least a little, anyway. He was hard to dislike, even if you were always a touch on guard when you were in his company. Any involvement with something like this seemed unlikely, but Ashley had been wrong before.

She shouted up for them to come out. When they appeared, she thanked the PC, who appeared disappointed to be venturing back out into the cold and wet.

'Geoffrey,' she said. 'Have you got a change of clothes on the boat?'

'Of course.'

'Bring them with you.'

Geoffrey scowled but went back into the wheel-house, grabbed a sports bag, and hopped down off the boat.

'Where's your car, Hector?' asked Ashley.

'Near a café. I parked at some gates and walked past a small boat pond and another coffee place. I've lost my bearings.'

'Come on. You too, Geoffrey. We'll talk in the café at the traffic lights.'

They left the beach and strolled towards North Lodge Park. Ashley stared at Hector, who didn't seem fazed by being wet through. She'd been told a few weeks back that a constable was joining them from the Fast Track promotion programme. The idea was that they gave these constables experience in a variety

of different departments. Then they were rapidly promoted through the ranks.

It wouldn't be an overstatement to say the programme was contentious. The rank and file waited
years for positions to arise, whereas it felt like the
young university leavers had all the opportunities
given to them. It got many people's backs up, because
eventually, these kids would end up as the managers
and their experience was limited, or even missing. It
would also be fair to say that one or two of them had
been utterly useless.

Ashley was generally okay with it, though. The
force needed bright young minds in a rapidly devel-
oping world. Technology was changing almost daily,
which affected the crimes they investigated as well as
the techniques they used. She also thought a touch of
competition in the team helped people keep up with
these changes. It would be interesting to see what
type of person Hector would turn out to be, and,
more importantly, if he saw this as an opportunity to
learn, or just a box to tick.

She scowled at the graffiti that had been scrawled
on the walls of the lovely building inside the park,
which could be hired out as a wedding venue. Ashley
tutted. Someone had painted the number thirteen in

black on the left of the door and the number seven on the right.

It was a large nineteenth-century stone and brick house built in the Tudor style, dressed in flint stone. She'd occasionally imagined getting married there.

'Unlucky if you're tying the knot today,' she said with annoyance. 'They might have at least had a go at cleaning it off.'

'Perhaps it's recent,' Hector replied.

'Yeah, maybe. Shame graffiti isn't a major crime, it's just so annoying and pointless.'

They exited the park, turned right, and entered Henry's café, which was empty save for an old guy tucking into scrambled egg on toast. Geoffrey asked for a skinny latte, which made him and Ashley chuckle seeing as he didn't look the type. She ended up ordering three of them while Geoffrey found a seat.

'Were you in CID before this?' she asked as she and Hector waited at the counter.

'Yes. Six months at the Yard.'

'And how is Scotland Yard?'

'Busy.'

'Let me guess. Tonnes of paperwork. Few investigations except for those that are the proverbial fish in barrels. Lots of domestic and mental health cases.

Plenty of pissing in the wind, while placating a dis-
gruntled and unhappy public.'

Hector raised an eyebrow.

'Pretty much.'

'Would you like to lead this chat with Geoffrey?'

'It's your turf. Are we taking a statement?'

'No. I know Geoffrey, so someone else will need to
do the full initial account. I'll get Barry to pick him up
and he'll take a statement at Wymondham after
taking Geoffrey's prints and clothing. Take notes
while I have a quick probe and butt in if you have a
thought. I'll talk to Geoffrey if necessary later on, but
I've no idea where we're going with this at the moment. He's not a suspect. Let's see what he says.'

'He might disappear afterwards.'

Ashley ignored the comment as she paid for the
drinks.

'Take these to Geoffrey at the table and make
small talk. I'll ring Barry Hooper to pick him up.'

She nipped outside and stared at the minimal
traffic while the phone rang.

'What is it?' answered Barry.

'Morning, Barry.' She couldn't help emphasising
the Barry part. He'd been a solid member of the team
for years now, but he could be less than professional.
When he first arrived, he told everyone his nickname

was Hoops, because he loved basketball. Obviously, they all called him Barry to piss him off. 'You heard about the murders?'

'Yes, an hour ago. I'd be leaving for the office if you weren't wasting my time.'

She laughed and gave him an update of what she wanted him to do.

'I'll see you in half an hour,' he replied.

'And, Barry – that fast-tracker started today. He seems all right, and on the ball, so be nice.'

'Wanker,' said Ashley to herself after Barry didn't reply and just cut the call. She called the office. Emma picked up.

'Hey, Emma. Glad you made it in.'

'Yes, my poor mum stepped up.'

'Got a pen?'

'Fire away. We've had news filtering in that two have been killed on the beach.'

'Yes, it's a Ron and Ruby Jerrod. I'll double-check the surname, but I think that's right. No fixed abode. Can you and Sal look for next of kin, see what we have on file, if anything? He's got minor previous, but years old. I suspect she's clean. We're talking to the two witnesses we have so far who were both on the beach, but there's nothing obvious. Barry is going to bring in a fisherman called Geoffrey to the station for a statement. We'll need to take his clothing just in case, but he's not a suspect at the moment.'

'Sound's intriguing.'

Ashley smiled at that comment and said goodbye. Geoffrey and Hector were sitting in silence when she returned to the café. Hector had his notebook out.

'Okay, Geoffrey,' she said. 'We'd like to hear about your morning, from getting out of bed until I turned up.'

Geoffrey's big, calloused hand raised the latte, and he took a noisy slurp.

'Woke up at five, as normal. Kicked Kate Moss from my sheets, after giving her the time of her life. Then went to the beach to work on my boat.'

'Even though you knew a storm was likely coming?' asked Hector.

'That was why. I had a wheelhouse window rattling, and I like to double-check everything nowadays. I'm more forgetful, so I wanted to be certain that anything loose was tied down.'

'When did you arrive?' asked Ashley.

'Just before six, as it was getting light. Everything was sweet, so I was gonna call it a day when I saw a woman staggering towards me on the beach.'

'Dora Thorne,' said Hector.

'If you say so. I hadn't met her before. Lots of dog walkers visit the beach. I pay 'em no heed.'

'What did she say?'

'She was gasping but managed to say there was a woman buried in the sand, and a head. I thought she said *ahead*, so maybe there were two people in trouble. You get a lot of folk who don't give the ocean its respect around here, and more than a few who are drunk and fall asleep below the high-tide line. Not in spring, so much, but the summer, for sure.'

'So, you left her and ran down the beach,' said Ashley.

'My running days are finished, babe, but I've got long legs. Couldn't believe my eyes. Ruby was dead, or good as. I looked for the other person and saw a head further up, but out of the water. I thought it was another buried woman but hoped they were alive cos it was closer to the shore and moving a bit. Then a big wave rolled it up the beach and onto the rocks. I paused and had a moment.'

'What were you thinking?' asked Hector.

Ashley noticed Geoffrey's knuckles tighten on the mug. He leaned towards Hector.

'I was wondering whether to have pie or steak for tea. What the fuck do you reckon I was thinking?'

'I don't know. That's why I'm asking,' replied Hector calmly.

'I was wondering, what sick bastard would have done this, and are they still about?'

'Was anyone else there?'

'No, or you'd have three bodies. I rang 999 and said there'd been a murder. There wasn't much to tell them apart from the obvious.' Geoffrey took another slurp. 'It's close to home, this is. I knew Ron and Ruby both reasonably well. Went to school with Ron's older brother. He was a bit of a prick, God rest his soul, but Ron was harmless. Him and his wife were part of the scenery down here. I haven't got a clue what kind of sicko did this to 'em.'

'They weren't involved in crime?' asked Hector.

Geoffrey leaned his head to the left and sneered at Ashley.

'Who's he? Youth Training Scheme?'

'Remind me of Ron's surname, please,' said Ashley.

'Jerrod.'

'Cheers. So his brother's not around.'

'Nah, overdosed, yonks back.'

'Other family?'

Geoffrey shook his head.

'Doubt it. They were in a children's home. You must know them from working and living here?'

Ashley smiled.

'I gave Ron a caution for marijuana a long time ago. Seemed to think it was legal to smoke it in the town centre despite me constantly telling him it wasn't, but, other than moving him on the odd time he was begging, that's it. I still occasionally saw them mooching around. What else do you know about them?'

'Nothing much. Never saw them in the pub. Used to say hi when I bumped into them and maybe pass a bit of time. Sometimes he'd be there when I brought my catch in.'

'You said he used to come out on your boat.'

'Yeah, occasionally.'

'Well, what did you talk about then?'

'Not a lot. He just loved it, enjoyed watching the waves, seeing the sunrise, chill out, that sort of thing. When you're doing it for a living you take the tranquillity for granted, you know, so I liked him being there. Made me realise I'm lucky in many ways. Gave me some peace.'

'Any idea why they'd be killed, or anything that might help us in our investigation?' asked Hector.

Geoffrey was still looking at Ashley. 'He's a keeper, ain't he? Look, I'll catch you later.'

Geoffrey's seat scraped the floor as he rose from it. Hector slowly rose from his.

'Sit down, please. We're not quite finished yet,' said Hector.

Geoffrey's shoulders tightened. Ashley shook her head at him.

'Geoffrey. Calm down, please. We need a full statement from you,' she said. 'I also asked you to get a spare set of clothes for a reason.'

'Do I have to?'

'Yes. An officer will be here in a minute, and he'll take you in. You'll be back by lunchtime if you cooperate.'

'And if I don't?'

'We can't force you to, Geoffrey, but it might not look good if you don't tell us what you know. Now, did the Jerrods sleep on the beach all year long, and every night, or did they have a place for their things?'

Geoffrey dropped back down, looking exhausted.

'They were nomads. Ron wasn't about in the winter. He said they stayed in a caravan out in the countryside when it was out of season. They got it for nada for keeping an eye out for thieves and they received a little extra for helping on the farm. Winter veg, re-

pairs, you know. He reckoned they didn't claim benefits. They lived how they liked. Free. I respected it.'

'Any close friends you know of?'

'No idea, darling.'

'Thanks, Geoffrey. You've been very helpful. I
might want another word with you this afternoon.
Will I find you in The Cabin?'

Geoffrey's eyes narrowed.

'Who told you about that place?'

'I know everything. Don't ever forget that.'

The new, calmer Geoffrey rolled his eyes. 'Come
down, then, and have a few. Get drunk. I'm a great
shag.'

'That's not what your wife says.'

Geoffrey winked at her. 'Yeah? How would she
know?'

9
___

Outside, the rain had stopped, but a chill wind was blowing when Barry's car arrived. Ashley opened a rear door for Geoffrey and he clambered in. Barry gave the smallest of waves but no smile as he drove away.

Ashley directed Hector towards The Grove, which was a fancy restaurant and camp site a few minutes down the road. Fond memories of a tipsy sparkling afternoon tea with an ex, Rick, slipped into her mind. She grimaced as the memory of how the relationship ended elbowed its way in.

'Geoffrey could still be involved,' said Hector.

'Haven't you heard the phrase about not shitting where you eat?'

'You mean like not using the toilets at McDonald's?'

'Ooh, a joke. Things are looking up.'

As they walked past a new MG electric vehicle in a stunning azure blue, it beeped. Ashley watched with amazement as Hector opened the boot and took out a soft leather case and an umbrella. He strode after her, tapping the tip on the pavement every few paces.

'I thought you said you were twenty-two, not sixty-two.'

'I forgot I had it, and I didn't tell you how old I am.'

'Nineteen?'

'Twenty-four.'

'Thank you. Only rich people have umbrellas like that.'

'My father gave it to me when I became a detective.'

'Aren't you learning to be a detective?'

'Look, just because I'm on the Fast Track and own a nice umbrella doesn't mean I know nothing.'

'Okay, detective. How should we locate Ron or Ruby's next of kin if they live off the grid?'

Hector scowled as he thought, then smiled.

'A call-out on the news for anyone who knows

them. Check local dentists. There will be only a couple in a town this size. GP records. They're both in their fifties, so it's likely one or both will be on medication.'

'Pretty good. Media can be long-winded. My bet is on CSI finding a bank card under that canvas.'

'Didn't Geoffrey say they were nomads?'

'Don't fall for that poetic nonsense. They'll be on benefits. There was a phone charger in that tent, too. Their next of kin will probably be each other on their GP records, but these two don't appear to be shady criminals, so they'll have an address somewhere for post. That could be a relative or, more likely, a close friend.'

'Ah, and it's possible they'll know what they've been up to.'

'They might be involved.'

'I was getting to that.'

Ashley couldn't stop herself from rolling her eyes.

'Look,' said Hector. 'People are always making judgements about me. So go on, tell me what you're thinking.'

She stopped at the big sign for The Grove and turned to him.

'I don't think we're ready for that.'

'No, I insist.'

Ashley stuck her bottom lip out, then decided what the hell.

'Okay, you're a university type, probably after attending public school. This is your first proper job. You've had a privileged upbringing, and generally peer down on anyone less fortunate, which mean you haven't made any friends since you started. Being here is just a stepping stone on your way to superintendent, at which point you'll order me about with the experience I've given you.'

She checked his face, but it was expressionless.

'Then your father will give you the money to set up a security business and you'll toddle off with all the years of training we've wasted on you and make a fortune. Meanwhile, back at the ranch, I'll continue talking folk down from buildings and delivering death messages on little more than minimum wage.'

Hector didn't break stride as they crossed the road, but she detected a wince.

'Some of that's true, but not all of it.'

Ashley considered her words for a moment and realised she'd got on her soapbox.

'Actually, I've seen enough of you to change that assessment slightly. I reckon you joined up wearing rose-tinted glasses. You have a family member in the force who's told you a load of pony about noble policing. But seeing as you clearly aren't daft, you've quickly understood that it's a shitshow. We're under-funded and understaffed. Not only that, but the shocking lack of investment in community health care means that people everywhere are falling off the rails, and there's only us to get to them before the next train arrives.'

Ashley crossed the road and stopped outside Dora Thorne's house.

'Meanwhile, the tabloid newspapers are hellbent on destroying any goodwill that the public might have for the police. They focus on the 0.01 per cent who are bad apples, so we aren't even respected. This career was all you ever wanted, but perhaps, now, you don't want any part of it at all.'

Hector stopped too, took a deep breath through his nose, then looked down at her. There was a twitch at the side of his mouth.

'Maybe I can learn something from you, after all.'

10

Ashley didn't press the bell straight away.

'What's up?' asked Hector.

'We need to do a full initial account with this lady before she forgets things, but I don't want to drag her to the station. It's a shame I haven't got a recorder with me.'

Hector raised what Ashley would be calling his man-bag and tapped it affectionately.

'No problem.'

Ashley pressed the doorbell with an appreciative smile. Dora greeted them and ushered them into the spacious bungalow to a clean and tidy lounge. Her hair had been combed and there was a touch of subtle make-up. She'd also changed into grey slacks and a yellow jumper and looked ten years younger.

'Care for a cup of tea? The ambulance lady was going to stay, but she took a call as soon as we got back and had to take off.'

'Sure,' replied Ashley.

'Few biscuits?'

'Definitely.'

'Happy, my dog, usually sits in here with me, but he's fast asleep in his basket. We've had a rough morning.'

Dora left them in the lounge, and they heard crockery rattling as she busied herself in the kitchen. Ashley rose and glanced at the family pictures that adorned the walls and fireplace. There was a lovely picture of a beaming Dora with a handsome chap who had to be her husband. Dora looked twenty years younger. There were no recent photos of the couple together. The bungalow felt quiet.

'Would you like to hear my first impression of you?' asked Hector.

'No, thanks,' replied Ashley, sitting in an armchair beside him. She felt a frown growing on her face as she disappointed herself by being intrigued. 'Go on, then.'

'Middle-aged detective, bit of a drink problem.

Jaded from doing the job too long, but committed. Personal life a mess.'

'Rather cliché. Have you been watching *Line of Duty*?'

'You are middle-aged and a little dishevelled. Those jeans are ill-fitting, and that fleece looks old.'

'They're wet.'

'You barely batted an eyelid at the scene.'

'I'm a professional.'

'And I could smell alcohol on your breath at the café.'

'That was Geoffrey.'

'I smelled whisky on him. My dad's breath smells the same way sometimes. Yours was different.'

They both looked up as Dora returned to the room and put a plate full of biscuits down on a little table between them, before retreating to the kitchen to bring their teas.

They both reached over to grab one but paused in tandem, realising there were only Rich Tea biscuits on the plate. Ashley hadn't had breakfast and took two.

'It's supposed to be my day off, and I came straight from a friend's,' she said when her mouth was just about empty. A piece of biscuit flew out with the last word.

Hector didn't reply as he watched the missile flying past his knee.

'Are you always so forthright?' asked Ashley.

'No, but I'm bored with hiding what I really think. Nobody else does it. People have been making negative assumptions about me in every department I've been to.'

'So instead of rising above it, you've sunk to their level.'

'You started it,' he replied. 'Am I wrong, then?'

Ashley was saved from answering by Dora bringing in a tray with three very full wobbling cups on it, which Hector rescued from her.

Ashley explained that they were going to take a statement, which they'd record, but to speak freely about what happened that morning.

Dora began animatedly telling them about her and Happy's walks, but she slowed when she got to the bit about seeing the buckets. That part of the tale was revealed in a monotone. Hector and Ashley let her talk until she reached the part where she uncovered the heads.

'You're saying that someone had put buckets over both their heads?' asked a visibly shocked Hector.

'Yes. They also placed a large stone on top of the buckets, so they didn't blow away.'

'And the woman was definitely alive?' he asked.

'Yes. I didn't hear everything she said because of the wind, and she had shouted herself hoarse, but she begged to be saved.' Dora's face curled up into the beginnings of a sob, but she fought it. 'I couldn't help, though. I had to leave her.'

'You did what you could,' said Ashley. 'So, then you rushed to Geoffrey and asked for his help, and you didn't see anyone else on the way?'

'No. Maybe. My glasses were misty. I thought I saw movement up by the cliff, but I might have been mistaken. I'm sorry I can't be more helpful.'

'You've done amazingly well. Few would have kept your composure.'

'I suppose I haven't processed it all, but I'm not the same since my husband passed. He died in bed next to me, which was a real shock. Perhaps I've become numb to it all. I never expected my life to be so raw and ruthless.'

Ashley smiled at her, but her stomach lurched at the familiar thoughts. They probed more, but Dora grew tired. Ashley made polite conversation while she drank her tea to make sure the lady was all right after reliving her ordeal. Dora perked up at the mention of grandchildren and Ashley was pleased that she got to see them a few times a year despite them living in south London.

'Okay. You'll be assigned a family liaison officer, but I'll return shortly to see you,' she said. 'Are you sure you're okay? We can take you to be checked out.'

'Stop worrying, but it'd be nice if you popped in.'

'Maybe something will come back that you've forgotten.'

'That's more than possible. Let me write down my phone number. There was one thing, but it seems so silly now, I wonder whether I imagined it.'

'Please, anything might be important.'

'The lady under the bucket was exhausted and croaky-voiced, so I think she was under there for a while.'

'Okay, that's helpful.'

'I asked who it was who buried her because I was concerned they were still around. I think I heard her reply, but it was one word, and it was faint.'

'What do you think she said?'

'Monster.'

11

Ashley and Hector left Dora and paused outside her property. There was still a fresh breeze and billowing clouds filled the sky, but it seemed the worst of the storm was over. That was typical of the Cromer micro-climate.

'After eating those Rich Tea biscuits, I can't help wishing it had been the cookie monster,' said Ashley.

Hector raised an eyebrow but didn't comment.

'Do you remember seeing any black buckets at the scene?' he asked.

Ashley shook her head. 'That wind was blowing a lot of litter about. A bucket would end up next to the cliffs in the direction of the wind.'

'I'll ring the DI to search for them. They might have fingerprints.'

'I doubt you'll get through calling. There's no signal down there unless you're on the Three network and most of us will be on Vodafone. We'll have to go in person.' Ashley involuntarily shivered. 'I need to change these wet clothes and eat. I only live around the corner. You can come in and wait. Have some cereal or toast.'

Hector's expression made it seem as if she'd suggested he come to her house and clean the toilets.

'No, I'm fine. I'll run down the beach and update the DI and DCI. What was his name, Kettle? If they're struggling to receive intel down there, I can ring Control on the way and see if we've had any breaking news to pass on.' Hector looked around the wet but peaceful street. 'It's hard to believe what's just happened down there. I assume Cromer hasn't got an impressive network of CCTV.'

'Nope. If we don't get a break with this case fast, it's the long haul. We'll have to check into the victims' backgrounds, scour the town centre's sporadic CCTV, follow up on any media calls and that includes the cranks, chase down family, ex-partners and those farms they stay at in the winter. That won't be easy if they've been working off the books. Look at bank and phone records. All the stuff that takes ages.'

'Meanwhile, we pray that Ron and Ruby Jerrod aren't the first names on a long list.'

Ashley looked up at Hector.

'That's quite a leap. You sure you don't want to come to mine and freshen up? I've got a lovely little pink turtleneck jumper that I reckon you can pass off easily as a tank top. You could get away with a bit of Frank Spencer.'

'Are you implying that I'm camp?'

'Nope, just wet and cold.'

'I'm young, I'll be fine.'

She gave him her address and phone number. As he sauntered back to his car, she couldn't work out whether he was being a cheeky twat by implying she was old, or if she should just be grateful that she didn't need to attend the beach herself.

Her home was a small mid-terrace five minutes' walk away. She trudged past the hospital and up Mill Road. The front gate always needed a good shove to move it. She could remember her dad cursing at it many years ago. He'd died in this house, as had her paternal grandfather. As an only child, she sometimes wondered if it was also her destiny.

Ashley pushed open the front door into a small

lounge and was immediately relieved that Hector hadn't come back to what looked very much like a student's digs. She shrugged. Few people came here. What was the point of keeping it spotless? She thought about a rapid tidy-up, but quickly concluded food, shower and a change were her priorities.

After Hector's comments about her appearance, she found herself blow-drying her hair after the shower and putting on her best suit, although the competition was poor. She considered court shoes but decided that was pushing it and pulled on a pair of scuffed black pumps. Last night was catching up with her, so she put a touch more face paint on than she normally would do for work and was checking her mobile when it beeped.

A text came through from an unknown number.

With you in ten

It had to be Hector. For the second time that day, Ashley couldn't stop herself and felt compelled to frantically clean the lounge while the kettle boiled so at least there was an air of respectability. She hoovered the carpet while eating two cereal bars, receiving a strange tinny rattling sound in the machine as her reward, which made her remember having misplaced an earring the previous week. There was a knock at her door at the exact moment she realised she had no milk. Cheese in a milk carton, if she remembered correctly, but no milk.

'Come in,' she said. 'Mind the light.'

Hector stepped into the room and bonked the lightshade with his forehead. He was much taller and thinner than he'd appeared on the beach. Almost as though he knew how to hide it. He took his coat off and passed it to her. It was so damp and heavy, she almost dropped it before she hung it up.

'Do you want tea or coffee? Something to eat?'

'No, just orange juice if you have it.'

Result, she thought as she padded away to fetch a glass. He was slumped on the sofa by the time she returned, looking like a man who'd been out in all weathers. She offered him a Mars bar, which was the most calorie-dense food she could locate in the house. He thanked her, put it in his pocket, then drank the juice in one. He asked permission to use her bathroom.

'Did you find the buckets?' she asked when he reappeared.

'No, I used the toilet in there.'

Ashley laughed out loud. 'Very good.'

'Yes, both black buckets were against the cliffs, in

the thick grass. We might have one of the stones, too, now the tide's gone out a bit. I've got photos of them, so we can speak to Dora this afternoon and confirm. There's an interesting feature.'

'Yeah?'

'There are drill holes in the top and side of one bucket only.'

'Which would mean Ruby wouldn't suffocate underneath it.'

'Yes. That indicates a significant degree of planning and intelligence.'

'The plan must have been to kill Ron, or they'd have put holes in that bucket, too. Clever. What else?'

'CSI are unlikely to get footprints from outside the tent, although there is a clean footprint on a slice of bread, which might help. I took a photo of it. It's not either of the victims, whose shoes were all present. Ron and Ruby were discovered in their socks.'

'Let's see it.'

Hector showed her the picture. She compared it to her shot of Geoffrey's boot sole.

'It matches Geoffrey's boot print.'

'I agree,' said Hector. 'He told us he put the head back in there, so that's not surprising.'

'That's true. Pity. The fact they know about her socks must mean they've dug up Ruby.'

'Yes, I'm glad I missed seeing that. It was tough enough seeing her under the sheet. Ruby's clothes still have red stains on them because she was buried in the sand, but she doesn't have an injury that would cause her to lose that much blood.'

'So, she may well have been next to Ron when he was decapitated.'

'Yep. Her hands were tied behind her back with cable ties and her ankles connected in the same way. She was buried nearly half a metre down in a kind of racing-car-driver position. There was no chance of escape being so encumbered.'

'Encumbered?'

'What's wrong with encumbered?'

'Carry on.'

'Whoever did the cutting would have been drenched in blood if the victim were still alive. They'd also need to be strong to drag a full-grown woman forty metres to the hole, and fit to dig a trench in solid sand to begin with.'

'I agree. Maybe he didn't bother to hurt Ruby because he was confident she wasn't a threat. So, we're likely looking for a mature man in good nick, possibly with an accomplice.'

'The more killers there were, the easier these kills would be. Could even have been a sacrifice to the gods, or similar, the way they were lined up.'

'Christ, I didn't think of that,' said Ashley. 'Anything else?'

'DI Ibson was gone when I got back. DCI Kettle was like a wrecking ball, ordering people around. They're organising a house-to-house team to knock on the properties near North Park, and also the large ones up on the cliff top.'

'Cliff Drive?'

Hector took his notepad out.

'Yes, that's it. Teams are already knocking on all the chalets in the site near somewhere called Happy Valley. They'll continue onto Overstrand Road and into town in case those responsible made their escape that way. They've organised search teams starting this afternoon along the beach, through the foliage in the cliffs, and into the woods. It's a large area, so that'll take days.'

'It's needle-in-a-haystack time.'

'Yep. Big meeting at twelve at the main office with all involved. Kettle said you'll need to be ready, whatever that meant.'

Hector looked uncomfortable.

'Anything else?' asked Ashley.

Hector replied while analysing his fingernails.

'It seems their rucksacks pretty much held all their belongings.'

Ashley laughed.

'I won't say I told you so. Did they find a bank card?'

'Bank card, library card, NHS appointment card. There was even a current account statement for an address in North Walsham, which their benefits were paid into.'

'Bingo.'

Ashley looked at the clock on the wall. It was ten thirty, so there wasn't enough time to visit Walsham and still make the meeting at OCC in Wymondham. They needed to find out who lived at the Walsham address first before just barging in, so she handed him his coat back.

'We can go in your car if your mum doesn't mind you having passengers in it.'

Hector stood up and pulled a dismissive face.

'You detectives really love your piss-taking.'

Ashley opened the front door but didn't step out.

'Hector. You may think you know it all, but you don't. We're not investigating shoplifting and common assault here. You believe you're coping well, but it might not be apparent until tonight, next week, or even six months down the line when you're shouting in the faces of the people you love, that today's events have damaged you. We rely on humour to ease the pressure. It's an instant release in times of extreme stress. It helps.'

'I can cope without it,' he growled.

Ashley gave him a concerned glance and let him pass to go outside. She locked up and followed him down the road, realising that, for some reason, she liked this young man. Despite his bravado, she felt a motherly concern for him, even though there were less than twenty years between them.

Ashley suspected that was because her instinct was screaming at her that things were going to get much worse.

12

Ashley caught up with him, and they walked to his vehicle in silence. The car was as lovely inside as it was outside. It was far from an average policeman's ride, and that was before you considered the electric angle. Hector pulled out and drove steadily through the streets on the way to Wymondham. Ashley couldn't be doing with an hour journey filled with tension, so she turned the radio down.

Something had irritated Hector since he'd left, and she could only guess it was from when he returned to the scene.

'Was someone rude to you on the beach?'

'Just the usual piss-taking you Neanderthals enjoy.'

'Excellent, I'm included too, am I? Very kind. Take it on the chin, Hector. There'll be more where that came from. Everyone gets a bit of grief when they first arrive. Consider it a lesson in human nature.'

'I understand enough about human nature, thanks. I'm just sick of people thinking I don't know anything.'

Ashley considered what he was saying. Hassle for new starters was part of the culture in the past, and still went on now, but it had calmed down considerably. Banter was rife at crime scenes, though. Dry, cynical, dismissive language and inappropriate jokes were an emotional defence against getting overly involved in the misery and suffering they were facing.

Ashley had worked on teams where it hadn't been present. The pressure had built, and arguments had raged. She said as much to Hector.

'Yeah,' he replied. 'I've read about the WhatsApp groups where they share jokey photos of dead victims. You can count me out. People need to grow up.'

Ashley had heard enough. She respected that he was prepared not to take any bullshit, but he'd be poison to her team with this sort of attitude.

'*You* need to grow up,' she said quietly.

'Right,' he said with a sneer.

She reached over and turned the radio off.

'I'll only say this one time, because, as I said earlier, we were all new once, and we all had to learn. You, my friend, know fuck all.'

She looked across at him. His eyes were steeled on the road, jaw bunching.

'You've spent your whole life hearing how great you are, and now you believe it, and maybe you will be. But right now, you haven't lived.'

'Just because I come from a wealthy family doesn't mean I know nothing. At posh schools they teach you this thing called reading.'

Ashley shook her head.

'The people you're going to be working and dealing with will have had every type of trauma there is. What do you understand about chronic sickness, burying your parents or one of your children, or being homeless, pointless and futureless? What about not being able to have kids, can't get them into a local school, divorce, domestic abuse, a thousand different types of mental illness? Losing your job, can't find a job, never working again? Experience and understanding of all that doesn't come out of a book. It's learned in the field. You need to live it.'

'So, I should put up with being the punchline.'

'No, you have to drop the attitude. What kind of person can't cope with a little bit of ribbing? If it goes too far, tell me. Talk to me. Don't get wound up and do anything daft. If we laugh together, it becomes easier to put things right.'

Hector didn't reply.

'You know, ten years ago, you'd be nowhere near MIT. You'd have done two full years on the beat, maybe a couple more. Then you'd have spent time in Traffic, some in Surveillance, before scraping into CID. Three years of that would have hardened you up, so you were finally ready to join us. We deal with those who murder, torture and kidnap. There'll be things you can't forget.'

'So now I shouldn't be here?' said Hector, turning to glance at her.

This time, it was Ashley who kept her eyes on the road.

'No, I'm just saying tread carefully. You're in for a dark ride.'

13

They pulled up at Wymondham OCC, where they were based, and parked. The Norfolk Constabulary Operations and Communications Centre was a modern red-brick building with plenty of glass. There were spacious offices and, for once, sufficient interview rooms. Ashley enjoyed working at what was commonly called OCC. It was nice to have a place fit for purpose compared to some of the decrepit smaller stations she'd worked at.

Hector got out of his car, took his wet coat off, and swapped it for a suit jacket off the back seat. Despite him spending most of his morning on a beach, Ashley still felt like the grubby one as they walked in. As they waited for the lift, Hector sniffed.

'My point is, if you've had a stressful day, instead of insulting everyone, why can't you just go for a jog after work?'

Ashley opened her mouth, then closed it again. It was a fair question. She'd been her school's cross-country champion and had jogged for years to keep fit. It chimed very much with what she'd already been thinking.

'I used to run,' she said, surprising herself.

'Why don't you now?'

She was about to mention another ex, Dillon, but stopped herself. It had been easy to blame him for everything, but it had only taken three sessions with the shrink to realise Dillon had done nothing wrong. That was nearly a decade ago. It was horrifying to think that was when she last felt fit. But it was Richard, or Rick, or whatever the hell his real name was, who'd completely destroyed her confidence.

Hector indicated for her to get in the lift first. He was starting to look at her as if she were mad again when she clicked her fingers.

'Eddie Redmayne!'

'He stopped you running?'

'No, I was trying to work out who you reminded me of, and it's him. You're much taller, but same hair and skin, same freckles.'

As she stared at him, she noticed his face was harder, though. She wondered whether he had looked like that on the first day of police training, or if he was already changed by seeing society's underbelly.

'Thanks, I think.'

'I used to have freckles.'

'Aren't they permanent?'

'I killed them with booze, cigarettes and sunshine, and, what's the opposite of hope?'

'Despair.'

'That's it. All of those, and sometimes all four of them at the same time in a deckchair.'

The lift pinged to save her from spouting more rubbish. Hector gestured for her to get out first. She walked towards their department, nodding at people she knew on the way. It was usually pretty quiet on a Saturday, but rare events like today's brought in representatives from most areas.

In their office, Sal and Barry were the only ones present. Ashley sauntered in and slapped Sal on the back.

'This is Salvador Freitas, from Greece. We call him The Freitas Trainus because he's like a speeding bullet. He also likes dressing-up games.'

Hector looked down at the squat character in the same manner you would at seeing an interesting exhibit at the museum. Sal did not resemble a TV super-cop. Barry had started calling him The Mole a while back, because he slowly burrowed to the truth, until Sal had a discreet word with him about giving him a moniker that was too close to the bone. That was what Ashley loved about him. Sal had a quiet air, but he was no pushover. He enjoyed a joke as long as it didn't go too far, and there was a shrewd mind behind those wire-frame glasses.

The two men shook hands.

'Call me Sal. I'm originally from Portugal, and I'm not ashamed to say I enjoy role-playing games and battle re-enactments. And they nicknamed me Freitas Trainus because I am steady and reliable, like a freight train, unlike Barry here, who's neither.'

Barry came over and shook Hector's hand too firmly.

'I almost met you earlier,' said Hector.

'Fast Track?' asked Barry.

Hector nodded.

'Brilliant,' said Barry. 'You can call me Hoops.'

'Sure thing, Barry.'

Ashley managed to bite her lip, but Sal chuckled loudly.

'Okay,' said Ashley. 'What's the intel on the North Walsham address CSI found in the tent?'

'It's for a Mrs Edna Watkins, eighty-five years old, lives alone according to voting records,' said Sal with a wink. 'No previous or current charges.'

Ashley grinned.

'Excellent. And bank and mobile phone records have been requested?'

'Of course,' replied Sal. 'Barry took the interview with this Geoffrey guy.'

'Is Geoffrey still here?'

'He's just gone,' said Barry. 'Aggressive bloke. You sure he's not involved?'

'What did he say?'

'A lot of one-word answers and little more than he walked to the scene and found two dead bodies.'

'I reckon I know where he's going after all this stress. I'll have another chat with him later. Any idea who this Edna Watkins is?'

'Barry unearthed the marriage certificate for Ron and Ruby,' said Sal. 'She used to be Ruby Watkins.'

'Great work, Hoops.'

'Fuck off, Ash.'

Sal laughed again.

'Right,' said Ashley. 'I'm going to nip to the toilet

while our young apprentice makes the coffees, then we'll head to the meeting. Is the DI back?'

'Not seen him,' said Barry. 'He sounded a bit weird when he rang me earlier. I reckon he's finally lost it.'

Ashley chose not to comment.

'Nice shirt,' she said instead.

Barry had great dress sense for a man. He was a labels guy. His checked shirt was a fitted Ted Baker and his brown brogues shone. It was strange that he was often so grumpy, because he'd been lucky with his looks and, even though he was mid-thirties, his hair was still thick. There was more than a hint of Zac Ephron about him, at least when he wasn't scowling.

'Perhaps people who come to work looking like they've just left a funeral shouldn't express opinions on my attire,' he replied.

'I was being honest, you cheeky sod. Anyway, this is my best suit.'

'I rest my case.'

'See!' said Ashley to Hector. 'One big happy family.'

At midday, the four of them with around fifty others filed into the big meeting room. DCI Kettle was at the front with Detective Superintendent Zara Grave. She was another fast-tracker whose career had been on a rocket path. She'd been promoted so swiftly, Ashley suspected she knew diddly squat about what it was like to live the job, but operationally she was effective and organised.

Ashley sometimes wondered about her own ambitions. It had taken her five years to get to sergeant, but she'd always believed she wasn't on anyone's hot list for DI. Especially not after the accident and everything that followed when she worked in Sheffield. Even so, she'd passed her inspector exams, and lately Peter had been asking about her plans as though an opportunity was coming.

DCI Kettle rose from his seat, thanked everyone for coming and gave them a rundown of that morning's events. He paused, then looked around the room once before continuing.

'Post-mortems are being arranged as we speak, which isn't easy on a Saturday. You know they take three hours each, so they won't be started until the morning. We'll have preliminaries by tomorrow night. The pathologist who kindly came out to the scene has given me a quick summary. These are unconfirmed thoughts, but obviously there's a maniac out there somewhere, and we want an idea of what occurred.'

Kettle checked his notes.

'Her guess at events is that Ron Jerrod was stabbed in the stomach to incapacitate but not kill him. Ruby was cuffed, then hog-tied.' Kettle paused again. 'Google that if you don't know what it is. Judging by the lack of obvious injuries on Ruby's torso but the coverage of blood, it's likely that she was beside her husband while his head was sawn off. She was then buried in the sand and her husband's head was set next to hers. Black builders' buckets were placed over their heads and kept in position with big stones.

'A dog walker, Dora Thorne, noticed those buckets, removed them, tried to assist Ruby, but couldn't get her out of the sand because the waves were already lapping at the victim's chin. Dora ran for help and found a fisherman, who returned to the buckets, but he was too late to save the woman.'

Kettle ran his hand over his head.

'I'll lead this investigation with DS Knight, who knows the area well, as the deputy SIO. So far, we have nothing. Just a gruesome crime. The town is being flooded with police and that includes door knockers and searchers, with the hope of finding the weapon. DNA tests will be done, blood-splatter experts notified, toxicology ordered, but, at the end of the day, it's an identify and apprehend.'

Kettle moistened his lips.

'DI Peter Ibson has taken a leave of absence. I would appreciate no gossip on the subject. DS Knight's team have spoken to both witnesses this morning. Come to the front, please, Ashley. What are your thoughts?'

Ashley rose from her seat and walked forward while the place buzzed with the chatter on Peter. She remained silent until the room quietened.

'The fact that one bucket was drilled beforehand indicates significant planning, as does knowing when the tide would be all the way in. There was a considerable amount of mental suffering inflicted on Ruby, which perhaps makes her the prime target. I suppose it could be a spurned lover, but I'm not feeling that particular theory.'

'What are you feeling?' asked Kettle.

'Good old-fashioned psychopathic killer fits the bill. It's possible that someone's had a mental episode, but this was a complex plot, which doesn't tally with a personality breakdown. Even so, I'll get my guys to find out who's left prison in the past year locally with violence on their records, and we'll look nationally for extremists of any kind. I know Cromer's community psychiatric care coordinator, so I'll check who's on his books. I'll need top-level sign-off for him to release their details if he's working with anyone promising.'

'You'll get it. Anything else?'

'I'm planning to visit who we think is Ruby's mother after this meeting. She's pretty old, so I'm not hopeful, but it's a start. Then I'll talk with our two witnesses again. They'll have had more time to see if their recall changes now the shock is fading, and I'll have extra questions as we receive more information. The romance angle is unlikely, but maybe there's been a fallout in the rough sleeping community. Geoffrey might have seen more of those types of people on the beach.'

'That's what I call a dirty love triangle,' shouted Barry.

There was a brief wave of groans.

'I forgot about Homeless Bob,' said Kettle. 'He'll have this solved for us in no time.'

Loud laughter echoed around the room.

Homeless Bob was a legend in Cromer. He'd been a feature in the community for as far back as Ashley could remember, even when she was at school. Five years ago, a thief had stolen a watch off a lady's wrist. Bob had sprinted after them all the way from the coach park at Cadogan Street, which was at the start of Church Street, before rugby-tackling the thief outside The Albion public house, which was nearly at the end. The following year, he'd given the police a tip-off about a drug operation that was functioning out of a caravan in East Runton.

'Actually, that's not a bad idea,' said Ashley. 'He's a real wanderer, going up and down the coast. I'll put out a be-on-the-lookout for him straight away, failing that I know where he kips at night if he's in town.' Getting a BOLO wasn't straightforward nowadays, but one on Bob would be granted. 'And that is where we're at. Let's hope something turns up in town or through searching, or we get a break on the PMs or CSI at the scene. I'll distribute the tasks while we wait for the HOLMES room to be up and running. My team will study the bank records. Did you find a phone at the scene?'

'Yes,' said Kettle. 'Old Nokia, unlocked. I'll email you the number. It's Vodafone, which for those who don't know is one of the systems we can log into and check recent calls. We'll use this room as the incident room. It'll be set up and operational with a HOLMES team and full admin backup by Monday morning. Let me know if there's anything you need. No expense spared for this. The world will be watching.'

'Excellent,' replied Ashley. 'To be honest, we don't have much to go on other than the method, which is unusual for this type of crime, so let's hope this was an intensely personal attack.'

Ashley wasn't going to add anything else, but the room was silent. She looked around at all the eyes that were still upon her.

'Because if it wasn't, this might not be the end of it.'

14

The team was stony-faced when they returned to their office. Peter had always been a distant boss, but he'd been instrumental in Ashley being given another opportunity after her wobbles in Sheffield. Then, when Peter left CID to join MIT, he took her with him. She also knew he'd backed up Barry on numerous public complaints about his attitude. Sal's sickness record had been shocking for an entire year, and there were rumours he was going to be asked to leave, but Peter stuck by him.

Sal's illness turned out to be thyroid cancer, which was one of the best cancers to get if you had to develop one, and he had recovered fully.

'Poor boss,' said Sal.

Even Barry had nothing sarcastic to say. DS Bhavini Kotecha arrived at that point and glanced around at their sour faces.

'Has Barry farted again?' she asked.

'Peter's gone long-term sick,' said Barry.

'We don't know that,' said Sal.

Ashley kept quiet. Few people returned to MIT after a breakdown, if that was what it was. She supposed he could be physically ill, having relationship issues, or maybe he had problems with kids nobody had heard about. It struck her again as odd that they knew so little about him.

'Bhavini,' said Ashley, pointing at Hector. 'This is the guy we were told was coming, Hector Fade.'

Bhavini shook his hand with half a grin on her face.

'So, this is the chosen one. I'm the tough sergeant here,' she said. 'Don't let my size and beauty fool you. When I punch, I aim for the crown jewels.'

Ashley grinned. Bhavini was a consistent performer who seemed to lead a quiet, healthy life. She and her uber-fit boyfriend spent most of their free time at the gym.

'Bee, I thought you were up all night with that domestic?' asked Sal.

'Yeah, and how come MIT are getting called out for run-of-the-mill stuff like that?' asked Barry.

'It was a really nasty one, that's why,' replied Bhavini. 'The girlfriend has serious mental health issues, and he seems unbalanced. It sounds as though they'd been knocking seven bells out of each other. He's in hospital with a bruised back after going down the stairs.'

'Going? Do you mean falling or being helped down them?' asked Sal.

'I think she pushed him, but he said he fell. He was in a lot of pain, but she was so crazed, I thought she was going to need sectioning. Uniform weren't sure what to do. Nor was I. Eventually her mum, who's in her seventies, came over and calmed her down. The mum has this couple's kid, who's about eight, full time, which indicates problems going back a while. I didn't get home until gone nine this morning after all the paperwork, so I crashed for a few, but I didn't want to miss this. Bring me up to speed.'

'Sal and Barry can do that,' said Ashley. 'We've got a death message to deliver.'

'Lucky you.'

'Yep. Did you spot if one of the FLOs was here on the way in?'

'Yeah,' replied Bhavini, with a mischievous look.

Ashley's face fell. 'Great. Come on, Hector. Let's find Flash and book a car out.'

Scott Gorton was seated at his desk but rose when he saw them. Death messages were delivered if possible with a family liaison officer (FLO), and if it could be done with an officer of each sex, that was preferred, too. Sadly, Ashley and Scott had done quite a few together over the years.

Scott looked a bit like a chunky Brad Pitt, but his nose and ears had been misshapen through playing semi-professional rugby when he was younger. Ashley booked out a Vauxhall Astra. She got in the driver's side, Scott took the passenger seat and Hector sat in the back seat with his head touching the roof.

'Buckle up, children,' said Ashley as she put her glasses on.

She gave Scott a full update as they drove. They shared a chequered history, having had a few big rows, but Ashley struggled to remember what it was they'd argued about afterwards. He was just one of those people who could get under her skin.

Family liaison officers were police officers who had been specially trained to work with families affected by serious crimes. Their work often involved bereavements. Scott Gorton was good at it. He'd been Ashley's mentor in CID when she returned to Cromer, which was around the time his marriage was collapsing.

Ashley recalled him carrying a dead sixteen-year-old out of a ditch one misty night at the culmination of an abduction case. Ashley had been trying to stop the bleeding from a head wound of the thirty-seven-year-old joyrider who had kidnapped her. Sometimes she regretted saving his life. That had been Scott's last investigation in CID nearly seven years ago. His own daughter had been sixteen at the time.

Ashley had thought it was odd that, when he wavered mentally, he moved departments and took on what most would consider the worst job in the force. Other people's misery had a habit of causing some of your own, although Scott appeared to be coping fine.

'Right, use my phone and try to get hold of the community care coordinator,' said Ashley, passing Scott her mobile. 'Put it on speaker if Dylan answers. Hector, take notes for the file, please. Hopefully, he'll be able to help the investigation.'

'Is he still in Cromer?' asked Scott.

'Yep. You know him, he loves it. I reckon he'll answer, even though it's his Saturday clinic.'

Scott rang Dylan Crabb's number, and he picked up on the second ring.

'Dylan Crabb speaking.'

'Dylan, it's Ash.'

'Ash, baby. How are ya?'

Dylan was mixed race, half Welsh, half Tunisian, and a Buddhist. It was the ideal religion for dealing with the mad, sad and the struggling of Cromer because patience and tolerance were needed. Crabb had both in abundance. Ashley updated him.

'Wow. I heard on the news that two people were killed on the beach, but the names haven't been released. Ron and Ruby, wow. Can't believe it. I only spoke to her a week ago.'

'Did you speak to her regularly?'

'Yeah, she's been struggling for about six months. I was beginning to consider stronger meds, but I wasn't sure what the root cause was. Strange how she deteriorated recently though. Something changed in her life, but I don't know what. She was so down but wouldn't talk about it.'

'Did you see Ron as well?'

'I usually saw him at the same time. I run a community day at the GPs for people who are too chaotic to see a doctor or who aren't in the system. He used to bring her down, but I think he self-medicated with a bong. She used to do the same, but Ruby said she'd stopped doing drugs. Said she couldn't deal with it any more.'

'Okay, so is it possible she was being threatened?'

'Yeah, something had spooked her quite badly.'

'How's your roster of clients? We're looking for a person capable of extreme violence.'

'Nah, I've got nobody like that. We had one volatile bloke with borderline personality disorder. He was a shouter and a shover, pretty unstable. He'd flare up at people in the street as though they were attacking him, when they were just walking past, but he's been back inside for a fortnight. Shame, really, because we were making progress, but he pushed a man through a shop window.'

'I'd have thought the magistrates would have kept him out if he was under treatment.'

'Well, he was drunk at the time. The judiciary don't tend to like that.'

'And no one else?'

'No, I seem to have plenty of very suicidal people on my hands. I've got a guy who we keep having to pull away from the cliff tops at Happy Valley. He stands there at all hours, cursing and shouting at the sea, as though it's somehow upset him. Tough thing is he was doing really well when he first came to us, so I was hopeful, but he's steadily deteriorating.'

'What did he do time for?'

'Actually, he came from a hospital, not prison. He was away for over thirty years. There have been a range of new drugs developed like olanzapine and a combination of meds seemed to have got him to a level of stability that meant we could attempt to reac-climatise him in the community. He's an interesting case.'

'Could he be responsible for what happened on the beach?'

'You can never tell what sick people are capable of. I've been astounded many times. Schizophrenics and the like aren't usually violent, though. They may lash out if they're threatened, so it's more than pos-sible one could kill. I don't know the gory specifics, but what is less plausible is him covering up his in-volvement in the crime. Any serious planning would likely be beyond him as well, if that helps. He some-times pops into the clinic on Saturdays, but I'm often visiting where he stays, so I'll have a word with him.'

'He doesn't sound like the culprit, but I might need to talk to him.'

'No probs. He's local. Do the paperwork and I'll come with you if you want.'

Crabb dealt with a lot of the prison leavers, but

not all of them. He would definitely have been involved with Homeless Bob over the years, though.

'I'm going to have a chat with Bob later, too,' she said. 'I don't suppose you've heard anything from the rough sleepers about arguments, that kind of thing.'

'Bob's a sad tale as well. He's back using.'

'No way. He's been clean for years.'

'Yeah, out of the blue. Maybe the last year or so. There must be something in the air at the moment. One of the others told us he was found sparko in the sand and the tide was coming in. He was on the nod. Would never have woken up if a passer-by hadn't rung for an ambulance.'

'Sounds like he was lucky. Is he sleeping in the same place?'

'Think so. Although the owners won't be happy when they come back to use it this summer. It stinks.'

'Cheers, Dylan. Catch up soon.'

'Deffo. We always say we're gonna get a beer or a coffee. Let's do it this time. I'll be at the Doggie Diner tomorrow at ten if you wanna hook up. Augustus is in his element there.'

'Sure thing. Flash says hi, by the way,' said Ashley.

'Cool, Scotty Dude is with you as well, is he? Nice one. You guys finally got together. Bring him too.'

Ashley felt her face reddening and cut the call.

Scott coughed and shrank in his seat as though the car were closing in on him. Ashley looked in the rear-view mirror to find Hector staring at her with a big smile.

* * *

North Walsham was a small market town nine miles from Cromer with a busy vibe to the centre, but Edna's address was on the outskirts. Ashley's phone beeped as she parked up. It was a text from her partner, Bethany.

I leave next Sunday.

Great, thought Ashley. It was becoming one of those days.

They quickly deduced Edna Watkins' home in North Walsham was a retirement apartment in an over fifty-fives development. Scott and Ashley left Hector in the car and walked towards the block of flats' main door. He poked the buzzer for number two and waited but there was no reply.

'Bollocks. Perhaps we should have rung first,' said Ashley.

Scott pressed the buzzer for flat number one.

A surprisingly youthful voice blared out.

'Hello!'

'Hi, we'd like to chat with Edna. Do you have any idea where she might be?'

'Who are you?'

'We're police.'

'Ooh, I'll buzz you in. Come to my flat.'

They pushed open the door when it buzzed and walked in to find a short lady in a wheelchair in the doorway of her downstairs flat. She gave them a big grin.

'You can't speak to Edna.'

'Why not?' replied Ashley.

'I'm afraid she's dead.'

15

Ashley and Scott shared a look.

'When was this?' he asked.

'Only two days ago.'

'I'm sorry to hear that.'

'There's no need to be. She was suffering, and it was a good death. I think she was happy to go now that everything was sorted out.'

Ashley didn't want to be tactless, but she didn't have all day.

'How did she pass?'

'She died in her sleep. We were supposed to be going to the café, but she never arrived. I asked the warden in the end, and he opened her door and found her in bed. She'd struggled with heart problems and emphysema for years. The doctor only told her last week it was a miracle she was still here.'

'And what was recently sorted out?'

'Her daughter had been in touch again and was visiting regularly.'

'Okay, had they become estranged?'

'Not really. Ruby was just flaky. I've met her a few times. Edna often brought her around to show her off, but she seemed a miserable woman to me. Edna hadn't seen her for over five years because Ruby lived a free life, whatever that means. All she did was text every now and again. I suspected she was after money, but Edna said she wasn't. Edna even offered her some, but Ruby turned her down.'

'Ah,' said Scott. 'So Edna was pleased to be in touch with her daughter before she died. It made her feel that the scales were balanced.'

'That's it, young man. Edna had a large inheritance to leave her.'

'Really?' said Ashley. 'How big?'

'Half a million.'

Ashley whistled while her mind churned.

'I don't suppose you know who'd receive that money if something happened to Ruby?'

'Why wouldn't Ruby get it?'

'I'm sorry to say that she's died as well.'

'Oh, my, that's terrible! How? She was so young. Early fifties.'

'I can't confirm anything at this point.'

'Ooh, that's why you're here. Are there people after the cash? Edna said her only other living relative was Ruby's cousin, so maybe they were a beneficiary too, but I assume Ruby would have been the main one.'

'Do you know his or her name and where they live?'

'It was a man, but I'm not sure she ever mentioned his name. She never saw him. It was her brother's only child but the brother moved away and died years ago. I think they lived in Stockport.'

'Near Manchester?' asked Scott.

'Or was it Stockton, or Stockwell? Something like that.'

'Had Ruby been told about her mum's death?' asked Scott.

'Yes, the warden rang her. She was supposed to come here yesterday. I wondered why she didn't show up.'

Ashley took the details of the warden, then handed her business card to the lady and thanked her for her help before they headed back to the car and brought Hector up to date.

'People have been killed for much less than half a mil,' he said.

Scott nodded.

'I've heard about a lot of violent fallouts over inheritance.'

'Me, too,' said Ashley. 'Although, if Edna predeceased Ruby, Ruby would have inherited it all, anyway.'

'Some wills are set up that if the beneficiary is dead, it goes to their family. Let's assume Ruby was the sole beneficiary,' said Scott. 'It would have then gone to her estate when she died. I'd be surprised if Ruby had a will. Her husband also predeceased her, because she was alive under the bucket when he wasn't, so who would inherit from her if she had no children?'

'I'd assume it was the cousin again, as her only living relative,' said Ashley. 'That's a circular way of ensuring your inheritance.'

'He's someone else we need to talk to, then,' said Hector.

'The list is getting longer,' said Ashley. 'I'll ring the office and get them on the job.'

She placed her phone back in the hands-free kit and rang OCC. Barry picked up and she gave him as much detail as she had.

'What you're saying is you don't know Edna's maiden name, her brother's name, or the cousin's name or the address.'

'Correct.'

'And it could be Stockton in the north-east, Stockport in the north-west, or Stockwell in London.'

'You love a puzzle.'

'Great. You want me to put a hold on the body?'

'Which one?'

'This Edna. Who's to say she wasn't knocked off?'

'I knew we kept you around for a reason, Barry. The GP would only have given her a once-over and there wouldn't have been a post-mortem because she was in ill health and had seen a doctor a few days beforehand. Inform Michelle. She's going to have a busy weekend.'

'Let's hope she gives us something,' said Barry. 'We've had no breaks here. The mobile records look normal. There's a private number in North Walsham, which I'm guessing is the mum you're visiting now, and that's more or less it apart from one to the GP in Cromer. They've cleared the tent at the scene and looked through their belongings. A small amount of marijuana was the only slightly dodgy find. There were blood-pressure tablets in Ruby's name, and we found seventy-five pounds in the pockets of the jeans he was killed in. That makes it unlikely to be a mugging for money that ended with his head being cut off.'

Ashley wouldn't have expected any mugger to go to the lengths that this killer had, but didn't comment.

'Bank records?'

'In progress. Grave has rushed authorisation through so we could get the information this afternoon. They might be interesting if there's a possible financial element to the crime.'

'I don't suppose the prison service have accidentally released Charles Bronson.'

Barry chuckled.

'No. DS Ally Williamson's team is checking into that. There's been nobody with a history of serious violence released recently in our area. There are two who left Manchester and Liverpool who have significant records and got out in the last week. Ally's liaising with Probation up there as we speak.'

Ashley's team were 'twinned' with Ally's so if either needed extra resource, the other team were familiar with having helped each other before and ready to help out.

'Okay, keep me posted. I'm going to visit Geoffrey and Dora, then check on Peter.'

'Good idea. I'm worried about him being on his own after all this.'

Ashley ended the call and nodded. Barry could be decent when he wanted to be. Ashley, Hector and Scott drove to Dora Thorne's house in Cromer, but there was no answer to the doorbell, so they continued on to Northrepps Road where Geoffrey now drank in The Cabin.

During the last lockdown, one of the older guys who used to socialise in The Cottage pub, Billy Speechley, converted a small barn on his land into a bar, which he called The Cabin. Ashley had heard about it a year ago through Joan. Most of the drinkers had returned to the pubs for the social scene when the restrictions were lifted. The Red Lion had embraced real ales and had a friendly vibe, so some had headed there, but a few continued to drink at The Cabin because they could bring their own alcohol at supermarket prices, and Billy let them smoke inside.

Ashley left the others in the car. The mostly older men who drank here wouldn't appreciate the police coming in mob-handed. She liked to keep people like this on side because if she wanted to hear casual gossip, then regular drinking holes were a good port of call. Promises were broken and secrets revealed over one drink too many.

The weather had settled into a nothingness that made the barn a depressing vision set against a grey sky. Her first glance inside didn't raise her opinion, either. There was only the bar owner, Billy Speechley, in there. Ashley recalled him retiring on his seventieth birthday three or four years back. The man in front of her was a shadow of that robust fisherman. He had two crushed cans of stout in front of him and another one in his hand. Ashley cleared her throat.

'Oh, it's you, Ash. Long time since I saw you. Come for a drink, or is this a raid?'

'I'm looking for a busload of Scandinavian pornstars, Billy. Know anything?'

'Yeah, they left disappointed. Told them my hives had flared up.'

'Shame. Geoffrey about?'

'He's been gone about half an hour. Wasn't in a good way. He gives it the hard-man act, but even he won't easily forget what he saw this morning. Caught who did it?'

'Not yet. Was Geoffrey going home?'

'Doubt it. She threw him out a year ago.'

'Really? What for?'

'They argued a lot over money. No tourists meant no demand for crabs, but he still drank the same amount of beer each week. He's been sofa surfing. I let him crash here for a few days, but he drank all the beer.'

'Okay, thanks for that. Are you okay, Billy?'

He looked around his empty barn and shrugged.

'Not really. Some of my mates are depressed, others are angry. A few are going mad. Life seemed okay not so long ago but it's hard to see the point now.'

'Start going to The Red Lion like the others. It'll do you no good drinking on your own.'

Billy nodded. She gave him her card, saying to ring her if Geoffrey reappeared, but she wasn't too worried about finding him. Geoffrey should be fishing on his boat in the morning.

Ashley left the sombre scene and made a note in her pocketbook about Billy's comments and then tried Geoffrey's phone, which went straight to voicemail. The first tendrils of concern had started encircling her heart with the possibility Geoffrey might be involved with the deaths. Money made people commit evil acts, but she pushed the thoughts away. Someone with a more twisted mind than Geoffrey was responsible for that morning's murders.

When she returned to the car, she drove to Peter Ibson's house. He lived only a mile down the road. Scott had known the DI for a long time, too, so

Ashley figured he might be able to lighten the load if Peter was struggling. Scott knocked, but nobody answered. Peter's car was on the drive, so Ashley and Hector headed around the back of the property in case he was in the garden.

The gate was unlocked, so she pushed it open. The lawn was immaculate, but there was little else of note. She stared at the weed-free borders, but there were no flowers that she could see and Ashley imagined him working away on his own. The garden was like the man himself. Presentable and smart, but instantly forgettable. She noticed the side door to the garage was ajar, so she poked her head around it to find a pristine array of exercise machines and free weights, which appeared well maintained, but there was nobody using the equipment.

She peered through the kitchen window. Inside looked like one of those show homes where none of the appliances have ever been used. Poor Peter, she thought. What kind of life was he living? Why hadn't he reached out to her?

After another knock at the front, they got back in the car and returned to the office to crack on with what was still called paperwork, even though it was mostly done on computers.

They headed to the incident room for a further

update from DCI Kettle at 6 p.m. It was a less formal affair as the lack of progress and the fact it was a weekend meant many had gone home. Kettle had big bags under his eyes.

'There's no further concrete intel,' he said. 'Although there have been some interesting calls to a hotline number that we had broadcast on BBC news and radio. A man in a long black coat with a deep hood has been seen in the streets of Cromer over the previous weeks at night. One caller described him as looking like the Grim Reaper.'

'Jesus. The newspapers will love that,' said Ashley.

'Brilliant,' replied Barry. 'I can see the headlines now. Death comes to Cromer. Business trip.'

Once they'd all stopped laughing, Kettle continued.

'He could be here to recuperate with the sea air, because two callers mentioned him having a limp. I've released what we have to the other news outlets. The added publicity can only help. Do we have anything at all from bank or phone records?'

'It doesn't seem like there are any suspicious calls,' said Bhavini. 'I've had a look at Ron and Ruby's bank account, too. There's been a bit of extra spending for the last few months. A lot of thirty- and fifty-pound withdrawals, but there is ten grand in there, which is ten grand more than I've got in my current account.'

Ashley put her hand up and Kettle nodded.

'We went to deliver the bad news to her next of kin, but Ruby's mother had recently passed away. Ruby had been visiting her, so those withdrawals could be to pay for taxis. Public transport isn't great to North Walsham.'

'When did she die?' asked Kettle.

'Thursday.'

There was a burst of chatter at the two deaths being so close together.

'Was it suspicious?' asked Kettle.

'I don't think so, but none of us like coincidences. We've got numerous leads to follow up tomorrow, and that's one of them.'

'Did the daughter know her mum was dead?'

'Yes.'

'Okay. Anything else before we go home?'

'Has the beach been reopened?' asked Ashley.

'Not all of it, but there's access along it now. I called in some favours, and we had CSI from other counties assisting with the area search and scene processing, but nothing's turned up so far. There are no prints on the hacksaw or the spade. They're both really old tools. It's not a fact you want to think about too deeply, but the saw blade was rusty and dull. There was no paint left on the spade, but it still had soil around the top of the blade as though it had been used recently.'

'Will CSI check the soil?'

'Yes, but it's a long shot. The age of them means there's no point in checking local shops for recent purchases. We'll release to local media that we're interested in hearing if anyone has had any tools stolen from their garden or allotment recently. Tomorrow, we'll feed the fingerprints they've managed to find in the tent into the machine, and hopefully we'll get a match.'

There were no further questions, so Kettle continued.

'The weather's ruined the scene, so CSI will be finished shortly and off home, as should you guys. I appreciate everyone coming in today, and there's obviously overtime tomorrow. We'll meet at noon when we should have more information. The council is sending us their CCTV from the town-centre cameras. Let's see if Dr Death shows up on film and we catch a glimpse of his face.'

Barry offered to give Ashley a lift home after the meeting. He said he'd come with her to chat to Homeless Bob. Barry lived in Sidestrand, which was only three miles from Cromer. She checked her phone while they walked to his car and found a message from Dylan Crabb saying that the guy who shouted at the sea hadn't turned up at his clinic, but Dylan would drop by his place that night.

Jesus, she thought, where the hell was everyone disappearing to?

Ashley often joked that detectives' hunches were just trapped wind, but there was something very unsettling about this investigation. She had a sinking feeling that tomorrow would bring more bad news.

16

An hour later, they were parking up behind the large properties on Cliff Drive that backed onto Cromer's promenade. Homeless Bob had an unusual arrangement with the owners of one of the bigger homes. They'd caught him crashed out in their shed on a cold Christmas Eve when they'd arrived to check on their property but, instead of chucking him out, they said he could stay. The rich owners only used the home in the summer months, so having someone there to keep an eye out in winter would give them peace of mind.

When Ashley initially found out, she couldn't decide if they were being kind, or if they should have let him sleep in the house, although she suspected that might have been a risk they didn't want to take. Bob had told her a few years back that they'd offered to give him access to the conservatory, but he'd declined. Said the shed felt like luxury compared to the tent he'd been sleeping in.

Like Ron and Ruby, Bob was a regular sight in the town. Bob was another one who disappeared for months on end, but, unlike them, he left in the summer. He stuck to the coast and begged and did odd jobs as far north as Wells and as far south as Great Yarmouth. Barry knew him well, having done years of local response.

'You don't think he's responsible for any of this, do you?' he said.

'I would have said no, but Dylan told me he was back on drugs.'

'That's a pity. He was a shambling, thieving wreck, who was forever in and out of Norwich nick when I was on the beat, but I still kind of liked him. What's that phrase where you take the piss out of yourself?'

'Self-deprecating?'

'That's it. He assaulted me a few times, though, trying to evade arrest.'

'Let's get on with it,' said Ashley, getting out of the car. 'I've had enough of today.'

The front of the house, which faced away from

the sea, was secure, so they headed down Cliff Lane and turned right. There was still an onshore breeze, and the clouds scudded across the sky as though fleeing from trouble. Sunset wasn't until seven thirty, but it already looked the type of night you'd think twice about venturing out in.

As if on cue, a flash of lightning lit up the horizon. The rumble of thunder was only a few seconds after, and the first drops of rain began to fall.

'Great,' said Barry. 'If there's anyone in there with a scythe and skeletal fingers, then I'm clocking off.'

Ashley found the rear gate and gave it a solid knock to no avail, which caused Barry to grumble. He jumped on the spot, just tall enough to see over the wall.

'There are porch lights on. It seems to be deserted, except for the bloke in a mask playing the piano.'

'Ask the phantom if he's seen Bob.'

The gate was locked, so Barry dragged himself onto the wall and slid over. Ashley heard a bolt scratch back and a latch lift, then the door opened inwards. Barry stood there with his face frozen. His arms outstretched.

'What are you doing?' whispered Ashley.

'That's my Nosferatu impression.'

'Yeah? You look like you followed through.'

Barry pulled the gate shut after Ashley had entered and pointed at the bolt.

'Bob would be able to thread his hands through at the top of the gate and move the bolt, so that must be how he's getting in and out but keeping it relatively secure.'

'Which means he isn't likely to be home.'

'Maybe he always slides the bolt across whether he's in or out. I like what he's done with the place, though.'

Dylan had been right. The owners would be most displeased with the state of their low-maintenance suntrap. Bob had covered virtually every surface with rubbish. Some of it was pizza and cereal boxes, stacked in corners, but the rest was a shifting mass of litter and what looked like used toilet paper. Strong gusts swirled the detritus around as though it were a whirlpool, which quickened as the wind strengthened.

'I don't fancy getting sucked into that,' said Barry, reading her mind.

The shed was in the left-hand corner with its door creaking in the breeze. It appeared well constructed and was approximately three metres square, with a glass window at the side. The panels seemed to have been varnished recently but Ashley wasn't looking forward to checking inside.

Barry had put on a sports jacket. He reached into a pocket and pulled out a thin torch before nodding at her. They approached the shed head-on. The door was slowly swinging open and shut, but it was too dark inside to see if it was occupied.

'Bob!' shouted Ashley. 'It's the police.'

They both listened, but all they could hear was the sound of the coming storm. Barry strode forward, held the door open with his foot, clicked his torch on, and shone it into the abyss. Ashley made out a camp bed at the back with a bunched-up sleeping bag on top, but it was impossible to say if anyone was in it.

Ashley shouted again, but there was no movement or a reply. She puffed out her cheeks and walked past Barry and inside. The right wall of the shed was covered in hanging tools, with the other side having a smeared window. The wall behind the camp bed was adorned with shelves. It was hard to see what was on the floor due to the litter, but there was clearly foil and needles and other drug paraphernalia on a very small table.

Ashley shook her head, even though she knew relapsing was part of addiction. The council and outreach programmes had made progress over the last few years, moving many of the rough sleepers into accommodation and helping them access support services, but it was a roundabout for many.

Ashley knew too well from her years on the beat how easy it was for people to end up struggling. Sometimes it was a single event, like a relationship failure or a lost job that could cause everything to fall in on itself. Other times it was the death by a thousand cuts before a safe home and good health were just memories.

Barry had boots on and he stomped forward and nudged the sleeping bag. His nose wrinkled.

'Let's get out of here,' he said. 'We can come back in the morning.'

Ashley let him past and took another look into what was in effect Bob's home. Had he lain here, plotting those terrible murders while thousands of people had walked past him just metres away on the way into town?

After Barry dropped her at her place, she tried to shake off the rising worry that Bob was another person who was missing, but it wasn't easy. Ashley deliberately didn't keep alcohol in the house, but she was tempted to nip to the shop. She recalled what Hector had said about finding a healthy way to cope, which made her lean on the kitchen work surface and think about her broken promises.

She'd known for a while she had to turn her life around, and that started with her health. Ashley had even written a list six months ago describing how the new 'her' would be different and extroverted. She would make the first move to try to develop friendships. She would arrange drinks and meals out. She would stop spending all her leisure time alone. She would get fit. Ashley took two deep breaths. When was *she* going to start?

Ashley rooted through the cupboard under the stairs and found a pair of trainers, which she hoped wouldn't cripple her. She made a promise to herself to run along the promenade first thing in the morning. Ashley was certain Bob was living in that shed and he'd be getting an early visitor.

17

Candice Sweet opened the front door of her little council house in Felbrigg. The man's car was parked further down the street, as he'd said it would be. She struggled to remember what he'd come for, but not going with him hadn't been an option. Candy thought of the photograph that she'd been sent three months before and knew she deserved no sympathy.

It was cold and damp outside, but all she felt was a detachment from her existence. In a way, that was how she'd been her whole life. She plodded towards the vehicle. The rustling trees overhead often instilled a childish fear in her, but not this time. She somehow understood the real danger had just flashed his headlights.

She turned and looked back at her home. They'd had good moments there, but last night's madness seemed to have coated her memories with black paint. All she could think of was her partner shouting at her and throwing himself down the stairs. If she was going to kill herself, then Elliott wanted to die as well.

The thought of returning to the shore on a night like tonight was horrifying. That evening all those years ago had been in the middle of August and she imagined that the gentle waves had lapped at their feet as they danced, but she couldn't recall anything about it, although the truth had been preserved in a photograph.

She got in the vehicle and shut the door, automatically pulling the seat belt across even as she spoke her fears aloud.

'I'm too scared to go,' she whispered.

He stared out of the windscreen, put the car in gear and turned in the street.

'You have to. She needs peace.'

It was ten miles of empty single carriageway back to Cromer, and they were soon threading through the quiet back roads. He parked on the corner of Ellenhill, a quiet street opposite the Kings Chalet Park. He reached down by his knees and, after fumbling around, straightened up and leaned closer to her. She was frozen with fear. Grabbing her chin with steely fingers, he poked something between her lips. Her mouth filled with bitter fluid, which she couldn't help swallowing.

'Good girl. We have to finish things. Let her be free.'

She watched him get out of the car, zip up his black raincoat, then open her door. She stepped out of the vehicle into the cold night, but the chill that had enveloped her was worse than anything the weather could cause. This was really happening. Candy caught a glimpse of his face, which was twisted and tormented.

He put his hood up, seized her wrist, and dragged her across the road and up the steep path between the chalets and Cromer Country Club. She stumbled in the dark, which made him curse under his breath. He fumbled in a pocket, then torchlight danced in front of them, and she staggered on. At the edge of the trees in Happy Valley, they were lit up by the lighthouse. The beam appeared to pause above them, directing them seaward.

It was a peaceful place during the day, with ramblers and dog walkers filtering through the network of paths and passages that snaked through the ferns and bushes. Many of the visitors came from the holiday villas and chalets nearby, but the season was yet to begin in earnest. An owl hooted in the treetops above, seemingly warning her. Humans shouldn't come here at night.

The path down to the beach was steep and unforgiving. The lighthouse couldn't penetrate the dark under the tree canopy, and his torch cast strange shadows. Candy tripped, and this time she fell and twisted her ankle.

'It hurts,' she cried out, but she was pulled to her feet by leather-gloved hands and shoved onwards, causing her to stagger through a thorny bush at the side of the path. The sting on her bare shins was as if she'd been whipped.

Candy didn't recall him having gloves on earlier.

She regretted the dress and cardigan that she'd chosen to wear. It was similar to what she'd worn that fateful night so many years ago. As she reached the last step of the stairs to the beach, that evening seemed like yesterday.

The tide was some way out when they stepped onto the sand. She couldn't make out the waves, but she could hear them rumbling in the distance.

The wind had a bite down here, and it cleared her head from the marijuana she'd smoked earlier. The weed she now believed this man had posted to her since he came to visit her that day not long after the photograph arrived. It was a habit she'd broken long ago, but relapsing came easy when the goods were free.

At the water's edge, halfway down the beach, she stared around, feeling disorientated. With a click, his torchlight vanished. There was no moonlight. Just madness. She didn't want to die.

Then her thoughts went back over the years. He was right. She had wasted her existence. The biggest success in her life, her son, had ended up her greatest failure. If it hadn't been for her mother, Timmy would have been in care. Even though he lived down the road, Candy didn't see him much. After a while, kids weren't so forgiving of failed parents.

'It's time,' said a voice next to her. 'You know what you did. There have to be seven.'

She shook her head.

'Why me first?'

Her voice tailed off. She wasn't the first. Natalie, her best friend, had been, and Candy was to blame. She'd sacrificed her friend, and now the sea wanted her to pay the price. A memory flashed through her mind. Seven people, high on life, but too high. Staggering around in the shallows, screaming as though they were neck deep.

She had to leave. Her hands tensed and she backed away from the tumbling waves. The air seemed to charge before a long, jagged flash of fork lightning lit up the sky. She stared into his face, which was too close to hers. His eyes blazed with righteous purpose, and she felt a fool.

Whatever he'd squirted in her mouth began to take effect and her heart raced as though the lightning had entered her body. Blood pulsed through her veins. She turned to run.

A hand on her upper arm stopped her while another on her neck twisted her around and propelled her forward until she was splashing in water. She tried to tip her head back to scream, but only a brief cry came out.

It sounded tiny in such a vast open space.

She was violently shunted forward, falling head first, and a wave slapped her in the face. The sea rolled over her, forcing her nose into the shifting sand on the bottom.

As the force of the turbulence subsided, she managed to hold herself in place on all fours, fingers clawing and sinking. She lifted her head clear and spat out the salty liquid, retching and coughing as her throat burned, before she sensed a bigger wall of water coming towards her.

She attempted to get to her feet, but the pressure had returned to her neck. This time, the grip on her neck didn't let go.

18

Ashley woke in the dark to a cool draught coming through the window, but the malice of the previous day's wind was gone. She swung her legs out of bed and almost twisted her ankle on the running gear she'd deliberately left there. The familiar pull of toast and jam made her mouth water. Be strong, she thought.

She was pleased that she'd only drunk tea when she got in because her head felt clear and, to her surprise, a small part of her was excited. Her jogging days had been a much happier time in her life. After half a glass of orange juice and a few stretches, she walked outside. If she was quick, she might catch the sun rising above the North Sea.

As she was locking up, Ashley noticed her neighbour's door was open, and he stood in the doorway with a mug in his hand. Arthur was a pleasant, quiet, elderly chap, whom she barely knew despite living next to him for nine years. In fact, she only knew his name because a letter was accidentally posted through her letter box with her own mail.

'Lovely morning, Arthur,' she said.

'I suppose so.'

'Coming for a run?'

'Just got back.'

'Excellent.' She was about to leave when she noticed a dampness on his face. 'Everything okay?'

When he finally looked at her, his eyes were red.

'Sorry. Today's a sad anniversary for me. It's funny. I could never remember our wedding anniversary, but I can recall the last time we spoke like it was yesterday. She was only going to the shops.'

Ashley had never met his wife, so she'd assumed she must have died a while ago. She had to wrack her brain to recall if he had many visitors. A woman came on a Saturday, but Ashley wasn't sure if it was a daughter come to clean, or just a cleaner.

'I'm sorry to hear that. How many years ago did she pass?'

His face fell.

'No, you misunderstand. It's the anniversary of when she left, although she'd already moved most of her stuff out of the house into the apartment of the bloke who ran the greengrocer's in town. I hadn't noticed. She said afterwards she didn't want to make a fuss. We communicated by text and email with the odd phone call, but we'd somehow become strangers.'

Ashley looked to her right and observed the blue sky starting to beat back the grey. There went her sunrise, and she needed to check in on Homeless Bob.

'Look, I've got to head off. Do you want me to pop by later and make you a cup of tea?'

He blinked a few times. 'You don't have to do that.'

'It's no hassle. I'm not overrun with friends either.'

She wondered whether that was rude, until he smiled.

'Okay. What's brought this on?'

'What do you mean?'

'You've hardly spoken to me in years.'

She was about to say that he hadn't talked to her either, or maybe explain that she'd been really busy at work, but she stopped herself.

'I think I'm having an epiphany.'

'Sounds painful. You can tell me about it later.'

Arthur gave her an endearing salute and closed his door. Ashley checked her phone was turned on, put it on the exercise app so she could see her stats when she got back, slipped it into her thin fleece pocket and zipped it up. She decided to jog through the chalet park. The cliff edge beyond was the best place to watch the sun rising, although it was quite a steep slope up to the top. She set a slow pace but was sweating profusely even before she'd reached it.

'Christ,' she gasped as she almost ground to a halt halfway to the summit.

She looked around to see if she was on her own and spat out the weird toxic phlegm that had collected in her mouth. Sweat beaded on her brow as she drove herself forward. Ashley was almost running on the spot by the time she reached the cliff fence, but a gentle breeze chilled her skin, and the view lifted her.

She'd missed the sunrise, but a golden globe hung above a row of clouds that resembled castles. She pulled the sea air into her wheezing lungs, which felt good and, at the same time, bad. She turned left and walked towards the cliff-top promenade and Bob's shed. Other runners were out and about. They all nodded or said good morning, which spurred her into a kind of lurching stagger.

She felt a twinge of guilt at letting herself get so unfit. When she was in Australia, she'd scuba dived and rafted. In the Far East she'd swum most days. She was a wreck in comparison to those days.

The last time she'd run anywhere was probably three summers ago when a wasp had got in her blouse while they were investigating what turned out to be animal remains at the back of a disused warehouse. Bloody insect had stung her on the tit as well.

Barry had been with her, and he'd started slapping her chest to kill it. She'd slapped him with the shock of it all, but they'd laughed afterwards over a coffee.

She gathered herself outside the gate to the back garden, then put her hand through the gap at the top of the gate and slid the bolt across. It was clear someone had been inside the garden because Barry had shut the shed door and it was now ajar.

'Bob! Are you there?' she shouted.

Ashley considered if she was in any danger. She was pretty certain she'd be able to fight off a sickly Bob, so she nudged open the shed door, letting the daylight flood in. It looked as if the sleeping bag had been moved from the bed, but it was unzipped and there was nobody in the room. She had a quick look around with the better light and saw dirty clothes scattered amidst the general rubbish.

In one of the corners next to the door, she lifted up an old newspaper to reveal a neat pile of folded clothing. She crouched next to it. On the collar of a plain white T-shirt was a streak of dark red. She took her phone from her pocket and used it to lift the edge of the T-shirt uncovering a pair of white trainers underneath. Ashley's heart sank when she saw they were also splattered with blood.

19

Ashley stepped out of the shed and called Control to report what she'd found. She got through to Jenny, who'd first given Ashley the call to go to the beach what seemed a long time ago now, and Jenny confirmed she would contact all the necessary teams.

Ashley pondered what she'd found. Could Bob be responsible for the horrific events of the day before? She pictured him in her head, and he did not look like the type of guy who'd be burying people in thick, wet sand or cutting off their heads. Drugs sent people crazy, though.

She bent down at the shed door and looked at the clothing again. Ashley had seen a lot of bloody clothing in the past, and she'd be surprised if it wasn't that. Sirens sounded in the distance. She looked at her watch: 7 a.m. It was going to be another gruelling shift.

She unlocked her phone and checked the fitness app. Four hundred metres run, four hundred walked. Eighty calories burned. She reminded herself it was only the first moment on a positive journey. It wasn't judgement day.

Ashley had a thought. She poked her head back in the shed to see if there was a big black coat with a hood but there was nothing like that in there. She opened her phone contacts and brought Dylan's last text up. It was unlikely he'd be at work on Sunday, but she also wanted to know if he'd been to visit the man who hated the sea the previous night at his hostel. She texted.

Does Homeless Bob have a limp?

The first response vehicle arrived with two keen-eyed youngsters. She smiled at their energy as they cordoned off the garden and the immediate space out of the gate. It would be nearly an hour before backup arrived if they were coming from Norwich. She scanned the garden, which wasn't a great scene for CSI to operate at again, and all the rubbish would need to be photographed and tagged. But she couldn't worry about that now, her priority was finding Bob.

She stayed until she could hand the scene to a sergeant and then headed to Henry's café. It was gone nine by the time she finished all the ringing around to get the town searched and update the teams who needed to be informed.

Ashley knew where the homeless chose to sleep in Cromer, the various parks, the cemetery, the beach, and the many local churches, which gave good protection from the wind and rain outside, even if their visitors weren't always allowed inside.

She headed back to her house the same way she'd come earlier and even managed a little jog down the hill. A search team was already combing through the ferns in Happy Valley, and it looked as if a dog handler was involved in a discussion with a uniformed group.

An armed response vehicle (ARV) was on its way to search the house in case Bob had broken in and was hiding inside. With the bloody clothing found, caution was needed with Bob. They were trying to contact the owners. The police were always being given short shrift about not investigating burglaries and lesser crimes, but the Norfolk team was impressive when it came to a serious crime like murder.

Back at her place, Ashley took a quick shower, then ate a bowl of Cheerios while her mind processed the information. She then ate two slices of toast with thick butter on before she remembered her new healthy-living regime.

'Fuck,' she whispered.

She saw she had missed a call on her mobile from DC Emma Stones so Ashley rang her back.

'Hey, Ash, how are you?'

Ashley smiled. The world could be burning, and Emma would always ask after your health. Barry had gone to school with her, and they'd joined the force at the same time. He told Ashley the bullies in sixth form gave her the horrific nickname of Twenty because of her weight. Apparently, the moniker had crept into her police training course until the tutor crushed it. Ashley wondered if Barry was to blame for that, but hadn't asked.

'Good, Emma. What's up?'

'We've found Bob.'

'Excellent. That's assuming he wasn't crouched over another victim.'

'He was staggering around on the beach, north of the pier.'

'Off his face?'

'Completely. Collapsed and vomited when they confronted him.'

'Was he armed?'

'Nope. The new guy, Hector Fade, was first on the scene. He has a lovely phone voice, by the way. Said that Bob was encrusted, which made me chuckle. I assume that means he was minging, but no weapons. We won't get any sense out of Bob for a few days.'

A message came through on Ashley's mobile. She asked Emma to hold, and saw it was from Dylan Crabb.

Bob doesn't limp, he lurches. Funny you should say that, though. I went around that guy's house we spoke about in the early evening. He seemed out of kilter, but I calmed him down. Now, Eddy does have a pronounced limp.

20

Ashley's mouth went dry. She told Emma, who immediately thought of how the new information would help with combing through the CCTV footage.

'That sounds promising.'

'Yes, are you at the station?'

'Yeah, my mum agreed to have the kids all day again.'

Ashley scowled. Where was that horrible husband of hers, and why wasn't he having them? She was pretty sure town planners didn't work weekends.

'Chat soon,' said Ashley, and finished the call before ringing Dylan.

'Hi, Dylan. Thanks for getting back to me. I don't suppose this Eddy guy has a large black coat.'

'I haven't noticed him in one.'

'How did he seem out of kilter?'

'Eddy was doing well. He's got himself fit and healthy, said he's been working out at a local gym, but this hollering on the cliffs is a worrying recent development. He reckoned that's where he was last night. I'd describe his state as extremely stressed.'

'I'm going to need to speak to him, Dylan. Pronto.'

'I know. I just don't think it can be him, though. He's a good kid.'

'Didn't you say he's been in prison for thirty years?'

'No, I said he was in a secure unit. Kind of a hospital. You'll understand the *kid* comment when you meet him, so I'm not sure how he'll react to questioning. Can I be present?'

'Definitely. You said he's fit. Is he strong?'

'Yes, I'd say so. Why?'

'Just wondering. We've picked up Bob in a right mess, but it looks like he could be involved.'

'Really?'

'I'm afraid so. What are your plans today?'

'Like I said, coffee at the Doggie Diner at ten. I normally chill Sunday afternoons, but of course I'll come to the station today. This sort of thing unsettles the entire community. Do you want me to sit in with Bob, too?'

'No, I don't think so. Bob won't be suitable for interview for a while, but what he needs is a bloody good solicitor. I tell you what, I'll pop down to the café and you can give me the background on this Eddy guy. It's a murder enquiry, and he's now a suspect, so that trumps any patient-doctor privilege. I'll get the forms done. What's the guy's full name?'

'Edward Balmain.'

'I'll see you at the café.'

So Edward Balmain was strong. That fitted the profile better than Homeless Bob. Could they be working together? How bloody angry did you have to be to saw someone's head off while they were alive? Or how mad?

Her brain instantly brought an image of Geoffrey up. He was fit and mad. Ashley had seen him digging for lugworms and he'd seemed like a machine. It was time to talk to him again, too, assuming they could find him. She knew he would normally have brought his catch in by now and be tidying up, so she texted Hector to head down there. If he was about as usual, she'd be less concerned.

She wasn't going to arrest Eddy Balmain on her own, so she put a call back to Emma and gave her an

update about the latest intel. Sal and she were
trawling through CCTV. Ashley then rang Control
and informed them of her movements and explained
her requirements. DCI Kettle would organise everything as the SIO.

They had the ARV in the town centre, and they
were mob-handed with all the personnel helping
with the inquiry, so manpower wasn't a problem. Unfortunately, they weren't dealing with an average
hard-faced criminal who might even get off on being
dragged past his neighbours. Eddy was going to be
unpredictable. If they could pick him up quietly, it
would be better all round. After all, he might have
nothing to do with it. Limping around town didn't
necessarily make him the murderer.

Ashley put yesterday's suit on without thinking
but chose a different coloured blouse. She had a pair
of black trainers that were a bit like shoes, so she
pulled them on. The detective team wouldn't be
leading the charge into Eddy's property. They would
need strong men or women in stab vests for that.
Kettle would probably call for help from the Operational Support Group. OSG officers were trained for
arrests that had an element of heightened risk.

She cursed as she left the house. A Taser team
would need to be present as a minimum but that

complicated matters. Eddy was probably living at a stepdown property, which would have at least three other residents with varying issues, maybe even as high as twenty others, depending which establishment it was. Incapacitating people like him with a Taser, in front of others, was a poor option, fraught with danger.

'I heard that, lady.'

Ashley looked up and saw the cheeky young lad from next door hanging out of his bedroom window. Oliver had a habit of shouting down to her when he saw her leave. She always gave him a minute, because he seemed desperate to be noticed.

'I said fudge,' she replied.

'Okay. I won't tell if you watch me play football later.'

'Who are you planning to tell?'

'My gran.'

'Your gran's not the boss of me.'

'Come anyway?'

'What about your mum?'

'Nah, she's stuck in London. Helping people.'

'Helping people escape jail?'

'Funny! Nah, I told you. She's a great lawyer.'

'What about your gran?'

'She's poorly and in bed.'

'Sorry, Oliver.'

'Please watch. My mum even got Oliver put on the back of my shirt.'

'Isn't it supposed to be your surname?'

'Not if you're the best, like the Brazilians. You know. Pele!'

'I'd love to, but I'm working.'

'On a Sunday?'

'Yeah, next time.'

'Do you always work Sundays?'

'Not usually.'

'Cool. Because we're playing the top of the league next Sunday. Do we have a deal?'

Ashley growled, but she'd only be lying on the sofa otherwise.

'Sure.'

'Promise.'

'Yeah, I promise.'

She was about to let out another growl, but he looked so chuffed that she just chuckled at the youth's impudence. Ashley felt a twinge of sympathy that he wouldn't have anyone to watch him today, but she cleared her mind and strode down the street at a fast pace.

Doggie Diner café was a ten-minute walk from hers at the edge of the town centre. Not having the time for a dog of her own, she'd never visited, but she'd often seen it busy. When she arrived she spotted Dylan inside and her eyes widened as she saw him talking to Dora Thorne. Ashley then recalled the chihuahua in her basket, so that kind of made sense. It was nice to see her smiling. She really was tough.

Ashley's phone rang as she was about to enter the café. She accepted the call.

'Yes, Hector.'

There wasn't an immediate reply, but she could hear the slap of running feet.

'Hello?' she said.

Heavy breathing came on the line.

'Ashley?'

'What's going on?'

'I was down the beach with that Geoffrey guy. A jogger pelted across the sand towards us. He said there's a dead body further down the beach. I'm almost there now.'

21

Ashley sat down on the bench outside the café to think. Uniform would have taken Homeless Bob handcuffed to Norwich hospital, so he was secure and could be interviewed when he wasn't under the influence. Eddy Balmain seemed a more likely suspect but you didn't have to attend detective training to wonder about the fact that Mad Geoffrey was nearby when both crime scenes were discovered. She needed to warn Hector.

'Have you called for backup?'

'No, I was worried it might be a mannequin.'

She supposed it was possible. Jokers had pulled similar pranks over the years.

'Okay, ring in whatever it is. Get uniform down there. Control the scene. Where's Geoffrey?'

There was a pause, which Ashley assumed was Hector looking for Geoffrey.

'He's following me down the beach, but walking. He's bringing a spade.'

Alarm bells went off in Ashley's head. How well did she really know Geoffrey?

'Hector. Be careful of Geoffrey. Keep your distance.'

There was another pause and Ashley could imagine Hector's stomach clenching.

'Understood. Barry was with me at the other scene. I'll ring him to get straight down here. I was debating arresting Geoffrey but decided to see how he acts.'

'Good plan. Don't let him leave, though. We need to talk to him at the station so arrest him if you have to.' She told Hector about talking to Dylan to get the low-down on Eddy Balmain. 'I'll call you back afterwards,' she said. 'Hey, how come you have a signal?'

'I had an old pay-as-you-go phone on Three, so I've charged it and put some credit on.'

Ashley smiled. This arsehole was going to make her look bad.

'I'm at the scene now,' said Hector. 'There's quite a

crowd, so I'm more relaxed about the risk of Geoffrey burying me alive.'

Ashley listened to him shooing the people back.

'It's not a dummy, definitely not a dummy. Female. Maybe fifties. She's almost submerged at the end of a breakwater. No obvious signs of trauma, but only her back is visible, not her face.'

'Give me ten minutes,' said Ashley, and cut the call.

She entered the café feeling dazed. After what she'd just heard, it felt odd going in somewhere that felt like a party that was in full swing. Dylan was laughing with a tall guy wearing an apron. Dylan's little mongrel, Augustus, was licking a sausage, then looking up all pleased with himself, then lapping away at it again.

Dora Thorne waved from behind a huge slice of cheesecake. Happy, her chihuahua, was lucky that Ashley was on more important business, because whatever he was doing to the fluffy bear he had on the floor with him was most certainly a crime in a public place.

Ashley waved back and stood next to Dora.

'Is everything okay?'

'Yes. I had a restless night, but a bit of cake and pleasant company will put the world to rights. You might think me cold, but it's the reverse. Events like my husband dying and those poor people yesterday have taught me to try to enjoy every moment I have left.'

Admirable sentiments, thought Ashley, and you had to love the resilience of most old people. Her dog was certainly making the most of things.

'I came around to see you yesterday afternoon to see if we could add to that statement but you were out, and you didn't answer your phone.'

'I popped to a neighbour's house and left my phone on charge.'

'Did you remember anything else?'

'No, sorry, love.'

Ashley showed her the picture of the stone that Hector guessed was on one of the buckets. Dora nodded.

'Yes, that's it. The other one was more like a well-worn brick. You get a lot of them down there.'

A young woman came over. She had a bit of a goth vibe going on.

'What would you like?' she asked with a genuine smile.

Ashley glanced at her name badge.

'Sorry, Lola, I haven't got a dog with me.'

'That's okay, well-behaved humans are allowed too.'

Ashley ordered a hot chocolate to go, then took a seat in the corner where a foursome had just left. Dylan, who wore a flannel shirt and trousers, came and sat next to her. With his wavy hair, he looked as if he should be on the cover of a hairdressing magazine. Even though he appeared different from the average person in the street, he was one of the most moderate and reasonable people she'd ever met.

'Okay, Dylan,' said Ashley, getting her pocketbook out. 'We shouldn't be overheard. I hate to do this officially, but we need the details on what you know about Eddy.'

'No problem. He was in a medium secure unit called Brancaster House not far from here for most of his life. I'm not sure what the initial cause was, or if it was a run of things, which had him sectioned. I've had him under my care for a year on day release and stopovers, but he's been permanently discharged from the hospital for over six months.'

'So, he's better now?'

'Not as such. If you're diagnosed with something like schizophrenia, there's no cure, but a combination of drugs and support can help patients manage their condition. In his case, the new medication helped curb his anger and confusion, and therefore reduced his threat to others.'

Ashley's order arrived. She then remembered she was supposed to be on fruit teas.

'So, he was coping,' she said. 'But now he's deteriorating again. Is there a recall procedure for you to take him back off the streets?'

'After so long out, he would need to return to court, and the magistrates would need evidence of him being a significant danger to himself or others, which is quite a high bar. Eddy probably broke the law to get sectioned when he was ill three decades ago, but he's served his time. He's just trying to be a regular guy now.'

'Unless he's our beach killer.'

'Fair enough, but the link between violence and mental health problems is grossly exaggerated.'

'You said he was violent in the unit he was in.'

'Yes, but apparently only when they tried to make him leave the unit. When he was left to his own devices, he was reasonably compliant. Then they had a breakthrough, and he was reintroduced into society.'

'Reasonably compliant?'

'Yes, if you or I were put under conditions like those in a secure unit, we'd blow up at times, too. It's a tricky balancing act between maintaining security and providing a therapeutic environment.'

'I suppose that if you sent him back, he may never get out again.'

'Correct. He's come a long way, but, like many before him, it's a serious struggle to rejoin society.'

'Can you explain?'

'Do you remember the film *Awakenings*?'

'Just about. The patients woke up after being given a new drug. It stopped working, so they went back to sleep.'

'Kind of. The medication worked, but they're still unsure as to why the patients' mental and physical health deteriorated. Part of the problem was their subjects had been asleep for decades. How do you cope with life when you return to it after missing so many years? Your parents are likely dead, your friends gone, the opportunity to have children has passed without you even being aware of it. No career, no money, no pension. And, except for in a hospital environment, they have no experience of making, building and maintaining relationships, either sexual or platonic.'

'Sounds a bit like me,' said Ashley.

Dylan laughed. 'In your case, there's an element of choice.'

Ashley raised an eyebrow at him, but let it pass, seeing as it was mostly true. Another plate of cheese-cake came out of the kitchen, Ashley couldn't help licking her lips, but managed not to order any.

'Okay. My team are arranging to bring Eddy in. I suspect they'll have a Taser team at the front of the property so you'll have to stand back behind the offi-cers who'll go in first. We'll see how he reacts. What does he look like?'

'He was chubby when he came out, but he's slimmed down now. The limp was caused by a car ac-cident in his late teens. His neck and the left side of his face were burned, so he's no beauty, but he has a nice smile, thick blond hair and very blue eyes. They'd be handsome features on a different person, but his mannerisms aren't always natural. And, like in *Awakenings*, I fear dyskinesia is appearing.'

'What's that?'

'Violent tics and sudden movements. His aren't so pronounced, but his left hand is showing signs of spasticity, even though it's not a symptom he's shown before. It could be the new drugs. They have all manner of side effects, which sometimes worsen the longer they're taken.'

'Okay, what's the address?'

Ashley took the details, grabbed her drink and

left the café. She rang Kettle and discussed the plan. He told her he would personally attend and said DC Salvador Freitas and DS Bhavini Kotecha would be on hand to assist at the station. Although the custody officers there would be able to cope with anything, it helped if the investigating team could see behaviours first hand.

Eddy's home wasn't far from Ashley's favourite Chinese takeaway. Lucky it wasn't open, or she'd be tempted to completely blow her new healthy lifestyle while she waited for everyone to turn up.

Ashley took the opportunity to ring Hector on the beach. He picked up after a few rings.

'How are things?' she asked.

'Uniform have the scene controlled. CSI are on the way, but there's very little here. The pool she was in has drained, so she's half exposed. I rolled the woman to see if she has any wounds on the front of her body, but there aren't any. It looks like she might have drowned. Our pathologist is already doing those two post-mortems, so she can't attend.'

'I assume you're against the tide too, being further out.'

'Yes. Geoffrey said this section of sand will be three metres under in a little over five hours. A coroner's officer is on the way. Barry arrived. He got annoyed with Geoffrey's attitude, Geoffrey then threatened Barry, so Barry's arrested him and stuck him in the back of a patrol car. We'll be bringing Geoffrey in shortly.'

'Great. I'm hoping to fetch an Edward Balmain and bring him in, too. We'll crack on with the interviews and see if we can find out what the blazes is going on here.'

Dylan was leaving the café as Ashley cut the call.

'This stepdown place for Eddy must have CCTV,' she said.

'Yes, of course,' he replied.

'We normally barge in and arrest people at 5 a.m. while they're asleep, but we need to speak to him today.'

'That wouldn't work, anyway. He'd be groggy and confused and more likely to lash out.'

'Okay. What's your best guess? Will he be violent now if we ask him to come with us to the station?'

'I don't think so. Not if I'm in the car with him.'

'But isn't this like the secure unit?'

'I don't follow.'

'Aren't we about to take him from somewhere he doesn't want to leave?'

Dylan shrugged, but Ashley noticed he swallowed deeply afterwards.

22

Ashley stood a hundred metres up from the address and glanced up and down the road. They'd easily set up a cordon because there was a circular route for traffic to move around. The ARV, which was a big 4x4, was parked up near the house, and the officers were prepared, but Ashley didn't expect them to be needed. A Taser officer was ready to go, just in case. They were waiting for DCI Kettle's imminent arrival to make the final decisions.

Dylan had given them the mobile number for the support worker on duty in the property, who had confirmed that Eddy Balmain was there. He'd come out of his room, had his breakfast, and behaved normally. The warden was working days, so he wasn't sure about Eddy's nocturnal movements, but he said he rarely saw Eddy. He couldn't say if that was because he was out, or if he was in his bedroom but he'd heard nothing out of the ordinary from that room.

He said that wasn't unusual because many of the eight residents in the place were on strong medication, which made them drowsy. More promising was that none of the others had moaned about Balmain. Resident complaints were usually a good indicator of worsening behaviour because even though they generally supported each other, they also knew the signs to look out for, as most had relapsed themselves in the past. Those people had also jumped through quite a few hoops to get to this point in their lives and they were protective of their space.

Ashley was checking her watch when the front door opened and a thick-set man with blond hair and sunglasses appeared. Nothing unusual seemed to register on his face as he looked up the street. It had to be Eddy Balmain. He turned, locked the door behind him, and placed his key in his coat pocket. There was a metre-high gate that separated the pavement from the house. As Eddy stepped towards it, Ashley strolled over and stood a few metres away.

'Eddy. My name is Detective Sergeant Ashley

Knight. Do you have a minute? I've got a few questions.'

Eddy put both hands on the top of the gate, but didn't push it open. He raised his sunglasses and rested them on his head, then squinted at her.

'I don't know you. Why do you want to talk to me?'

Ashley was encouraged by the fact he sounded lucid and sober. Even from three metres away, she could tell his eyes were a light shade of blue that was quite unnerving above a heavily scarred lower face.

'There's been an incident. Will you help us with our enquiries?'

'I'm not breaking the rules on the cliff tops,' he replied slowly.

He looked down the street again and seemed to realise that there were many officers in uniforms staring at him. His eyes returned to her face. Any calm in them had vanished. When he spoke next, he lowered his head in the same way a charging bull would, glaring up from under his eyebrows.

'People need to be warned about the sea.'

'It's not about the cliffs,' she said. 'It's the beach.'

Eddy's moody face constricted into one of horror. He took a step back, then another, before raising his chin.

'No, I won't go back. I'll never go back.'

Eddy frantically glanced around himself, but, even in his stressed state, he could see there was no escape in front of him so he got his door key out again.

'Calm down, Eddy,' said Dylan from across the road.

Eddy's head shot in the direction of the voice. His neck arched as he shouted.

'Dylan, stop them. I told you, and I told them. I told everyone. Not the beach.'

Eddy yanked the gate open, then stomped out onto the pavement. Ashley retreated as his head swivelled in her direction, like the turret of a tank. The OSG officer next to her stepped forward.

Eddy raised his fists, but Ashley sensed it was more a defensive pose.

'Taser, Taser, Taser. Sir, lower your hands or I will deploy my Taser!'

Eddy's teeth clenched as he turned his focus onto the officer.

'Eddy, no, we're not going to the beach,' shouted Ashley. 'We want to chat to you at the police station. In an office.'

'That's right,' shouted Dylan. 'I'll come with you,

Eddy. It's just questions about what you can see from the cliffs.'

Ashley detected a further spark of anger in Eddy's expression, but then his shoulders dropped, and his arms lowered. He scratched his head and squinted, but his teeth were still bared.

'It's okay, Eddy,' said Dylan.

Eddy pulled his sunglasses back down. The tension in his lips relaxed, covering his snarl.

'Okay. If Dylan says it's fine, I'll go.'

The Taser officer looked back at Ashley, who nodded.

'The officer will sit with you in the back of the car. That's for everyone's safety. Is that okay?'

Eddy strode towards the officer, then stuck his arms out in a way that showed being handcuffed was not a new experience. Ashley wasn't arresting him, so hadn't planned on using cuffs, but she noticed Eddy's bulging forearms, which had a network of pronounced veins on them. He looked at Ashley.

'Not the beach.'

She shook her head and smiled.

Eddy was put in the back of an estate car with an officer next to him. Ashley sat in the front seat and studied Eddy through the grille.

'Are you okay now?' she asked him.

'Yes, yes. Sorry, you surprised me. I don't like the beach.'

'We need to peek inside your room at the house. Is that all right?'

'Why do you want to look in there? That's my private place.'

'We'd like to rule certain things out.'

'What's happened?'

'We're not sure yet. These officers will take you to the main office and we'll get this cleared up, okay?'

'Where's Dylan?'

'He'll be in the front seat here in a minute. I'll see you back at the station.'

She got out and went over to Dylan, who was standing a little away from the others. He gave her a sad smile.

'I thought he was going to blow up then. Will he be safe in the police car?'

'Yes, a six-foot-four constable sitting next to you is a great neutraliser. The officer in with him has options, if necessary, but he seems calm. We'll have an extra unit follow them. Just talk to Eddy on the way back, keep him chatting about whatever he likes.'

Before Dylan had a chance to get into the car, Kettle arrived in an expensive-looking BMW and Ashley brought him up to speed.

'What is it you want?' he asked, cutting to the chase in his usual blunt manner.

'I need to search the property and gardens of Balmain's place, but I didn't arrest him,' said Ashley, hoping for authorisation.

A smile threatened to appear on Kettle's face.

'Nice try, but you'll need to get a warrant. Then get it searched. Find me sandy shoes or bloody clothes. Get the CCTV. Find him going out last night or the night before. Let's have this sorted, before anyone else dies.'

Dylan was hovering behind her.

'I thought I'd mention something I forgot to tell you earlier,' he said. 'I walked through town on the way to the café this morning. When I passed that big white building next to the sunken garden, I noticed there was graffiti on it. Well, it was a poem of some kind.'

'You think it's connected to this?'

'God knows, but it was the way Eddy talked about the sea as though it was alive that reminded me. I went to the boating pond afterwards and my hunch was right. It looks like the same black paint and style of writing that was used to put those numbers on the council building.'

'Okay, what did the rhyme say?'

'Hang on. I took a photo.' He pulled his phone from his jeans.

'Look, Dylan, you'd better get going,' said Ashley. 'Eddy might become agitated in the car. Send it to my phone.'

'Will do. I'll see you at the station. Remind me to talk to you about how thin he is.'

Ashley had a quick word with the PC who was driving and the one who was following to support, but they were veterans and didn't need advice. She watched as they drove off and a minute later, her mobile beeped.

She opened the message and looked at the picture. She had to use her fingers to expand the shot on the small screen, but the black words were clear and bold on the white background of the house.

Only when there are seven
Can they rest in heaven
For nobody can deny
The Hungry Sea

A shiver ran up Ashley's spine.

23

Ashley rang Sal back at the station to organise the warrant. They probably could have searched the room with the warden present, but because Ashley had chosen not to antagonise Eddy by arresting him, it was better to wait for an hour or two and do it by the book. There was no point in rushing the search, either. Kettle redirected the second CSI van that was on its way to the beach, so it would be there when the warrant came through.

Kettle and Ashley looked in the room from the door to make sure it wasn't a gorefest in there. They would have wanted to warn those transporting Eddy if that were the case, but they saw nothing obvious, although it was messy with clothes strewn over the carpet. Ashley thought of the mess in Homeless Bob's shed. Outside, they asked the support worker how these places ran.

'When the residents arrive, there's a contract signed where they agree to one-to-one meetings with staff, having their medication supervised, behaviour observed, and regular room checks. We keep a close eye on them, especially at the beginning, but Eddy's been here six months. He wasn't allowed out all night at the start, but he's free to come and go as he pleases now. The next step for him is a more independent place, maybe a shared bungalow with only daytime support, but we've noticed his struggles, so we've reined back in for now.'

'Might it be to do with his meds?'

'Perhaps. Eddy's been managing his own meds without our involvement for quite a while.'

'Isn't him shouting at the sea from cliff tops cause enough for an intervention?'

'I've gone and fetched him myself. It's only through the chalet park. When I've got near him and he's noticed I'm there, he stops.'

'And that's okay?'

'Yes, it means he has an awareness of what he's doing and, even though it's unusual behaviour, it's not illegal. Maybe he had a terrible experience at the seaside when he was younger. You also have to accept that the people who live here have been very unwell. They may now be much better, but they aren't like you and me. Unusual conduct is expected. If we returned them to secure care the first time they shouted at a wall or an imaginary friend, we'd have a lot of empty rooms.'

Kettle blew out his cheeks.

'It seems as though you're waiting for them to do something really serious.'

'Isn't that what you do?'

Kettle smirked, but then nodded at the truth of the statement.

'Would he have the mental capacity to disguise his behaviour?' asked Ashley.

'Of course. Eddy is a long way from stupid. He can beat me at draughts, so yes, he could.'

'What about murder?' asked Ashley.

The care worker wasn't daft. He knew they were talking about the horrific events on the beach.

'Yes, he might have changed his clothes afterwards and had a shower here, or I suppose he could have swum in the sea to wash blood off. I hope it isn't him, but his behaviour has deteriorated considerably. I've stopped turning my back on him.'

Kettle grimaced at that.

'What about dealing with the emotional after-math of taking a life?' he asked.

'Not everyone wears their heart on their sleeves.'

Ashley couldn't help a chuckle. That was damn true.

She told Kettle she was off to have a look at the graffiti near the sunken garden next to North Lodge Park. It was a fifteen-minute walk, but that was fine. She needed to wrap her brain around all the different angles, because right now there was too much confusion for her to even have a hunch.

Ashley took her time and stopped at a newsagent's on the way for a snack. She stared at the Double Deckers but chose an apple instead and grabbed *The Sun* newspaper after seeing the headline. The front page had one word on it. Saw. She supposed that wasn't a surprise considering the gruesome findings on the beach.

When she reached the white house with the paint on it, she read the rhyme again with a frown. She really hoped it wasn't connected to their case.

Up close, it looked as though a matt paint had been used. It was something else to get analysed, but again it would probably only be valuable as evidence when they caught who'd done it.

Painting was messy. It would leave residue on

someone's hands or clothes. Or under their finger-nails, unless, of course, they had gloves on.

There was a strong police presence in town, but it would also be much busier, because, although the clouds were grey, it was warm. That always brought day-trippers to the town. She wandered through to the café in North Lodge Park and was disappointed to see it closed. A nice coffee would have gone down well. It hadn't reopened consistently since the pandemic.

Ashley sat on the wall of the boating pond, got her penknife out of her pocket, and began to cut the skin off the apple. As she was Deputy SIO, the rest of her day was going to be frantic. There'd be meetings, absorbing gathered intel, paperwork, and updating command staff. Once she got back to the main office, she probably wouldn't get the chance to eat again. It was unlikely she would get any peace to quietly think either.

As she took in the scene, she flicked the bits of skin to a fat seagull who swallowed them piece by piece, as if they were coming on a conveyor belt. Part of the apple thing was Emma had once told her about a diet if you were prone to snacking on crap. The idea was that if you were hungry out of mealtimes, your only option was an apple. If you didn't fancy an apple, you weren't hungry enough and therefore you should have nothing.

She studied the writing on the council building again, which she was surprised to see had been added to. Thirteen now had a four next to it and there was a mark through the three. She slid off the wall, took a bite of apple, and wandered over.

Up close, she could see that someone had attempted to put a line through the three *and* the one, but it appeared they'd run out of paint. She heard a trundling behind her.

'Morning, madam.'

Ashley recognised the man pushing the wheel-barrow as a council worker, by his hi-vis work clothes, but she also recalled him drinking in the town pubs. She couldn't remember his name but remembered him as being affable.

Drinking in a small town could be problematic, but Ashley hadn't been one for getting absolutely steaming in public. Not until she hit rock bottom, anyway. Then Peter had given her a little advice, and she'd drunk at home. Was that any better? She doubted it was better for her.

When she was in the pub, she wasn't on duty, even though she could still exercise most of her powers. Didn't she deserve the same opportunities and social life as everyone else? Wasn't she allowed to make mistakes, even make a fool of herself when she wasn't being paid? She guessed there were lines, but they were thick, grey ones.

'I'm here to clean these off,' said the guy.

'Do you know how long they've been painted on here?'

'Only a few days. People get married in this place, so we try to keep it nice. That number one and the seven turned up Friday morning, but I was off. The number three appeared on Saturday morning, then the four this morning. They're paying me double to work today. They have important visitors arriving Monday.'

He gave her a wide-eyed nod, as though the prime minister were coming, which she doubted.

'I'm sorry, but we're going to need to take samples from these first.'

'Oh, that's a shame. Will you be finished today?'

'I'll ask them to ring you when they're done.'

As she took shots from a distance and close up, her mind whirred. With it being either side of the door, the numbers could have been fractions. A seventh, three sevenths, now four sevenths.

'I don't suppose you know who did it. Would it be kids?'

'They told me that a woman from the third floor of the holiday lets behind us noticed when they were painting the three, but the person had a big coat and hood and their face was concealed, so she couldn't describe them.'

Ashley's brain clicked it all into place. First it was 1/7, then 3/7. The 1 should have been crossed out, but they were disturbed. Last night was 4/7, and the other numbers were supposed to be struck out, but it seemed the paint had run out.

What did the rhyme say? Only when there were seven, could they rest in heaven. Were two and three Ron and Ruby? They were murdered Saturday morning. Was number four being pulled out of a rock pool at that very moment? So, who was number one? Had the person been killed on Thursday night or Friday morning and they just hadn't found the body yet?

If there were going to be seven, then there were three more to go. Was number five lined up for tonight?

Ashley swallowed and the piece of apple stuck hard. She coughed it out, bringing tears to her eyes. What the hell was happening?

24

By the time Ashley returned to the stepdown house, the warrant had been authorised and CSI were going through Eddy Balmain's room. An hour later, there was nothing definitive, so Kettle offered to drive Ashley back to OCC. Even though Ashley knew little about Kettle's private life, they worked well together. Although the first detailed conversation she'd had with him and his boss, Det Supt Zara Grave, had been after a mistake which nearly let a serial rapist off the hook.

She and Barry had been instructed to attend Grave's office. While they were waiting outside, Barry had said, 'We're about to be Kettle and Graved.' She hadn't had a chance to query the phrase, as they'd been called into the meeting, but it meant you lost. Top Brass were either time-served coppers who knew their stuff, or politicians who raced through the ranks like wildfire. Kettle was one, and Grave was the other. That meant no bullshit worked when they grilled you at the same time.

Kettle, who had always been called by his surname during his time in uniform, at least had a sense of humour, and he often wore the expression of an old-fashioned stern policeman, whereas Grave, who insisted on being called Zara, looked like a friendly accountant.

Ashley admired his car when she got inside and they set off but didn't comment on it.

'Any news on Peter?' she asked.

'I spoke to him last night. I was planning to pop around, but he's gone to stay at a friend's. Says he's going to turn his phone off and try to relax. Hopefully, he'll return soon. We told him to have a fortnight off, get his head together, then come back for a chat.'

'Fair enough.'

She knew he wouldn't say any more, and, as if to prove that, he quickly changed the subject.

'What's your gut reaction about these three suspects?'

'Geoffrey, Bob and Eddy?'

'Yes.'

'My gut's in turmoil. But first let me tell you about this graffiti.'

Kettle groaned when she'd finished.

'Don't you love it when a case gets worse and worse?'

'Yep. We're going to have to put someone on that beach tonight.'

'Two, I would say. Shame I can't swing an ARV, park it on the shore with flashing lights, just to be certain.'

'Pity we can't lie in wait. It'd be a good chance to catch the killer in the act.'

'I think the boss would take some persuading to agree to that.'

Ashley laughed.

'I suppose if nothing happens tonight, then it's more likely that we have the person responsible in custody.'

Kettle smiled.

'I think a manned patrol car will be an adequate deterrent to any more sacrifices.'

Ashley swung her head to look at him. 'Hector mentioned Ron and Ruby's deaths felt like sacrifices.'

'I was being facetious. The death this morning was different.'

'I suppose suicide is likely. People do strange things at crime scenes.'

'They certainly do. Not that I'd want one, but another incident would help our line of inquiry.'

Ashley chuckled. It was gallows humour, but with an element of truth.

'What's that phrase?' she said. 'One for sorrow, two for joy.'

'Three for a pattern that even CID can't miss.'

They both grinned at that.

'I want you to do all the interviews,' he said.

'Okay. I assume I can choose who to do each one with.'

'Nope. Do them with Hector Fade.'

Ashley considered that. It wasn't a big deal. Hector would have been the most recently trained when he first joined CID and he was young, which was sometimes a good contrast with a more mature detective like Ashley.

'I was thinking of Emma Stones,' she said.

Kettle shook his head.

'Nah, she's too nice for this, and Barry's too nasty. Pederson and Freitas would probably freak them out. This Hector comes well recommended, and they have great plans for him. He solved numerous tricky cases in the Met, and he wasn't there long.'

'Is Daddy pulling strings?'

'Ah, you managed to make the connection.' Kettle smiled.

'Him having the same surname as one of the Met's big cheeses was a clue.'

'Ex cheeses.'

'Oh, I hadn't heard.'

'Yes, although it was fairly sudden.' Kettle rubbed his chin for a moment. 'I want you to have Hector's corner. I know how some of the guys can be when we have these fast-trackers.'

'You're the boss,' said Ashley, but she suspected Hector could hold his own. 'I'll talk to Eddy Balmain first, while we have his care coordinator with us. We'll also need a lot more bodies to check so much CCTV.'

'That's sorted. We've got staff from all over and they're on it now. I think we have enough to hold Balmain for a couple of days. If that limp of his is identical to one of the persons seen painting the town black, then we certainly have enough. If he's on the CCTV at his premises coming back at 6 yesterday morning in a different set of clothes than he went out in, then he'll be under lock and key until the trial.'

'I agree. Same as Homeless Bob. How long for the DNA check on the trainers and shirt? If the blood came from Ron or Ruby, then Bob will be clucking in a prison cell in a few days. Have you heard how he is?'

'While you were sightseeing in town, I was on the blower. DNA's being hurried. Should get the results Tuesday morning. Bob's withdrawal is so bad that he's been sedated. He's not going anywhere until we've had a chat with him. Tuesday will be a good time if we know the test results. What about this Mad Geoffrey guy?'

'He's struggling at the moment, too, which is making me suspicious when normally I wouldn't have considered him. The thing is, these aren't simple crimes. If this graffiti is connected, then it's a complex old plot, and I can't imagine the Bob and Eddy show are running it. Maybe Mad Geoffrey's the high priest in this production, and those two are his disciples.'

Kettle parked up and they entered the building together and headed for the incident room. There was a buzz and energy about the place that didn't diminish when they arrived. The air was thick with heated conversation.

Emma Stones rushed over to them.

'We've just had word of a missing person. A woman called Candice Sweet has vanished from her house. She hasn't been seen since last night and is a bit of an agoraphobic, so she rarely leaves home. Mrs

Sweet, her mother, is on her way here with a photograph of her. Candice matches the profile of the middle-aged lady found on the beach this morning, but obviously we're only in the process of taking the body to the mortuary.'

'Straight to the punchline, please,' said Kettle, picking up on there being something more.

'Sorry, sir. DS Kotecha has just informed us that Candice Sweet is the same woman who was involved in the nasty domestic in Felbrigg on Friday night.'

25

Ashley sighed. This was one of those cases where new information was arriving so fast that it was a struggle to keep up. The computer system, HOLMES, was brilliant at making connections, but it needed the information keying in first, and there hadn't been time for much of that. When the room was set up on Monday, thousands of pieces of information would be entered each day by a team of experienced data-in-putters.

Ashley was rubbing her temples when Hector and Barry returned from Cromer beach. They came straight over to her, and Hector showed her a series of photos he'd taken from different angles at the scene. She flicked through the pictures twice. A few had caught the horrified expression of bystanders as they looked down on the deceased.

'Still no obvious signs of foul play?' she asked.

Hector shook his head.

Ashley concentrated on the last close-up of what was obviously going to be Candice Sweet, as if the waxen face were somehow going to talk to her. The question she wanted to ask was why would a middle-aged woman head to the beach on a dark night?

'Barry, there's no family liaison officer about this afternoon, can you and Emma talk to Mrs Sweet when she arrives? Hector, let's prepare for our talk with Eddy.'

An hour later, Ashley was in the interview room with Hector. They'd decided their direction of inquiry was going to be dictated by what Edward Balmain said. Dylan Crabb and he had been waiting in one of the quiet rooms that were kept for people who had not been arrested but were helping with enquiries. The duty solicitor also sat in with them.

After the preliminaries were finished and Eddy was cautioned, Ashley steepled her hands. Eddy looked presentable and was clean-shaven, even though there were patches around his chin that he'd missed. He clearly hadn't lost all control, although there was a slight tremble to his fingers, which he'd rested on the table in front of him. Perhaps significantly, there was no black paint under his fingernails.

'Do you think you've done anything wrong over the last few days?' she asked.

'No. No, I haven't,' replied Eddy.

'But you acknowledge that you have been warning people about the sea. You stand on the cliff tops, and shout.'

Eddy shrugged.

'Yes.'

'Why?'

'It's alive. They say it has no memory, but it does. She wants what she wants, and she can't be denied.'

Eddy nodded after he said that, turned to Dylan, and nodded at him as if he'd delivered obvious advice.

'And what does the sea want?' asked Ashley.

'It wants seven.'

'Seven what?'

Eddy's eyes narrowed, but he didn't reply.

'Brides, seas, perhaps dwarves?' asked Hector.

Eddy glanced at his solicitor and pointed a thumb at Hector. He barked out a laugh. His cackle faded and the gaze that returned to Ashley was stony.

'The original seven.'

'Who are the original seven?' she asked.

Eddy's face curled up as though he was trying to recall something long forgotten.

'The girls and boys,' he said after a painful, silent minute.

'Which girls and boys?'

'I can't remember.'

Hector leaned forward.

'Did you write the graffiti on the council building in town or on the white building next to the sunken garden?'

Eddy blinked at them as if they were talking in riddles. He released a deep sigh, but again, he didn't reply.

'Were you on the beach in the last two days?'

'No, no, no. I don't go on the beach.'

'When was the last time you were on the beach?'

A line of sweat had broken out on Eddy's forehead.

'Not since the thing.'

'What thing?'

'When it all started.'

'When what started?'

Balmain waved his finger at them.

'I won't go back. I can't. I'm special, you see. Someone else can be seven. They explained every-thing. It made sense.'

Eddy's head jerked upwards, which caused everyone in the room to twitch. His eyes wandered around the room before settling on Hector.

'It'll be over soon, so don't go to the beach.'

Eddy leaned back in his seat and winked at Dylan.

'Have you seen anything when you're on the cliff top?'

'Only her.'

'Who?'

'The sea. She's waiting.'

'For what?'

'The end.'

'The end of what?'

Eddy nodded. 'Just the end.'

After five more minutes of chasing fragments of Eddy's memories, Ashley decided that it was time to get to the point. She understood he was a vulnerable person, but people had died. She had to mention what had happened to observe his response.

'Eddy. Listen carefully. Three people have died on the beach.'

'When? When did they die?'

'Yesterday, and this morning. Do you know anything about these deaths?'

'No. Who was it? Who died?'

If it was an act from Balmain, it was a convincing one.

'Ron and Ruby Jerrod.'

Balmain shook his head and squinted.

'No, I don't think I know them.'

'Do you know anyone called Candice?'

'Yes.' He grinned. 'From school. Candy. Foxy's friend.'

'I'm afraid we believe she died, too.'

Balmain covered his face with his hands.

'Talk to us, please,' said Hector.

Eddy slid his hands down his sweaty face.

'I know Foxy's dead. That's when it started.'

'No, Candy's dead.'

'When did she die?'

'We think early this morning?'

'Oh, dear.'

'Who's Foxy?'

'Candy's friend. We were friends. All friends. Good friends.'

'Was she killed?'

Eddy sniffed, then scratched his neck hard.

'I don't think that was me.'

The solicitor, who'd barely said a word at that point, leaned forward.

'I'll need a word with Mr Balmain.'

Eddy pouted at Dylan.

'I want to go home.'

Ashley paused the interview but kept an eye on Eddy, who had begun to strain in his seat as though ready to explode. Dylan was right. His mannerisms and language were like those of a child, although Ashley could see his chest muscles flexing under his T-shirt.

'Calm down, Eddy,' said Dylan. 'Look at me.'

Eddy looked at him in the same way a loyal dog would look at an owner who had suddenly mistreated it for the first time.

'Take me home,' whispered Eddy.

Dylan gave him a reassuring look.

'You know I'm looking out for you, don't you?'

'Yes, we're friends,' he replied, unconvincingly.

Dylan nudged him with his elbow.

'What should I change my name to?' he asked with a wink.

Eddy frowned, then barked out a laugh.

'Cromer.' He looked back at Ashley, then at Hector. His face split into a wide grin. 'He can be Cromer Crabb.'

Ashley smiled at him.

'Very good, Eddy. Thanks for talking to us.'

Eddy closed his eyes until he was taken from the room.

Ashley and Hector returned to the office.

'How'd it go?' asked Sal.

'You know a slam dunk?'

'That good?'

'The opposite.'

'Oh. Well, I have a couple of bits of news. Emma's still in with Mrs Sweet. We've said she can wait here until the mortuary is prepared for her to ID the body, but Barry said the photograph she brought with her is a good likeness to the ones taken at the beach.'

'Poor woman.'

'Yes. Emma had time to study the CCTV from the stepdown house before she started her interview. Balmain leaves around 10 p.m. on Friday, and he stumbles back at about three-thirty in the morning. I'll show you.'

Ashley pulled a chair up and waited for Sal to find the footage. She watched it back twice. Did Eddy look as if he was coming back from a double murder? After that interview, anything was possible. Ashley would say he looked more drunk than exhausted.

'And he doesn't leave again?'

'No, the front door cam shows no movement until gone seven, and then it's someone else.'

'Dora Thorne found the bodies just after six that morning. That would mean Eddy went down to the beach, where he doesn't like to go, cut off Ron's head and placed it on the sand, then dug a hole next to it, where he buried Ruby up to the neck, before putting a bucket and stone over them both. After that, he changed his clothes, and came back home all tired after a busy night.'

'Maybe. No normal person goes to a beach in early April when it's pitch black. It's possible they wouldn't have been found until dawn.'

'I suppose he could have been working with another criminal genius like Homeless Bob.'

Sal smiled. 'I've found the closest living relative for Ruby Jerrod by tracing her uncle. She does have one cousin, by the looks of it, up in Stockton-on-Tees.'

'How far away is that?'

'More than two hundred miles. Shit journey from there to here, too.'

'Have you spoken to him?'

'No. I've spoken to local plod. They're arranging a senior detective team to visit his house in case he's involved. I'm guessing we'll be able to rule him out pretty quick if he can prove he hasn't left Teesside this weekend.'

'I suppose that leaves Geoffrey.'

'You want me to sit in with you?'

'No, you keep trudging on. Try to get as much keyed in as you can and get the rest of the paperwork to the admin team. Same as Emma when she gets out.'

'You think Geoffrey's involved?'

'The Pope could be involved at this point. Balmain said some cranky stuff about an event from years ago so we're going to need to look into that. He half implied he was involved in someone else's death, so we have enough to arrest him and keep him overnight.'

'Do you want to speak to Candy's mum?'

'Good point. I wonder if she knows anything about it.'

'You could drive her to Norwich hospital to see the body and ask her then. She'll probably open up to you.'

'Oh, Sal, very sneaky. Which would save you or Emma a journey.'

'Oh, yes. That's a stroke of luck because Emma wants to get home to her kids. I want to give my missus a break before she goes back to work. We'll be back tomorrow first thing. I'll make sure the town CCTV is looked at for those hours. They've given us bodies from the admin team to help out.'

'Okay, cheers, Sal. I wouldn't mind a chat with

Michelle about the post-mortem results. I take it nothing glaring has turned up.'

'No, the first report is in. I've had a flick through. She said to ring her. You know how she loves drownings.'

Ashley grinned.

'Kettle said to tell you the force support unit have agreed to patrol the beach this evening. If anyone goes down there tonight, they'll get a nasty surprise.'

'Good. We don't want strike five, or whatever this "seven" thing is, happening under our noses.'

'It's probably not a nice thing to say, but this is a really meaty case. I'm enjoying it.'

Sal always loved the development of complicated cases, but Ashley's pleasure came with the resolution. She tapped Hector on the shoulder to say she was ready for Geoffrey just as her phone rang, and she saw it was Dylan.

'Will Eddy be released tonight?' he asked.

'No. We'll have to wait to see what CSI finds in his room. And we need to study the CCTV for the town centre to check if it was him doing that graffiti. We'll need to talk to him again about this Foxy thing.'

'Okay. He isn't going to be a flight risk if you let him go.'

'No, but he didn't seem that stable, so who knows what he might do if we release him?'

'Eddy couldn't function on his own. He feels safe at the house. I don't believe he'd jeopardise that. By the way, I'm sorry I forgot to tell you he never went on the beach.'

'That's okay. We'd have had to talk to him, anyway.'

'I'll have a chat with the others who deal with his care plan about this latest behaviour. He won't like spending the night in a cell.'

'I understand. Don't worry about the cell. We'll arrange for an assessment at the hospital and keep him there overnight. Hopefully that will be less stressful for him. You wanted to tell me something about his weight?'

'Oh, yes. I really noticed how much he's lost, so I'm going to ask the warden if he's been eating. Obviously, that's another sign of deteriorating mental health or perhaps an issue with his medication.'

'That makes sense. Dylan, what is this connection with the sea? Does he talk to you about it?'

'Before, all he'd say is that he doesn't like it. He'd shut down the conversation if we probed further. This obsession is a recent change, which is concerning.'

'Can you come back in the morning?'

'Sure. What time?'

'I'll ring you first thing because it might depend on what we find out in the meantime.'

'I assume his solicitor will tell him not to mention any more of that Foxy stuff.'

'Yeah, that's likely.'

'So, if his room is clean and CCTV draws a blank...' Dylan left the statement hanging.

'Yes,' said Ashley. 'We'll have to let him go.'

26

Ashley and Hector sat next to each other in interview room four while they waited for the custody staff to bring up Geoffrey Sullivan, which Ashley thought was a nice name. It was the first time she'd heard it in full, which again made her consider how well she knew him.

'Still think this town is boring?' she asked Hector.

'I never said that.'

'Bet you didn't fancy coming to Norfolk.'

'You can't guess everything about me, you know, just by looking at me.'

Ashley pulled a face. Hector took a deep breath, as though to centre himself.

'Sorry,' he said. 'I didn't sleep that well last night.'

'No problem. My skin's like a rhino's. Thank God for make-up. Any thoughts about how we do this?'

'Yes. You've known the guy years, so how about I do the bulk of the talking? You can focus on whether you think he's lying.'

'That makes sense. We're not going to charge him for threatening language to Barry, but it might make him more likely to cooperate if he knows that. We need to make Geoffrey think he's helping us with enquiries. He's refused a solicitor, which I don't think he'd do if he was involved. He's actually a good man to have on side because the town community is quite tight and they don't tend to talk to the law.'

'Okay. I suppose if he *is* innocent in all of this, then he's had two very trying days.'

'Exactly. We signed up for this. Every day we get up, we're prepared to hear about abused or tortured people, look at dead bodies, or delve into society's worst perversions. Geoffrey probably wakes up thinking about fishing.'

'I reckon this guy's involved.'

'If we think he is after our discussion, then we arrest him for murder, and I'll ask Bhavini to do the interviews with you.' She smiled. 'I've known Geoffrey since I was a schoolchild. It was one of my dad's few pleasures in life.'

'Geoffrey?'

'Hilarious. No, eating a crab. We were okay for money because my father never went anywhere to spend any, so his one little treat was a crab every now and again. You could get them dressed in town but, back then, he used to send me down to the gangway and I'd buy one off Geoffrey's boat when he returned to shore. My dad always said you can't get fresher. It had to be Geoffrey's boat, even though there were a lot more fishermen at that time.'

Ashley had a little smile as she thought back.

'You might not believe it, but I was a pretty kid. That line of freckles across my nose I was telling you about made me look like a choir girl, even if I could be a devious strong-willed little madam. I used to barter with Geoffrey, and he always let me off twenty pence. I'd not tell my dad and use the change to buy a chocolate bar.'

'No wonder you can see into the minds of criminal geniuses, because you were once a crook yourself.'

'Precisely, although that was one of life's learning curves, too. Dad passed away not long after I finished my A-levels. Few people came to the funeral because he was such a loner, but Geoffrey did. After the service, which a distant aunt sorted, we had a few drinks at The White Horse. Geoffrey told me that my father often visited the dock for a chat, and they used to chuckle about the twenty-pence pieces. He used to ask Geoffrey to keep an eye out for me.'

Hector looked a little uncomfortable, as though he didn't know what to do when a person shared something heartfelt with him.

'You know, I hardly ever tell people about my past,' he finally said.

'That's because you're too young to have one.'

Hector gave her a mock sneer.

'Sorry,' said Ashley. 'Maybe give it a try. It's liberating.'

'I'm not sure I'll be giving the crab a try.'

'Do you know what? I haven't had once since Dad died.'

'Why not?'

'I was worried it'd bring up too many sad memories, I guess. Perhaps it's time. I'll treat you, if you hang around long enough.'

Hector nodded at her, but he didn't reply, so she guessed that was a no. She noticed what he was wearing that day. He was in a dark green suit and black slip-ons and looked relaxed and comfortable in it. Even Barry would struggle to carry a green suit off.

There was a knock at the door and they brought

in Geoffrey. There were two chairs on the other side of the table and he chose to sit in the one opposite Ashley.

'Right, Geoffrey Sullivan,' she said. 'I'm DS Ashley Knight, and DC Hector Fade is also present. Our conversation today will be recorded. I do need to caution you that you do not have to say anything. But it may harm your defence if you do not mention when questioned something which you later rely on in court. Anything you do say may be given in evidence. Is that clear?'

'I understand.'

'We have a duty solicitor who is here for legal advice. If you are in any way implicated in what's happened, I would take advantage of that. Would you like a solicitor present?'

'No,' he replied, looking directly at Ashley. 'I'm not involved.'

Hector led the interview and did a thorough job of revisiting the previous day's events but there was no new information, and Geoffrey refused to tell them where he was sleeping. Geoffrey barely looked at Hector throughout.

Ashley was surprised to find that Geoffrey seemed diminished in this environment, smaller somehow. That was interesting because, through Ashley's many years of interviewing, she knew that people shrank under the weight of their lies. If she tugged and pulled at the loose ends of their stories, conviction and confidence rapidly drained away. Until everyone in the room knew all that remained unsaid was the truth.

Hector wasn't making much progress, so Ashley took over. She leaned forward, forearms on the table.

'Geoffrey. It's important you help us. We need to know where you live.'

'Why?'

'Because we have to check it for bloody clothing.'

'What if I say no?'

'Geoffrey, we've known each other a long time. You know me.'

Geoffrey scowled.

'At the moment, I believe you. My partner here doesn't.' Ashley gave Geoffrey a tight smile. 'This is murder, so the common assault charge against my colleague isn't as important as resolving this case. If I hear about any squatting while I'm making progress in solving the case, I'd probably not pursue that either.'

Geoffrey reddened. 'You know about that?'

'I told you, Geoffrey. I find out everything eventually. Where are you living?'

Geoffrey sank lower into his seat.

'I've been breaking into a caravan on Laburnum Caravan Park.'

'How long have you been doing that?'

'Four months, on and off.'

Ashley drummed her fingers on the table.

'That site hasn't been open long, so you must have been living without electricity. The manager's on the ball there. How has she missed seeing you around?'

'I leave my motor at the car park further up. I used to sleep in the back of my truck, but I nearly froze to death once when it was cold and dead windy. The next night was bitter. I couldn't face it so, when it was dark, I picked the lock of an older van on the edge of the site. Now, if it's really chilly, I kip in there. It's just the lock that might be a bit knackered. I've touched nothing else. Not even used the gas.' Geoffrey scowled. 'Maybe I ate some food.'

'Breaking and entering, and burglary.'

'That's why I didn't want to say.'

'You need to say. Why didn't you tell someone you were struggling?'

She was wasting her words. He'd be like a lot of older Norfolk men who preferred to suffer in silence due to pride.

'Assuming you aren't in prison at the end of all

this, I'll have a word with Catherine at the caravan park. She's the manager. Nice lady. She might be able to find you a cheap rate while you get sorted.'

'Fair enough, but it's warmer now, so I'll be back in my truck tonight.'

Ashley still believed he wasn't involved, but Geoffrey was going nowhere until they'd searched his truck and the caravan. He gave them the details of their locations, and seemed quite pleased he had a warm cell for the night. He visibly flagged as they tied the interview up.

'Ash,' he said as she stood up when they'd finished.

'Yes.'

'I want to help. I know Cromer like the back of my hand. I've spent all my life here. Locals have noticed strangers in the town.'

'Yeah, like who?'

'A guy in a big blue coat with his hood up. Another one shouting off the cliffs near Happy Valley. There have been a few complaints about someone watching the women walking their dogs or being followed too close on the beach. There's graffiti everywhere.'

'Why not mention all this earlier?'

'We don't talk to Old Bill.'

'Unless you're pissed in a pub.'

He laughed, and she saw a glimpse of the old Geoffrey.

'Yeah, it's fine then.' He paused, then took a deep breath. 'Until I looked at your pal here and realised that he thinks I'm the killer, I never really thought about it like that. I've been all at sea, if you excuse the saying, since Sandra left me.'

'Threw you out.'

'Yeah, that.'

Ashley sat back down.

'Tell me about the graffiti. Do you know who wrote it? Did you read it?'

'It'll be kids. We always get one or two bouts of it each year, but there's been more recently. And no, I don't read kids' graffiti.'

Hector cleared his throat.

'You must have seen plenty of drownings over the years.'

Geoffrey's eyes sharpened. He growled his reply.

'I have. People take liberties with the ocean and that's a mistake. Folk perish on the beach all the time. Suicides, a lot of them, but others didn't plan to die. You get idiots jumping off the pier, straight into the Devil's Throat, which is dangerous as hell. The current is strong around there and people panic when they're dragged out to sea. Nowadays, I fish close to shore for crab and lobster, but back in the day, we went after a catch much further out in all weathers. I've lost good friends in the past.'

'Do you remember a death on the beach perhaps thirty years ago?'

'I can't recall how many beers I had yesterday.'

Ashley smiled. 'That's not very helpful.'

Geoffrey clicked his fingers.

'Actually, I do recall one sad tale. Long, long time ago. Some teenagers had a party on the beach and a girl drowned.' Geoffrey's eyes misted over. 'God, I still remember that girl. She was a live wire from a rough family. Foxy. That was her name. What a girl. Young kids were always messing around in the town back then. No computers, see, so they'd get drunk in the parks and the cemetery, or they'd mess about under the pier or have bonfires on the sand. My generation did that, too.'

'Why do you remember her in particular?' asked Hector. 'If it was so long ago.'

Geoffrey stared long and hard at Hector for the first time.

'You must have read the ugly duckling story. That was her. We all knew Foxy.'

At Hector's falling face, Geoffrey replied quickly.

'Not like that, you melon head. We looked out for her. Her dad was on the piss, mum on the game, so she was always out and about. Foxy was part of the fabric of the town. Well, she turned into a right beauty. But one morning, she was discovered drowned on the beach.'

27

Ashley and Hector escorted Geoffrey to the custody suite. Geoffrey grudgingly told them which of his keys fitted his truck and said most of his clothes were in the back of it, including the ones he wore when out fishing. He said none of his things were in the caravan and he only slept there at night. Ashley made a mental note to ask Barry to look in both on his way home before they were searched properly.

Ashley ensured the custody officers knew to give Geoffrey her business card when he left, in the hope he would come good on his word to poke his nose into things for her.

'Is that so Geoffrey can ring you after he's killed

someone else on the beach?' asked Hector on the way back upstairs.

'You won't be laughing if Geoffrey's the next person to die,' replied Ashley.

Sal Freitas shouted out when he saw them returning to the office.

'Michelle called in. The body of the drowning victim is ready to be identified. The coroner's officer is en route. I told her you'd bring Mrs Sweet, who is an American, by the way. Been here a long time, but lovely southern accent. Michelle said she'll wait to do the PM with you if you're heading down. She'll talk to you about the other two as well when you arrive, but there's nothing that raises new alarms.'

Ashley checked her watch. It would soon be five. Bhavini yawned at her computer. Hector was checking his phone messages next to her.

'It's getting on,' said Ashley to him. 'You need to be somewhere else tonight?'

'By your side is fine by me.'

'No sarcasm before nightfall, please.'

'Nope. No plans.'

'Seen a post-mortem?'

'No.'

It was impossible to fully prepare anyone for

seeing a human body being cut open, so she didn't bother even to try.

'Have you eaten?' she asked.

'Nothing since breakfast.'

'Good. That'll help.'

'That doesn't bode well.'

'Let's collect Mrs Sweet from the waiting room. Take notes while we drive her to the hospital. We won't get much out of her afterwards.'

'Do you reckon there's an angle with this historic stuff?' asked Hector.

'Do you?'

'Yes.'

'Why?'

Hector paused to arrange his thoughts.

'People of all ages are murdered all over the world. Generally, those who die are young men unless the perps are spree or serial killers. Spree killers hit schools or communities, but they're rare in this country. Our gun laws help. Serial killers often target marginalised parts of our society like prostitutes. Our three victims are old. The people we're talking to are old.'

'Fifties isn't that old,' said Ashley with a glare.

'Not to you, maybe.'

'I think you could argue that older folk are often marginalised.'

'I suppose that's true, so perhaps that's what connects them. Eddy Balmain probably knew Ron and Ruby and this woman who drowned last night. Another female friend of his died thirty-odd years ago, but what if Geoffrey was present then as well? He lived in the vicinity at the very least.'

'Aren't you more worried about Balmain?' asked Ashley.

'Do you mean that more people he knows are dead now he's free?'

'Yes, that thought had trickled into my mind.'

'I don't like him for it. He's too unstable. Let's get as many details as possible about that incident. We must have investigated Foxy's death back then. Was it deemed a suicide, or just a tragic accident? Maybe Mrs Sweet will know and can give us more accurate dates. I doubt anyone was charged with murder, because Kettle or one of the older officers would have recalled it, and we'd have files on it.'

'Perhaps Balmain was involved, and the episode ruined his mental health. But if there weren't any convictions, the records are going to be patchy at best and definitely incomplete. Things got done differently then.'

'Is Kettle local to Cromer?' asked Hector.

'No, far side of Norwich.'

'Okay. We should talk to retired officers from Cromer to see if they remember anything or were even involved in the investigation.'

'Not a bad suggestion, although think how many cases an officer investigates over their entire career. Would they recall one with no convictions?'

'It seems nobody forgets this Foxy,' replied Hector.

'True.'

'You went to school here. It's a small community. Do you remember it?'

'There's only about eight thousand people here, and no, I don't. I'd have been at junior school.'

'So, perhaps the mayor might know, or, seeing as Foxy was still school age, your old headmaster or her teachers would recall a dramatic event like that. Teachers will be easier to locate as well.'

Ashley was beginning to see something special about how Hector's brain worked.

'Yes, although Cromer school doesn't have a sixth form, so we might need to speak to the other places that do. It seems unlikely that Eddy or Candy progressed to further education back then, but we can check on that.'

Ashley had a quick chat with Bhavini about her and Hector's thoughts around there being a connection to the historic death. Ashley liked to include Bhavini because she had a habit of thinking outside the box.

'That sounds like a great angle for tomorrow,' said Bhavini, rubbing her eyes.

'Yeah, I just wanted to lodge the ideas in your head. I'll see what specifics I can get out of Mrs Sweet, but it looks as though she's about to experience one of the worst things a human can.'

'Bell me if anything comes up.'

'Will do.'

'Is Dylan Crabb coming back tomorrow?'

'Yeah. He's happy to come in when we want another talk with Eddy Balmain. It would be safer for Eddy if Dylan took him home afterwards, assuming we don't find anything. He might even say something to Dylan about everything when he's off guard.'

'What about looking at Eddy's health records?'

'Dylan's given us a heads-up on them.'

'No, I meant before Dylan became involved with him. You said Eddy was at a secure unit called Brancaster House before he came to Cromer. They'll have his file going back to his childhood, or at least when he was detained. It'll tell us why he was sectioned and provide a detailed map of his mindset over the years. He might have confessed to a part in a crime as his health improved.'

'They aren't likely to email that out on request.'

'Balmain said he was innocent. Why wouldn't he want us to look at his file to confirm that?'

Ashley high-fived Bhavini, then left the office with Hector. They picked up Mrs Sweet, who seemed to be quietly praying, booked out a car and set off. It was rush hour, so the five miles would take up to thirty minutes, and as they crawled through traffic Ashley glanced across at the poor woman, who would still be clinging to the tiny chance that she was about to stare down at the body of a stranger.

Instead, her life as she knew it would end.

28

Mrs Sweet looked sprightly for someone with a daughter in her fifties. She was slim with lovely skin and Ashley suspected she'd once been pretty. The years had left their mark, though. The big bags lodged under her eyes appeared as though they were present long before her daughter went missing this morning.

Ashley waited until they'd been driving for a few minutes before she began quizzing her.

'Can you tell me about Candice?'

'What would you like to know?'

'The usual. Marriage, kids, job, hopes, dreams, plans.'

Mrs Sweet rubbed her hands for a while, then she surprised Ashley by smiling.

'My husband and I struggled to have children so we were over the moon when I fell pregnant. He liked the name Candice, but I told him she'd end up being called Candy Sweet, so we agreed that was stupid. But we lovingly whispered Candy to the bump, and when she arrived, we couldn't call her anything else.'

Her smile drooped a little.

'Candy was a happy kid, but she wasn't very bright. My husband joked that she got his looks and no brain. She was quiet and easily led, but she had mates who looked out for her.'

'What were the names of her friends?'

'Natalie Fox was her best friend. She was lovely. Hair like spun gold. I have happy memories of those two when they were young.'

It was obvious something had gone wrong. Ashley kept the conversation easy.

'It's a shame we have to grow up.'

'Yes, poor Candy was too daft for more schooling at sixteen, so she took a job in a shop, but she couldn't deal with the maths around money and hated it. We got her into care work, but she found the snappy nature of the dementia patients hard to cope with so she quit and stayed at home a lot. Foxy visited still, even though she was at school doing A levels. Foxy had the world at her feet.'

A tear slid down Mrs Sweet's cheek and ran into her mouth but she didn't appear to notice.

'What happened?'

'They had a party.'

After a sniff, she gazed out of the windscreen while she carried on talking.

'We don't really know what happened that night. They found Candy asleep on the beach. Well, they said asleep, but I think she was unconscious. Everyone else had gone apart from her and another friend. Foxy's body was rolling around in the surf. She'd been dead for hours.'

'When was the party?'

'I can tell you exactly when: 15 August 1989. Candy's birthday. Foxy's was the day before.'

'That's well over thirty years ago.'

Mrs Sweet's quiet smile returned.

'You must think me demented. The reason I'm telling you about it is because, even though she survived, Candy was never the same again. She's never worked properly since, never married, and she barely spoke for ten years.'

'I'm sorry to hear that. Did they find out what happened?'

Mrs Sweet frowned.

'Misadventure was the word the coroner used.'

'And you don't reckon it was.'

'No, I do not! Drugs were involved. Foxy tested positive for LSD and cannabis and alcohol.'

'Did you know they took drugs?'

'I suspected. A lot of kids experiment with them around here. It's a boring place for most children. Public transport is poor at night, and it's like a ghost town in the winter. But it was the amount of drugs they consumed. They had enough LSD in them to send an elephant to Mars.'

'So, it was an overdose that led to the drowning.'

'I think it was murder. Those bloody hippies with their narcotics killed Foxy and ruined the others' lives.'

'Which hippies?'

'Ron and Ruby.'

ROSS CLIFF AVOID

29

Ashley glanced into the back seat at Mrs Sweet.

'Do you believe they deliberately gave them too much?'

'They were reckless. Foxy and Candy were just eighteen.'

Mrs Sweet's voice broke, but she quickly gained control.

'What kind of idiot gives out LSD on the beach when the tide's coming in?'

'Do you think the girls were tricked into taking it?'

'No, for a smart girl, Foxy was wild and adventurous.'

'And she was beautiful.'

'She went from being a leggy, gawky, laughing kid

to a stunner nearly overnight not long after she turned fifteen. A touch of make-up and tight clothes and she had boys struck dumb and grown men's jaws hitting the floor when she strolled by. She became popular and was invited to everything that was going. Everyone wanted a piece of her, but she never forgot my girl. She always said Candy was her plus-one.'

Ashley moistened her lips while she considered how to frame the next question.

'You mentioned that boys had started paying Foxy attention.'

'Yes, but she wasn't that interested. She said there were a few nice ones at school, but she was in no rush to settle down. In fact, I recall her telling me she wanted to date them all. She was desperate to get out of Cromer and see the world. I hoped she'd take Candy with her.'

'Were there other boys at the party that night on the beach?'

'Yes. The fool. He was there. I remember that. They found him incoherent and staggering around a campsite five miles away. They got no sense from him. He had some kind of breakdown later.'

'Edward Balmain.'

Mrs Sweet's eyes connected with Ashley's in the rear-view mirror.

'Yes, that's him. Eddy.'

'Did you know him well?'

'We lived on Holt Road near to him. He was always coming over, at all hours, but we didn't mind too much. Now that lad was simple. I think he liked Candy because she wasn't much brighter than him. They played nice as kids, but he was a boy who never grew up. When Foxy and Candy became women, they wanted different things while he'd still come around with toys and stickers.'

'Were they mean to him?'

'No, Candy tried to calmly push him away from them because he started making odd comments. I think he was hearing voices. Foxy enjoyed having him about, though.'

'Would he have harmed anyone?'

'No. He was gentle, like my Candy. People like them, they hurt themselves, that's all. Although, even when he was little, he had real strength in those hands. I used to get him to open all my jam jars and carry my shopping from the car.'

They'd pulled into the hospital car park by now and when they got out of the vehicle, Ashley decided to ask Mrs Sweet one last question.

'We think there were seven at that party. Candy, Foxy, Eddy, Ron and Ruby. Do you know who was the one found with Candy or who else might have been there?'

They walked as they talked.

'No. Candy mentioned some names at the time, but it's been too long now. Ron and Ruby disappeared afterwards, the bastards. They didn't return for years. I confronted them when they finally slunk back into town, but they reckoned they left the party early and everything was fine at that point. In true Cromer style, it was all swept under the carpet. Things like that aren't good for tourism, are they?'

'I suppose not,' said Hector.

'Besides, Cromer has always kept its secrets. Candy couldn't function afterwards. She wouldn't go anywhere near the sea. I moved us out of town to Fel-brigg, where it's woody and quiet, and a long way from the beach.'

'Was she better there?'

'Not really. She'd somehow got a photograph of that night she couldn't put down. It near sent her catatonic.'

'What was the picture of?'

Mrs Sweet avoided Ashley's stare and took a few seconds to answer.

'Them enjoying the party, splashing about in the sea.'

'Does she still have it?'

Mrs Sweet looked up at the huge hospital building and slowed as they approached the entrance doors. Ashley only just heard her reply as Hector opened them.

'No. I went in her room and destroyed it when she was out.' Mrs Sweet stopped walking. 'I can't see her like that in there. I can't do it.'

Ashley watched in amazement as Hector let the doors close, returned to Mrs Sweet's side and held her hand. He lifted it up, then patted it. She peered up at him. His expression didn't change. He just nodded, and on she walked.

All three of them came to a halt at the entrance to the mortuary, as though they recognised the horror of what lay ahead. Mrs Sweet would bear the brunt of it. Her face was crushed.

'She was my baby. She was all I ever wanted,' she sobbed. 'All those years. All that love. All the memories. They're gone. To the bottom of the sea.'

30

Ashley guided Mrs Sweet through the double doors. The first mortuary Ashley had attended was in Sheffield and had been very similar. Cream walls, few features, sterile air. It always felt as if the air were sparse in these quiet places.

A member of staff came out to greet them. She would escort Mrs Sweet to the viewing suite, which was a quiet room where she could be alone after confirming her daughter's identity.

It seemed that Mrs Sweet didn't want to release Hector's hand so Ashley nodded at him to go with her.

'Take your time. Is there anyone we can ring for

you?' she asked the woman. 'Perhaps they could pick you up and stay with you.'

'No, there isn't anyone. It wasn't just Foxy who died that night. My husband worked himself to the bone so we could afford the move from Cromer to Felbrigg. I think that's why he's so frail now. The only other adult we're close to is Elliott, and he's already in this hospital.'

Ashley smiled, but cursed inside. She'd forgotten about the domestic involving Candy and her partner. Surely this had to be connected somehow. She could have done with time to think things through, but they had a post-mortem to watch after Mrs Sweet had finished her goodbyes. It might be tough to leave Mrs Sweet on her own, but a murderer was at large. They had to crack on.

Ashley dismissed the thought as they entered the viewing suite. Identifying a body wasn't a time for being alone.

'Hector will sit with you if you'd like,' she said. 'Then he'll take you home.'

'Thank you, dear. Maybe it won't be her.'

Ashley reached out and gave her arm what she hoped was a comforting squeeze. Hector looked relieved to have escaped his first post-mortem. He'd be unaware that being with Mrs Sweet would probably be worse. Ashley left to find the pathologist, Michelle Ma Yun.

Ashley was sitting in Michelle's office, drinking a glass of water, when she heard the howl of confirmation. Michelle, who was on the opposite side of the desk, nodded at the sound, then continued.

'Okay,' she said. 'Let me sum up the first two post-mortems. Ron was definitely alive when he was de-capitated. He lost a lot of blood. Much more than if he was already dead from the stab wound to his stomach.'

'Could that have killed him as well?'

'Eventually, yes, but it missed the major organs, so if he'd been treated within half an hour, he'd have survived.'

'You think it was done to incapacitate him for the main event.'

'Correct. Maybe the attacker really knew what he was doing.'

'That's worrying.'

'Yes. You know how I love it when dead bodies give up secrets?'

'Yep.'

Michelle looked over her glasses.

'No secrets here.'

'Boo!'

'Except one!'

'Hurray!'

'There's a puncture wound in the median cubital vein.'

'Neck?'

'No, it's the vein which we donate blood from. Ron doesn't appear the donating type, so I'm guessing he was injected with some kind of sedative. Toxicology will definitely tell us because the body won't have had time to eliminate it.'

'Okay. Let's hope he was asleep when the saw came out.'

'Did you say they were homeless?'

'I'm not sure how I'd describe them. Nomads maybe.'

'Well, they were healthy nomads. Good lungs, heart, and liver. Very little dental problems for him, worse for her, but on par for her age.'

'The cause of death for him was neck pain. Got it.'

'Spot on. Very sore in this instance. As for the others, drownings are BS.'

Ashley laughed, which was a pleasant release from the tension that had built in her body. Michelle's family had come to the UK from China a long time ago. She had a strong Norfolk accent, which was at odds with her Eastern Asian looks, and she loved supporting Norwich City Football Club. The previous pathologist had been a tweed-wearing elderly academic woman who called Ashley *madam*. Even in the mortuary, things were changing. Michelle was professional, cool and efficient, but for some reason she seemed to think BS wasn't any kind of swear word. Or perhaps, more likely, she said it to lighten the atmosphere that came with looking at dead humans.

'Big bullshit, or little bullshit?' asked Ashley.

'The biggest BS. You want me to explain again?'

'Please. It's been a long day.'

'Forensic diagnosis of drowning is considered one of the most difficult in forensic medicine, even for me. It's worse than time of death, which you guys believe I can give to the minute. People don't respond the same way when they drown. The throat closes sometimes, and they die of heart failure without the lungs filling up with water, like in this case. We did a thorough PM, but your findings at the scene were as important.'

'Okay.'

'Ruby was in a reclined, sitting position, so she may have closed her airwaves as the tide came in. No oxygen to the heart makes it stop, no blood flow from that non-pumping heart means no fresh oxygen to the brain, and brain death occurs in less than five minutes.'

'Unconscious in two minutes?'

'Yes. Usually I need to wait for the histology and toxicology reports to come back. Obviously, in Ruby's case, we have timings and eyewitnesses for her. I would say time of death for the husband was close to when his wife died.'

'So, the murderer had probably not left the beach for long when Dora discovered the scene.'

'Yes. It's the other lady who's going to be the problem.'

'Brilliant.'

'I thought that would cheer you up. The coroner's officer is waiting for us in the mortuary. I'll talk while we scrub up.'

They left the office together and went to the changing room.

'An autopsy for a deceased person found in water where there are a lot of unknowns makes it much trickier.'

Michelle had been in position for five years. She used autopsy and post-mortem interchangeably, whereas the stuffed shirt who she replaced had insisted that autopsy was American, when apparently it was Greek. *To see for oneself.*

'I'd expect the lungs to contain fluid because she was found submerged. The body relaxes after death and the muscles contract, which includes the airways. Therefore, we can't say for sure if she was dead or alive before she entered the water.'

'Is it bad of me to think of the *Night of the living dead*?'

Michelle smiled.

'Think overdose on the sand or thrown in the sea by the killer.'

'That seems more likely.'

At that moment, the woman who'd escorted Mrs Sweet and Hector to identify the body appeared, having pulled on her scrubs. She pushed in a trolley, which had a body on top.

'Mrs Sweet is happy for the PM to proceed,' she said.

'This is Tina Brown, my APT today. She's already photographed the corpse. This is Ashley Knight.'

'Hi, Ashley. Your partner has taken Mrs Sweet to visit her daughter's boyfriend on his ward. She says it's only fair he hears the news from her, even if he is useless. Hector said he'll see if either has anything to say, then he'll drive her home.'

'Okay, thanks.'

Contrary to popular belief, pathologists rarely

opened the body cavities. That was a role done by highly trained Anatomical Pathology Technicians like Tina. Michelle carried on talking while she waited.

'Bodies roll around with the motion of the waves and get damaged, which makes it difficult for us to guess what happened before they entered the water. Cells change at a different rate due to the cold, so time of death is even harder to estimate. As a rough guide, a warm but not stiff body hasn't been dead for more than three hours. That includes Ron and obviously Ruby. Hence them dying around 6 a.m. A cold and stiff body has generally been dead for anywhere between eight and thirty-six hours, while a cold but not stiff person has been deceased for over thirty-six hours.'

'I'm following,' said Ashley.

'I took a temperature earlier when she first came in, for the lady we now know to be Candice. We use a chart, which is notoriously inaccurate, but it's the best we have. My best guess at the moment is she died around midnight.'

Ashley knew the coroner, Zane Walton, who then arrived in blue theatre scrubs and white wellies.

'Evening, Wally,' she said.

'Evening, Plonker.'

Zane was a tall, fit-looking man who had a constant tinge of pink under his tawny skin as though he'd been exercising. He always looked the picture of health and the perfect contrast to the marble body that had just been wheeled in. Ashley had considered him dating material until she noticed he mentioned his wife and kids in most conversations.

Ashley sat on a seat and glanced at her watch. If everything went to plan the post-mortem would finish around nine. Michelle and Tina consulted the paperwork, then began the slow process of examining the body, starting with confirming it was the right person.

It was a gruesome thing to think about, but the reality for most police was that observing post-mortems was fascinating. Ashley didn't know the victim, so she was able to be analytical. She made notes, even though it was being recorded.

Hector came back twenty minutes later. Someone had told him to scrub up. He took a seat next to her, but Michelle asked if this was his first one. She asked him to stand closer, or he wouldn't see anything. Hector nodded, then looked at Ashley.

'Mrs Sweet's staying with Elliott all night. He's devastated. The nurse up there said that's fine in the circumstances.'

'You didn't have to come back.'

'I'm here to learn.'

Hector's Adam's apple shuttled up and down like a faulty lift.

Three hours later, Michelle was done, Hector hadn't uttered a word, and Zane left.

'In summary, then,' said Michelle, 'there are no obvious causes of death anywhere on or in the body, and the stomach is empty. Toxicology will confirm the possibility of an overdose. There was water in the lungs, and they appeared water damaged, but they need to be analysed under a microscope, as will the heart. There are no obvious indications of trauma, which could have caused prior death, or signs of considerable incapacitation, which would have led to drowning.'

Ashley nodded.

'There's also no clear evidence of restraint, unlike with Ruby, whose wrists and ankles were damaged by her struggling against the cable ties. It appears Candy went to the beach of her own volition. Sorry, but that's all, folks.'

Afterwards, Ashley and Hector took their scrubs off and put their jackets back on, then returned to Michelle's office.

'Cheers, Michelle. We've all had a tough day. I appreciate you doing it.'

'Sadly, I didn't have anywhere else to be.'

Ashley was going to leave it at that, but Michelle was one of those who'd mentioned meeting up out of work. It was another offer that Ashley hadn't followed up on.

'You know we said about meeting for a drink or something,' said Ashley. 'How about next weekend?'

'The Canaries are playing at home on Saturday.'

'That's okay. Thought I'd ask. We keep saying we'll catch up but never do.'

'I'm free Sunday.'

Ashley beamed at her.

'Perfect.'

'I'm sorry I didn't have more for you today. It's a shame the last one was so inconclusive.'

'Yes, you haven't given me much to go on, so I'd guess at this point the evidence is pointing to suicide. I'll ring you in a few days.'

Ashley wondered how Candy had got to the beach from Felbrigg when she didn't seem the driving type, but she supposed it was less than an hour's walk.

'Don't forget, though,' said Michelle. 'Drowning post-mortems can be BS.'

Ashley chuckled as she left the mortuary and staggered back to the car. Hector took the keys out of her hand and guided her into the passenger seat. She would have been asleep on the way home if the young bastard next to her hadn't kept talking.

'That story you shared with me about your dad,' he said. 'Thank you. And you're right. I made no effort to make friends in any of the departments or stations I've worked in. Many of those secondments were lonely experiences, which was partly my fault.'

'See. I said you'll learn something, even if it's just my horrible history.'

Hector pulled up outside her house.

'My life isn't all roses, you know.'

'No one's is. Thanks for coming back to the mortuary. I wouldn't have minded if you didn't fancy it.'

'No, I enjoyed it, if that's the right word. In fact, I quite like it in Norfolk, with you guys. It's different from London. You're still mean to each other, but in a supportive kind of way. Despite just arriving, I've already seen some horrific things, but I feel more part of the team than I have anywhere else, so the impact is lessened somehow.'

Ashley dragged herself from the car and slapped her hand on the roof to let him know to leave. Talking seemed too much effort. She stared at Arthur's house next door to hers and saw the light was on. Oh, no.

Was it only this morning that she offered to go around after work?

She stood motionless for a moment with her eyes closed, then dragged them open, and went to knock on his door.

31

Ashley stirred in a strange position with an unfamiliar smell in her nostrils. While not unpleasant, it was a little pungent. She cracked an eyelid and glanced around. This wasn't her lounge. It had the same dimensions, but there were old pictures of people she didn't know on the fireplace and on the walls.

'Ah,' said a voice at the door. 'The Kraken awakes.'

Ashley peered blearily up into Arthur's smiling face.

'It's been a while since I had a pretty woman wake up under my sheets. Tea or coffee?'

'Coffee, please,' she said, pushing off the blanket and stretching. 'Sorry, did I nod off?'

'You asked me if I remembered a young girl drowning years ago. I didn't, so I was telling you about the business I owned. I was in full swing until I realised you were snoring.'

'Do I snore?'

'You did last night.'

'Damn. I never used to. Can you hear it through the walls?'

'It's not your snores I hear.'

Ashley winced. She didn't want to probe into that comment. She jumped off his sofa with a rising sense of panic. God, she was going to be late for work. She turned her mobile phone on to check the time as Arthur brought her drink in. It was five to six.

'Arthur. Why are you having breakfast so early when you're retired?'

'I don't sleep well these days and this is my favourite part of the day. My paper used to be delivered at six on the dot years ago, and I'd have mackerel on toast most mornings.'

'Is that what the smell is?'

'Yes. Do you want some? I've got plenty.'

Ashley was about to make her excuses, then realised there might not even be bread in her kitchen. Her gurgling stomach tipped the internal argument in favour of staying. Soon, they were eating at a little table next to the window. The décor in the property was clean and neat, but everything about the place had the silent scream of a solitary existence about it.

Arthur had shaved and put cologne on, which had to have some strength to fight through the stinky mackerel.

'How long ago did your wife leave?' she asked. 'If you don't mind talking about it.'

'It was a bit after the financial crash, so 2009. She often fell asleep when I talked to her as well.'

'You have a unique talent. You should record your voice and play it next to your bed in the morning. Have yourself a lie-in.'

Arthur chuckled.

'How was the fish?'

Ashley looked down at her empty plate. 'Tasty.'

Arthur grinned.

'You said you were having an epiphany. What brought that on?'

Ashley used the napkin that Arthur had put out to wipe her greasy mouth. She idly wondered if he always set the table this way.

'I guess I had an event a decade ago, which was tough to cope with.'

'Life can throw hard balls.'

'Yeah, but I kind of let it beat me. My boss at work,

Peter, saved my career and gave me a second chance, but I've been living on autopilot. I had another terrible experience and nearly had another breakdown. Peter helped me through that, too. I used the pandemic as an excuse not to go out, then I've never started again. I've been sitting in the house drinking at the end of the week, just so I don't have to think about anything. I've realised I have to get off my arse and do something. People keep asking me to meet out of work, but I always fob them off. It's like I'm choosing to be lonely.'

'What happened?'

'The worst event was a car accident ten years ago. I wasn't legally at fault, but I've always blamed myself. I wasn't seriously injured, cuts and a bit of whiplash, but my colleague was. I didn't deal with it at all well. My long-term relationship suffered, and I barely realised.'

'Did it finish your relationship?'

'Yes. Dillon and I had met travelling and I eventually moved to Sheffield to be with him. Anyway, that's another story. He tried to talk to me afterwards, but I couldn't focus on us. I ignored him until we were living as strangers. Someone else noticed and took him off me.'

'You got hurt, and you came home. Back to Cromer.'

'Yes. I can't blame Dillon.' She paused. 'Actually, I can, but he did try. It wasn't my finest hour after he dumped me. There was begging and bombarding him with calls. He was really good about it, actually, but he owned the flat we lived in, so I had to go. Funnily enough, my dad left me his house next door when he died, and I'd rented it out. The tenants had just left, so I brought all my stuff home and moved in. I've been here ever since.'

'That was about 2013, wasn't it?'

'Somewhere around then.'

'I remember. I used to hear you shouting late at night. You know, through the walls. I wasn't sure if it was at the TV, God, or the moon.'

Ashley felt her cheeks burn.

'That's embarrassing. Sorry.'

'It's okay. My story is really similar. I'd occasionally join you. In spirit, at least.'

Ashley laughed. 'What happened to you?'

'Nothing so dramatic, but I worked hard. Too hard. I never spent any time with my wife, and when I did, I talked about work. She wanted children early in our marriage, but she couldn't have them. My business was successful. I spoiled her rotten, with everything but attention, which I now know was all she craved. Like you, I created a gap, and someone else filled the space. And, like you, I realised too late.'

'Weren't we a pair of fools?'

'We were.'

'Not to be nosey, but if you're rich, why are you living next door to me in one of these pokey two-up two-down terraces?'

'My wife got my pension and the house. I got the business, which I thought was a good deal for me, but it never quite picked up after the recession. I ended up selling it for peanuts and this was all I could afford. It was too late to start again at my age. I've pretty much wasted the years since. Like you, my confidence disappeared.'

Ashley watched him clear the plates away and briskly wash them up.

'Why do you get Age UK to deliver your groceries? You seem mobile enough to me,' she asked.

'They go to the supermarket and fetch my favourites.'

'Why don't you do your own shopping? It's not like you're busy.'

'It's hectic in there, and they're so quick at the tills, and I haven't got a car—'

'What?'

'Nothing.'

Ashley chuckled. 'You look forward to the company!'

'I see why you're a detective.'

'Too right. Look, I better run. Thanks for breakfast.'

'Thanks for visiting.'

At the door, she had a thought.

'I can take you shopping with me, if you like. I usually go Wednesday nights.'

Arthur smiled, then his head bobbed. He grinned.

'It's a date.'

He stood there beaming in his pressed trousers and shirt and tie. He could even give Barry's trouser creases a run for their money.

'Oh, before you leave,' he said. 'You must have dislodged something in my mind, because when I woke up, I remembered that girl who died years ago. I read about it in the weekly paper. She looked like a model on the front page. My wife was really upset about it.'

'That's the one. It sounds like there was a tragic accident at a beach party. We think there were seven people there, and one of them drowned. The thing is, I think that, over the last few days, three more who were present that night have died under suspicious circumstances.'

Arthur sucked in a breath.

'Do you believe the others might be next?'

'Maybe. I reckon I know one of them and I've got him in custody, but I've no idea who the others were, and I'm not sure how to find out.'

'You should ask the headteacher about it. She'd remember that kind of scandal because I think there were drugs involved. My wife obsessed about it for a while.'

'Do you think your wife would mind me ringing her?'

'She'd be fine with that, but the headteacher was our next-door-but-one. I told you I was wealthier back then. If she's still alive, I assume you could visit her this morning.'

32

Ashley returned to her house and took a long, hot shower. Despite her sofa sleep, she felt good. Better than good.

She rang Control to see if there were any incidents during the night but thankfully there were none. Nothing on the beach and nobody reported missing. For a case like this, there would usually be a meeting at nine to update everyone on any progress or developments. Plans would be made for the week ahead. Knowing Kettle, she'd be expected to talk and, no doubt, present the plan.

Ashley smiled and jotted down some notes, then got dressed in her second nicest suit, which was grey, and left for Wymondham OCC. It was a bright morning. The clear sky gave a hint of sunshine to come, which further improved her mood. She'd missed her jog, but she could feel the tightness in her calves as she drove, so perhaps that was for the best.

By eight thirty, her team were in, and Jan Pederson was back from holiday. Ashley gathered them around her desk to catch up before the meeting to make sure they were up to speed. Kettle might fire questions at anyone present and being unprepared under the laser beam was a poor start to anyone's week. Other departments would have queries, too. Uniform handled the initial incidents over the weekend, but if there had been no further crimes last night, the baton would head MIT's way.

She discussed her findings with them and asked if anyone had preferences for roles. Sal preferred to work from the office. It suited his methodical style, and his little hands typed faster than everyone else except for Bhavini. Emma said she'd stay and help him, while dealing with the CCTV.

With five minutes to spare, Ashley remembered her date with Michelle on Sunday.

'Right, ladies. I know we keep saying we'll catch up out of work for drinks or a meal, but it never happens. Well, Michelle, the pathologist, and I are meeting up on Sunday lunchtime. I've rung Joan, the paramedic, and you two girls are invited.'

Bhavini and Emma looked at her, then at each other, then back at Ashley.

'Yeah, baby,' they said in unison.

'Hey, what about the guys?' asked Barry.

'I'm already on call, so don't worry about me,' said Jan. 'I'll cover in the office if needed.'

'Sorry, Jan, I forgot to introduce you. This is Hector Fade,' said Ashley. 'He'll be with us for a while learning the MIT ropes.'

Jan Pederson was six and a half feet tall and willowy. He looked a bit like a young David Beckham despite being in his thirties and he was more than a little geeky. There wasn't anything special or different about him. He just turned up and did the job. Whatever was thrown at him.

'This is Yawn Peterson, from Daneland,' said Barry. 'Don't mention golf, or you'll be ninety when he's finished.'

'Hi, Jan,' said Hector, pronouncing it properly as Yan. 'I like golf. Maybe we could organise a game.'

Barry groaned.

'Trust Hector to play golf. It's not a sport, it's a rich person's pastime.'

'Is the small ball game you play in your underpants a sport or a pastime?' asked Jan.

As per usual, Barry had been leaning back on his chair with one of his hands wedged under his belt half into his groin area. He slipped his hand out and gave Jan the finger. Jan raised his palm to Hector next to him, who, after a painful pause, high-fived him. Budding bromance, thought Ashley.

Kettle convened the meeting in the incident room, which now had a collection of whiteboards, and files already piling up, despite it allegedly being the twenty-first century.

'Here's the latest,' he said. 'No crime last night on the beach, or anywhere else for that matter, except for a couple of DUIs in the Broads, and a stolen sheep near Holt. If one of you lot is answerable for the latter, please return her this morning, and we won't say any more about it.'

Kettle liked a joke to break the ice, but he was soon staring intently around the room as he spoke. There were around fifty people present. Ashley could sense the energy.

'Two deadly incidents, two nights in a row, on the same patch of beach, is obviously very concerning. We've had nearly two days of searching and questioning and house-knocking and found little. A lot of media exposure has given us some bizarre calls about the Grim Reaper or his lookalike wandering around, possibly painting cryptic messages on various buildings. That's it.'

He kept quiet and leaned back on his heels for effect.

'The beach has been combed and the woods and cliff tops were scoured. Test results will be arriving all week, so let's keep on top of this. We have a gargantuan amount of material from those searches, not to mention hours upon hours of CCTV. I really hate using good personnel time sorting through that lot when we could be talking to suspects. So, let's focus.'

Kettle turned to the uniformed inspector beside him, who rose from his seat.

'We'll have a continued strong presence in the town for one more day if nothing else occurs,' he said. 'You know how tight we are for staff these days. Zara and my super would very much like to see a quick result when we're front page in all the papers.'

Kettle nodded and took over.

'DS Knight is stepping up to run the investigation on the ground while DI Ibson isn't here. All teams report to her. We'll have daily meetings now until the case is solved. Ashley, what have you got for us?'

Ashley stood up.

'The picture is still rather messy, but we're making connections between the three victims. There's a link with a party some years ago, but that line of investigation is still in its infancy. The party also connects to graffiti that appeared in town at the same time as the deaths. The good news is that we have Edward Balmain, Geoffrey Sullivan, and Robert Redding, AKA Homeless Bob, at the station today.'

'That's encouraging,' replied Kettle.

'Although there are caveats. Bob and Eddy don't appear capable of complex crimes, to say the least. Geoffrey was present when both scenes were discovered, and he lived in the town over thirty years ago when there was an earlier death. He is the more competent of the three, but it seems a leap that he'd be responsible.'

She paused for effect.

'Bob was also here back then, and it's just occurred to me now that the young woman who died, Foxy, and the girl who drowned yesterday, Candy, and the man we have in the cells below, Eddy, were likely all in the same year at school. I have a feeling that Bob was in that year as well.'

'Okay. What's the connection with the victims who were found under the buckets?'

'We think maybe they were also at this party years

ago, but any number of angles could come from those two. There is more bad news.'

A general groan went around the room.

'Pathology results won't be back for a while, although the most important ones will hopefully return tomorrow, but Michelle thinks that the third death could be a suicide.'

Kettle nodded.

'That's certainly possible,' he said. 'People watch the TV. They hear about people dying in places nearby and take their own lives at the same place. I believe this Candy had mental health issues.'

'Yes, but she hated the beach. Returning there to kill herself seems unlikely.'

'Or poetic,' said Kettle.

Ashley nodded.

'Eddy also struggles to cope with the beach after the death at the party all those years ago, so his presence on it is a stretch, but he might have assisted another person. Also in Eddy's defence is the fact that the pathologist puts Ron's time of death around 6 a.m., shortly before Ruby's, and we have Eddy returning to his hostel place at three thirty so this might point to another person being involved.'

'Which could be one of the seven people from the weird rhyme you mentioned,' said Kettle.

'Yes, the best guess is that four are dead, one is Eddy, and that leaves two more. Bob is possibly another, but who is the final person? Perhaps it was someone who believed the others were responsible for the death of Foxy.'

'Why wait so long for revenge?'

'I've no idea. One theory is that Eddy is involved in this because he was put on day release a year ago, and has been fully free from the psychiatric unit for the past six months. These deaths and other unusual behaviour have all started since he got out. His preceding thirty years were spent under secure conditions.'

Kettle blew out his cheeks.

'So, what's the plan?'

'DCs Freitas and Stones are pursuing intel on those mostly likely to have been upset by Foxy's demise. DC Hooper will supervise the searching of Geoffrey's vehicle and sleeping addresses, including his boat. There's another angle we need to consider, where Ruby had an inheritance coming, so we'll investigate that in case Ron was collateral damage. DS Kotecha and DC Pederson will attend Norwich hospital to speak to Candy's partner and mother. We need more background on Candy's mental state and the argument between her and her boyfriend, which resulted in his allegedly throwing himself down the stairs. They can also see if Bob is fit for interview.'

She checked her notes, then continued.

'DC Stones searched the database and there's a brief incident report for the death on the beach thirty-three years ago, and nothing else. When everything was scanned and digitised, we lost no end of crime reports, so it's not surprising there's little on what would probably have gone down as a tragic accident. There'll be coroner records, but they'll need to be ordered and located. We'll be on that today, too.'

'Let me know if I can help speed up any of this process,' said Kettle.

'Don't worry, I will do. DC Fade and I are going to talk to the headteacher at the time of Foxy's death at the party. I'm hoping she'll point us to who else was at that party. Bob might know, but I suspect his brain cells have been gobbled up by drugs like a Pac-Man got loose in his head. The blood in his shed means he is more likely implicated than not, and it's reasonable to think he was at the scene of Ron's decapitation. He may well have done it.'

There was a whisper through the seated staff as they digested that horrible image.

'Are you going to interview Geoffrey and Eddy this morning?' asked Kettle. 'We don't have enough to hold them if these searches reveal nothing damning, so we should finish them, pronto.'

'Yes, we will do, but I want to chat to the head-teacher first to get some background. She might even know Geoffrey's history. What I need from the other teams now is the meat and bones of the case. There's a mountain of CCTV to look through with huge sections of the town where there's no cover. I'm hopeful for a break today where we can narrow the focus of our searches further. I'll also instruct a team to gather mobile phone data, both calls received and sent, and information from the masts.'

'I thought there was very little signal on the beach.'

'There's no signal for most carriers. Three seems to function, and I got a text offering the services of a naval something or other, so that's worth looking into as well. Geoffrey's phone is on Three, which might be important, because it could confirm if he was at the beach if he said he wasn't.'

'Although he's obviously down there a lot. I assume you'll need the other teams to act on whatever HOLMES throws up.'

'Yes. We have a busy few days ahead of us.'

Half an hour later, after the meeting finished, Ashley and Hector were headed to the old headteacher's house. They'd found a phone number, but the call hadn't been answered.

After two minutes in the car, Hector's nose wrinkled. He sniffed the air suspiciously, then looked across at Ashley in the passenger seat.

'Have you been kissing that Geoffrey character?'

33

Arthur hadn't been joking about once being rich.
Even Hector nodded appreciatively as they drove
down the tree-lined avenue. The large detached
houses each had an individual style and were on impressive plots with massive drives and lawns. It was a
far cry from Ashley's terrace. Mrs Lythgoe had still
been the headteacher when Ashley was at school.
She had to be well in her eighties. Ashley remembered a small, thin woman with a hawklike face that
was terrifying on your first day of school.

Ashley pointed at the only vehicle on the drive as
they walked past it: an old Fiesta with rusting wheel
arches.

'That doesn't look good,' she said.

'Why not?' he asked, knocking on the big wooden door.

'That's unlikely to be her car, and people who start their lives off in places like this don't tend to drive bangers like that. So, if she's got any children, it won't be theirs either.'

'Could be the cleaner.'

'I bet you an ice cream it's her carer.'

'Okay, you're on.'

The door opened to reveal an attractive youngster in a healthcare tunic. Her eyes widened at Hector's frowning face.

'Hi,' said Ashley with a grin. 'We're here to speak to Mrs Lythgoe. We're police officers, but it's nothing to worry about.'

The woman had the hint of an accent, but it was so slight, Ashley couldn't place it.

'I'm Jo, one of her carers. She's not really with it any more. She won't know what you're talking about unless you're interested in something before about 1995.'

'That's lucky. We're after 1989.'

Jo didn't ask for their IDs, she merely stepped back to let them in. They flashed their warrants to put her at ease. Mrs Lythgoe was in a sunroom at the rear of the property. It was cosy and warm in there, with bright fresh flowers in a vase. A traditional riser chair engulfed her, giving her the look of a child having a nap. Jo came in and held her hand.

'Visitors are here.'

Mrs Lythgoe awoke in the same way a toddler would: with a smile and an innocent stretch. Ashley often felt that when she woke, she opened her eyes to problems.

'Do I know you?' asked Mrs Lythgoe.

'Kind of. I've got some questions about the secondary school in Cromer. I went there when I was young.'

'Okay, dear, are you considering sending your children there?'

Ashley looked at Hector and smiled.

'Yes, we are, but not for a while yet.'

'It's a great school.' A little frown arose. She blinked twice. 'I'm the headmistress there.'

'Yes, and that's why we'd like to ask you about some former students of yours.'

'I pride myself on remembering all the children, even the ones who've left.'

'Do you recall a Natalie Fox?'

Mrs Lythgoe scrunched her eyes, then nodded. Her eyes widened and she leaned back in her seat.

'Poor Foxy. Even I called her that, you know.' She

pointed at the bouquet next to her. 'She was like those sunflowers. Bright, fun, and she lit up any room she was in. Such a terrible shame. It's been a few years now, but I still think of her often.'

'Can you remember her friends?'

'Yes, of course.'

Mrs Lythgoe's eyes seemed to cloud up. She tapped the arm of the chair. Ashley was feeling bad about confusing her, when the frail lady smiled.

'I can picture Foxy. She matured late, so she didn't hang around with the popular children, but her group was a tight clique. That changed in the fifth form. Foxy was one of those who started her last year here as a girl and finished it as a woman. I think she tried to be loyal to her old pals, but it's quite a pull when all the cool kids want to be with you.'

'So, who did she spend her time with?' asked Hector.

'Her best friend was Candy Sweet. Such a lovely name for a very nervous girl. They were a fivesome. There was a simple lad called Teddy Batman and a brilliant boy called Kenneth Markham. He lives at 99 MacDonald Road. I remember going around to tell him and his parents that he'd won a science award. They were thrilled.'

'Do you think it might be Eddy Balmain, not Teddy Batman?'

Mrs Lythgoe frowned.

'No, I don't believe so, although Batman would be a strange name, I suppose.'

'Who was the fifth one?'

'Pardon?'

'You said their gang had five. Foxy, Eddy, Candy and Kenneth. That's four.'

Mrs Lythgoe's frown deepened.

'Sorry, I'm not sure what you're asking.'

Ashley smiled at her.

'You were telling us who Natalie Fox's friends were at school. We've had Foxy, Eddy, Candy and Kenneth. I need one more.'

Mrs Lythgoe's grimace faded. Then she gasped in relief, like someone who was tripping and had found their feet.

'Robert Redding.' Her smile returned. 'But everyone called him Bob.'

Ashley's and Hector's eyebrows raised in unison.

'Is this the guy who became known in Cromer as Homeless Bob?' asked Hector.

'Yes,' she replied, her voice strengthening with the confident recall of old memories. 'He was a weak boy back then. Mentally frail. Children like that can cope while they have friends they've known for years and the structure of school, but life changes. It speeds up after secondary school and the whole world opens up before them. Some can't keep up and fall by the wayside. Bob was one of those children.'

'So, Foxy got popular, then she left for sixth form in Sheringham. Did she hang around with those cool kids before she finished her time at your school, or did she resist the urge?'

Mrs Lythgoe's calm faded again.

'Angela was a pal, I think, and Bill, or was it Ben? Definitely a B, or a D, and, and, um...'

Mrs Lythgoe attempted to smile, but there was panic in her expression. She strained her neck to look over their heads at Jo for help.

'You tell them, Claire.'

'It's perhaps time we call it a day,' said Jo. 'She gets easily tired.'

'What do you mean, I get tired easily? I'm going to my office.' Mrs Lythgoe tried to rise from her seat, but she wobbled and slumped down. She shut her eyes, face tense with concentration.

When she opened them, she looked around, as if she'd fallen through a rabbit hole.

'This isn't the school?'

'No, it's the weekend, silly,' said Jo, crouching next

to her. 'You must be half asleep still. We're all reading here at home. I'll get you a nice cup of tea.' Jo patted her hand. 'And maybe a chocolate biscuit. We can relax today.'

Mrs Lythgoe blinked a few times, then nodded.

'Okay, Claire.'

'I'll show you out,' said Jo, standing.

The officers followed Jo to the front door.

'Sorry,' said Ashley. 'I didn't mean to upset her.'

'That's fine. She'll have forgotten all about it by the time I go back in with the tea.'

'Who's Claire?'

'Her niece. She never had children of her own, so I assume Claire was once an important person in her life, but I've been here for a year now and she's never rung or visited. The mind does unusual things as we get older.'

'Okay, thanks again. I don't think we'll need to return, but ring us if she somehow pulls any names from the past.' Ashley gave her a business card and was about to leave when she had a thought. 'Is she happy?'

Jo contemplated her answer for a few seconds.

'I like to believe she's content when I'm with her. It's as though she passes all responsibility for her life onto me, so she can sit and daydream. She's fading now. I think she would be lonely if she realised how few people come to visit.'

Ashley and Hector returned to the car and began the journey back to Cromer after agreeing to first visit Kenneth's childhood home, seeing as they were only five minutes away from the address Mrs Lythgoe had given them. Hector glanced across at Ashley.

'Why did you ask that?'

'About her being happy?'

'Yes.'

'I'm not completely sure. She's obviously receiving great care, but the whole set up made me feel very sad. I assume she was a spinster, which is depressing.'

'I suppose so. Although I would have thought the schoolchildren were her world. If she loved her job she'd probably make the same choices again.'

'Perhaps. It just feels as if I'm turning into a spinster, too. I never expected to get to my age and be completely alone and back in Cromer.'

'Why are you alone?'

'I don't like to think about it too much.'

Hector paused at a busy junction, looking left and right.

'Maybe you should.'

'Maybe I shouldn't.'

'I'm a great person to talk to. I won't be here long.

You kindly pointed out that I was young and inexperienced, so my opinion doesn't matter too much.'

Ashley sneered at him, but Hector continued.

'You said partners should get to know each other. How can I do that if you don't tell me anything?'

Ashley groaned.

'All right, fine. Even though I was exonerated, I still feel terrible about something that happened and there's a lot of self-blame and regret involved. I have survivor's guilt, but mostly it's shame. I did try to deal with the feelings, but I couldn't. So I've been hiding them away where nobody can find them, not even me.'

'Does ignoring everything mean you can carry on functioning?'

'I used to think so.'

Ashley blew out a deep breath and decided it was about time.

'Okay,' she said.

34

Hector indicated and pulled into one of the car-parking spaces at the seafront.

'Can't you drive and listen?' asked Ashley.

'I want to give you my full attention.'

'Fair enough. The accident happened in March 2013. I'd met a guy while I was backpacking around the world and decided it was time to stop being a bum. We clicked so well, but I let him leave without me. A month later, I knew I'd made a mistake and booked a flight home. He lived in Sheffield, so I turned up at his house when I flew back to the UK.'

'Life travelling is very different from real life.'

'Yeah, but surprisingly it worked. I applied for the police and, after a bit of a wait, got taken on. I'd been in about five years and moved around a few departments. I enjoyed trying new roles. We'd begun to think about kids, or at least a dog. Anyway, surveillance involved too much quiet time for me, so I'd asked for Traffic.'

Ashley had to moisten her lips.

'It was a typical drizzling, murky Sunday evening in Yorkshire. I was out with a top bloke called John Stagg. You know how some names suit people.'

'You mean like my poncey, rich person's name?'

'Exactly like that. John was larger than life, large in every way except he was only five feet six tall. Anyway, we received a call for a failing to stop. Little black Fiesta, blacked-out windows, big exhaust, normal hot-hatch bollocks being driven by teenagers.'

'Gotta love boys in fast cars.'

'Yeah. We were one of two response vehicles in the vicinity, so we gave chase. It was Parsons Cross, S6, and we often pursued joyriders through those tight streets and rat runs, up and down hills, but these kids gave us a real chase. It was their manor. They were hurtling around in circles. The other response driver finally got eyes on for just a few seconds. I can remember him swearing down the radio. He said the Fiesta was going like greased lightning. We pulled the satnav up and spotted a place to trap him. You worked in Traffic, right?'

'Not for long. I didn't see anything especially dramatic.'

'Any pursuits?'

'Plenty, but only two really high-speed incidents, and they were both on A roads. One ran out of petrol, and the other crashed into a muddy field.'

'Okay. Well, it's the same adrenaline rush, but the streets are narrower and you're in a built-up residential area. You've got to stop them because it's only a matter of time before a pedestrian is hit, especially if they're driving on the pavement.'

'Sounds perilous with only two RVs.'

'It was. It's dodgems, sometimes at high speeds. Doesn't get any more dangerous. But there's a buzz and it's exciting, even if it probably isn't supposed to be.'

'That's normal.'

'Yeah, but that's part of the reason I feel so guilty. The speeding car followed the route that John Stagg had pointed out. We moved into position and blocked the road. The Fiesta came towards us at speed towards the passenger side of our vehicle, so John's door would have taken the impact. I was just about to move away, or John would have been in danger, when they rapidly slowed down.'

Ashley swallowed, even though there was no moisture in her mouth. There was plenty on her brow. She felt a trickle run down the side of her face.

'I was looking around for other vehicles, so I didn't see what the Fiesta was doing. When I turned back, the car was charging at us. It was so fast, like a fucking rocket. They later found it had been chipped and had a nitrous kit in it.'

'So, it *was* a rocket.'

'Yes. John screamed. I put the car in gear and tried to pull away, but I was too slow.' She paused and her voice dropped to a whisper. 'I should have been quicker.'

Ashley closed her eyes. She was back there. Her nostrils flared.

'I remember the look of horror on the kid's face who was driving as he tried to steer past us, but the boost from the kit was too much for him. I don't re-member the impact. I just remember coming to. The Fiesta hit us side-on and smashed us into a lamp post. It must have ruptured one of our fuel tanks. I groggily focused and looked past John. The other car's bonnet had smashed up and the engine was belching black smoke and spitting flames. Most of our windows were smashed. I could hear screaming. Young men crying out as they roasted. There was steam and dust from the airbags and a hissing in our vehicle, so I was worried about burning, too. There's a particular smell of steaming oil, flaming petrol, and burning plastics that instantly constricts your throat. John's side of the car was crushed. He was unconscious.'

Ashley wiped her forehead, then continued in a quiet voice, which gradually rose in intensity, until she was almost shouting.

'I got out my door, no problem, then raced around to him, but their vehicle was in the way, so I returned to my side. Petrol was on fire under our car. His seat belt undid when I pressed it, and I tried to haul him out, but he was too heavy for me. The other response vehicle arrived and between us we lifted him half out of the crushed car, but his feet were stuck. Flames started flickering out of our mangled bonnet. I was worried the engine was going to blow. Then there was a rush of flames from their car, which entered John's footwell, and he woke up.'

She didn't want to close her eyelids again, because she knew she'd see John's face. His bulging eyes and yawning mouth.

'The seat catch for those models was under the seat in the middle. I'd usually have to move it every time we swapped driver, so I knew where it was, but it was on fire.'

Ashley raised her hands. Her left was much redder than her right. She opened and closed it.

'I watched him burn for a few seconds, then rammed my hand in there, scrabbled around and thankfully the seat came back quarter of an inch. We dragged him out screaming. John survived, but he'll never walk again.'

35

Hector fidgeted in his seat, but then he reached across and patted her hand in the same way that Jo had done to Mrs Lythgoe. Ashley supposed that was on-the-job learning.

'I'm sorry. That would take anyone some getting over.'

'I should have kept my eyes on the approaching vehicle. I knew they were driving erratically, and I also knew they were moving fast. Toxicology on their remains afterwards showed high levels of cocaine and alcohol. There were two canisters of nitrous fitted, which put too much pressure on the old engine. They even had petrol containers in their car. Crashing into us was basically suicide.'

'I'm guessing images and sounds like that stay in your mind.'

'If I come into contact with a similar burning smell, it drags me straight back.'

Ashley's phone rang and she was relieved to answer it.

'DS Knight.'

'Hi, Ash, it's Sal. Barry's rung in. Geoffrey's car is clean, and the caravan and boat are too. Jan visited his wife's house. She confirmed his story that he doesn't live there. Obviously, there was sand everywhere. We'll have Geoffrey's DNA checked against the clothing in Bob's shed to be sure.'

'Any news from Eddy's place?' asked Ashley, trying to get her brain to catch up with what he was implying.

'There's virtually no sand in Eddy Balmain's room. Specs on his trainers. Nothing incriminating in his place at all, in fact. No big coat. The clothes he went out and returned in are relatively clean. I know he could have got changed, but apparently he hates the sand. I don't think he was ever on that beach.'

'Okay. I'll be back to interview them before they leave. Maybe one will confess after a night on our uncomfortable beds.'

'Good luck with that.'

'Bollocks,' said Ashley, after finishing the call.

'Bad news.'

Ashley cocked her head to one side.

'No, actually. I didn't like Geoffrey for it, so I'd have looked a muppet if he was our guy. As for Eddy, everyone automatically blames the people with mental health problems, when they're usually the last person who's likely to commit this type of crime. Eddy hasn't got a criminal record, remember?'

'Homeless Bob has.'

'Yes, but he's unlikely to be a Moriarty type, either. I can more imagine him being involved, but not running the show. There's someone else pulling the strings here.'

'Perhaps one of the others who was at that party.'

'Unless it's a madman who's killed them for fun, and Candy's death is just a consequence. Maybe it was a trigger for her, and she decided to end it all.'

They shared a look. Neither liked that hypothesis. Hector turned the engine back on and pulled out to continue to Kenneth Markham's house. After a spell of silence, Hector picked up the thread from earlier.

'That car accident doesn't fully explain why you returned to Cromer,' he said.

'Well, I basically had PTSD afterwards, as well as two black eyes. The Federation was excellent. I got counselling and loads of leave, but I couldn't deal with it. The time off just meant I had more time to think about the accident. I went back to work after three months and being busy helped. I used to do all the overtime I could, and when I was at home, I'd have a four-pack and a bottle of wine and get through it that way.'

'Every night?'

'No, mostly I'd only have the beers. Wine was for the long weekends. My boyfriend tried, but I don't think he knew how to respond. I was a classic example of someone who couldn't find a way through a traumatic episode. They say talk about it, but it was too raw. I coped by shutting down all my feelings. My bloke kept saying I was a zombie, and ours was a zombie relationship. After a while, we drifted into two people living together. Roommates, not soulmates.'

'So, you came home to your parents.'

'No, they were already gone, but I still owned my dad's house here. I had planned to come back and clean it to sell because the tenants had moved out. I fancied dropping out and going travelling again, but when I arrived, I smelled the sea air. Everything was so familiar, yet nobody knew me after being away so long. After a few long walks, I asked for a transfer.'

'How did you end up in CID?'

'They had a few positions in CID down here. Two older guys had taken retirement, and the uniformed youngsters aren't as keen on the move nowadays. They enjoy getting their antisocial-hours allowance and the knowledge that when their shift ends, they can go home. Detectives have to stay and get the job done.'

'I suppose everyone wants to catch murderers, but that's done by MIT.'

'Yes. You usually need to go through CID to reach MIT. For a couple of years, you spend your time trawling through evidence taken from people's mobile phones and their computers. CID is a long way from a starring role in *Luther*. General detective work can feel like a safeguarding job, where you deal with a succession of individuals with mental health problems. Sex crimes, domestic abuse, modern slavery, stalking. That's not to mention the fact it's all stuff where, if you get it wrong, there are serious consequences.'

'Doesn't being the Senior Investigating Officer on a murder inquiry carry a lot of risk if there are mistakes?'

'Of course. If the shit hits the fan in this case, it'll go in Kettle's direction, but in MIT everyone gets their share. We're all in it together because they're complex crimes. Anyway, I came for an interview with Peter. He took me on, even though I was honest with what had happened in Sheffield and how I needed a fresh start. Do you know what he said?'

'I'm surprised he didn't say no.'

'Me too, but he told me that when I got through it, I'd be better at my job.'

'Interesting angle.'

'No, he was right. I could only focus on the bad, but he gave it a silver lining. I moved back into my house where I still live now, put my head down, and got promoted. When Peter progressed to MIT, I went with him.'

'And here we are today.'

'Yes. Any more questions, Bamber?'

'Who's Bamber?'

'Never mind. You're probably too young.'

'You shouldn't feel guilty. They deliberately rammed your car. You weren't to know their vehicle was jet-propelled, and you burnt your hand getting him out. That was noble.'

'I can see all that, but I visited John three months after the incident. I was only there for a minute. It was too hard. I couldn't even look at him. He was in so much pain. So, I left and never went back.'

Hector pulled up outside a guest house, which

seemed to be out of business, so he parked on their forecourt. Kenneth Markham's home, number 99, was next to it. If he still lived there. Hector got out and strolled towards the front door. Ashley took a moment in the car. She hadn't told anyone that story properly since Peter interviewed her. She'd been a wreck then, but Peter still took a chance on her. It was why she was so defensive of him when others moaned about his brusqueness.

Ashley got out of the car and walked towards Hector. Perhaps this guy was going to be good for her sanity after all.

She wondered if she'd tell him the rest.

36

The door had an opaque glass panel, so Ashley could see if anyone was approaching. A shadow loomed, but it seemed to take a long time to reach them. The door opened a couple of inches, then a chain jolted it to a stop and a man's head slowly appeared in the crack.

'How can I help you?' asked a subdued, croaky voice.

'Good morning, we're police officers. We're looking for Kenneth Markham.'

The light-green eye they could observe blinked.

'What do you want him for?'

Ashley smiled and held up her warrant. 'Are you him?'

'Yes. Hang on.'

The head edged out of sight, and the door shut. The chain scratched back, then the door yawned wide. Ashley was expecting an old man from his voice, but the trim person before them looked to be about fifty and was smartly dressed in black trousers and a white shirt.

'Is it about my mother?'

'No, we're here to see you.'

'Oh.' Shock registered on his face. 'You'd better come in. We'll go through to the parlour.'

Kenneth turned around and walked slowly and carefully through a doorway on the right of the front door. He put his hand on the back of a chair in the far corner. Ashley spotted a new-looking black wheelchair further down the corridor as she followed him into the room. On the open door was a small picture of a fisherman with his dog in a boat. He had a bottle to his lips and under it was written, 'What will we do with a drunken sailor?'

Kenneth turned, gave them both a weak handshake, then sank into a similar riser chair to the one that Mrs Lythgoe had been sitting in. Ashley looked around the walls at an abundance of framed photographs, mostly of Cromer at dawn or dusk. Whoever took them had talent.

'Nice,' she said.

'Thank you. A hobby of mine.'

'Why did you ask if it was about your mother?' asked Hector as he sat next to Ashley on the sofa opposite Kenneth and took his notebook out.

Kenneth leaned forward with a conspiratorial expression and spoke quietly.

'She says whatever's on her mind. There was an altercation at the butchers a while back. I've often thought she'd end up in court with her antiquated ways. Still, she's good to me, so I can't complain.'

'Is that wheelchair yours?' asked Ashley.

'Yes, I can potter if I'm careful, but I need the chair if I want to go anywhere. They've started calling it fibromyalgia, but it's chronic fatigue to me. I developed it at university.'

'I'm sorry to hear that.'

'Don't be. I'm used to it, and others have much worse luck. So, what is it you wanted to talk to me about?'

'We've been investigating the murders on the beach. I'm sure you've heard about them.'

'I have, and that's precisely what I mean by worse luck. Those two were all out of the good kind.'

'Someone else lost their life down on the same stretch of beach a couple of nights ago.'

'Really? Another murder?'

'We're not certain yet.'

'Wow. And what's my connection to all this?'

'We think you know her,' said Hector.

'Okay. As you can imagine, I don't get out much or have too many acquaintances. Who is it?'

'Candice Sweet.'

'Candy Sweet?'

'Yes, do you know her?'

'I did.' Kenneth's expression softened as his mind transported him to the past. 'Must be over thirty years ago. We used to be pretty good friends at senior school, but we lost touch.'

'And you know Edward Balmain.'

'Yes, of course. I called him Fast Eddy. It was our little joke.'

'And you were mates with him.'

'Yes, there was a gang of us. We were the geeks. Bob and Foxy were the other two.' Kenneth's eyes glazed. Then he sniffed and smiled. 'It was a long time ago.'

'Do you still see Bob or Eddy?' asked Hector.

'Not really. I didn't fancy returning to Cromer after university. I moved around a lot and was gone for big chunks of time. My mum and dad had a business they ran here, so I came back once in a while, but, apart from Bob, everyone had left.'

'So, you still saw Bob,' said Ashley.

'No, not to speak to. He had a bit of a breakdown, drugs I believe, but he was always erratic.' Kenneth leaned back in his seat. He shook his head. 'There was an accident.'

'What sort of accident?'

'A beach party. Foxy and Candy went with Eddy. Funnily enough, I think that Ron and Ruby were there too. They all got drunk, and in the morning, Foxy was gone. The tide had turned, and it brought her body back to shore. She'd drowned. This town was a tighter community then. It was a big shock.'

'And you didn't go to the party.'

'No, even then, I used to get tired quickly. Running down steep slopes and walking on sand didn't appeal. We weren't close by then, anyway.'

'Had you fallen out?'

'No, nothing like that. Cromer school doesn't have a sixth form, so the brighter kids like me went on to sixth form elsewhere, and the thickies got jobs.'

'And the others were thickies?'

'They were different times. Candy wasn't completely daft, but she was highly strung, and there wasn't a lot of point in her going on to further education. Bob was already taking drugs and skipping school. Fast Eddy was living up to his nickname. It's funny you should mention him. I got told he'd gone crazy and was in whatever they call asylums these days, but I saw him about six months back.'

'Did you talk to him?'

'Kind of. I was with my mum at the supermarket and he spotted me. He kept staring at my chair and saying sorry, as though he was to blame for something. He looked funny, too. Sort of bloated. Weirdly, he asked if he could push me in the chair. I let him scoot me around for a bit, then he said, "See you later." It was all very odd, but made me wary of seeing him again. Anyway, so, out of our gang, it was just me and Foxy who attended Sheringham Sixth Form college.'

'Did you two remain friends there?'

Kenneth tipped his head and laughed, but he put his hand over his mouth. Veins showed in his neck as he rocked in his seat.

'Sorry,' he said, when he'd calmed. 'I wish. No, I'd already lost her in the final year of secondary school. We all loved her, because she was gangly and boyish and great fun, but so unaware of how being with her was so intoxicating. She was one of us outcasts. Then she grew a big pair of titties, and you know how it is.'

Ashley watched him glance down at her flat chest.

'No,' she growled. 'How is it?'

Kenneth cringed, revealing large, uneven and crooked yellow teeth. He closed his mouth when he saw her staring at them.

'Sorry. She became very popular. Too cool for us.'

'Did that make you feel sad?'

'A little, I guess, but I made a couple of new pals. There were other kids who were academic. Look at my face. I was never going to get her, and she still said hi and would stop and chat. I don't blame her for dating the cool kids. I'd have been with the pretty girls if they'd have had me.'

Ashley didn't doubt that for a minute.

'So, back to the party. Do you recall who was on the beach?'

He leaned forward again with the same expression on his face, which appeared more creepy than mysterious now. It was little wonder this guy had few friends, thought Ashley.

'Everyone was freaked about it afterwards. There were rumours. Foxy was popular with the townsfolk, despite the mischief she got up to. It was right at the end of the summer holidays, so I left for university shortly after and didn't think too much more of it. Bob, Ruby and Ron all seemed to vanish into thin air afterwards. I don't really know what happened, but kids kept joking that the people at that party were doomed.'

Kenneth clicked his fingers then spoke with enthusiasm.

'An idiot wrote a poem on one of the buildings around town that more would die. That a creature from the depths would come back and kill the rest of them. Something like that.'

'Do you remember who the rest were?'

'No, although the rhyme said there were seven. Funny what you recall.'

'How about an Angela or a Bill?'

'God no. There was an Angela who also went to Sheringham sixth form when we did, but she'd never have taken drugs, but I can hazard a guess who might have been there.'

'Go on.'

'It will have been Brad and Pete.'

'Why them?'

'They were captain and vice-captain of all the sports teams. Super popular. Good-looking, fit, best friends, rich families. Dream lives, you know. But they both lusted after Foxy, and they battled for her. She chose Pete, and Brad was furious, but only one could win. It was probably tough for Brad because I bet it was the first time he'd wanted something and not got it.'

'Did they stop talking?'

'Yeah, for a bit. Brad Garrett was a robust kid, with a reputation as a scrapper, but they buried the hatchet towards the end of school.'

'Do you know what happened to the pair of them?'

'Yes, they both did great for themselves. They left Norfolk but returned to live near here after university. Brad Garrett runs Garrett's Car Sales in Holt. We bought a car from them once, although I didn't meet him there. Sells quality second-hand motors. I bet he's rich, although I've not seen him in the flesh since we were at school. The other guy did well, too, but then you'd know all about that.'

'Why would I know?' asked Ashley.

'I see his name in the paper all the time.'

'Who is it?'

'Detective Inspector Peter Ibson.'

37

Back in the car, having managed to keep their cool in the house, the detectives turned to each other.

'Holy shit,' said Ashley.

'Yeah. I can't get my head around it.'

'It's my heart that's struggling. Peter was initially in charge when we were down on the beach for those first two murders. He must have known it was the exact same spot where his beautiful girlfriend died. The girl he fought with his best friend over. Passion and love at that age are all-consuming. Nothing stands in their way. He would have remembered instantly, yet he didn't comment on it.'

'It was the distant past. Perhaps he didn't connect

the dots, although he did seem uncomfortable. Would you have mentioned it?'

Ashley took an apple out of her pocket, then a penknife, and opened the short blade.

'Hmm, maybe not,' she said. 'Saying, "Hey, guess what, the love of my life died here three decades ago," would have sounded very strange. As for him being uncomfortable, that's kind of his style.'

'Yeah, but now he's off sick, so perhaps it was the thing on the beach that finally pushed him over the edge. You said he's been acting a little odd for a year.'

'Whatever's going on, we need to talk to him and this Brad guy. Either could be the killer for all we know.'

'Or they could be next,' said Hector slowly.

'Oh, God. Yes. We'd soon be at seven.'

Ashley began to peel the apple and Hector raised an eyebrow.

'What?'

'Why don't you just eat it?' he asked.

'I find the texture of the skin off-putting on the first bite. To be honest, I'm not that mad about apples.'

'Why not peel an orange, then? It'd be quicker, and less unsettling for me.'

Ashley chuckled.

'I smoked for ages. At times of tension, like now, I'd fire up. I often tried to quit using sweets instead, but I'd pile weight on and would start up again. This is what helped me stop. It's a distraction, and the knife is the only thing I have left that meant anything to my father, apart from our house, of course. He used to do this too. It was good for his mental health, because to take the skin off in one go takes patience and concentration, and you forget the urge to smoke or eat crap, or, in his case, it kept the dark thoughts at bay. Bollocks.'

She put the half-peeled apple and knife in a small bag she kept in her pocket as Hector started the car.

'It also gives me time to think,' she said. 'I was going to say let's head to Peter's house, but Kettle mentioned he was leaving town for a while and turning his phone off.'

'Maybe he wanted to be out of reach.'

'Perhaps. We can drop into Holt and visit Brad later, but let's go back to Wymondham first and interview our friend Eddy. See what he has to say about Peter and Brad's love triangle. We'll be stuck in the car half the day, but I need as much background as possible before I tackle Brad and Peter. I want to know if they're lying to me.'

'That's assuming they're both still alive.'

Ashley nodded, but she was finding Hector's ability to cut to the chase almost unsettling.

38

Ashley and Hector found Emma and Sal in good spirits when they returned to the station. It appeared they'd made progress. Sal was dressed in light-blue suit trousers and a matching waistcoat, which seemed to emphasise his short stature. Ashley didn't comment, knowing her wardrobe was something else she should have an epiphany on. Emma hadn't taken much time choosing her grey blouse and black slacks, either.

'As per usual,' said Sal, 'we have the good news and the bad news.'

'Give me the bad news first,' said Ashley.

'It's intermingled, so you'll get them together,' said Emma.

'So why ask?'

'I didn't. I said there was good and bad,' said Sal.

'Spit it out, please.'

'A quick-thinking CSI was able to find four big spots of blood along the concrete promenade where the beach huts are,' said Emma. 'You know how blood soaks into things, so she should manage to pull a DNA test off it and match it to Ron. Cutting some-one's head off would be messy, so it's likely the suspect was covered in it.'

'So perhaps the killer stabbed Ron first, which caused the blood on Ruby, then he buried her, before he got sprayed with blood while cutting Ron's head off,' said Hector. 'Then he fled past the beach huts leaving drops in his wake.'

'That would make this guy really warped,' said Ashley. 'Imagine Ruby being buried up to her neck and seeing Ron's head placed next to her, before the bucket came down.'

'It sounds utterly savage,' said Sal. 'But that new evidence helps with timings. It wasn't doing any more than spotting rain at about six-fifteen, so the blood was certainly spilt before that and maybe quite a good hour before that for it to dry. Once blood is in stone, it's very hard to get out, so the later rain won't have washed it off.'

'So Eddy could have been involved,' said Ashley.

'This makes it more probable. He could have been there at the beginning, then couldn't cope with the beach or the memories. It could have been his partner in crime pulling a saw out that scared him away.'

'Shit. I didn't think of that,' said Ashley. 'I assume we've been checking for someone carrying a saw or a holdall when the CCTV was being analysed.'

'Of course,' said Emma. 'And the new evidence also helps us narrow down the CCTV search because there was a drop of blood right at the end at the last hut, which indicates the killer exited in that direction towards Geoffrey's boat and the town centre.'

'Cool. So, we're looking for a person running through Cromer, covered in blood and carrying a tool bag at around 6 a.m.'

'Precisely,' said Emma.

'And was there anyone doing that?' asked Hector.

'No,' said Sal.

'Not that we've found,' replied Emma. 'Which is obviously more bad news.'

'Wait,' said Ashley. 'There's a flight of steps up the cliff face. It starts in between the beach huts and leads right up to Warren Wood. Bob's shed is only about fifty metres away, so if Bob was involved, it's likely he'd have gone up there.'

'The killers might have split up, and the other person headed into town with nothing incriminating in his hands because Bob had it,' said Emma.

'It makes it tough with so many access points,' said Sal. 'I'd guess that this wasn't a long job, so the perpetrator would probably arrive an hour or so beforehand. We're searching all the routes, but it's also fair to say that just because he made his escape that way, doesn't mean he arrived by the same route. If he was smart, he wouldn't have done, because people would be more likely to remember him if they'd seen him twice.'

'Let's really hope he's not too smart,' said Ashley. 'Get onto the council and find out who owns those beach huts. Just in case he's using one as a changing room.'

'That's already on the list,' said Emma. 'Uniform knocked and checked but none were in use. I suppose a guilty occupant would have ignored them.'

'Well, we haven't caught him yet, so he's no idiot,' said Hector. 'If I was heading for a slaughtering, I'd also wear something waterproof like a raincoat.'

Hector winked at Sal, who grinned.

'Or a blue or black Macintosh!' he replied.

'Yes,' said Hector. 'The creepy guy in town who's been wandering around scaring people and drawing rhymes and numbers on walls looks very much like a person we need to speak to.'

'I'm pretty sure we've found him on CCTV,' said Emma. 'Although he wasn't carrying a saw.'

'That's lucky, with all that footage to check,' said Ashley.

'No, remember we knew what time frame to check because the perpetrator was spotted writing on that house. Unfortunately, the picture is grainy and distant, but the person clearly has an unnatural stride.'

'Bollocks. If that means he has a limp, it brings us back to Eddy again.'

'Yes. I can search the CCTV from the stepdown place and see if he left at a similar time. We should be able to rule him in or out.'

'Okay,' said Hector. 'Although we've made some pretty big leaps there. I don't suppose anyone's seen our DI Ibson in a blue waterproof coat?'

Sal and Emma both said, 'Eh?'

Hector told the stunned pair about Kenneth Markham's educated guess. Emma was the first to recover after about ten seconds.

'Bloody hell. Could Peter be the killer? He's smart enough. He knows all the victims, including Eddy and Bob. He's lived here or near here for nearly all of his life and he'd know how to get away with a crime. He's been distant for a while, and you said he seemed really out of sorts that day.'

'Peter's been out of sorts for the best part of a year, but he's still done a good job,' said Ashley.

'Maybe he's been planning it for that long,' replied Emma. 'Perhaps he waited for Eddy to leave the madhouse, and they planned it together, then at the last minute Eddy choked, so Peter had to do it all himself.'

Hector tutted, before replying.

'Then Peter ran through the town, wrote more graffiti, went home and got changed, then turned up on the beach as probable Senior Investigating Officer. Shame we didn't check his fingernails for blood and paint.'

'Yes, but he's currently conveniently out of reach, and Candy's also dead,' said Sal.

'What's the motivation? Why wait until now?' asked Ashley.

'Maybe he was burning up with it for years, then Eddy got out and it all came rushing back,' said Emma.

'Perhaps he waited until Eddy was out, so he could pin it on him,' said Hector.

Ashley considered that for a moment, then groaned.

'I can't believe I'm actually considering this! Peter believed in his oath. He lived it every day.'

'Peter Ibson was also a brilliant detective,' said Sal. 'If he wanted to fit Eddy up, he'd have put sandy trainers in his room.'

'Or bloody trainers in his shed,' said Hector.

Ashley blew out a breath.

'I'd forgotten about Bob and his bloody trainers and T-shirt. It'd be a bit of a coincidence if he'd just had a nasty nosebleed that day. Well, by the end of tomorrow, we should have spoken to Peter, Brad and Bob, and have the DNA results back. Let's break for a coffee, then see what Eddy's got to say for himself about all this. I need to run this by Kettle, too. It goes no further about Peter until I've spoken to the DCI.'

An hour later, Ashley and Hector had interviewed Geoffrey again and released him on police bail. They returned to the interview room to wait for Eddy Balmain.

'Still fancy Geoffrey for it?' asked Ashley.

'I can't help thinking he has some kind of interest in it all, but I can't see what it that is.'

'Okay, don't forget those thoughts. Maybe you've had a detective's famous hunch.'

'Yes, but Kettle didn't seem focused on him.'

'Kettle knows we're closest to the case. He's known me long enough to trust that I'll investigate all the angles including Geoffrey, and if that includes Peter Ibson, then so be it.'

Eddy had been given a mental health assessment the previous evening at Norwich hospital and spent the night there, but they'd cleared him for interview. Uniform had brought Eddy back an hour ago, but it was Dylan and the same solicitor that had represented Eddy the previous day who entered the room first and took a seat.

The solicitor cleared his throat.

'I've been in to see Eddy, and it's not good. Last night was tough for him.'

'We'll be the judge of that,' said Hector.

Ashley made a mental note to give Hector feedback about needlessly pissing people off. It wasn't like TV. Most of those in the legal profession were far from millionaires and were working lengthy hours, often for little money. They also tended to be fair and reasonable.

'I agree,' she said. 'He doesn't seem to have the rationale for this kind of crime, and he clearly doesn't like the beach. I just want to ask him a few more questions about something that happened a long time ago.'

'Good luck with that.'

Ashley didn't have time to query that comment, because Eddy was brought in, and it was immediately obvious that a night in hospital had taken its toll. His limp appeared more pronounced, as though the knee could give way at any moment. Geoffrey had seemed refreshed after his sleep on a blue mattress, whereas Eddy did not look at all well after a night under lock and key. He sat down opposite them and avoided eye contact while his left hand jerked uncontrollably into a little thumbs up.

'Hi, Eddy. We have a few questions. Then we can get you home. Is that okay?'

'Sh-sh-sure.'

'We're wondering if you know anything about a rhyme and a few numbers that were written on some of the buildings in town.'

Ashley thought Eddy was looking at her, but he was actually staring above her to avoid eye contact.

'No. I've done nothing like that.'

'I noticed you're limping a bit. Have you hurt your leg?'

'I had a car accident. Years ago. Can I go now?'

'Last few questions. We've chatted with an old

friend of yours, and he was telling us about a party on the beach. That was over thirty years ago, too.'

Eddy's head twitched to the left. He peered back at her, then it jerked away again. His eyes widened.

'No, no. No talking about the party.'

'We need to talk about the party.'

Eddy's head jiggled back and forth. He looked down and seemed to freeze.

'We spoke to your friend, Kenneth Markham.'

'Not my friend. Not my friend.'

'And he told us about you, Brad Garrett and Peter Ibson.'

Eddy's head shot up. His hand did a succession of mini thumbs-ups.

'Foxy died. Foxy died. I didn't do it. I wanted to go home.'

'Who did it?'

Eddy scratched his face, marking it. He looked left at his solicitor, then right at Dylan. Eddy shook his head again.

'Who killed her?' asked Ashley.

Eddy jumped to his feet, eyes straining. He snarled his reply.

'It was the sea. The sea called for her, and we couldn't stop her. I didn't push Foxy. We tried. I ran, but I heard her cries as the ocean took her.'

'Please sit down, Eddy. It's okay.'

Eddy sat down. There was one more jerk of his head, then he went limp.

'Where exactly are you going with all this?' asked the solicitor. 'You have nothing. No weapon, no DNA, no bloody clothes, no corroborating CCTV, and no witnesses. You certainly don't have enough to charge him. He's clearly unwell. My client won't be answering any further questions. It's obvious he's not up to concocting a complicated crime like this one. He'd have left sand and blood everywhere.'

'No sand,' said Eddy. 'Can't touch the sand now. Not after Foxy.'

'I agree,' said Dylan. 'I need to get him home and relaxed. This dyskinesia that he's displaying now is a common response to stress. If you persist, he'll have a complete breakdown and there'll be no other choice but to return him to secure conditions. If you let him calm down for a few days, I might get more information out of him, but all you're doing by questioning him now is pushing him closer to the edge.'

'Okay, Eddy,' said Hector. 'I know you want to prove you're innocent.'

Eddy sneaked a glance up, then gave another thumbs-up. Ashley thought he intended this one.

'Can we talk to the hospital and check your medical records, Eddy?' she asked.

'Then we can really understand your history and rule you out,' said Hector.

'My client doesn't need to provide evidence of his mental health.'

'Do it,' said Eddy loudly. 'Look, look at it. I've done nothing wrong. I haven't hurt anyone. You'll see. No violence now. No violence.'

Ashley read from her notebook.

'"Only when there are seven can they rest in heaven. For nobody can deny the hungry sea."'

Eddy violently shook his head from side to side. He whispered his reply.

'That's what he says. No rest until there's seven.'

'Who says, Eddy?'

'The sea wants seven, but I don't want to die.'

'Eddy, are you protecting someone? Have you spoken to Peter or Brad? What do you know?' demanded Ashley.

'I can't go back. No more beach, and no more hospitals, please!'

'That's enough!' shouted the solicitor.

Eddy scrunched up his eyes, bunched his fists on his lap, and seemed to swell. The veins were pronounced on his muscled arms. Ashley was again

taken by how toned he was. With his expression constricted like that, his cheeks bulged in strange places.
The car accident must have really damaged his face
as well as his leg. It was a scary sight.

'Interview terminated,' she said.

Eddy was escorted from the room to be released.
When he'd gone, Hector remained in his seat, staring
at the wall. He slowly tapped his fingers on the edge
of the table almost as though he were playing the piano. Ashley leaned back and waited until he spoke.

'I reckon he knows something. He's stressed all
right, but I don't think it's from being here. More
likely from something he's done.'

'I agree, but perhaps it was something he's seen or
heard. Let's find Peter Ibson, because I've had a nasty
thought.'

'Go on.'

'Dylan said that Eddy's been going to the gym.
Can you imagine him rocking up at a posh gym, or
even affording one?'

'No, not at all.'

'Exactly. But when we went to Peter's house, he
had a gym in his garage.'

39

Ashley and Hector returned to the office and updated the team. Bhavini and Jan were back from the hospital.

'How's Bob?' asked Ashley.

'Spaced out. They let us have a word, but he was too sleepy to get much sense out of him. Although I had the impression he was putting it on,' replied Bhavini. 'The nurse told me the doc will examine him tomorrow morning at ten and discharge him afterwards if he seems all right. There's still a uniform present, so he won't be sneaking out.'

'And how's Candy's mum?'

'Stunned,' said Jan. 'They let her sleep next to Candy's boyfriend, who's in pieces. Candy's mother didn't want to talk to us. She even tried to shut Elliott up, saying there's no point going over spilt milk.'

'Crying over spilt milk,' corrected Hector.

'Yes, that's it. Nice phrase. But Elliott kept sobbing. He felt responsible.'

'Did you ask for his take on the stairs incident?'

'Yep. Said he hurt himself on purpose. Elliott seemed a bit simple as well, so I don't reckon he was lying. He believed he should have done more to stop her from killing herself.'

'Why does he think it was suicide?'

'He said she'd been really down lately. She was at rock bottom a few weeks back. When he asked her about it, she said someone she knew had visited, and that had upset her.'

'Distraught enough for suicide?'

'Yeah, that's why he was arguing with her. She kept saying she had to die, not that she was going to die. It was like she deserved to. He told her he couldn't live without her and threw himself down the stairs. She started shouting at him at the bottom for being so stupid. A neighbour called the police.'

Ashley considered what Jan had said. Deserved to die would mean she'd done something wrong. What could that be? Maybe she was somehow responsible for her friend, Foxy, dying. Perhaps she should have been looking out for her on the beach, and when she died, Candy felt guilty. Ashley could understand those thoughts.

'A lot of suicides make little sense,' said Ashley. 'It's the horror and tragedy of mental illness.'

'That was the strange thing about Homeless Bob,' said Bhavini. 'We're still waiting for toxicology, but the doctor reckons the amount of heroin Bob took was immense, because he was out of it for so long.'

'What's odd about a heavy habit?'

'It was too much. Bob would know more than anyone the quantity for a safe dose. The doctor reckoned it was a deliberate overdose.'

'Unless someone else gave him too much,' said Ashley.

A hush came over the team as they considered it.

She gave them a moment to absorb that, then issued instructions to set up a meeting at Eddy's recent secure unit.

After the discussion, Hector and she left the station for Peter's house in the hope that, despite what he'd said, he was home. Hector signed for the same car. He seemed puzzled by the prospect of their DI's involvement.

'I can't find a strong motivation for him being part of this.'

'No, me neither. Peter was anti-violence. He frowned at Barry's overzealous arrests. I don't see him doing anything like this, but what I mentioned earlier applies here, too. Many people are closer to the edge than you think. All reason can go when they snap. I think Kettle is more worried about Peter's mental health than his involvement.'

Hector bobbed his head.

'You said he began to act differently about a year ago, which was about the time Eddy was having day visits to Cromer. Maybe it brought all the terrible memories of his loss back. Losing your big love as a teenager would be extremely destabilising.'

'I would say that's an understatement. Perhaps the death of Foxy was what caused Eddy to completely lose the plot. It's odd how he said he had a car accident. That must have been after the party, but before he was sectioned.'

'That could have been the incident that had him sectioned. His hospital notes should be at his last unit. They'll probably include his psychiatric sessions, so hopefully we'll find out.'

The traffic was light and they reached Overstrand in good time. They knocked on Peter's door, but there was no answer. Ashley tried to go around the rear again, but the gate was locked, and Peter's car was nowhere to be seen. She pulled out her mobile and gave his number a ring. Straight to voicemail.

Ashley shook her head in disbelief at what she was about to do. She called the office and spoke to Emma.

'Hi, Ems. I'm going to need you to get Kettle to authorise a BOLO on the boss. Also look on ANPR to find out if his car's been near these scenes.'

Hector smiled at her as she finished the call.

'What do you reckon?' he said. 'Is Peter hiding from the killer, or is he looking for his next victim?'

Peter Ibson was a good man, wasn't he? She wouldn't think the worst, but, deep down, Ashley had to admit she didn't have a clue.

40

The next stop was the car showroom in Holt. It was only ten miles from Cromer, but, whereas Cromer's pleasures were widely known, Holt almost kept its charms to itself. The people who lived there were proud and protective of their charming cobbled-wall buildings and eclectic architecture. Those who visited always returned.

'You'll like Holt,' said Ashley.

'Why's that?'

'Rich people live there. I once paid a fiver for a Scotch egg at a farmer's market. Best damn one I ever had, but still.'

'My parents are wealthy, not me.'

'So, you'll become rich.'

'Maybe, but my folks aren't even sixty yet. They've lived healthy lives. I probably won't inherit for at least another twenty years, so I need to make my own way in the world.'

'Yeah, but when it comes to buying your first property, I bet you get a helping hand.'

'Of course. Isn't that what all parents do? You said your father left you his house, so what's the difference?'

'Do you really want to know?'

'I wouldn't have asked otherwise.'

'My mum vanished when I was two. She walked away and left my father literally holding the baby. So, it was just me and him, and he had his own struggles. I grew up in a house empty of emotion with a man who I now understand had serious depression. It wasn't all bad, but our home quietened further as I got older. I took on the cooking, then the shopping, even managing the bills.'

Hector glanced over.

'That can't have been easy for a young girl.'

'Actually, I liked the independence, and it was a gradual thing. My dad never cared where I was, so I was a free spirit. I was doing the same as this Foxy and her friends did over thirty years ago. Parties on the beach, smoking and drinking in the cemetery, hiding from the ticket collector on the Norwich train.'

'Okay.'

'Let me ask you a question. What's strange about most domestic abuse cases?'

'Why people put up with it.'

'Spot on. In a way, it was similar. He slowly slipped away from me. You probably don't know what young teenage girls are like, but I started trying to provoke and taunt him. I was so rude, just hoping for a reaction. I was jealous of my friends' normality. Their folks were interested in their school lives. They had foreign holidays and family get-togethers, birthday meals out. I craved all that, but it was beyond my father.'

Ashley had a sneaky glance over at Hector as they arrived and he was distracted by the eighteenth-century Georgian buildings. He drove slowly through the centre, past the art galleries, antique shops and bookstores. There was a range of tempting places to eat located along the high street and lurking down charming courtyards and alleyways. Hector had a small smile on his face when he turned to her.

'Sorry, carry on.'

'The worse I behaved, the more distant he became, until he barely functioned and I rarely spoke to him. After I'd finished my A levels, I came home one morning after staying out all night and found him lying on the sofa, dead. He'd taken all his pills and choked to death while unconscious.'

'I'm sorry. That must have been terrible.'

'At the time, I didn't think it was terrible.'

'But you do now?'

'It only sank in halfway through my travels, which made me reckless, but that's another story. It's only after doing this job that I realise in some ways he can still be my hero. He struggled with his mental health for sixteen years and was clearly suicidal a long time before he took his own life. He managed to wait until I was ready.'

Ashley knew the area where the garage was, and they were soon pulling into a forecourt with a choice of gleaming vehicles on it. The big sign simply said: Garrett's. Hector pulled into a visitor's space and stepped from the vehicle. She had been meaning to buy a better car, but it had always seemed like a hassle.

She wandered down the line of cars at the front. There were BMWs, Mercedes and Audis, all of which were too new for her price range.

'Morning, madam. Lovely day. What is it you're after?'

Ashley turned around expecting to see a young woman in a sharp suit, but it was a middle-aged woman in jeans and a casual checked shirt.

'I'd like one of these,' said Ashley, patting the bonnet of a BMW. 'But I can't afford it.'

'They still seem expensive to me, and we own the place.' The lady had a huge American sitcom style friendly smile. There was an air of Barbie about her blonde hair and make-up, but it was relaxed and suited her years. 'I'm Lorna Garrett.'

Ashley shook her hand.

'I'm Detective Sergeant Ashley Knight, and this is Detective Constable Hector Fade.'

Lorna's face fell.

'Oh. How can I help?'

'It's Brad we're after.'

'He's at the MOT garage. What's he done?'

Ashley stole a glance at Hector, who'd picked up on the assumption of guilt too.

'Could we have a quick word with you first?' he said.

'Of course. Come to the office. Mondays are always quiet, but we sold four cars yesterday.'

Mrs Garrett took them through the showroom, which had a selection of cheaper vehicles in it more within Ashley's budget. They all looked immaculate.

Ashley crouched to peer into a Mini Cooper, which was clean inside and out.

'One careful lady owner,' said Lorna. 'I can do you a great price if I don't have to go to prison. Sorry, I'm rambling. Come through here.'

She guided them to a smart and tidy office with a laptop on an otherwise empty desk. There were flowers in a vase and pictures of family on the walls. The room smelled fresh and airy.

'Nice place,' said Ashley.

'Thank you.'

Ashley expected Lorna to sit behind the computer, but she pulled the chair around and sat opposite them.

'Would you like a drink?' she asked.

'Water would be fine.'

Lorna glided her chair to a small fridge at the back of the office and grabbed three bottles of Buxton. Ashley liked this woman's style.

'So, my husband.'

'Yes. What kind of person is he?'

'I would describe him as serious. He's a hard worker. Too hard. Calling him driven is maybe not strong enough.'

Ashley thought of Arthur saying the same words as she glanced at a family picture, which looked as if it was taken on an exotic beach. A tall, handsome man stared intently at the camera with his arm draped over Lorna's shoulder. She seemed tiny beside him. A younger woman with longer blonde hair and a pretty face was laughing next to them. The photograph could have been an advert for high-end swimwear if Brad's expression hadn't been so distant.

'Good-looking guy.'

'I know, but he's not easy to live with.'

'How so?'

'He can be a bit controlling and hates receiving advice. He can be grumpy and aggressive. Sometimes he'll argue with the customers if he believes they're in the wrong.'

'Sounds charming,' said Hector.

Lorna put her head in her hands, then gave them a sheepish grin.

'Sorry, I'm being unfair. They're all his bad points, but we really haven't been getting on well lately, which is a pity, because he has mellowed. He was very protective of our daughter, but she didn't mind. She's at college in Scotland now though. I reckon she chose the farthest place possible that did her course.'

'Do you think that affected him?'

'I think he was pleased she was spreading her

wings, but wished she hadn't spread them so far. He was out of sorts before she left though.'

'What do you think was bothering him?'

'To be honest, I'm not sure. He's been a bit cloak and dagger. He had a visit from what he said was an old school friend, which is weird, because he doesn't really have any friends.'

'When was this?'

'Perhaps six months ago. Brad hasn't been the same since. He wouldn't talk about it, apart from that the guy accused him of something, but he was wrong, and it wasn't anything to do with us.'

Ashley could see that Brad's behaviour was taking a terrible toll on his wife.

'That must have been hard for you, especially seeing as you work together.'

'Yes, exactly. He refused to give me any details, and it's kind of soured our relationship.'

'Do you have anyone you can talk to about this?'

'No, not really. Most of my friends are here in Holt. Our business is here, so I don't want word to get out that Brad has become erratic or unstable. I've been hoping he'd snap out of it, but he's been even worse these last few weeks. Is that why you're here, because he's upset someone?'

'To be honest we're doing background checks, but

his change in behaviour might be connected to the recent incidents on Cromer beach.'

'What? Surely not those people who were killed.'

'We don't know, but Brad knew some of those victims from a long time ago.'

'You surely can't think he's involved?'

Ashley remained silent as she could see Lorna wasn't convinced by her own words. Lorna took a big gulp of her water and ran a hand through her hair.

'He often used to have a beer or two on Sunday nights in the local. After a long week, it was a good way for him to wind down. I'd meet him there sometimes. We'd do badly at the quiz, have a meal maybe, but he goes most nights on his own now, and he drinks too much. Then he might not come home. He's been sleeping here a lot. I found him yesterday morning fast asleep in the chair looking about eighty years old.'

'If you don't mind me saying,' said Hector, 'he doesn't sound the greatest catch. How did you end up with him?'

Ashley bit her lip at the rude comment, but Lorna didn't seem to notice.

'You aren't the first person to say that. We met at the start of university. He was so handsome, albeit a bit dark and moody. He pursued me relentlessly.

Flowers, meals, cinema trips, the lot. I suppose I was flattered and gave in. It was an intense romance and then I fell pregnant near the end of my third year. I was worried he'd run a mile, but he was ecstatic, and we got married. He built this place up from scratch and we've lived a good life. I'm sure I can be grouchy as well.'

A sleek red Mercedes car drove past the window to the rear of the building, which Ashley could now see was a large compound full of dirtier cars, some of which looked as though they'd been there a while. A few seconds later, a tall man in a black wool overcoat walked by. He glanced into the office. Then his face twisted with anger.

Ashley rose from her seat.

'I think we'd better talk to Brad right now.'

41
___

They heard Brad Garrett bang the showroom door open and stomp his way straight to the office. He visibly calmed himself when he appeared at the door.

'Can I help you?' he asked.

Ashley stood, introduced herself and Hector, and told him they needed to talk to him. Brad's eyes bored into her.

'Where and when?'

'Here and now is fine. Obviously, it depends a little on what you say.'

'Okay. Lorna, if you'd like to give us a moment.'

'She doesn't have to leave,' said Ashley with a smile.

Brad didn't reply, but continued to look at Lorna.

'I'm staying, Bradley, and don't you say otherwise!'

'I don't want you here. Get out!'

'Okay, okay, I'm going,' she said.

Ashley stole a peek back at the seaside photo-graph on the wall as Lorna stamped from the room. Brad appeared well groomed and fit, but the man in front of them was much changed. He removed his jacket and revealed a surprising paunch. His hair had thinned, or that might have been because it was damp despite it being a dry day. The excess weight he was carrying had made his face jowly instead of fuller.

'Why do you think we're here, Mr Garrett?' asked Hector.

'I've no idea.'

Ashley kept quiet and was pleased Hector under-stood to do the same. It took Brad about ten seconds to break.

'The incidents in Cromer.'

'Yes. My colleague will take notes. Take a seat, please.'

Brad collapsed into the office chair. He mopped his forehead with a hanky while Ashley gave him the caution.

'What can you tell me about the murders, Brad?'

'Nothing.'

'Mr Garrett,' said Ashley. 'We're here to talk with you about the recent deaths on the beach. I'm sure you've heard about them. Old friends of yours, we believe.'

Brad shook his head.

'But you knew the victims.'

'Sort of. From years ago.'

'How did you know them?'

'Socially.'

'You had a party with those people on that same stretch of beach not long after you finished at senior school.'

Brad nodded while loosening his tie and undoing his top button.

'And a girl died.'

'Yes,' he whispered.

'Did you kill her?'

Brad shook his head, but he avoided eye contact.

'Did you murder Ron and Ruby?'

He glanced at Ashley.

'No, of course not. I wouldn't have been able to recall their names until I heard them again. It's brought it all back.'

'Can you prove your whereabouts last Friday and Saturday night?'

'I was here most of the time. There are always jobs

to do. We have a reputation for fairness and honesty, which means we're often busy. There's CCTV at the front of the lot and everywhere in the showroom, so I'll be all over it.'

'When do you start?'

'At 6.30 a.m. without fail. It's my favourite part of the day. Opening up and seeing all the cars makes me feel like I've achieved something.'

'Your wife said you had a visitor who upset you.'

'I wasn't upset.' Brad's voice strengthened. 'Look. This has nothing to do with me. I don't go to Cromer unless I can help it, and I certainly haven't revisited that spot on the beach. The whole thing nearly ruined my life.'

'What exactly happened back then?'

'Who told you I was there?'

'Kenneth Markham.'

'Who's he?'

'He went to your school.'

Brad put his head in his hands, but Ashley could see his eyes moving as though he was thinking about how much he should reveal.

'Will my wife hear about this?'

'I should think so.'

Brad folded his arms, then wilted.

'Okay, okay. There was a guy called Peter. He and I

go way back. We were best friends throughout school, from infants up. We were good at sport, so there was a bit of healthy rivalry, but nothing more than that. At the start of the sixth form, we got new starters from Cromer's senior school because they didn't have one. Natalie Fox was one of them and it was love at first sight. Sadly, that applied to both Peter and me. She kind of played us off against each other, but said she wasn't interested in dating me at the beginning.'

The sides of Brad's mouth briefly twitched upwards.

'God, she was something else. Tall and willowy, but curvy, and she was wild and fun. Sort of untame-able. She had odd friends from her old school who she hung around with at the weekends. Peter and I spent time with them too because that was the only way we could be with her. She wouldn't be separated from them, despite our best efforts.'

'Kenneth was one of them?'

Brad frowned.

'I don't believe he was part of their close crowd, but my eyes were on Foxy. The only ones I can think of were three misfits with whom I barely exchanged more than a few words. There was a simple guy named Eddy. He was pretty harmless, but he was a big unit. I think Foxy liked him there because he was happy to just be her friend. Her best mate was a drippy thing called Candy, and there was a druggy called Bob. Peter and I came from quiet backgrounds, so we hadn't got tangled up with drugs, but they all took them.'

'So, who was there that night?'

'It's all hazy, but I think there were five of us. Bob was supposed to be scoring for us, but I don't recall him arriving. Foxy wanted to get high. She had a thing for LSD and knew these hippies that lived on the beach in the summer, so maybe we asked them. I suppose they gave us a tab each, but I can't remember.'

'Why can't you be sure?'

'I couldn't remember anything afterwards. It was as if the whole evening had been erased from my mind.'

'So, the five of you were Peter, Candy, Eddy, Foxy, and you. Ron and Ruby would make seven.'

'Yes.'

'Wait,' said Hector. 'Weren't Peter and Foxy a couple by then?'

Brad gave them a painful nod.

'Why would you take drugs and watch them being romantic right in front of you?' asked Ashley.

'I had to be near her.'

'Wouldn't that make you angry? Your best friend had stolen your girl.'

Brad gritted his teeth and looked away.

'I don't think I planned to stay the entire night. She'd been telling me for a while that she liked me after all and maybe she'd split up with Peter. It was horrible. I felt like I was just a plaything.'

'What happened then?'

'I woke up in bed the next morning at eleven with Peter hammering on the door. My mum let him in, and he rushed up the stairs and started hitting me. He was out of it still. My dad threw him out. Peter kept shouting that I'd killed her.'

'This is Foxy.'

'Yes. I don't know what he meant because I never spoke to Peter again until recently.'

'Never?'

'No, the police interviewed me, but I said I left the party early, even though I didn't know for sure. I went to university in Leeds as soon as I could and couldn't wait to go.'

'Why?'

'It seemed Cromer had gone mad. Somebody started putting graffiti on the walls saying that all of us had to die. My parents lived in West Runton, so I stopped going into Cromer. Another friend who knew

Peter and me said that Peter disappeared off travelling a few days after I left. Apparently, he'd delayed his year at uni because he was so upset.'

'He vanished?'

'Yup. There was an article in the newspaper about what they think occurred, but nobody really knew. It said that a jogger had run down the sand and found Peter and Candy cuddled up together. At first, she thought crows were circling above a dead seal which had washed up much further along the beach.'

Brad looked out of the window, Adam's apple bobbing up and down. His voice quivered.

'But it was Foxy?' asked Ashley.

'Yes.'

'What about the hippies?'

'They'd gone. It was pretty obvious to me what had happened. The drugs had been too strong. We'd all had a mad trip and Foxy had drowned. It happens all the time at places like Thailand's Ko Pha-Ngan's full moon party. People get so high they wander into the sea alone. I assume the hippies legged it because they would be blamed.'

'Rightfully so. It's culpable homicide, or in other words, manslaughter. So, you didn't see any of the people present that day again.'

'Just that Eddy guy. He went crazy afterwards. I

expect he already had issues, which wouldn't have been helped by taking alcohol, LSD and marijuana. About a week later, I saw him off his face lying in the churchyard talking gibberish. Then he stole a car and drove it down the slip ramp next to the No. 1 restaurant. I assume he was going to drive into the sea, but he lost control and hit the concrete defences and nearly died. My mum told me he was sectioned after that.'

'So, you never returned to Cromer after university.'

'I only came back to my parents' for a day or two on holidays. I've always loved cars, so I got a job selling them for BMW in Norwich, and when I had enough experience, I opened this place. I steer clear of Cromer, and I'm still not a fan of the sea. That night changed me. I felt responsible and guilty for a long while after. I still see Foxy's face all this time later, which is crazy. She was so alive. It upended my world that she died, and I couldn't remember if I had anything to do with it.'

'It sounds like a heartbreaking accident.'

Brad finally looked straight at them through eyes that were now bloodshot and watery. He frowned and twisted his head from side to side as though waging an internal battle.

'Later that day and the following days, marks came out on my hands, face and arms. There were huge bruises over my back and chest. It was like I'd been in an almighty fight, but I couldn't recall a damn thing. We must have been tripping our heads off, but I guess we'll never know what happened.'

'I've yet to understand the attraction of LSD. Isn't it notorious for flashbacks?' said Hector.

Brad looked pained.

'Yes. I had terrible nightmares at university. I stopped drinking and never started back up until years later. Any loss of control terrifies me. I can only assume the others went through the same thing.'

'What were those nightmares?'

'Just rubbish. Dancing, twisted faces. Beasts in the water. Foxy kissing me, then laughing in my face.'

'Was that the first time you'd taken it?'

'No, we'd done it once before, but that time it was mellow and funny. We laughed until our sides hurt. It was hilarious and gave us a sense of belonging to all be wasted together, but Foxy dying damaged me forever. I lost the girl of my dreams, my best friend, and my childhood in one night and I can't remember why.'

Ashley paused for a moment.

'Have you heard that another body was found at the same spot on Sunday morning?'

'Yes.'

'It was Candy.'

'Oh God. Was she, you know, killed in the same way?'

'We can't say at this point. But four of the seven from that night are now dead.'

'And you think I did it?'

Ashley held his stare until he looked away.

'Where have you been this last week?'

'Working. That's it. I've been picking up cars all over, but not near Cromer.'

'We're going to speak to Peter next,' said Hector.

He said it in a way that made Brad's head jerk to look at him.

'Maybe Peter did it,' he said.

'It was Peter's visit which upset you recently, wasn't it?' asked Ashley.

'Yes. He must have had flashbacks, too. The girl was his, and he lost her. It kind of explains things.'

'What things?'

'When he visited me, we almost came to blows.' Brad swallowed hard. 'He kept asking why I'd sent it to him.'

'Sent what?'

'I don't know. He bellowed that I knew well enough. I was shaking when he left.'

'Did he mention anyone else's name?'

'I was barely listening. I didn't recognise Peter at first,' he said, then paused for a moment. 'He was just so incredibly angry.'

He looked at her with the same trapped expression that Eddy had in the interview room and just then Ashley realised Brad wasn't nervous. He was scared.

42

Ashley and Hector returned to their car more informed, but none the wiser. Brad said he would forward the CCTV from the garage forecourt to them to confirm his movements. He gave them a list of the registrations of the cars and the addresses from where he'd collected them. It seemed detailed, but, realistically, Brad might have been in any number of vehicles.

Ashley paused as she put her seat belt on. The mention of LSD again had got her brain whirring.

'LSD really complicates this case,' she said.

'Which part of it?'

'I don't think it was a common drug by the late eighties. Stimulants were more popular by then, which makes me think Ron and Ruby were perhaps more involved than we think. By then, people were well informed of the unpredictable Russian roulette of flashbacks, which you wouldn't get with drugs like ecstasy.'

'People have ignored health warnings forever. Look at smoking.'

Ashley chuckled as they drove away.

'True. Loads of us kids smoked back then, despite the health implications. I really miss it. It's a shame it's so bad for your health. You could say quality phrases like crash-the-ash, bum-a-smoke, and I-fancy-a-fag, and nobody said a word. I'd be suspended for using such fruity language nowadays.'

Hector shook his head as though she were talking about the Victorian age.

'What's the plan, then, boss?'

'Let's go back. Type all this up. A good night's sleep will let our minds sort through the avalanche of intel we've received today. We might have missed a connection.'

'Okay. I'll ring Dylan Crabb when we get back and explain that DI Peter Ibson might be on his way to kill Eddy.'

'Do it now, although I'd prefer it if you worded it slightly differently.'

While Hector rang Dylan, Ashley ruminated on Peter being missing. He could be anywhere in the country. He didn't have a job to come back to, so he could stay away as long as he liked. Getting authorisation to look at his bank records was an option, but Peter would know not to use his card if he was involved. Kettle had said he'd look into that side of things.

Hector finished the call.

'Dylan's going around to spend the evening with Eddy. Make sure he's okay. Eddy calmed down a lot after he left the station, so he's hopeful.'

'Great. Let's pray nothing nasty happens this evening. We've got surveillance on the beach tonight, but I should think it will be the last night we'll get it.'

'I'll ring the office. See if Emma or Sal have made any progress. We could really do with looking at that coroner's report for Foxy's death.'

'Chase it up, then. That was good work back there, Hector.'

'I know.'

'And so modest.'

'It's a bit like computer programming. One step leads to the next. There's a finite number of possibilities. It has to be one of them, and so on.'

'Yes, but computers don't want revenge, or hold decades-long grudges.'

'True. Humans can behave in infinitely unusual ways.'

Hector rang the office and Barry picked up. Hector explained what Brad had told them, then put the call on speaker.

'Right,' said Barry. 'We'll crack on.'

'What progress have you made?' asked Hector.

'Get you. You're not in charge yet, mister.'

'Barry, stop being an arse,' said Ashley.

'Sorry, Sarge. I didn't realise the sneaky sod had me on speaker.'

'Spit it out.'

'The council are sending us a list of who owns those beach huts. We considered getting a warrant to look inside them, but there's a register which lists all the details. ETA for that is tomorrow. There's no sign of the DI. His car's on ANPR when he went home from here on Saturday, but it's not been on a major road in Norfolk since. You know how shit the coverage around Cromer is, so that's not unexpected.'

'What about his HR file? He'd have next of kin on there, or a beneficiary for his pension fund.'

'Kettle's checked. It was just his mother, and Kettle remembers Peter going to her funeral. I'll see if we hold the pension beneficiary, but I assume that'd be the same.'

'Okay, how about the latest toxicology reports?'

'Tomorrow morning.'

'Excellent. We're on our way in to write all this stuff up.'

'Hang on. Kettle's arrived with news.'

Ashley heard muffled talking in the background.

'Right,' said Barry. 'We can downgrade the mad panic to find the DI. We've got the DNA report back from Bob's clothing.'

'Is it Ron's blood?'

'Correct.'

Ashley's mind raced.

'We'll need to increase and warn those watching Bob at the hospital.'

'Chill, Ash. Kettle's arranged that already. I guess that's case solved.'

'Great. Well done,' replied Ashley, quietly.

After a pause, Barry tutted.

'You don't think so, do you?'

'These aren't the crimes of a heroin addict, but I suppose we'll talk to him tomorrow. Did you speak to the secure unit?'

'About Eddy? Hang on. Jan!'

A few seconds later, Jan came on the phone.

'It's all go here, Sarge. I spoke to Reception at the hospital Eddy was in, then the manager rang me back quite quickly. She was pleasant. Said Eddy was her favourite resident.'

'Has she sent you the reports?'

'No, she said there's too much of it, and anything over the last twenty years is in boxes. She knows his history well, though, and she's happy to speak to you Wednesday afternoon. If you attend in person, she'll get everything out of storage and refresh her knowledge, but it'll take a day. I mentioned a few details about the case, and she thought that a visit might be helpful, particularly regarding his feelings about the beach. Do you still want to go in light of the Bob news?'

'Definitely.'

'Okay, I'll confirm with her.'

'Anything else from anyone's phone or bank records?'

'Nothing obvious.'

'Keep everyone focused,' said Ashley. 'I'll see you in a bit.'

Hector cut the call.

'Case closed?' he asked with a wry smile.

Ashley shook her head.

'Not a chance.'

43

Ashley's alarm woke her on Tuesday morning. The clock said five-thirty. She was about to roll over when she remembered she was supposed to be jogging or walking as many mornings as possible. Ashley had laid out her kit, so she was soon leaving the house and stretching as she walked to the hill by the lighthouse.

It was a fresh morning with a few spots of rain in the air. The light grey clouds hid the sunrise, so she decided to run along the cliff top towards the town centre. The place where Bob had been sleeping still had police tape fluttering outside it, but the door had been secured to keep people out. Her mind started working as she jogged onwards.

She turned left to the council building on which the death tally had been painted, and was pleased to see there wasn't a number five to be seen. The cleaner had done a good job and completely removed all the paint. There was only a brighter white patch to show where the numbers had been.

Ashley then took a detour and stared at the big white house at the cliff edge and read the poem or sea shanty or whatever it was that was still present. The writing was quite orderly considering it had been done with a paintbrush, which again made her doubt Eddy or Bob had written it. She ran down the slipway and turned left to jog along the promenade next to the pier. Geoffrey's boat was heading out. She waved, but there was no response.

Ashley was blowing hard and her stride had shortened considerably by the time she passed the boarded-up funfair and the small beach chalets, and she had to stop when she reached the beach. One day she'd just keep going, all the way past the Runtons and on to Sheringham and back. Twelve miles of beach would be quite a task, but she was sick of her lifestyle. Why hadn't she looked after herself better?

As she began the return journey, which was mostly uphill, she thought about the interview later. If Bob was responsible and those trainers and shoes were his, then where was the knife he'd used, and where was the coat he'd been wearing? That didn't make sense. Why be so reckless with his T-shirt and trainers but not his other clothes? It was a shame the weapon hadn't turned up, but Bob still needed a pretty convincing story if he didn't want to be charged with murder.

The final incline beat her, but she still smiled to herself as she took a long shower when she got home.

The clouds had been rapidly breaking up, so she put her third best, beige suit on, which was also her last suit and had seen better days. She paired it with a white short-sleeved blouse seeing as the aircon in the interview rooms was hit and miss.

Kettle had sent her a text saying that Surveillance hadn't seen anything suspicious the previous night and would be stood down.

Ashley clambered into her old maroon Vauxhall Vectra at eight and arrived at her desk by half past. Hector was already in and chatting to an animated Jan. It had only been a few days, and he was enthusiastically proving her first assumptions wrong. Sal, Bhavini and Barry were next in, and finally Emma.

Ashley watched them arguing about who used the last of the coffee. There were seven other teams in MIT, but she was glad to be the sergeant of this one. The bickering gave her the family she was lacking.

Barry and Jan left to collect Bob from the hospital. Sal had found the front-page article from the archives of the *Eastern Daily Press* about Foxy's death, but it didn't tell them anything they didn't already know. There was a picture of Foxy holding a balloon with seventeen on it, which she assumed was a photo from the year before. She had an extremely short but quite classy full-sleeved blue dress on with heels. Her smile was goofy.

Things had moved on rapidly over the last few years. DNA tests, which used to cost thousands, and toxicology reports, which took ages, were now cheap as chips and the process computerised. They'd get an email this morning regarding the results. Michelle or CSI might be contacted to interpret them, but the team would soon have the information they needed.

By eleven o'clock, Bob had been brought to the station and was with the duty solicitor in an interview room with a supervising officer from Custody. Barry cursed when he returned to the office after being part of the escort.

'That doesn't sound promising,' said Ashley.

'He's here and just about with it, but it's like he's got shell shock. They've got him on a big old dose of methadone to stabilise him, but physically, he's an absolute wreck. I've arrested him on suspicion of murder, but he didn't seem to care. The hospital tested his blood, and the levels of heroin when he was taken in were high enough to stop his heart, so he was lucky not to be dead. I'd probe into that because it doesn't make sense. Bob would know after all this time how much to use for a fix. Any more than that, he'd see as a waste.'

'Yes, we thought the same,' said Ashley. 'If I remember rightly, he was a happy chatty type on drugs, as opposed to just blanking out, so taking too much wouldn't suit him anyway. I wonder what put him back on it. Dylan said it was in the last year, which is the same time period as the changes in behaviour of everyone else in this case. It's hard to think they aren't linked.'

'I reckon one of this lot provided the spark, but the blaze got out of hand,' said Jan.

Ashley nodded at that. There had to be someone else involved. She took Hector with her to start the interview.

Ashley was shocked by Bob's state. He'd clearly not been eating properly in the midst of his struggles, because, in its desperation to survive, his body was consuming the flesh on his face.

Dull eyes peered at her from a skeletal skull as she asked him for his name.

'Robert Redding.'

Bob merely nodded to confirm he understood the caution, but he gave the rest of his details.

'Would you prefer I called you Bob?' asked Ashley.

Another grudging nod came her way.

'How are you?'

'No comment.'

'A person who says no comment clearly has something to hide.'

'No comment.'

'Either you were involved in some way, or you weren't. Which is it?'

'No comment.'

'The picture has become much clearer to us. If you aren't responsible, but know who is, you need to explain now, before the person who is tells us a different story and implicates you.'

'No comment.'

Ashley analysed Bob's features and frame. His clothes had been taken for analysis when they'd first discovered him on the beach, so it perhaps wasn't surprising that the ones they'd found him didn't fit well. Yet he resembled a bag of bones. His arms were so thin it was almost painful to look at them. His eyes were cloudy, and blackheads covered his skin.

When she'd worked in Sheffield, Ashley had been present at an exhumation and it would have been a coin toss on whether Bob looked worse.

It made her wonder when his life fell apart. Someone must have loved Bob at one point, or maybe that was where it went wrong. Perhaps there was no love. Ashley herself knew the attraction of oblivion when life seemed worthless. The wretch in front of them was more Hopeless Bob than Homeless, and he'd been that way for quite some time.

'Okay, Bob. Here is exhibit A42585, an old Nike T-shirt, which I'm pretty sure I've seen you wearing. Is this your T-shirt?'

'No comment.'

Bob glanced at it.

'After DNA testing, we can confirm that the red stains on it are from blood which belonged to Ron Jerrod, who was murdered on Saturday morning. Can you explain how his blood came to be on your clothing?'

'No comment.'

'Here is exhibit A42586, a pair of battered, sandy Reebok trainers, which were found where you sleep next to the T-shirt I just showed you, which also have

Ron's blood on them. Why is Ron's blood on your trainers?'

Bob stared at them for a few seconds longer than the T-shirt. His forehead wrinkled.

'No comment.'

Ashley was about to continue when Hector put his hand on her arm.

'Bob,' he said. 'Are those trainers yours? You just looked at them like you'd never seen them before.'

Bob held eye contact with Hector, then smiled, revealing a handful of cracked and yellow teeth with obvious black decay.

'No comment.'

'I'll cut to the chase,' said Ashley. 'Did you murder Ron and Ruby Jerrod on the beach on Friday night or Saturday morning?'

'No comment.'

Ashley paused, having expected him to deny it.

'This is the time to confess. We understand you have your problems, but this needs resolving now.'

'You can ask as many questions as you like. No comment will be my answer to all of them.'

'Bob,' said Ashley. 'No comment isn't a defence when the evidence is so damning. If you can't give me an explanation of why Ron's blood is on these items, we *will* charge you with murder, and you *will* be re-manded in prison.'

'Jail isn't much of a threat when you're homeless. I've got long days ahead trying to get off H. Might as well be banged up where I see a nurse every day, re-ceive three square meals and, if I'm lucky, visit the dentist.'

'That might be nice in the short-term, but thirty years will soon become a heavy cross to bear. Perhaps even unbearable.'

Bob leaned back in his seat. Ashley had assumed the gaunt, sweaty face and haunted eyes were evi-dence of his addiction, but it was only partly that.

Like Brad before him, Bob was scared.

Yet Ashley always thought that was the confusing part for folk like Bob. Life could still be hard for those who had a support network, friends, and the routine of work. Bob had none of that. Everywhere he went and every face he looked in, he'd be judged, and found wanting. But somehow, he found the strength each day to survive, which meant, with the right sup-port, he could achieve so much more.

'Your issues with heroin aren't the only reason you want to be locked up, are they?'

Bob shook his head. He gave her a ghastly smile.

Her nose twitched at his rotten breath as he snarled his reply.

'I don't know what's going on, and I'm damn sure you don't. There's something out there killing vulnerable people.' Bob raised a finger and pointed it at Ashley. 'And I'm homeless. So, fuck that.'

Bob leaned back in his seat.

'At least in prison, I'll be safe.'

44

Ashley tried many ways to loosen Bob's tongue, but she eventually gave up. It was odd how he'd said something was killing people, not someone, but he refused to explain his choice of words. Hector had at least got him to agree to them taking another swab. Bob refused to give her any other names, so she had him taken back down to the cells. She couldn't think of a reason why the CPS wouldn't charge Bob. He'd be off to court, where they'd remand him in prison. When Bob was gone, she asked Hector why he'd asked for a further swab.

'Just to be certain. I don't reckon those trainers are his. If his DNA doesn't show on them, then we're right, there is another party involved. The test will show if there's any other DNA present. Perhaps we'll get a match on the database.'

'Maybe Peter Ibson's name will come up.'

Hector chuckled. The police gave a swab when they joined the force so their presence could be excluded from a crime scene.

'You're right. You said Bob's clothes were disgusting,' said Ashley.

'Exactly. That T-shirt is filthy, but those trainers, while old and speckled with blood, look clean. It's possible they've been put through a washing machine, which Bob is unlikely to have done.'

'He didn't have one in his shed.'

'What about a Nespresso coffee maker or NutriBullet?'

'Very funny.'

There ensued a tonne of paperwork, inputting and scanning to prepare the case for the magistrates' court the next morning. Usually, Ashley didn't mind too much because it was the conclusion of an investigation, but this time, she was distracted. Bob was obviously involved, so him being remanded was not unjust if he wasn't going to tell them his side of things. But who else was pulling the strings? Was it someone they hadn't spoken to?

Mid-afternoon, Ashley's phone rang. The call was from the pathologist, Michelle.

'Hi, Ash. Just ringing to confirm we're still meeting on Sunday.'

'Of course, twelve in The Welly. We can just have a few drinks and maybe some of their amazing street food from the restaurant at the back. There's plenty of sport on the big TV, or we could play a bit of pool. It'll be a good laugh.'

'Yeah, I can't wait.' There was a brief pause. 'I suppose I should talk to you about the murders.'

Ashley smiled.

'Go on, then, but let me update you first. We've arrested the guy whose clothing had Ron's blood on, so we're busy putting the case together. What did Ron's toxicology say?'

'To be honest, it wasn't what I was expecting. Do you remember the injection site where we suspected he'd been injected with a sedative?'

'Yep.'

'The reports show no evidence of any drug in Ron's body except marijuana.'

'Could the injection site have been historic?'

'It might have been a from a day or so ago, but that would be a coincidence.'

'A recent habit. Heroin doesn't stay in the system long?'

'Tests nowadays are really sensitive. I can get his hair follicles checked for historic use, which would show up, but I'm not sure it would help us.'

'What about Ruby?'

'Her result shows LSD in her system, but no marijuana.'

'What?'

'Yes, not loads, but it was present. There was more present in her stomach than her bloodstream, so it was recent.'

'Christ. That would be some trip with your head under a bucket.'

'I know. But again, is that another coincidence, or did whoever bury Ruby give it to her?'

'What exactly does LSD do to a person?'

'It's a powerful hallucinogenic drug made from lysergic acid, hence the slang name. There's a buzz, sweats, dizziness, euphoria and laughter like many other drugs, but it also rapidly intensifies the senses and blends them.'

'What does that mean?'

'Visual hallucinations are common. Such as hearing colours or seeing sounds. It can feel like you're leaving your body.'

'Sounds terrible.'

'They're the plus points! It also distorts time, causes panic, fear, paranoia, amnesia, nausea and anxiety. These may occur at the start of the trip and throughout, lasting up to fifteen hours. Flashbacks are common. They can cause persistent psychotic symptoms many years later, especially if there are underlying mental problems.'

'And could you die if you were given a huge amount of LSD?'

'Not as a direct cause, but accidents are common. For example, sometimes people believe they can fly.'

'Or swim to Norway?'

'Yes, people die due to their actions while out of their minds. Flashbacks are the long-term cost. Sufferers see things that aren't there, believe facts that aren't true, or hear people talk who aren't present, sometimes many years later.'

'I assume the bigger the dose, the worse the effects.'

'Correct.'

'Brutal. Poor Ruby. What about Candy's tox reports?'

'Yes, that's really why I'm ringing. Candy also had LSD in her system, and marijuana. I suspect she was a habitual smoker, judging by the state of her lungs and yellow-stained fingers. Her levels of LSD were much higher. She'd have been on a different planet.'

'So, she might have just smoked a big spliff, necked a tab of LSD, then walked into the sea.'

'Yep. There are no marks to indicate intravenous drug use, although she took a significant dose of LSD, so it's more likely she took drops of it than a tab.'

Ashley shook her head. Was this simply another case of someone taking drugs, so they didn't have to deal with being alive? Or was she forced to take part in a reenactment of the beach party three decades ago?

'Are you thinking she got deliberately off her face and then committed suicide?' she asked.

'I was, until one last thing arose. You recall I said there weren't any signs of a struggle on the body.'

'Yes.'

'Bruising on dead bodies works the same as bruising on the living. It takes a few days to become fully pronounced.'

'And she now has bruises.'

'Yes, not heavy marking, but I can see it around the neck and the shoulders.'

'Candy was involved in a domestic Friday night, so could it have come up from that?'

'Maybe, but I think I'd have noticed Friday's

bruises sooner. I've seen examples of this type of bruising before in another domestic murder.'

'Murder?'

'Yes. It's the same bruise pattern as when a woman's head was held under water in a bath.'

45

Ashley had a terrible night's sleep. When she woke the next morning, her brain felt as stiff as her limbs. There'd be no running today. She rolled around in bed trying to picture who would want to kill everyone at that party. Was it someone on the beach, or somebody who was furious not to be invited?

Had there been a killer living in Cromer for over thirty years? If so, had he been dormant since Foxy's death, or had he been killing all along and just got away with it? Norfolk had thousands of missing people, like all counties. Children often fled to coastal resorts in the pursuit of happy futures. Some were never seen again. The sea held many secrets.

Ashley hobbled downstairs and looked in her

fridge for breakfast, even though she knew there was little in there. After a black coffee and four cheese triangles, she spent ten minutes putting her body through stretches and was feeling livelier by the time she drove to the office.

The first thing she did when she got to work was to bring Bob back in for more questioning, but he refused to even say no comment so the interview just ended in frustration.

The council still hadn't replied with the names of the owners of the beach huts, which was infuriating. The person dealing with it had apparently called in sick.

'Why don't we just break into them?' asked Hector. 'Seems to me there's a risk to life and they could easily contain evidence of an indictable offence.'

'Are you paying for the damage, Fast Track?' asked Barry.

Hector looked confused.

'If there were six huts,' said Ashley, 'it would be okay. Smashing our way into forty, on the other hand, would be quite a hit to the budget.'

Barry offered to go down to the council and thump a few skulls. Ashley ignored him and asked Emma to see what she could do because it was an important relationship to maintain, and the council were as understaffed as some of the police departments were.

That was one of the benefits of working in MIT. When it came to major crimes, few resource requests were denied. It just took ages to trawl through CCTV, even with extra manpower, and that was the trouble they were having. The area of interest was too big. Nobody had been seen looking suspicious around the time of the murders, but there were too many escape routes that had no coverage at all.

After checking her emails, she booked a car out for the journey to Great Yarmouth.

'You'll have to drive,' she informed Hector as they approached the Vauxhall Corsa. 'My calves are in rehab.'

'You're keeping up the jogging, then.'

'Trying to.'

'Well done. I can never understand people letting themselves go.'

Ashley opened her mouth theatrically as he pulled away.

'Just when I begin to think maybe you aren't a robot, you say something like that.'

'It was you who said you haven't been looking after yourself.'

'Yes! Implying that I could try harder, not that my hideous fat ass was dragging on rock bottom.'

'That's why I don't have too many friends. It's so exhausting worrying about offending people. By the way, I saw someone checking out that ass yesterday.'

Ashley gritted her teeth, but, much to her disgust, she couldn't resist the bait.

'Who?'

'The family liaison officer. Scott Gorton. Actually, I meant to mention the tension in the car between you two. You should get it on, as you oldies say.'

'I think that's the problem. Flash and I almost did once.'

'Ooh, do tell.'

'No, it's too early for that kind of secret. But be careful. If you don't do relationships, you end up alone.'

'I like my own space. Not everyone wants to live in their own soap opera.'

'Loneliness is a killer.'

'Perhaps we should see if he's been on the beach.'

'Ooh, funny.'

Hector frowned as a tractor and trailer pulled out in front of him.

'Do you mind if I ask you a personal question?' he asked.

'I'm beginning to wish I'd come on my own.'

'You said partners should bond with each other, and I think I'm starting to understand you, but when you talk like this about not being isolated, it's confusing.'

'Why's that?'

'You're an orphan who lives alone without children and you're pushing fifty.'

'Jesus. You're so lucky I left my PAVA spray in my desk.'

'You still have admirers. Some men love the Velma look from *Scooby Doo*. Why are you on your own?'

'I wasn't until a few days ago, if you must know. I had a girlfriend.'

Hector looked over and nodded.

'Now I am surprised. I hadn't got a lesbian vibe from you.'

'Should I have a sticker on my shirt?'

'Don't be tetchy. We all make assumptions. I saw Flash blushing when Dylan mentioned you too, so I presumed.'

'Well, Bethany dumped me, so I don't think I was a great one.'

'Was it your first time?'

'Yes. It was weird. Apart from a trippy weekend at a mad house party in Sydney, I'd never considered it. I liked Bethany, though, and it felt natural. Although she reckons that I don't fancy women, I just despise men.'

'And do you?'

'Some of them.'

'What happened?'

'Something horrible.'

'Tell me.'

'Why are you so keen to hear all this?'

'I'm not stupid. I know I have little experience of life. My dad made police work seem like good versus evil, but most of it is dealing with people's struggles. My school was full of rich kids who had issues, but everyone was wealthy, so if it got too bad, they went to rehab, or Aunt Clara's estate in the country. They didn't go and live under a bridge and sniff glue.'

'I'm not quite on the Bostik just yet.'

'I know. I had a chat with Jan over the phone last night. Nice guy. We talked about his career and how it took him a while to get his head around what the job really entailed. I'd been finding it hard to see where I fit in, and what the point of it all is.'

'But you feel different now, despite only just arriving here?'

'Yes. I'm fired up like I was on my first day, when I

was going to change the world. Maybe it's because the crimes are so serious.'

'Murder does grab people's attention.'

'Stop changing the subject and tell me about the horrible thing.'

'It's not that exciting. I threw myself into the role when I returned to Cromer and couldn't be bothered with dating. I used to socialise in the local pubs. That kind of casual environment suited me. You turn up and get chatting to whoever's in there. Eventually, I met a guy in the pub, Rick Jones, who was on holiday here. Nice bloke, very tall, but he lived in Southampton, well over two hundred miles away. We started seeing each other once a month when he was nearby on business, or he'd book a hotel halfway in London. Before we knew it, two years had gone by. I liked the arrangement, but my clock was ticking. He went on a work trip, flying in and out of Stansted, which obviously isn't far, so I thought I'd surprise him when he got back.'

'Oh dear.'

Ashley nodded.

'Yes. I bought flowers, but I wasn't planning to go down on one knee. All I was going to say was that we should try to make it work. I don't have strong roots here any more, so I was prepared to move.'

Ashley imagined flames were leaping out of her face as she remembered.

'Arrivals was packed because three planes came in close together. I was nervous and excited, so much so that I had to go for a poo.'

'Too much detail.'

'You wanted to know. When I got back, I saw the top of Rick's head walking past. I was behind all the people at the barrier, so he couldn't see me. When he walked through the last gate, his expression broke into a big grin and he crouched. A little girl ran into his arms.'

'God.'

'Yes, he picked her up, then strode to the heavily pregnant redhead with the face of a model who was sweetly waving a few metres away.'

Hector gasped.

'I'm sorry. Did you kill him on the spot?'

'I bloody well wanted to. Instead, I slunk home. He even had the cheek to ring me two days later about meeting up. I told him I'd been at the airport as a surprise.'

Ashley blinked back the tears that were trying to escape.

'And?'

'He put the phone down. We never spoke again.'

'Brutal.'

'Do you know what the worst bit was?'

'There's more?'

'Afterwards, I wondered why his pregnant wife would drive with a toddler all the way to Stansted from Southampton to meet him. It'd be a five-hour trip.'

'That is odd, unless he doesn't live in Southampton.'

'Well done. They live in Fakenham.'

'Which is twenty miles away.'

'Yes. I felt stupid and angry for a long time. He'd implied he didn't do social media, but I don't either, so I didn't check. I used Emma's Facebook account and found Rick's account under Richard Andrew, Andrew being his middle name. His profile pic was one of the family from a distance, but I could recognise his height and the ginger hair of the woman who met him at the airport.'

'You must have been absolutely furious, and vengeful!'

'I was stunned at the time. Of course I was angry later, but I kept thinking of her and those kids. After a while, my rage or sadness, depending on which was on top, faded, and I tried to date again. Poor old Flash became collateral damage.'

Ashley stopped talking after that. The hurt was still there, but the edges were softened with time, and she knew she hadn't done anything wrong. They drove in silence through the farmland and quiet villages. Ashley stole a peek at Hector, but his face was impassive. She felt something loosen deep inside her soul.

It was good to finally tell someone.

Death On Cromer Beach

46

Ashley had been to numerous secure units through the years. A couple had been large psychiatric hospitals, while others had been much smaller. This place seemed more like a medium-sized retirement home from a distance, but it was clear the security was elevated with strong-looking doors and barred windows.

Hector pressed the buzzer, and a guard was soon opening up with a smile.

'Police?' he enquired.

'How did you know?' asked Hector.

'You're the only ten o'clock visitors. Take a pew. Stephanie will be right over.'

Ashley was expecting the unit manager to be in a white coat, but she had a similar suit to hers, and she also wore the same harried expression that Ashley often had. Ashley guessed her to be around fifty.

'Thanks for coming,' said Stephanie. 'Please follow me. We'll walk through the low secure unit, so you can get a sense of the place.'

It had the feel of a retirement home, but there were only a couple of people around. A young man was doing a jigsaw on his own in a day room. He gave them a friendly nod as they passed.

'Morning, Tommy,' said Stephanie.

'Morning, miss.'

When they reached her office, she pointed at two seats opposite a busy-looking desk with at least ten red box files at the side of it.

'Please, take a seat. So how is Eddy?' asked Stephanie with a sad smile as she stepped past the boxes and sat in her office chair. Ashley realised she would know they weren't visiting for anything positive.

'Not great,' said Ashley. 'But he was happy for us to speak to you, which is to his credit. I assume you've received the necessary paperwork from our team.'

'Yes. I'm not entirely surprised you rang, although I was optimistic about him when he left. What's happened?'

'To be honest, we don't really know. Three people

died on Cromer beach recently. One was a decapitation, another either torture or a sacrifice to the sea,
for want of a better phrase, and the other was found
drowned.'

'Yes, I saw it on the news. Horrifying. And you
think Eddy's involved?'

'Possibly. It might be connected to a party many
years ago on the beach. Of the seven who were there,
four have now died at the same spot, even though
three decades have passed since the first one
drowned.'

'Sounds complicated.'

'It is. Is Eddy capable of something like that?'

She sat back in her chair and contemplated for a
moment.

'Yes, I suppose. Although he wasn't when he left
here.'

'Can you explain?' asked Hector.

'Let me give you the background on what we do
here and the people we normally deal with. First, I'm
sure you're aware from your own line of work, mental
health diagnosis is notoriously hard. Conditions like
schizophrenia often cross over with other conditions
such as borderline personality disorder and bipolar.
No person fits any one diagnosis exactly. Everyone,
regular folk included, is in a constant state of flux.

Some days I'm a touch crazy, others I'm a little depressed, but functioning people tend to have narrower ranges than the extreme patients we treat.'

'We all have friends who swing from pole to pole,' said Ashley with a smile. 'Although I would say most congregate around the south pole.'

Stephanie laughed.

'That's a good explanation. Life isn't plain sailing for a lot of us, and it's easy to feel depressed. We have to do many things we might not want to, like going to work. We see and experience events that upset us, like deaths of people close to us, or we can become jealous through social media, but we still operate within an acceptable range of emotions. The extremes of those poles are where it really goes wrong. Destructive behaviour at one end, like gambling, shopping and sex addiction, perhaps drugs and suicidal thoughts at the other, but no two cases are the same.'

Stephanie steepled her fingers.

'Simply put, our patients become unable to function in our modern world and need to be in places like this after an acute episode. Few recover completely. Relapses are common. Perhaps warden-controlled housing is the best end result for them.'

That seems to fit Eddy, thought Ashley.

'People are often first brought to our notice when they've committed minor criminal offences. Low-level secure units are usually enough for us to find the right combination of support for them to get balanced and leave. Cases like schizophrenia can be more serious because they may suffer from delusions and need stronger medication. Young people's metabolisms are faster, so that might involve giving them a bigger dose, which might have a tranquillising effect. Patients like Eddy usually start in the medium secure unit here, with the hope of moving them to lower secure, then into the community at a later date, but that's a much longer process.'

'So that includes Eddy. Could those delusions make him kill?' asked Hector.

She smiled in a way that made Ashley realise there was genuine affection for Eddy.

'Eddy was unique in a unique community. I've been here for twenty years. Some would say I've served a life sentence, but Eddy certainly has.'

Ashley grinned at her. Like many who worked in these environments, humour was the main coping mechanism.

'I was clinically involved when I first began working here,' continued Stephanie. 'Eddy was already a resident. I've reread his previous history from when he arrived in the autumn of 1989. He was very unwell then.'

'In what way?' asked Ashley.

'I would guess he had undiagnosed schizophrenia, which probably started presenting itself as he headed towards maturity, say maybe fifteen. Without treatment, it can get progressively worse, and he would have started to lose a grip on reality. He was anxious in the extreme and would lash out at any contact.'

'Wouldn't people who knew him have noticed this?'

'Perhaps not completely. It can be a gradual process. Teenagers are usually swept up in their own problems and parents struggle to get a clear picture. Often the police are the first to see how ill a person has become.'

'Right,' said Ashley. 'I think he was deteriorating back then, but still hanging around with his school friends, one of whom was a girl called Natalie Fox. Perhaps she was helping him function. The problem was they were taking drugs, including LSD.'

'Drugs that shift reality are incredibly dangerous to people who are already wrestling with everyday life. He wouldn't have known what was real and what wasn't, even after most would normally have sobered up.'

'At a party,' said Ashley, 'this friend who was important to him drowned. I'm guessing he couldn't cope with the aftermath, and he drove his car towards the beach in a suicide attempt.'

'That's interesting, but what he told us here doesn't match that. There was a girl who died called Foxy in his records, so that fits. But any mention of her would send him into a depressional spiral. He wouldn't talk about the details of her death, just that the sea took her, as though it was a living thing. Eddy said he hated the sea and wanted to hurt it.'

'He was using the car as a weapon, then,' stated Hector.

'That would be my conclusion. All this was before I arrived here, but his files are here for you to read if you wish.' She gestured to the stack next to her. 'After ten years, they're computerised, so I can forward them. I've flicked through his entire first year. The accident damaged his face and his leg got crushed. Both are visible injuries, and he walks with a limp.'

'He seemed strong as a bull when we interviewed him.'

'Oh, now that's concerning.'

'Isn't it good that he's healthy? He's been keeping fit and going to the gym.'

'We had him on clozapine because without it he was prone to rages. He was on that for years, but it's got side effects and has long-term heart issues for some patients. With that drug, he could function in low-security conditions, but if we talked about progression to the community, he would relapse immediately and become violent, even on a high dose. He would shout about the sea.'

'So how come you released him?' asked Hector

'The years mellow most folk. I realised that if we stopped talking to him about leaving, then he didn't actually need clozapine. He became like a volunteer worker here, helping with others, setting tables and wanting to clean. I liked him. He was always funny, and he got healthier then, lost a bit of weight and he began to care about his personal hygiene and appearance.'

Stephanie frowned as she recalled that time.

'Such a shame for him to be in this place for all those years. We attempted a different smaller unit with him elsewhere, but he struggled, so we brought him back. I think it's fair to say he was only living half a life here. We're making plenty of progress with medicines, but it's debatable with mental health care.

New antipsychotics have come along, but they all have side effects. There are newer atypical drugs such as olanzapine, risperidone, and aripiprazole, and we tried them all on Eddy.'

'And he got better?'

'Yes. He could eventually talk about everything that had happened in a rational manner. We began to take him on days out. He functioned. It took a long time, but a year ago he was ready for us to look at day release and then finally to put him in a stepdown unit.'

'So why is it bad if he's fit and strong?'

'All those drugs have side effects from weight gain to diabetes to cardiovascular damage to premature death. That's why some physicians don't agree with them. Feeling very sleepy and having an increased, perhaps even uncontrollable appetite is common. Getting organised and fit in a gym is rare for our clients.'

'Which means he might have stopped taking them,' said Hector.

Stephanie nodded.

'Okay,' said Ashley. 'You mentioned he shouted about the sea.'

'He did. We once took him to the seafront at Great

Yarmouth, but he refused to walk on the sand. It was as though he believed it would suck him under.'

'Why did he move back to Cromer, then, if he despised the beach?'

'He wanted to be close to his only friend.'

'He had a friend?'

'Yes,' replied Stephanie, looking confused.

'Was it a woman called Candy?'

'No, it was a man.'

'Surely not Bob. Was he a man called Robert Redding?'

'His surname has slipped from my mind after six months, but his first name was Peter.'

Ashley's mouth went dry.

'Peter Ibson.'

'Yes, that's it! Lovely bloke. Friendly. I sincerely think he was the biggest influence on getting Eddy ready for a return to society.'

'And he often visited Eddy here?'

'Yes, he came every month without fail for over thirty years.'

47

Stephanie gave them a little more background, but it seemed Peter had been a benign visitor who was good for Eddy. What Ashley really wanted to probe now was Eddy's ability to kill.

'Stephanie,' said Ashley, 'with everything you've told us, and all that's happened, isn't Eddy better kept off the streets? We don't have enough to remand him in prison because I can't imagine what would get him to put his feet on the sand again to do these things, but he's involved in this. My fear is that someone's been pulling Eddy's strings.'

Stephanie scooted her chair over, so she was closer to them.

'People like Eddy are easily influenced. They usually know on some level that they can't be left to their own devices, so they'll attach themselves to a person who'll look after them.'

'Someone they believe will take care of them, but might not?' asked Hector.

'Yes, Peter was very protective of Eddy. It seems strange to think he'd use him as a pawn for murder, but there's one important thing to remember in all this.'

Ashley nodded at her to continue.

'LSD is well known for flashbacks years later. It should never be mixed with other drugs like it often is. Who knows what Eddy's going through? Without his prescription, and being near the site of his best friend's death, would amplify all the risks. As I mentioned earlier, he really could do anything.'

'What are the chances of him being sectioned again? At least that way he's out of the equation if any more crimes are committed. Is that something you'd support?'

'It's not as easy as that. The clinical care co-ordinator team would be responsible for any decisions regarding that in conjunction with a psychiatrist. A case would be heard at magistrates' court. Dylan Crabb is your man over there, but it doesn't seem like

Eddy's done anything wrong that you can directly point to.'

'Well, he has been standing on the cliff tops screaming out to sea.'

Stephanie sighed.

'Poor Eddy, but that's not a crime. With re-sectioning, the courts are cautious. Care here is incredibly expensive, and the risk of harm to himself or others needs to be high. You have to remember the old adage. It's hard to prove you're crazy enough to get into these places, but once you're here, it's difficult to prove you're sane enough to leave.'

Ashley and Hector thanked Stephanie and returned to the car. They were pulling away when Ashley's phone beeped to say there was a message from Dylan Crabb and she rang him straight back.

'Hey, Dylan. We've just visited Brancaster House and got the lowdown on Eddy's condition. What's your view on putting him back in a unit?'

'That's sort of what I'm calling about. It's obvious he's struggling, but it's not that easy to re-section someone. We had a talk with him this morning at his GP's surgery. A better and quicker option is if he volunteers to return to secure conditions and so we asked him what he thought of that.'

'I assume he wasn't enthusiastic.'

'No, he was far from keen. He kept asking if we knew where Peter Ibson was. I told him we didn't, and he got really agitated again. That is your inspector he's talking about, isn't it?'

'Yes. We want Eddy back in the station. He's too much of a risk to the public. Can you meet us at the stepdown unit, and we'll pick him up?'

'That's why I'm ringing. We tried to calm him down, but Eddy jumped up and said he was leaving. I stood in his way, but he just threw me to one side like I was made of paper. When I asked him where he was going, he displayed more tardive dyskinesia.'

'Which is again?'

'Involuntary movements of the face or body. He shouted sorry at me, then ran out into the street.'

'Where was he heading?'

'Towards Morrisons' petrol station.'

'Okay, I'm going to get authorisation to put out a BOLO for him. Do you agree that he should be brought in for his own safety and the public's?'

'Yes. I wonder if I've been naïve. I didn't think he had the ability to kill, even if someone else was urging him to do it.'

'But now you do?'

'Yes. He seized me so violently, I felt like prey.'

Ashley frowned. That didn't sound good.

'Look, I found out that he was having a visitor in the unit nearly all the time he was there, and it was Peter Ibson. I have a horrid feeling Peter's in touch with him now somehow.'

'What? Why didn't Peter mention that?'

'We'll be asking him that when we find him, but he's on sick leave at the moment. We're beginning to have concerns about DI Ibson, so make sure you let us know if he gets in contact. I'll be in touch when we've found Eddy. What was he wearing?'

'A dark blue coat with a hood.'

'Brilliant. Now we really need this guy in custody.'

Ashley rang Control to update them. They would instruct a response vehicle to head down to the petrol station. Then she called the office and spoke to Barry, who said a group of them would get down to Cromer and join the hunt for Eddy. Barry passed the phone to Emma, saying she'd just returned from visiting the local authority.

'Hi, Ash. The council has given me a list of all the chalets and beach huts. It's a bit of a disaster. Some are owned by the council and others are private. They have details for the private ones, but it looks like quite a few of the huts have been owned by families for decades because they have old dialling codes or no contact number or address at all.'

'Shit. I didn't think about that. They could have been rented out by the council or let privately.'

'Yes, I asked for details of who'd rented them from the council, but apparently that's a different data protection form.'

'Big surprise.'

'Yeah. They reckon I can have it tomorrow. Bhavini's heading down to the huts today to knock on doors again, but it's hardly beach weather, and there's a lot of them. I've requested one of those cadaver dogs that can sniff blood as well. Who knows, there could be a corpse in one already.'

Or a monster, Ashley thought idly, and good luck with getting a dog any time soon. Hector drove another mile down the road, then pulled in at a roadside café. He nipped out and brought back two polystyrene cups.

'Mochaccino latte with almond milk and sprinkles?' he asked.

'Yeah, sounds great.'

'Ah, sorry. I'm hoping it's two white coffees, but I struggled to understand him because of the cigarette hanging out of his mouth.'

'Great, although I suppose we still get sprinkles.'

They didn't have time for a break, so they sipped their coffees as Hector drove.

'I had a few questions about what you kindly shared with me on the way here, but after all that, I've forgotten them,' he said.

'I reckon it's about time you shared something with me. For some reason, I've told you more than I'd tell a shrink.'

She watched him wage an internal struggle. Maybe despite the age gap and their vastly different upbringings, they were quite similar after all.

'Okay, but this mustn't go any further.'

'Of course. My lips are sealed.'

'Well, I'm not planning to stay in the police.'

'What?'

'I feel like I've been sold a pup. Anyway, I just checked my emails, and a university friend has more or less offered me a job.'

'Great. I devote my life to training Mr Golden Balls and he's going to leave. Or is it my fault?'

'It's my fault, and I suppose my father has his share of the blame.'

'Go on.'

'My parents aren't tactile, affectionate people. There were no cuddles, or I-love-yous. Their own childhoods were as stilted as the one they gave me, but my dad was an inspiration. He used to tell me all these stories, and I'd believe the cops were the heroes, and the baddies all belonged in the slammer. I used to watch him from my bedroom window when he left for work in his dress uniform and I'd say that, one day, I would be just like him.'

'All families are at least a bit messed up.'

'Yes, but he also taught me to be cold and distant like he is. I was cautious around him, but I don't really know why. He never hit me, or even shouted at me.'

'If you can't see warmth, it's not surprising a child would feel afraid.'

'You were right about what you said about me. I had no clue whatsoever about real life when I started this job.'

'Well, every enthusiastic rookie cop gets a big surprise when they first start on the beat. At some point, you think that everyone's up to no good, or they're drunk, or both.'

'That's part of it, but everyone hates us, and that includes the media. It's like they're hell-bent on destroying any trust the public might have in us.'

'Welcome to our world.'

'I'd been doing response for exactly one week when a woman spat in my eye. I had two people try to headbutt me the next week, and a bloke had pissed in my car by the end of the first month. I ended up part of a team that was more or less driving around south

London sticking Tasers into folk. When I joined CID, I was amazed that loads of stuff wasn't investigated. There simply wasn't the time or the manpower to probe into low-level crime even though it was traumatising for the victims.'

'So, you realised policing's a mess and nobody knows how to sort it.'

'We need to go back to beat cops and investigate every crime, or it's all a waste of time. I could see that straight away.'

'Yes, but all that costs money. And the government hasn't got any for us.'

'Are you saying we're expected to do our job badly, while letting down the communities we're supposed to protect?'

'Oh, so you do get it.'

'Quite. This isn't a career any more. It's a poorly paid position filled by mugs who don't understand what they're signing up for.'

'Yes, and you could have been the one in charge of it all.'

'Exactly. I've been looking for other stuff, while feeling guilty.'

'Because of what Daddy will say?'

'Yes, he'll be very disappointed, so God knows what I'm going to do.'

'What was your degree in?'

'Computer programming and digital media. I wrote a programme for the Met that analysed and linked people's social media footprints. They loved it.'

'I can see why private enterprise would lap you up, but it'd be a shame. To be fair to you, you've got great potential at this detecting lark, and you're at least enjoying your time with us.'

'Trust me, I'm as surprised about that as you are.'

Ashley put the lid back on her coffee. Even she wasn't that desperate.

'Talking of which, isn't it odd that everyone implicated in this case is off social media?' she said.

'I know. Geoffrey, Candy, Bob, Peter, Eddy, Ron and Ruby can't be found online at all. I was talking to Jan about it. He agreed it's rare. In an age where people plaster their deepest desires and most private demons over the Internet in desperation to be seen or heard, these guys are conspicuous by their absence. No Instagram, no Facebook, no LinkedIn. Bob had no mobile at all. Only Geoffrey's is a smartphone, but he uses it like it isn't. In some ways, if we don't hear any more about these people, it will be as if they've never existed.'

Hector started the car.

'Are you on those sites?' he asked.

'No,' she said. 'You?'

'Nope.'

They would have finished the journey back to the station deep in thought, but Ashley received a call from Barry saying a person matching the description of the graffiti artist had been spotted near West Runton.

'Where exactly was he seen?' asked Hector after she cut Barry off.

'On the cliffs just before Laburnum Caravan Park. That could be Eddy. He was heading that way.'

'Isn't that—?'

Ashley cut him off mid-sentence.

'Yes, that's the park where Geoffrey was sleeping.'

48

Ashley drove home later trying not to think about having a glass of wine, or two, but she'd been good so far this week. The call that hinted at Eddy being near Laburnum had been an anonymous one to a helpline that TV and local radio had broadcast. A man had been seen wearing a large, hooded coat, limping in the direction of Beeston Hill, but the intel was an hour old.

Ashley and Hector had spoken to Catherine, the manager of the caravan park, but the van Geoffrey had been sleeping in was secure. The owner, an eighty-year-old called Diana McCallum with a mischievous glint in her eyes, was cleaning it ready for the new season when they arrived. She seemed disappointed that Mad Geoffrey wasn't coming back.

Contacting nearly two hundred owners and searching their caravans was a step too far at this point in the investigation so, instead, they checked the doors of each to see if any had been broken into. It took a long time for no gain.

She could almost feel the wine sliding down her throat as she pulled up outside her house. Perhaps one glass. The urge was in her mind now, and it would be near impossible to deny it. She was contemplating a takeaway to go with it when she remembered her neighbour, Arthur. Thank God, she thought. She didn't bother going home, just knocked on his door.

Arthur appeared in a dated suit, shirt, and tie, but they were all in good condition. His shoes were shiny.

'Evening,' he said, looking relieved.

'You do know I'm taking you shopping, not dancing.'

'Of course.'

'Ah, you thought I'd forgotten.'

He smiled, tapped his watch, but kept quiet as he followed her back to the car.

'Hey, I didn't say a time. Seven thirty isn't late.'

She suspected he'd spent all day looking forward

to it. They got in her car, and she drove towards the town centre.

'Which shop do you prefer?' she asked.

'The supermarket.'

'Yes, which one? Lidl, Morrisons or the Co-op?'

'Isn't Lidl the posh shop that does Bavarian food and fancy olives and cheeses?'

'That's perhaps not how I would have described it, but I admire your positivity. Lidl it is.'

They made small talk on the way, then Ashley grabbed a big trolley to share. She laughed her head off as Arthur perused the aisles as though he were in Harrods.

'I take it your wife did the shopping?' she asked.

'Yes. I did used to go on my own before the pandemic, but it all feels too busy now. The checkouts are too quick. I've got arthritis in my hands, so I can't pack any faster.'

'You need to toughen up. You're retired, so tell the youngsters off if they're too rapid. I'll show you.'

They reached the front of the checkout and the attractive young woman with thick make-up scanned their food at warp factor ten.

'Can you slow down, please, dearie?' asked Ashley.

'Of course,' replied the girl with a Spanish accent,

and then took the speed down to warp eight. Ashley felt like a Duracell Bunny as she rammed their shopping into their bags.

Arthur and Ashley chuckled together as they returned to her car with the trolley, which had chosen to misbehave.

'It's got a gammy leg, like me,' joked Arthur.

He looked at her when she didn't reply.

'Are you okay?' he asked.

'Yes, sorry. There are a few gammy legs about at the moment. We've had so much information pouring in about my latest case that it's easy to get swamped. There's somebody with a bad leg who I need to talk to, who's vanished. Your comment made me realise that limps are actually quite common, especially in older people.'

'I assume you're talking about the deaths on the beach.'

'Yes.'

'Charming, I thought you were taking me shopping. Instead you were fitting me up. I'd better not find you've hidden a bloody knife in my freezer.'

'I think a jury would see through that. It's pretty clear to me that the killings were unlikely to be done by an elderly person, but it doesn't mean they weren't the driving force behind the crime. Whoever's responsible knows the town well, so it's made me consider the other fishermen. They might know something. One of my colleagues spoke to a few of them, but not many were about that day because of the weather. He also said they were a reticent bunch.'

'Ah, they'd know the beach. The killers could also have arrived by boat.'

'Yes, I did consider that briefly at the start, but only a loon would have gone out in that wind, even close to shore.'

'They could have used boats to hide their gear or tools, or even themselves, while you were investigating. Perhaps the RNLI or National Coastwatch have seen suspicious behaviour.'

'That's a fair point. If we don't get a break soon, that's one of the areas I'll focus on.'

'See!' said Arthur with a smile. 'You did a nice thing bringing me here, and God has rewarded you.'

'That would explain his actions when I've been less well behaved.'

Arthur's smile broke into a grin. 'I've had a few punishments myself.'

Ashley drove them back and carried his bag to his door.

'Come in for salami and cheese,' he said. 'I bought too much for one.'

'It's getting late, and I'm supposed to be losing weight.'

'Don't be daft. You've got a lovely, slim figure.'

Ashley puffed out her cheeks.

'Okay,' she said. 'Let me put my shopping away first, then.'

'Excellent. We can have a nice glass of port.'

She tutted with mock disgust. 'It seems the devil's work is going on here. I know enough about icebergs, ninety per cent below the surface, so watch your step.'

He raised his hands in surrender.

'I don't know what you mean.'

'One minute, it's a lift to the supermarket, the next I'll be cleaning your cooker. By the weekend, I'll be edging your back lawn and knocking the moss off your roof, while you've got your feet up on a seat inside, eating salmon sandwiches and watching the horse racing.'

Arthur winked at her. 'I'm not much of a gambler, but the rest is true.'

49

Brad Garrett put his empty pint glass down and stood to leave. It had been a busy night in The King's Head pub, but he'd kept to himself as usual. His mind was stuck at that horrible morning when Peter woke him up and told him Foxy had died. Brad's mouth was dry, despite all he'd drunk.

He had to steady himself by grabbing the chair of the woman next to him. Her head shot around, but the look she gave him was of pity rather than annoyance, which weakened his legs more than the many beers he'd consumed.

'Sorry, luv,' he slurred.

Brad never got as bad as this. In fact, he couldn't

remember ever being this drunk since that night on the beach.

He thought about saying goodbye to the manager, who often slipped him to the front of the queue if they were busy, knowing he drank on his own, but it was two deep at the bar with noisy students home from university for Easter. He lurched through the front door instead.

Outside, he sucked in the cold air in the hope of reviving himself, but his head spun as he staggered down the street. Brad thought of Lorna waiting at their house and felt worthless. She'd been a great wife and a good mother, but he'd never fully engaged in family life. He'd pursued her with a fervour that he hadn't understood at the time, but, with hindsight, he suspected it had been the rejection by Foxy that had caused his focus.

It wasn't fair to Lorna, although they had lasted longer than nearly anyone he knew, so perhaps that was something. The dark part of him laughed, knowing that he would gladly trade all those years for one night with the girl of his dreams and then, later, his nightmares.

As usual of late, he couldn't face returning home. It seemed there was an invisible barrier in their bed.

He felt as though he'd been living a lie, and now he was unable to maintain it.

His pace slowed as his vision blurred. Raucous laughter and shouts from the young as they left the pub made him turn around, but everything was out of focus. He'd only walked about fifty metres, but it felt like miles. Footsteps approached, so he put his head down and tried to stride out.

It was only a few minutes' walk to the garage, but it seemed to take forever. He worried about setting car alarms off as he staggered from one to the other using them for support. At last, he saw the lights of his forecourt. He pulled a bunch of keys from his pocket in preparation as he reached his red Mercedes, which was parked at the end of the customer car park. Maybe he should sleep in the back of that. It wouldn't be the first time.

His eyes became heavy, and the keys slipped from his fingers. They jingled as they hit his right shoe. Self-preservation made him crouch, so he didn't fall on his face, but he still toppled over and banged his head on the side panel of his car. He slumped to the ground.

The tarmac was cold under his cheek as his breathing slowed. His hearing was the last sense to go. The words that were whispered in his ear vanished like smoke, but he understood their meaning.

'Your time is up.'

50

Ashley woke to a terrible smell on her pillow and realised with horror that her breath had caused it. She lurched to the bathroom and brushed the remnants of port and Stilton off her teeth. She cursed the small pounding in her temple that she always got with port, but then recalled she'd only had two small glasses. She'd had fun though.

Arthur was an interesting guy. He'd taken a lot of risks and enjoyed some adventures when he was younger, many of which involved sailing, before managing his company had consumed him. They'd agreed to make Wednesday cheese and port night next week, too.

The aches and pains in her legs had faded, and

she felt good. Putting her running gear on didn't feel like a drag, and she was soon walking and stretching up the road towards the cliffs with a smile on her face. She again headed to the chalet park so she could power up the hill.

She ambled past a red Mercedes saloon in the car park closest to the gate through to the field, which looked familiar, but she couldn't recall why. After a second's thought, she pushed it to the back of her mind and began her jog. At the top of the cliff, the view was much changed. A light coastal fog had turned the beach grey and spooky. She ran past Bob's place, as she now thought of it, and trotted down the path into the centre of town.

The tide was out, and she could only just make out the crashing waves through the shimmering air. She worked the times in her head from the previous weekend and knew the sea would have started coming in about an hour ago. There was an expanse of perfectly flat, hard sand where the fishermen and women sometimes dug for worms. She decided to run to the pier and sprint back along the beach like the training scene in *Rocky III*. The climb up the steep cliff steps afterwards would be brutal, but, as the man said in the fourth movie, no pain!

When she arrived at the pier, she grinned. A fresh,

blustery breeze filled her lungs with the salty, cold air and she felt invigorated and fitter than she had in a long while. With the sea fret dropping the visibility, she felt completely alone, so she shot out a few uppercuts, jabs and hooks as she ran back, then scampered down the steps to the sand and jogged along the shoreline.

It was wetter in the sand next to the dark murky waves than she'd thought, and it began to creep into her trainers, so she moved into the middle of the beach. Geoffrey's boat was attached to a tractor, but it wasn't moving. He stood at the back of it, waving at her. She waved in reply, but soon realised he was trying to get her attention. When she neared him, he beckoned her onto the boat.

'Quick, come up here,' he shouted.

He held out his hand, and she took it. Geoffrey lifted her up as if she were a child.

'What is it?' she asked at his concerned face.

He handed her a pair of battered binoculars.

'I was about to ring 999,' he said, pointing into the foggy distance.

She put the binoculars up to her eyes and scanned the direction where he was indicating.

'I can't see anything on the beach.'

'No, it's in the sea.'

Ashley panned slowly left and frowned. She blinked her eyes as though they were deceiving her.

'Is that a wheelchair in the water?'

'Yes, keep going left.'

She edged over. A deckchair came into view with the sea about a quarter of the way up it. There was a man in a pair of jeans and a coat with a blanket covering his top half. He wasn't moving, despite the waves now lapping at the bottom of the seat.

Ashley's gaze moved to his hands, which were resting on the arms of the deckchair. She saw the fingers flex.

51

Brad Garrett had been on a cloud, or in a cloud, it was hard to say which. Rain speckled his face, but it was the lap of water on his bum cheeks that began to rouse him. He didn't have the strength to open his eyes, yet his mind was telling him something was wrong.

He managed to move his fingers. When he thought of his feet, he realised they were immersed in icy water. His ears picked up the roar of the wind and the crash of the waves. The smells and sounds were of the beach, which was not where he was supposed to be.

His heart thumped as his eyes became slits. He prised them open. His view grew into a mass of grey sea, out of which rose a rippling shadowy wave. It soared and wallowed, huge and billowing, and hurtled towards him. He opened his mouth to scream, but he couldn't. His lips were sealed shut.

The wave crashed down in front of him, although the water that reached him had little force. Even so, it flowed over his crotch in a white foam and soaked his clothes up to his chest. He tried to reach up to remove whatever it was that covered his mouth, but his wrist was secured to the arm of the deckchair. He flapped his hand back and forth like a fish out of water. It was the same on the other side.

A hungry sea rose again, this time with more purpose. The wave loomed larger, higher, keener, threatening, purposeful, but Brad couldn't move. The only scream he could make was inside his head.

52

Ashley shoved the binoculars into Geoffrey's hands.

'He's alive,' she shouted, and vaulted off the boat. 'Catch me up. We'll pull him out before it gets too deep.'

She dodged the other boats, stopped, and turned around.

'Bring your phone,' she hollered back.

Ashley trudged through the heavy stones next to the sand to the concrete path. She opened her stride when her footing was secure and sprinted. Adrenaline coursed through her veins, and it didn't take long for her to pass the beach huts. She dashed down the ramp past the Banksy, picked her way through more stones, then hit the sand and ran hard towards the area that she was beginning to know too well. It was where Ron and Ruby had been killed, and most likely Candy and Foxy, too.

Ashley gritted her teeth as a stitch took hold. She slowed to a fast walk when she was fifty metres away, in case it was some kind of trap. Who the hell would sit in the cold and wait for the tide to come in? Then she realised the significance of the wheelchair. That was how he was brought here. Most likely to die.

The beach was empty except for a slender figure and a small running dot much further up towards Overstrand. She checked back at the stairs and the face of the cliff, but there was no movement apart from that of the stunted trees in the wind.

At the water's edge, behind the man in the water's back, she cried out.

'Hey, what are you doing?'

Ashley watched with disbelief as the man started bucking backward and forward, then side to side as another wave rolled in and concealed him from the chest down. It lifted the wheelchair to the right of him and nudged it towards her.

She contemplated taking her trainers off, but thought better of it. Ashley splashed into the surf, shocked by how cold it was on her lower legs. She grabbed the wheelchair and pulled it back onto the beach, then she stepped forward keeping away to the side of the deckchair. She jumped a big wave as it broke in front of her. When she glanced across at the man, she saw the tape over his mouth.

53

Brad's mind began to spin out of control as his heart juddered in his chest. He was getting more and more breathless as water filled his nostrils. His vision zoned in and out. The seagull above swooped down on him, becoming pterodactyl-sized, then screamed in alarm and banked away.

Brad lurched to the side and realised his ankles were also secured to the deckchair. He was bucking and rolling when the surging water lifted the deckchair and him slightly from where his weight had pressed it into the sand. He dropped back down. His brain screamed at him to get out of the water.

The sea seemed to flatten out, as though pausing for breath from its recent efforts. Three large swells rose in the distance in front of him as he imagined it gathering its reserves. The first wave was dwarfed by the ones behind it. Maybe the surge would wash him into the shallows. When he felt his seat rise, he twisted and leaned, and the deckchair toppled onto its side.

He was left with only his right shoulder, right arm and right leg sticking out of the swirling briny sea. Panic heightened with his head submerged. The next wave crashed down and lifted him forcibly, washing him back towards the cliffs. He jolted to a halt as something under the water gripped his ankle.

54

Ashley watched the deckchair roll onto its side and expected the man to fall out, but he remained attached to it. She stepped through the next wave and noticed the black cable tie securing Brad's right wrist to the arm of the chair. There was also one around his ankle. Her eyes searched back up the beach. Geoffrey was making slow progress.

The sea retreated, giving the man just enough room to lift his head out of the sea and snort. Ashley was desperately tugging on the deckchair to pull it backwards, when a big wave took her by surprise and knocked her off her feet. The water surged over her head and up her nose. She scrambled to her feet and pushed herself up, spitting salty liquid out of her mouth so she could breathe.

She returned her focus to the man she'd recognised as Brad Garrett. Only his right shoulder remained visible above the water. Ashley reached into the sea, grabbed the deckchair arm with both hands, steadied herself and heaved with all of her might, but it was too heavy.

She released the wooden frame, plunged her hands into the froth, and lifted the top of Brad's head out of the bubbling sea. As the water level decreased in preparation for the next wave, she hooked her finger under the tape on his mouth and yanked it off.

Snot and froth flew out of Brad's nose, spit and slobber from his mouth. He hauled in fresh air, eyes shut, teeth bared. Another wave rushed in and smothered his face once more. Ashley heard Geoffrey splashing through the water next to her.

'He's tied to the chair,' she yelled at him.

Geoffrey's face was scarlet. He drew a large filleting knife out of his belt and stamped over to the deckchair. He seized the wood and sliced through the plastic ties, releasing the right side of Brad's body, so he slumped face first into the sea. Geoffrey froze for a moment, then handed her the knife. He reached down, supported Brad's head, then lifted the deckchair up with him still in it.

'Cut the ties!' he screamed.

She could see the one attached to Brad's arm and managed to get the edge of the knife under it. With a wiggle, it snapped off, and Geoffrey pulled Brad's head to his chest as the next wave hit. Brad's arms came around Geoffrey's bottom. He clung on with his face contorted in pain, buried in Geoffrey's groin.

Ashley realised Brad's ankle was still stuck and must be causing him agony. Geoffrey's lower back took the brunt of the next wave. Ashley had no choice but to follow Brad's leg to where the plastic had secured his leg to the deckchair. There was also a metal ring around his ankle. She lifted the deckchair onto its side and sawed at the plastic cable tie until it broke.

But Brad still didn't come free. Through the murky water, she realised it was a handcuff around his ankle with a chain through it. The chain stretched away, out of sight. She reached out and pulled the chain. After a bit of give, Ashley soon found it was rooted solid. She looked up into Geoffrey's grimace. He was soaked from head to foot. The water level now receding only to his thighs. He snarled, moved two steps out to sea, then jacked

Brad up so his forehead was level with Geoffrey's chin.

'Brad! You have to stand,' he bellowed.

Brad's eyes shot open and he managed to pull himself upright. The sea swirled around them. Ashley spat water out and wiped her face to clear her vision. The beach seemed distant, with a huge cloud bank rising up over the cliffs. She remembered Geoffrey's phone, but it must be ruined. A breaking wave slapped her on the back and shunted her metres down the beach. She turned, hopeless and horrified at what was about to occur. Geoffrey couldn't hold Brad forever.

They'd have to cut Brad's foot off, or he would drown.

As if he could read her mind, Geoffrey slowly shook his head, looking all of his sixty-odd years.

'I rang the police on the way,' he shouted.

'What about the fire brigade and coastguard?'

'All of them. I asked for everyone!'

Ashley turned to the beach and looked through the murk towards the pier and the church spire in the distance. In the early morning gloom, she could see flashing blues and golds. They were coming.

Ashley was bumped along by the surging water once more. She glanced out to sea. The waves had grown, or maybe Geoffrey and Brad were just lower in the water. Brad started to struggle in Geoffrey's grip.

She linked arms with Geoffrey to create a bigger barrier and to support him, but the top of the waves were up to her chest.

'Calm down, Brad, please, just a few more minutes.'

Brad's eyes flickered and disappeared into his head. He appeared haggard and broken. His eyes reeled back into place, and they fixed on her, but the focus within them was gone. He screamed. A sound so high and shrill that it was hard to believe that it came from a full-grown man. Ashley looked behind her as the face of a wave tumbled towards them. It swiped her upper back and barrelled her into Brad, knocking him out of Geoffrey's hands.

The wave sucked her under. She struggled on the bottom in the turbulent water, almost dropping the knife, before finding her feet. Ashley burst to the surface, then looked across at Geoffrey, who was peering down into the bubbling surf zone. There was no sign of Brad. Geoffrey stared hard, then leaned forward and plunged his hands into the chop to lift a choking submerged Brad's top half out of the sea.

'Bolt cutter. Tell them we need a bolt cutter,' he wheezed.

Ashley heard a high-pitched engine. She looked along the beach, but the police BMW that was racing up along the sand was too far away. A big orange object appeared behind Geoffrey. It had to be from Cromer Lifeboat Station. She half front-crawled, half jumped towards them as two figures slid off the side of it.

'He's chained and tethered somehow,' she gasped at one of them. 'His foot. Bolt croppers.'

The man raised an eyebrow for a millisecond, then swam briskly back to the boat, while the other crew member stood next to Geoffrey. Ashley watched as the woman grabbed Brad's left side. She faced the next wave while supporting him, jumping to ride it with ease as another one arrived.

'It's okay. We've plenty of time!' she shouted at Geoffrey.

There was a roar from the inshore rescue boat as it streaked away over the waves. The police 4x4 was forced to navigate a path through the thick grass and boulders at the bottom of the cliff and was only trundling closer.

'He'll only be a minute or two,' reassured the woman from the RNLI.

Ashley stood next to Geoffrey again, and the three of them jumped the waves together whilst holding a limp Brad. Time had slowed, but finally the boat returned and a man in a diving mask leapt out with long metal cutters in his hand. He dived under the water and emerged to give his buddy a thumbs up. She nodded at Geoffrey, then hooked her hands under Brad's armpits and heaved him towards the beach. Brad was a silent, dead weight.

The woman glanced at Ashley, then at the arriving vehicles, then at Brad.

'Actually, we'll take him back to the gangway by boat,' she shouted. 'It'll be quicker to the ambulance. Will you two be okay?'

Ashley nodded. The RIB reversed towards them, bobbing high, and the two crew members lifted Brad up into the arms of another rescuer, who heaved him on board. Brad was ashen. With a rev of their outboard, they departed at speed, leaving Ashley to wade back to shore with Geoffrey.

Geoffrey panted next to her. He put his arm around her shoulders. She hooked her arm around his waist, and they helped each other to safety.

55

When they got back to shore, the pair collapsed to the sand, grateful for solid ground. Turning around, Ashley noted the surf appeared less wild than when they'd been in its thrall. The waves were big but by no means towering. Perhaps the sea was sulking now, having been denied its prey.

'Are you all right?' said a waiting uniformed sergeant to Ashley.

'Yes, but have this man checked over, please,' she said with her teeth chattering.

Geoffrey didn't have the breath to reply.

'I think you should both see the paramedics after that. There are two ambulances back at the gangway. I'll get an officer to drive you there in no time.'

'Wait, it's a crime scene.'

The sergeant glanced behind her.

'There'll be nothing here in an hour but sea.'

'Okay. Search as best you can.' She handed him the knife, which she had somehow managed to hold on to.

The sergeant, who looked in his late forties, gave her a reassuring nod to let her know he knew his job. An Asian constable took Geoffrey and Ashley back, and they were checked out. Ashley was tired but could still function. The ambulance's heaters were put on full blast, which helped, and they were wrapped in heat protector blankets.

Geoffrey just wanted to go home, and seemed to have forgotten he didn't have one. He had a change of clothes in his truck, which he grabbed, then Ashley asked the ambulance crew to take them both to her house. The other ambulance had left with its lights flashing and sirens wailing as soon as Brad was on board.

After they'd been dropped off, Ashley showered her numb body and put on fresh clothes. Geoffrey was slumped at the dining room table, but rose to go upstairs to shower when she handed him a towel. Her phone was full of messages, but before she had time to answer them, her front door vibrated under a heavy knock. She peered at her watch. It was nine o'clock.

Ashley opened the door to find DCI Vince Kettle, DC Hector Fade and DC Emma Stones. She felt like closing it again, but instead, slowly beckoned them in.

'Come in, guys.'

'Are you okay?' asked Emma, barging between the two men.

'Yes, tired, spaced out, hungry and thirsty.'

'In other words, absolutely knackered. Sit down. We'll sort everything.'

Emma asked Hector to go with her and they went through into her dining room, leaving Kettle and Ashley in the front lounge.

'Take a seat,' Kettle said with a sad smile. He sat in the armchair opposite the sofa.

Ashley slumped down. 'Oh, no,' she groaned.

Kettle nodded.

'He didn't make it, did he?' she asked.

'No, I'm afraid not. They got a pulse and had him breathing again, but he had a heart attack as they were putting him in the ambulance. He was dead on arrival. What the hell happened?'

'God, I don't know where to start. I'll pop in and do a statement, see where we're at.'

'No, that's why we're here. If nothing's urgent, come back tomorrow, or next week if you feel rough or just don't fancy it. You've been through quite an ordeal.'

'I can rest when we've caught this fucker. Any sign of Eddy or Peter?'

Kettle shook his head.

'Not a dickie bird.'

Ashley waited until Emma and Hector returned with cups of tea. She sent Hector upstairs to give one to Geoffrey. Then Ashley told them what happened. When she'd finished, she was met with stunned silence.

'Who would do something like that?' asked Emma.

'The same guy who did for Ruby,' said Hector.

'I'll up the ante on Eddy and Peter,' said Kettle. 'We'll watch their bank accounts and phone records in real time, but we've got so little to go on. Neither man has any family, nor do they seem to have any friends.'

'Except each other,' said Hector.

Ashley thought about Brad. He'd been Peter's best friend before it all went wrong. Ashley remembered Lorna, who must be beside herself with worry. She checked her phone and there were numerous voice messages. She put them on speaker, and they listened to a very concerned wife say that she'd arrived at the showroom this morning and there was no sign of Brad. It looked as though he hadn't been in there all night. She'd rung again at eight thirty, worried that he still wasn't home or at work.

'I'd better visit her and tell her the news,' said Ashley.

'You'll do no such thing. I'll go with Flash,' said Emma.

Ashley's tiredness began to weigh heavily.

'Okay, thanks. I'll be in tomorrow morning. Ring me if there's a break.'

Nobody held eye contact with her.

'Okay, fine, don't call me,' she said. 'Make sure you chase up those beach huts. I reckon they might be using one to operate from. And look out for more graffiti in town.'

They nodded at her.

'That makes five,' said Hector.

'Aye,' said Kettle. 'Only Eddy and Peter to go. This whole thing could end without us ever having solved it.'

'I really hope not,' said Ashley, who then let out a big yawn.

Emma and Hector moved towards the door.

'One last thing,' slurred Ashley. 'Brad was obviously in an emotional state, but I reckon he was drunk or maybe drugged. I could smell his breath even in the sea.'

'Okay, we'll get going. Have some rest,' said Kettle, standing up.

'Do you need shopping getting, Ash?' asked Emma.

'No, I only went last night,' she replied.

It felt as if that were a lifetime ago. She wracked her brain.

'Talk to the other fishermen, or folk, or whatever people insist they are called nowadays. They know the tides, the beach, the sea. Talk to local builders. Ron and Ruby were buried under builders' buckets. People like that are strong.'

'I'll get one of the teams on it,' said Kettle.

'Good. Did the deckchair wash up?'

'No,' he replied. 'It didn't, and it's unlikely we'll locate the cable ties, although we're hopeful the chair will be left behind when the tide goes out.'

At the door, she closed her eyes and imagined the scene on the beach. There was something on the edge of her memory. The door was closing when she shouted out.

'Brad's car. I saw it at the chalet park. Red Merc. He must have driven here in it for a reason.'

'Unless he was abducted from his garage when he was locking up, then that person brought him here in his own vehicle,' said Hector.

'Perhaps he was meeting someone,' said Emma.

Ashley clicked her fingers.

'No, the wheelchair. I bet he was incapacitated and taken down to the beach in the chair.'

'You'd need to be strong to pull a grown man across the shingle in a wheelchair.'

'Eddy is strong. Peter is strong. And the tide was out, so you'd only have to drag it for a few metres before you got to hard sand.'

'Hang on,' said Hector. 'We saw a wheelchair at Kenneth Markham's house. The guy who lived with his mum and went to school with Foxy and Eddy. I think there was one in the dining room of the step-down place as well. Was it either of them?'

Ashley shot him a look. 'Jeez, in all the drama, I forgot to check the serial number.'

Hector smiled.

'I meant was it similar in shape and style?'

'Oh, sorry.' She chuckled. 'I'm not sure.'

'No problem,' said Kettle. 'I'll ask Barry and Hector

to go around and have a chat with Kenneth while Emma speaks to Lorna Garrett. She'll hopefully be up to showing us the CCTV outside Brad's showroom, which might give us something. If Kenneth's chair has gone, we'll bring him in. We'll check the hostel as well. Now rest. We'll see you tomorrow, or, better still, Monday.'

When the door had shut out the sounds of the street, she could hear Geoffrey snoring. She traipsed up the stairs and walked into her bedroom. Sure enough, an unshowered Geoffrey was sparko in the middle of her bed in just a pair of faded grey boxer shorts. Ashley grabbed a blanket from the cupboard and pulled it over him. She spun on her heels, staggered into the spare room where there was a single bed, and crawled under the duvet.

She closed her eyes, but her mind dragged up a vision of Brad Garrett's leg attached to a chain that tethered it to the sea floor. As she dropped off, she was wondering what sort of person would use handcuffs.

56

Ashley woke up in the spare room at 4 p.m. She went to check on Geoffrey, but he'd disappeared. When she called him, his phone was turned off. She made herself a sandwich and a side salad, then texted Emma and Hector for an update. Nobody replied. The news only reported that a man had got into difficulty on Cromer beach, but nothing more. She went back to bed at ten and slept through until nine the next morning.

Ashley had planned to go in on Friday but woke up tired and out of sorts. A cough was threatening, so she stayed home and kept warm. Kettle rang around midday. He was pleased that she hadn't ventured in. He said there were no major developments, so she had a long bath on Friday afternoon, watched a bit of TV before retiring to bed early.

Ashley rose on Saturday morning at seven feeling rested and, even though it was the weekend, she decided to go into the office and see what progress had been made. It wasn't quite nine when she arrived and Kettle and Grave were deep in conversation in the office doorway. They stopped talking when they saw her.

'How you feeling?' asked Kettle.

'Rested.'

'Nice to see you back but take it easy.'

He smiled and let her pass. Jan and Emma rose from their chairs when she reached them.

'Are you okay?' asked Jan.

'I'm great. What did I miss?'

'A fair bit, actually,' said Jan. 'But we were told to keep you out of it unless it was absolutely necessary.'

'And it wasn't?'

'Not quite,' replied Emma. 'The council gave us a list of the names of the people they'd rented out huts to. Guess who's on it?'

'Peter.'

'No. One was for a Mr E. Balmain.'

'No way, Eddy.'

'Yes, the hut was the last but one towards town.

Right next to one of the blood spots, which the testing also came back for. Of the four spots, all were Ron's blood apart from that one, which had no match.'

'That's a bit annoying,' said Ashley.

'It's not that bad. We'd have still assumed they'd gone towards the pier because it's past the steps which go up to the top promenade.'

'So, Eddy could have used the hut as storage, or for getting changed, or maybe hiding out in until the police left the beach. Bob could have split off and gone up the steps.'

'Any or all of them,' said Jan.

'I assume you kicked the door down?'

Emma chuckled.

'The council met us there and unlocked it, but there wasn't much inside. A jumper and a baseball cap, which we're having tested, and two medical face masks. We didn't notice any blood, nor any food or drink debris, which would probably have been present if it had been used as a base. CSI is obviously all over it. It was booked fairly recently by phone. They record some calls but not all. We're hoping to get a recording to see if it was Eddy.'

'Okay, what else happened?'

'Michelle did the PM for Brad. He had a minor faulty heart valve, and it was enlarged, which means the cause of death is likely to be heart failure brought on by the trauma. Tests on the stomach contents were inconclusive, but they tested his blood and urine, and he clearly had a lot to drink. We know which pub he'd been to.'

'Tell me about the pub.'

Emma smiled.

'Bhavini and Barry attended last night. Brad is well known there, quiet, and causes no trouble. The barman said he seemed very tipsy, but that wasn't unusual of late. There's no CCTV in the bar, but his wife showed us CCTV from the forecourt of the showroom.'

'He was kidnapped.'

'He collapsed. Someone appears to help him into the rear of his car. Unfortunately, it's on the edge of the parking area and the abductor keeps his back to the camera. He has a large dark coat on with the hood pulled up, so it's probably the guy we're looking for.'

'Any joy with the road cameras?'

'One picked up the car, but it's too dark for details.'

'Pity.'

'Yes. We suspect Brad was drugged in the pub. Rohypnol or a sleeping tablet are most likely because it seems he was completely knocked out until he woke up in the water around the time you arrived. Toxicology will tell us on Monday or Tuesday what was in his system. You said he seemed crazed, so perhaps he was given something else as well.'

'Like LSD.'

Emma nodded.

'That's highly possible. It could have been put in his mouth while he was unconscious. Candy's blood test showed its presence, as did Ruby's results.'

Ashley could tell there was more.

'Was the wheelchair the one from Kenneth Markham's place?' she asked.

'No. Kenneth didn't answer his door. He'd left a note for the postman to leave any parcels with a neighbour, but Barry and Hector could see through the letter box. Hector said it was the same wheelchair from before, and it was still in the same position. The wheelchair from the hostel has gone, though.'

'Shit, Eddy again.'

'Yes, or someone who visits Eddy.'

'Did the coroner's report come back for Foxy?'

'Yep. She'd taken LSD, alcohol, marijuana, ecstasy and then drowned. Verdict was as Mrs Sweet said. Misadventure.'

'I suppose we suspected that.'

'Hector came up with a splendid thought to really

muddy the water, though,' said Jan. 'He pointed out that both Ruby and Brad could have been saved with an earlier intervention. Few people go to the beach when it's pitch black, but some do, and there are a lot of variations with the speed of an incoming tide.'

Ashley looked out of the window as she thought about it.

'God, he's right,' she said. 'Geoffrey might have dug Ruby out if he'd been five minutes earlier. Even the spade was left behind. If Brad's heart hadn't given out, then he'd have survived. Who knows how long Candy was dead before they found her? That means this rhyme doesn't make sense.'

'That's what Hector suggested. If there indeed was a monster, or if the sea was the enemy, then it would want there to be seven and no let-offs.'

'Or perhaps whoever wrote the rhyme would want seven deaths,' said Ashley with a shake of her head.

'Yes, but it's not as dramatic as the sea coming for them,' said Emma, smiling. 'If Ruby or Brad had been rescued, then we'd have whisked them away to safety until the case was finished. There'd never have been seven.'

'So, the rhyme's just all part of the drama,' said

Ashley. 'I suspect it's going to be about revenge, but someone's also enjoying this.'

'Either that, or they're very angry. Maybe they don't necessarily want the seven to die, but it seems all of them must suffer.'

Ashley nodded. Extremes of emotion produced dramatic actions. It was inevitable more terrible events would occur unless the case was solved.

'What was the chain around Brad's ankle attached to in the sand?' she asked.

'The handcuff had been linked to a chain at one end and attached to his leg. The other end had been attached to a large gym weight, which was then buried. The handcuffs were non police issue, and the weight was old and rusted. We're trying to ascertain where the weight and handcuffs came from, but I'm not hopeful.'

'Jesus.'

'Yes. That's significant planning again. There was also more graffiti found near North Park,' said Jan.

'Let me guess, a number five.'

'Yes. A black five on one of the pavilions down there and a seven on the one next to it.'

'Five from seven. Two to go. Eddy and Peter. Of whom there's no sign.'

Kettle cleared his throat. He and Grave had returned as they talked.

'Actually,' he said, 'that's why we're in early. We've been discussing who's going to do the interview and what questions we want to ask.'

Ashley cocked her head.

'I'm back now, so me. Who did you catch?'

'We think you might be too close to the suspect, and we didn't catch anyone. Eddy is nowhere to be seen, which is odd given his mental state. Someone has to be helping him. We suspected Peter. Until he rang us.'

Ashley had to forcibly shut her mouth.

'He called the station?' she asked.

'Correct. He'll be here in an hour.'

57

The tension in the office was palpable when word got out that Detective Inspector Peter Ibson had driven into the compound, parked his car, and walked to Reception. He was taken straight to the custody suite.

Ashley asked Jan and Barry to head off to Cromer and finish the interviews with the fishing community. She didn't want to waste any time if Ibson provided a good excuse for his evasiveness, although she struggled to think of why he hadn't mentioned he knew the victims.

An interview room was prepared with live viewing facilities, so Det Supt Grave and DCI Kettle could watch along with DS Bhavini Kotecha. DI Peter Ibson had declined representation. He had also threatened to say nothing unless DS Ashley Knight did the interview. Kettle told Ashley he'd thought long and hard about giving in to a threat. Normally, they'd get Suffolk's detective team to interview a Norfolk officer, but that would take time. It was important that Peter talked, so Grave authorised one conversation.

He gave her the choice whether she'd like to have a more experienced detective from another team in with her, or if she'd stick with Hector. She chose the latter.

While she waited for Peter to be brought up to them, she realised the conclusion of this case might have ramifications for how she saw the world. Peter had given her a chance in Norfolk when he had no real reason to.

Calling him a hero was pushing it, but she respected him. Many here did. He'd risked his life on many occasions over the years. Just because he chose to keep his personal life separate from his work shouldn't be a negative.

Peter didn't make mistakes. He was never late or sick, and he was often the first in and the last out. In many ways, he was perfect, which didn't make him popular with some folk. That was especially true for those who weren't as committed.

Ashley blew out her cheeks while they waited.

'Are you wondering how the hell Ibson got involved in all this?' she asked Hector.

'Yes. The more I consider it, the more I wonder if we've got this right, but, like Bob, he is connected at some level.'

'Maybe, like Bob, he got out of town to make sure he was safe.'

'And perhaps he was the puppet master who had Bob and Eddy doing his evil work.'

The custody sergeant knocked and brought Peter in. He looked relaxed, clean shaven and smart in a fitted black suit. He had a white shirt on but no tie.

'I assume you don't want him cuffed,' said the sergeant with half a grin.

Ashley smiled at him. 'Not yet.'

Peter nodded at them both, but remained standing. Hector cautioned him and let him know the interview was being recorded.

'Sit down, Peter,' said Ashley. 'Thanks for coming in to talk to us. We've been looking for you for a while.'

'No problem, and you have my apologies. I didn't know.'

'Okay. You've declined representation. Is that wise?'

'I don't want a solicitor. I appreciate you checking,

but I'm not going to say anything incriminating, so it won't matter either way.'

'Fair enough. For the benefit of the tape, those present are DC Hector Fade, DS Ashley Knight and Peter Ibson. You are under arrest. You don't need me to tell you how serious this is.'

Ibson didn't object to the exclusion of his title, offering a glimmer of a smile. Ashley had given Hector the list of questions to ask because she wanted to concentrate on his replies and demeanour.

'I think, sir,' said Hector, 'that it will be simplest if we start at the murder of Ron and Ruby on the beach. Can you tell me about it?'

Peter stared across at Hector.

'Call me Peter.'

'What happened that day, Peter?'

Peter took a deep breath.

'I always wake at dawn. I can't remember if it's always been that way, or if it's a punishment. I shower and sit on my porch at the back of the house and drink a coffee. Sometimes I'll have another cup, but I usually head to work early. I was in the car when the call came. I called you, Hector, because you were due in, but I left it for Control to try to get hold of you, Ashley.'

'Did you have any idea who'd been killed that morning?'

'No, I did not.'

'You arrived around thirty minutes after the incident was reported, took control of the scene, and ensured the necessary precautions were taken.'

'No, I left the scene to a uniformed sergeant. They know what they're doing. I knew that we'd end up with it, so I was focused. The first few hours can be so important, in particular for damage limitation.'

'At that point, you must have recognised the victims.'

'I did.'

'How did that make you feel?'

'I expect I felt like you did.'

'Explain, please.'

'Sad at an untimely loss, but tempered by the fact I barely knew them, and I understood I had a job to do.'

'Yet you'd been at a party with them over thirty years ago.'

'Yes.'

'Where your girlfriend died.'

'Yes.'

'Which occurred at the exact same spot on the beach.'

'Yes.'

'But you still didn't mention it.'

'I would have done, but it wasn't important at that point.'

Ashley shook her head.

'Not worth the smallest mention?'

Peter didn't reply.

'Had you had any contact with Ron and Ruby since then?' asked Hector.

'I've seen them in town. Not to speak to.'

'You were described at the scene as unbalanced, for want of a better word.'

'That's right. I've been battling my demons more than usual.'

'Do you usually struggle?'

'Yes. Each day is an effort, but I've coped until recently.'

'We'll come back to that. You were relieved of duty by DCI Kettle, who could see you were struggling.'

'No, I asked to be relieved, and he agreed.'

'Where did you go?'

'I drove home.'

'Were you upset or angry or confused?'

'I was tired, sad, and yes, confused. The effort to carry on gets more exhausting. The deaths of Ron and Ruby, while tragic for them and their loved ones, were not tragic to me. Having said that, it made me focus on that devastating event years ago. Even though she died so long ago, it's affected me ever since.'

'Are you referring to Natalie Fox?'

Peter swivelled his head to stare at Ashley before he answered, but retained his impassive expression.

'Foxy. Yes.'

Ashley decided to be blunt to see if it would unsettle Peter.

'And that still upsets you, all this time later.'

He kept his eyes on Ashley. His voice was steady.

'It does. I suppose you could say it was love at first sight, but that understates how I felt about her. Perhaps all first loves are as consuming, but I doubt it.'

'But I think it would be fair to say your performance at work had dipped before these deaths. Maybe as long as a year ago.'

'Yes, that's fair.'

'Why was that?'

'No comment.'

'So, what did you do when you got home after you were given permission to take leave?'

'I needed to get away, especially from this town. A plan had been forming in my mind of late, so I put it into action.'

'What was the plan?'

'That doesn't concern you.'

'Where you went concerns me.'

'I visited a place called Salthouse and stayed with a friend's family.'

'But you didn't drive there.'

'No.'

'Why didn't you drive?'

'I didn't need a car.'

'And how long did you stay there?'

'Until today.'

'Did you return to Cromer at all in that time?'

'No, I went for a few walks with their dog and the children, but I didn't leave the village boundaries.'

'Were you aware of the drowning the following night?'

'I was.'

'When did you hear about that?'

'Two nights later.'

'And you know Candice Sweet.'

'I do, but, like Ron and Ruby, not that well, and I haven't seen her since that night.'

'The night you woke cuddled up next to her on the beach.'

'We were not cuddled up together. She was in a patch of marram grass. I woke up in the sand.'

'And you never met her again.'

'No.'

'How close were you to Brad Garrett?'

'We were childhood friends. As close as can be.'

'Until Foxy arrived.'

'Yes. We fought over her. Not physically, but we almost came to blows.'

'Were you aware someone died on that section of the beach yesterday morning?'

Peter's jaw bunched.

'I keep up to date with the news, yes. I don't know who it was.'

'It was Brad.'

Peter swallowed.

'I see.'

'Did you have anything to do with it?'

'No.'

'Did you visit him a month or so back at his car showroom?'

'I did.'

'Why?'

'I thought he'd sent me something.'

'But he hadn't?'

'He denied it. That's not the same thing.'

'What was it?'

'I'm not telling you.'

'Can you understand how that would make us think you were hiding something?'

'I am hiding something.'

'Okay. Tell me about Bob.'

'Bob is a homeless guy who lives in Cromer and is my age. I met him a few times before the party in question, but barely knew him. I saw him in town when I was in uniform, but otherwise I avoided him.'

'Why?'

'Bob was a drug addict. When I had dealings with him as a constable, he was so spaced out that I don't think he had a clue who I was.'

'Bob's been remanded for murder.'

Ibson finally looked back at Hector.

'Here's a tip. I would say all this is a little complex for Bob to have been the perpetrator. I'd let him go.'

'Bob was clean, but he began using within the last year. Do you have any idea why?'

'No.'

'Which brings us to Edward Balmain. Do you know him?'

'I do.'

'When did you last speak to him?'

'A few weeks back.'

'Where was this?'

'At my house.'

'He called on you.'

'Eddy uses my gym. I leave the door open for him.'

'You visited him for the best part of thirty years in a psychiatric hospital.'

'A secure unit, yes.'

'Why?'

Peter took a few deep breaths and turned back to Ashley.

'He was there the night Foxy died. He loved her as much as I did, albeit in a different way. I felt responsible afterwards. He should never have been taking drugs like the ones we took.'

'Alcohol, marijuana, LSD and ecstasy.'

'I don't recall any ecstasy, but yes. I'm a clever guy, and it was obvious Eddy had issues. We should have known better.'

'That's quite a commitment. Seeing someone for thirty years when you barely knew him.'

'Foxy was rarely without him. I knew Eddy well enough, and I liked him. The more time I spent with him, the more I enjoyed his company. We were similar in many ways. He helped me deal with the loss as much as I helped him.'

'It doesn't seem like either of you dealt with it very well, if you don't mind me saying so,' said Hector.

'I'm still here, aren't I? For a long time, I didn't want to be.'

'We believe Eddy murdered some or all of these people.'

Peter didn't reply.

'What do you think?'

'That you're entitled to an opinion.'

'What's your opinion?'

Peter breathed hard through his nose.

'Could I have a glass of water, please?'

58

Ashley gave Peter fifteen minutes' respite, even though he said he didn't need it. They left him in the room with two custody officers and headed to where Kettle and Grave had been watching. Both wanted them to go harder. After the fifteen minutes were up Ashley started the recording, and Hector went through the preliminaries again.

'What's your opinion of the idea that Eddy Balmain is the killer?' asked Hector.

'It's possible.'

'He's your friend.'

'I like to think so.'

Hector paused. His tongue darted out to moisten his lips.

'Where is Eddy?'

'I've no idea.'

'Did you know he was going to do this?'

'No.'

'Do you believe he's capable of committing these crimes?'

'God knows. His mental health began worsening a few months ago. Although I knew as soon as Eddy was released, he would never be well enough to rejoin society. Not on his own. It was a shame.'

'How did his behaviour deteriorate?'

'It's hard to say. He spent too much time in the gym. Sometimes, he seemed drugged up. Eddy wasn't built to cope with this world.'

'Did he stop taking his drugs?'

'His medication prevented him from engaging after he came out. We reduced his dosage, then stopped his pills altogether.'

'You stopped all his tablets?' asked an incredulous Ashley, cutting in.

'I did.'

'That was a big responsibility for you to take on, Peter. Did you feel you were medically qualified to make that decision for him?'

'He was fine. All he needed was my support, then

he could function. Those drugs are a disgrace. They're nothing more than a chemical cosh.'

'But then he started to behave badly?' asked Hector, taking over again. 'So, he did need his drugs.'

'No, he was reasonably well for months and months. Then I got something sent to my address, which I thought was from Brad, and I took my eye off Eddy. I didn't know what was troubling him. Eddy wouldn't tell me what had unsettled him. He came to my house out of his mind a few times. Someone had been giving him drugs. I used to let him sleep them off. He said he killed Foxy. I said we probably won't ever understand what happened.'

'Eddy killed Foxy?'

'That's what he said.'

'In cold blood, or did he mean that he should have looked out for her?'

'Your guess is as good as mine, but he'd never have hurt Foxy, or anyone else, for that matter, if he hadn't been out of his mind.'

'You were all so out of it, any one of you could have done it.'

'Maybe it's better we don't know who did it.'

'Better for who?'

Peter looked at the table.

'Do you still take drugs, Peter?'

Peter's jaw bunched.

'I'd never taken them before I met Foxy, and I never took them again. Bad things happen to people who take drugs.'

'Where do you think Eddy is?'

'I've no idea.'

Hector shook his head and turned to Ashley. She'd been making notes.

'Peter. Your world was destroyed by Foxy's death. Is that right?'

'Yes.'

'Why did you carry on?'

'Why did you, Ashley?'

Ashley then realised why he'd employed her. He'd been broken by life, too. By giving her a chance, he was trying to convince himself that he too still had something to offer.

'I wanted to help other people,' she said softly.

Peter smiled for the first time, and it was genuine.

'Me, too, but I don't think I can any more.'

'Why not?'

Peter raised his hands up, as if to say, all this.

'You know where Eddy is,' accused Hector.

But Peter didn't reply.

'You don't need me to tell you that interfering in a police investigation is a criminal offence,' said Hector.

'You don't need me to tell you that you can do very little about it until you know I'm breaking the law.'

'Are you planning to break the law?'

Peter paused. 'I want this case solved.'

'And that's best achieved through official channels. You know that!' Ashley raised her voice.

'I suspect our definitions of solved may differ.'

Ashley studied her notes.

'Salthouse. Didn't Ethan Cane live there?'

'Yes, I was with his family.'

'He was your sergeant before he died. A stroke, if I remember. Very sad. You joined up at the same time. Why were you there?'

'I'm godfather to one of his children. His wife knew about my depression and always said I could stay if needs be. The kids are getting older, but she struggles on her own. I wanted to help.'

Ashley cupped her chin, then rubbed her eyes and blew out a long breath. She'd been to the wake at Ethan's house. Life could be so unfair.

'We're going to keep you in the cells,' she said. 'We need to search your house, your car, and generally sift through your life. How do you feel about that?'

'I have nothing to hide.'

'Aren't you scared?'

'Of what?'

'Being next.'

Peter leaned back in his seat and glared.

'The night Foxy died, I received a special gift. I've never been afraid since. To feel real fear, you must have something to lose. I'm not scared to die.'

Ashley shrugged.

'Perhaps you've been scared to live.'

Peter's eyes narrowed.

'I've said enough. Interview's over.'

'We need to speak to Ethan's widow and confirm your story. CCTV needs to be checked. It could take days.'

'I'm in no rush to do what I have to.'

'Tell us what you know, Peter. You're one of us.'

He looked down and studied his fingernails. Ashley rose slowly from her seat and slapped her hand down on the table. Hector flinched next to her at the unexpected movement but their interviewee didn't move a hair.

'Peter! Your attitude today only brings me to one conclusion. You encouraged Eddy Balmain to leave secure conditions a year ago. You've brought him back here, and you've manipulated him into helping you take revenge on the people you feel are responsible for the death of the love of your life. This case is about vengeance.'

Peter gritted his teeth and stared straight at her. She could finally see anger. No, more than anger. Rage blazed in those burning eyes.

'You,' she continued, jabbing a finger at him, 'planned this for a long time. Revenge is a dish served very cold. Perhaps it festered all these years until your fury left you unable to function at work. We watched you lose control over the last year. You killed the drug-dealing hippies because they were culpable. Next was Foxy's friend for not looking out for her. Maybe you think Brad did it because he couldn't have her.'

Ashley paused. The only sound was the air being forced in and out of Peter's chest. She growled the rest of the accusation.

'You've set Eddy up. He's your scapegoat. I wouldn't be surprised if he was already dead.'

Peter inhaled slowly and deeply through his nose, closed his eyes, and visibly relaxed in front of them. He kept his eyes shut.

Ashley had one last go.

'Why did you come to the station? Why not just go and do whatever it is you have to do?'

Peter's eyes pinged open. Again, the tiniest hint of a smile.

'I didn't know what had happened. The motive

and identity of whoever was behind these crimes is beyond me. I knew this interview would be a two-way exchange of information, so now I have a plan.'

'What the hell does that mean?'

'Between us, we'll get to the end of this.' Peter stood. 'Now take me to my cell.'

59

Peter Ibson was escorted to the cells, and Hector and Ashley returned to their office. As they walked back, Hector slowed.

'Do you think that might have been too much?'

'What do you mean?'

'While maybe not a friend, he's been good to you. His mental health seems to be hanging from a thread. You were hard on him.'

'That's a valid point, but we have a job to do. That man in there was a different Peter. He's not the man I knew.'

'Maybe the guilty party is someone who has a beef with Peter. He must have annoyed a lot of villains over the years.'

Ashley smiled.

'See. That's the problem when the answer isn't obvious. What remains could be almost anything.'

Kettle called a meeting for the whole team, saying that they might as well discuss the interview in front of everyone, and the incident room was full by five. Kettle stood at the front.

'Thank you for ruining your Saturday for me. I'm sure you've all heard that Peter came in and has been interviewed. One of the stranger sessions I've witnessed. He's given us enough to keep him here while we check his story, but he hasn't given us enough for the CPS to charge him with anything. He's been arrested on suspicion of conspiracy to murder, so he'll be with us for a while.'

Kettle waited for the hubbub to die down.

'If I was a gambling man, I would say Peter has had a breakdown. Maybe it began a year ago when his behaviour changed. We all noticed, but it was gradual. He wouldn't be the first to struggle at this job, but he declined any offers of help.'

Kettle looked around the faces in the room.

'At the very least, he's involved somehow. Like Homeless Bob is involved. Maybe it was Bob who shared his drugs with Eddy, and perhaps Peter knows that. Peter said we should release Bob.'

Kettle let that fact hang for a few moments before he continued.

'You might think Peter's one of us, but that's finished if he's taken the law into his own hands. He becomes the enemy. We need to find concrete evidence of Peter's innocence or guilt, so please come in and help tomorrow if you wish, but don't burn yourselves out. Take some down time if you need it. Most of the requests and tests won't be back until Monday or Tuesday morning. Peter won't be going anywhere until then. The rhyme said only when there's seven, can they rest in heaven. We have five down, one in custody, and Eddy's vanished, so unless he turns up, we'll hopefully have a quiet Sunday.'

Chuckles rippled through the room.

Despite his calmness, Ashley suspected Kettle was struggling with getting his head around the reality of what he was saying. She wondered whether he believed it, or if he was only talking like this to fire up the team. Kettle had his hands resting on the table in front of him with his head drooped and shoulders raised. Ashley observed from the side as he hid the grimace that was forming. He looked back up at them.

'I'm very concerned by what Peter might do when he gets out of here if all the searches and checks come

up with nothing. There's no chance of getting surveillance if that happens. Let's focus, people, because
if we can't remand him, Peter will be free to wander
around Cromer as he pleases. Free to finish what he,
or maybe someone else, started.'

There was more chatter, but it died off when
Kettle nodded at Ashley, and she walked to the front.

'I'm sure this is hard for a lot of you to get your
heads around. Peter has been a decent boss for a long
time and a safe pair of hands for all of us in this force
at one time or another.'

There were many nods from those present.

'I've just spent the last half-hour thinking about
whether I believe he's guilty, and I'm still not convinced, which may be how you feel. So, remember.
We gather evidence. Nothing more. The courts will
decide on guilt. But like the DCI just said, I'm extremely worried about what he could do next. We're
missing a piece of the jigsaw, but I have a feeling Peter
now knows, or at least he suspects, what that piece is.'

She stared around at the people in the room.

'I'm beginning to worry that we've made judgements about individuals in this case with unconscious bias. Maybe we've wanted to believe people are
involved when, if we're realistic, it's unlikely.'

She took a moment for that to take effect.

'I think this all relates back to Foxy's death. If Brad and Peter fancied her, then it's likely others did. I reckon Eddy is a pawn, as perhaps Bob was. We need to identify the King. Is it Peter?'

She had their rapt attention.

'Or is it a person or persons we haven't yet met? Next week, we could have to expand our investigation and look for other players. Different teachers from the group's school days? This Kenneth guy might know more than he's letting on. I'll go to Norwich prison and see if Bob wants to talk. Any other thoughts?'

Hector put up his hand.

'Perhaps Eddy talked to another patient at his hospital and got them involved. It was a low secure unit, so a lot of the residents would only have been passing through.'

'That's a good idea. Let's also start delving into the other occupants of the stepdown too. Who did Eddy speak to in town? Where did he go? Who did he associate with? We'll need to revisit Candy Sweet's mother and partner and really dive into their pasts. That goes the same for Brad Garrett's wife. Does anyone else connect them? Are there motivations we've missed? Who's lying to us?'

You could hear a pin drop in the room.

'For those who aren't working tomorrow, spend the weekend with this case at the back of your mind, because on Monday,' she continued, 'Peter might be out. If he's innocent, then someone's killing his friends. They're raking up his past. They're ruining his life. He is one of the best detectives this station has ever had. We need to find the person responsible before he does, because Peter is now a man with nothing to lose.'

60

Ashley enjoyed a glass of wine while watching the seven o'clock news when she got home. She woke up in her armchair at midnight, dragged herself to bed and surfaced at five thirty. She really didn't fancy a run, but it looked as if it was going to be a pleasant day, so she put on her walking boots instead and strolled down Overstrand Road.

At Peter's house, she nodded at the uniformed officer who was standing outside, stretching. He would have had a long night guarding the scene. The police tape hung limp in the still air.

'Do you want a coffee?' Ashley asked him.

The youngster squinted in the weak morning

light, obviously not having recognised her in casual wear.

'Yes, please, Sergeant Ashley.'

Ashley smiled. Close enough.

She continued into the centre of Overstrand. The village was small, but, unlike many in Norfolk, there remained a thriving general store and post office. There was a big hotel called The Sea Marge with wonderful grounds, and a nice local, The White Horse. The beach was a few hundred metres away. It was a desirable place to live or retire.

She bought two coffees from the Costa vending machine at the store and drank hers with the constable back outside Peter's place. It had been an uneventful night. Kettle hadn't managed to secure a CSI van until that morning, so he wanted the scene protected.

Ashley had promised her now ex, Bethany, she'd help her move, so she went home, got changed, and walked through the town centre to Bethany's place.

The house already appeared empty when she arrived. The curtains were down, and the wheelie bin was stuffed to bursting. Ashley peeked through the windows and could see rows of packing boxes and piles of clothes but no sign of her ex. She sat on the front wall and basked in the spring sunshine. Oddly, it was at times like this when she really missed cigarettes.

From her pocket, she took the apple she'd grabbed from the fridge earlier that morning. She retrieved the penknife but decided she couldn't be bothered with removing the skin. She cut a chunk off instead and munched away in peace. Maybe she could kick the peeling habit, too.

Her mind wandered over the previous few days. It didn't seem possible that only a week had gone by, because she felt a changed person.

Twenty minutes later, Bethany beeped her horn and pulled up at the kerb. She had oversized blue jean dungarees on over a small pink crop top and looked good despite the sweaty face and scraped-back hair.

'You came,' she said, giving Ashley a hug.

'I said I would.'

'I thought you might have the hump.'

'I'm not saying I'm not sad, but I'll take friends if that's on offer.'

Bethany peered at her.

'Of course. You seem different.'

'I'm sober, which we weren't very often.'

'Oh, yeah! Come on, then, there are like a million boxes.'

They settled into a rhythm and made good headway, stopping for the odd chat.

'Are you going to your mum's, then?' asked Ashley.

'Yes, in Sheringham. She says she's got a new fella with a posh house in Walsham, so she's not there much. I just can't afford to keep this place on.'

'I don't mind helping.'

Bethany gave her a stern look.

'Ashley. I appreciate how generous you've been, but I don't want handouts. Not from anyone.'

Bethany took another vanload while Ashley brought the last of the boxes to the front of the house. Bethany returned with a grin.

'I forgot to tell you this great joke.'

Bethany liked jokes.

'What do you call a psychic pygmy who's escaped from jail?'

'Go on.'

'A short medium at large.'

Ashley groaned. 'I should dump *you* for that.'

Bethany put down the box she was carrying.

'I'm sorry, Ash. It's not nice being dumped, but I need a partner who's, well, a bit gayer than you are.'

'Was I that bad at it?'

Bethany shook her head.

'No, you were great at that part of it. I suppose the best way to explain it is by asking, would you like to walk through town holding my hand, then snog me in every pub and shop?'

Ashley curled her lip.

'I wouldn't want to do that with anyone.'

'I know, and that's the thing, because I would. Come on, there's bound to be some hairy-assed fifty-year-old for you with their blurred name tattooed on each biceps.'

'I'm not keen on faded tattoos, or chicks with hairy bums.'

Bethany laughed.

'Ash, we'll all fade as we age.'

'Don't you think I'm much of a lesbian?'

'There's more to being a lesbian than having sex with other women. It's the support and understanding, the being present. You were rarely with me even when you were on the sofa sat next to me.'

Ashley stared into the distance, then looked back at Bethany.

'Perhaps you're right. To be honest, although of course I'm a little sad, I've made a shift in my thinking. I've kind of decided to get out more. Be in control of my own life for once. I've organised a girly liquid lunch today, which hasn't happened for years.'

'Wow, you're actually leaving the house for something other than work or food.'

'It's the new me.'

'Good for you. Focus on who you are and what you really want. You won't be able to find anyone else, male or female, if you haven't found yourself.'

The last few boxes went in, and Bethany turned to Ashley. She held out her hand.

'Nice knowing you, Sergeant.'

'You too, Private.'

'We'll catch up soon,' said Bethany, before climbing into the cab. She waved and drove away, leaving Ashley alone in the street, hair dancing in the warm breeze, staring long after the van was out of sight.

It was still a mild morning even though rain clouds were gathering in the distance, so Ashley thought she'd treat herself to a cheeky pistachio gelato from Windows Ice Cream in town, so named because they served out of the shop's windows. She was reminded of Geoffrey when she walked past the crab shop near Windows, so she rang his phone.

'Hey, girl,' he answered.

'Geoffrey. I just wanted to say thanks for what you did.'

'No problem. Can't believe we're still alive. Shame the guy we tried to save isn't.'

'Yeah. I was wondering if you're okay for a place to crash.'

'My wife took me back.'

'No way. That's great.'

'I forgot I had nowhere to go but the truck, so I went home. She had one look at me and asked me in.'

'Perfect. I would say you deserve a second chance.'

'Funny you should say that. I was thinking about what type of person would do that to the guy on the beach. They'd have to be sick in the head. I've chatted to Homeless Bob a lot over the years and I don't reckon he'd be involved in any of that. Perhaps you guys should give him a break.'

'It's not as easy as that if Bob has Ron's blood on his clothes.'

'Maybe the killer planted it on them.'

'That is possible, but Bob wouldn't talk to us, which surely he would have done if he's innocent. He didn't even suggest that someone else did it, so he knows something.'

'Okay, mate. I know you're doing your best.'

Ashley was taking the first lick of her gelato when

the penny dropped after Geoffrey's comment. She almost spat the contents of her mouth out with annoyance. Ron had been found with a needle mark in his arm, but the tox screen was clear. She now knew it wasn't an injection mark.

It was a withdrawal point.

61

Ashley left the house at pace to make sure she got to the pub at twelve. Oliver from next door was at the upstairs window, which she assumed was his bedroom. He opened the window and yelled down.

'Are you coming to the game?'

'What game?' she replied.

Kids struggle to hide their emotions, and Oliver was no different. He pouted.

'You promised.'

Ashley dredged her memory for the conversation, which was buried under heaped piles of police work.

'Does it start at three?'

'It starts at two.'

'Doesn't your mum come back most weekends?'

The young lad pouted.

'She's trying, but she's busy with an important case. I told you that.'

Ashley was aware time was ticking away.

'I'm sorry, Oliver, but I have a big case too, and I've made plans. How about next weekend?'

Oliver's face scrunched up, and he shook his head. 'You're all the same.'

Ashley opened her mouth, but Oliver slammed the window shut. Feeling rotten, she began the walk into town. She was a few minutes late when she arrived. The Wellington, aka The Welly, had been a place where she drank on and off ever since she'd returned to Cromer, coming here to play pool and darts, and the family team who ran it were always welcoming.

Ashley was excited and nervous about socialising with the girls, and she paused at the entrance doors and removed her coat. She tightened her chunky belt and shifted her yellow polka-dot dress around her shoulders. It was easy to understand how her neighbour, Arthur, had created a prison for himself by not venturing out. Her confidence had dwindled with not challenging herself to new experiences. She took a deep breath and stepped inside.

There were only a couple of old timers at the bar. They peered back at her through rheumy eyes.

'Shut the door!' they shouted in unison.

Ashley did.

'I needed to let your farts out,' she said when she was standing next to them.

The older guy of the two, who looked around ninety, gave her a gummy smile.

'Good job. I could barely breathe.'

Leona and Simone came swinging through from the back. They managed the bar now, although Ashley was old enough to remember when their parents ran it.

'Ash! What a nice surprise,' said Leona, who was made up to the nines. 'You look well.'

'You, too. We're having a ladies' catch-up.'

'No problem. What you having?'

Ashley ordered a Pinot Grigio that arrived in a bowl a goldfish could have got lost in. Bhavini came in next, all full of beans in a cream suit, looking as if she should be in Milan. Ashley bought her a mocktail. Then Hector arrived. Ashley had asked him to come in the end. He'd said that he wouldn't come if it was girls only, but she'd said he smelled like a woman anyway, so it was fine. Jan, Sal and Barry had agreed to work.

Hector asked for a single malt whisky, no ice, then leaned on the bar in loose jeans, a red and black checked shirt, and a buff leather jacket. He looked as if he'd been drinking there all his life.

The paramedic, Joan, turned up at the same time as the pathologist, Michelle, both dressed in blue jeans and nice blouses, and both had made an effort with their hair.

They linked arms and laughed together as they approached the bar.

'Two Fosters,' said Michelle when asked. 'Pints!'

They were in such good spirits that Ashley would have put money on them having been elsewhere if it hadn't been so early.

The final arrival was Emma. She had a checked shirt on too, and a cowboy hat. She even strolled in a bit like John Wayne. Her make-up was spot-on, and Ashley realised what a pretty girl she was when she wasn't looking exhausted. The two old men were getting off their bar stools when she reached them. They both looked up at her without expression, then walked past her in a line, giving her a mock salute.

'Howdy,' the older one said.

'Gulping or sipping whisky, Emma?' asked Ashley.

'Sorry,' she replied. 'Should I take it off?'

'Your hat? Heck no. One of those two has been rustling farts, so shoot him if you find out who it was.'

'I'll have a dry rosé if they've got it.'

'That's not very wild west.'

'I'm actually a damsel in distress, but the clothing doesn't suit me.'

Ashley had foolishly wasted time wondering whether everyone would get on. The noise in the bar went up a notch immediately. More regulars came in. She recognised a few who waved at her. Geoffrey arrived and bought a drink next to them. He checked Emma out, which made her blush, and said a quick hello to Ashley.

When he'd gone, Emma turned to Ashley and whispered in her ear.

'I used to dress like this all the time. It was my thing, you know, for going out. I'm six feet tall and nearly twenty stones, so what was the point in trying to hide? You ought to have seen me line dancing. Men loved it. I was never short of dates.'

Her smile slid away from her face.

'My husband told me to grow up. He said this get-up looks silly on a woman my age, and now, despite my size, I feel invisible.'

Ashley put an arm around her waist.

'You look fabulous. I'm jealous, but let's not tell

each other our sad stories today.'

Ashley kept hold of her and shouted out to the others.

'Emma's round. Please take note of her amazing hat!'

They all cheered and once they had another drink, they moved to the end of the pub and sat around a big table. Ashley loved this room with the large windows, high ceilings and huge fireplace. It still had a traditional pub vibe. Ashley hated that places like this all over the country were quietly and steadily locking their doors at closing time for good.

Memories flooded through the walls at her. She'd brought Rick Jones here. A shadowy image of him playing darts and grinning at her after each shot. Both punch drunk with love, or so she'd thought.

'Where have you gone to?' asked Hector.

'Drowning in the past.'

'I think we've had enough drowning for one week.'

'Ash has got a cheek,' said a flushed Emma, next to her. 'She just told me off for being gloomy and telling sad tales.'

'Perhaps we should all share a secret or a personal memory with each other. It'll be a tie that binds, like the fellowship in *The Lord of the Rings*. Maybe it's a chance to get something off your chest, too. A problem shared and all that.'

'Ooh,' said Bhavini, stopping her conversation with Michelle dead. 'Are you starting us off, Hector?'

'I can if you like.'

'No, I'll go first,' said Joan, who was already halfway through her second drink. 'I wear nappies.'

There was a quiet pause.

'Do you mean for medical reasons, or as a kinky thing?' asked Bhavini, with a straight face.

The table erupted into gales of laughter.

'And I've got false teeth,' said Joan when they'd calmed down.

'My husband's a right cunt!' bellowed Emma, who then put her hand over her mouth as though she couldn't believe such a word had come out of it.

'Mine, too!' shouted a female voice from a table near them.

They all hooted again, especially when a man hollered out from the bar, 'Oy, I heard that.'

'Ah, I get what we're doing now,' said Bhavini. 'My turn. You know my fiancé?'

Most of them nodded. She was often showing pictures of them in their workout gear looking all loved up and pleased with themselves.

'I'm not sure he really counts as a fiancé.'

Ashley held her breath while she waited for the revelation. Bhavini spoke down to the table, but they all heard her.

'Seeing as he's already happily married.'

The silence continued for a few seconds. It was Emma who knew what to say.

'Things will work out. You'll see.'

'I say drop the bastard. He doesn't deserve you,' replied Joan.

Michelle had been looking around the table with wide eyes, as though she had something truly terrible to reveal.

'I haven't had sex for three years,' she said.

'Me neither,' said Joan.

The two women linked hands.

'I haven't had good sex for much longer than that,' said Emma.

Hector knocked his second whisky down in one, then dropped his tumbler on the table with a clunk.

'I've never had sex.'

There was a brief pause, before Joan grinned widely, showing off her too-straight teeth.

'You're in luck!' she hollered. 'There's help for you here.'

Michelle went to the bar and bought another round of drinks. When she came back, Ashley felt the collective gaze upon her. It was her turn to share. There were numerous nasties in her past, but at that moment, her life was being dominated by one in particular. She looked around the table and shrugged.

'I can't have children.'

There was no pause or quiet that time. Hector put both hands on her arm next to him and the rest of them rose as one and gave her a group hug. And for the first time in quite a while, it felt as if things were going to be all right.

Everyone took a turn in getting a round. There were some soft drinks and coffees, but most present were becoming wobbly. Ashley wondered for the life of her why she'd decided she'd been better off staying at home.

Hector tapped another empty glass on the table.

'I'd just like to say thank you for getting me drunk. It's been a while.'

'It's been grand,' said Joan. 'But the afternoon's still young.'

Emma gave a whoop, then broke into a fit of giggles.

That's the spirit, thought Ashley. She was about to let out an appreciative cheer when she caught sight of the clock on the wall. It was ten past two. She looked out of the window at the drizzle.

62

As Oliver Robinson trudged back onto the field after half-time he heard a voice from the touchline.

'Keep going, you're doing well.'

It was the old guy, Arthur, from a few doors up. At least he'd bothered to come.

Oliver's team was losing by a goal. The opposition was a point above them at the top of the league, and Oliver was desperate to take something from the game, but he'd struggled to get involved so far. They were too organised.

The ball flew high from a free kick towards the corner where he knew one of their team's weaker players was. Oliver chased after it. There was a group of the visiting parents in that corner.

'Clear it, Johnny,' a woman shouted. 'Clear it!'

Oliver steamed towards him.

'Now, Johnny!'

As Oliver arrived, Johnny clipped the ball over his head. In his frustration, Oliver let his slide in the mud continue and took the lad's legs out.

'Hey, Ref! Book him,' a man bellowed.

Oliver looked up into the referee's face.

'I slipped,' said Oliver. 'It's the rain.'

'You get one slip for free. Next slip gets booked, or sent off,' said the ref, pulling him to his feet.

The second half was an up-and-down affair with few chances. The parents seemed to be getting more and more vocal. For the first time in his life, Oliver sensed the tension in the air, and, as he was his team's top goalscorer, the pressure was on his shoulders. The minutes ticked down, and they were still trailing by a goal.

After a messy corner, the ball broke out to Oliver, who was on the edge of the area. He instinctively kicked the ball hard towards the top corner of the goal. His eyes widened as it arced towards the net, then ricocheted off the crossbar for a goal kick. Oliver cursed as he ran back to the centre circle. The moisture in his eyes wasn't just from the weather.

'Chin up, Oliver,' called out a female voice.

Oliver glanced up but had to wipe his eyes to see who'd shouted it. Yep, it was a tall woman in a cowboy hat. When he got closer, he could make out his neighbour, Ashley, in a line of other women. He ran and stood in front of them.

'You can do it, son!' shrieked an older lady with long, wet, grey hair.

'Keep going,' said a pretty Asian woman with brown skin like his. They weren't dressed to watch a kids' football game in the rain, but they seemed oblivious to the heavy drops that had started to fall. Next to Arthur, on the end, was a cool guy who resembled a movie star.

'Head up, Oliver. There's still time,' he yelled.

Funnily enough, all of them were holding white coffee cups with Doggie Diner on the side. A lady who looked Chinese was pouring something into hers from a clear bottle. Oliver caught Ashley's eye, and she grinned at him, giving him a thumbs up.

'You've got time. Do your best.'

Oliver set his jaw and was about to focus back on the match when a familiar figure arrived next to the handsome guy. It was his mother in her work coat. She waved energetically at him. He took a deep breath and returned his attention to the game.

The goal kick was punted into the centre of the

pitch, and he stormed towards it. After a melee in the middle, the ball squirted loose, and he was quickest. Oliver could hear the shouts and screams from the touchline as if he were within a bubble. He kicked the ball through a player's legs and raced around him. Oliver wrong-footed the final defender, then, focusing on the part of the goal where he'd just hit the cross-bar, he pulled back his leg.

The goalie charged off his line and hurtled forward to close the angle, but he'd fallen for Oliver's ruse. Oliver slipped the ball to his left and circled the sprawling kid. Then, with all his might, he lashed the football into the middle of the empty net.

Oliver wheeled around, then dashed back to his half of the pitch. He pumped his fist while sprinting towards the people who had come to watch him. He jumped high into the air.

And the crowd went wild.

63

There was a large, solid presence in bed next to her when Ashley woke up. She could hear its heavy breathing, while its radiated heat warmed her back. She almost dared not look around at who it was. Last night's antics filtered into her brain. They'd bought wine, and all returned to her house. When they'd realised Ashley had no food in her house, teetotal Bhavini had driven into town to Artisan 2 Go on Church Street to order what she called the world's best halloumi fries. She hadn't been wrong.

Ashley rolled over.

'How ya feelin', cowboy?' she asked.

Emma lay fully dressed, boots and all, with her

Stetson resting on her chest as though laid out for a trip to Boot Hill. She slowly raised one eyelid.

'Kill me,' she whispered.

Ashley giggled.

'Come on, you can't feel that bad. We stopped drinking after the food.'

Emma rolled off the bed and stood up.

'Actually, you're right. Nothing a glass of juice and fried meat can't sort out. It's the first night I've had away from my kids in years and I slept like a log.' She grinned. 'I had a really good day.'

'Me too. I'm looking forward to your wedding.'

'My what?' Emma collapsed into a fit of giggles. 'Oh, yeah. It's not a bad idea. Arthur's a great dancer and more fun than the numpty I'm married to.'

Ashley smiled, although there was a bit too much vehemence in the statement for her to laugh. Everyone else had left the night before, so they each took a turn in the shower, then got dressed. Emma's car was in town, so they walked to fetch it. Ashley heard Emma's stomach rumble, so they sneaked into Browne's tea room on Bond Street and grabbed one of their amazing breakfast baguettes for the journey.

They nipped to Emma's so she could put a suit on and it was dead on nine when they arrived at the station.

Ashley signed in to her computer. Sal had emailed the team about work he'd done at the week-end, but she read one from Kettle first, which asked her to see him asap. She went straight to his office.

'Morning, good Sunday?' she asked.

'No, I struggled to turn off with Peter in the cells. Wherever we look, he's coming up clean. His house is spotless. Apart from the call here to say he'd visit the station, he's not used his phone since we put him on leave. His mobile doesn't appear on local masts, either. I suspect it was turned off. Peter gave us signed authorisation to check his phone and bank records.'

'They don't sound like the actions of a guilty man.'

'Unless the guilty man knows that they won't reveal anything.'

'True.'

'We're going to release him.'

'Okay. I take it no reports incriminated him at all.'

'No, obviously his DNA is on the database anyway, so it would have been noticed on any of the tests, but he'd know not to leave evidence. Have you read your emails?'

'Only the one from you.'

'Bob's DNA is present on the T-shirt, but the trainers have virtually no organic matter on them at all except for the blood. They must have been washed at a high temperature.'

Ashley told him about her theory that blood might have been squirted on Bob's clothes to incriminate him.

'Great. Sounds like someone else we'll need to release as well.'

'I assume there were no further incidents over the weekend.'

'No, but there's more conflicting evidence. Sal came in for a few hours yesterday and found more footage of Eddy in town walking around normally.'

'You mean not limping?'

'No, sorry, he was limping, but Sal analysed his gait. He has more of a collapsing-knee-type limp.'

'So?'

'The grainy footage of the person we believe responsible for the graffiti has a stiff, straight-legged limp.'

'Oh, Jesus. That doesn't help. Is it obviously different?'

'The CCTV is too poor quality to be clear, and it might just bother him in a different way at different times, but it confuses the issue.'

'I don't suppose he was in a big coat with a hood.'

'Nope.'

'How about authorisation for surveillance of Peter?'

'Not a chance.'

'Okay. I've had a thought. Let's get CCTV from the train. We know when Peter went to Salthouse. Let's see if he was in disguise.'

'It's worth a try, but the train company aren't the fastest at providing info.'

'Look, you were as worried as I was about what he's going to do when we let him go. Let's build our presence in Cromer, so if something kicks off, we're on the scene. If he's planning anything, we can monitor the CCTV in real time. If we happen to see Peter running through town with a tin of paint or a machete, we can put it down to luck.'

'That's a good idea. You know, I thought he was guilty, but I rang the widow he visited myself. She insisted Peter was a great guy.'

'Was he at hers the whole time?'

'Yes. She said he took long walks, but that's it. He came and went as he pleased.'

'Jeez. We're going to have to search her house as well.'

'It's happening today. I doubt she'll drop him in it. Apparently, he's been helping financially for years.

Peter told her while he was there that if anything happened to him, she'd be provided for in his will.'

'That sounds like he's expecting trouble.'

'I agree, and it's also the behaviour of a man who has his affairs in order.'

Peter Ibson was released at 11 a.m. He thanked them for their hospitality, got in his car, and drove away. Ashley and Hector followed shortly after, as she wanted to have a chat with Hector over a coffee, then talk with Candy Sweet's mum and her boyfriend, who had left the hospital. Bhavini and Jan had spoken to them on the ward, but she had a lot more background on the case now.

In particular, she had questions about Kenneth Markham. She'd dismissed him from being involved earlier because of his health, but she hadn't actually seen him in the wheelchair. It was also weird that Brad Garrett said that he'd never heard of him. Kenneth had told them he was okay with being cast aside, but if he'd fallen for Foxy as Peter had, that might have been a lie.

When they reached Cromer, they waited at the traffic lights next to Bann Thai.

'That's the best Thai food I've had in this country. I'll take you one day if you hang around long enough.'

Hector smiled, but made no comment.

Ashley found a parking space opposite The Gangway café on the edge of Cromer centre. They did the best cocktails at night, but during the day it had a busy hipster vibe, which Ashley enjoyed being part of.

Hector pulled himself up on a stool at the window.

'Is it too early for a Margarita?' she asked him.

'It's about a month too early for how I feel.'

She told him about her suspicions about Kenneth.

'Hmm, would you remember the name of every single person from your school sixth form over thirty years later?'

'No, maybe not, especially if they only arrived in the sixth form, but Kenneth is unusual looking. With those teeth, he would be hard to forget.'

A young waitress appeared, full of the beauty and vitality that only youth provided.

'Morning, what can I get you folks?'

'Latte,' said Ashley.

'Double espresso, please,' said Hector.

Before she could go, Ashley stopped the waitress. 'Is it okay to ask you a question?'

'Sure.'

'I read in the paper about the deaths on Cromer beach. I bet it's a bit worrying if you live here. Are people chatting about it?'

The girl looked at them as if she'd asked her what colour coffee was.

'Er, yeah! It's everywhere. There's a seriously demented dude running around killing old folk. I even had a nightmare about it where I woke up on the beach with a bucket on my head.'

'Any theories floating around, crackpot or otherwise?'

'One of the other waitresses reckons it's the ghost of Henry Blogg.'

'Wasn't he a hero in real life, saving people in peril at sea?'

'Yeah. That's her point. She reckons he's come back to punish us for climate change.'

'Charming.'

'My other mate says it's the weird guy who goes to the library, keeps shouting at the books.'

Ashley and Hector exchanged a glance.

'Okay, what does he look like?' he asked.

'Kind of rearranged face, as though he was in an accident, and he limps around talking about the sea.'

'When did anyone last see him?'

'I saw him in there a few days ago. I'm redoing my French A level because I want to live and work in France. This town sucks.'

Ashley laughed as the girl left to serve a man at the bar. Cromer's pull weakened for her age group, but she'd be back.

'So, Eddy's still about,' said Hector. 'Where's the library?'

'It's next to the coach park on the same side of Cromer as Kenneth's house. Let's drink these coffees and nip to Felbrigg first to see Mrs Sweet, then we'll do the library. Mrs Sweet must remember Kenneth if her daughter hung around with him at senior school.'

'Perhaps he's not as useless as he made out. I assume he didn't have a record.'

'His name didn't come up on any searches, but he might never have been caught.'

The waitress came back with their drinks.

'My brother's at the local school. He's only eleven,'

she said. 'They're all obsessed with it. He says that there's a monster in the sea, and if you go down to the beach after dark, it comes out after you, and you can't escape. Your body is left on the sand in the morning, but your soul has been taken to the depths.'

Ashley nodded, but the mention of the word monster again made her think of Eddy and Kenneth. Both had unusual features, one by accident and one by nature. In poor light, perhaps torchlight, would they appear gruesome enough to be described that way? Or had someone been wearing a mask?

They drank their coffees and headed off to Felbrigg. Ashley assumed that Mrs Sweet would be at her house with having a youngster to look after in the school holidays, but she didn't want to give her a warning that she and Hector were coming to visit.

Mrs Sweet answered the door. She had the haunted face and slumped shoulders of a parent who'd recently lost a child.

'Yes.'

'Hi, I'm sorry to bother you, but we just wanted to follow up on a few lines of inquiry.'

'I take it you haven't caught who did it yet.'

'No. Our findings haven't confirmed Candy was murdered either. You said yourself she'd been struggling.'

'I think I'd have known if she was suicidal. You better come in.'

They walked into a tidy room where a young lad of about eight was colouring. He looked up and smiled at them.

'I'm Timmy, and I'm drawing a tank. Look!'

Ashley took the picture. 'Wow, that's great.'

'Yes, I'm going to blow it up.'

They took a seat on the sofa, while Mrs Sweet disappeared. Ashley was expecting a hot drink, not the photograph that was shoved under her nose a minute later.

'I was thinking about ringing you, but then I decided to leave it alone. It's not bringing Candy back, and it's rather an incriminating photo.'

Ashley analysed the photograph. The glossy paper made her suspect the picture was new, but the colours seemed from another age. It had been taken at the beach from a distance. There was a bonfire on the right of the shot, which lit up the two individuals behind and to the left of it.

Ashley recalled the photo of Foxy in the blue dress. It didn't do her justice. Foxy was all legs in tight cut-off denim jeans and a bikini top. Even from afar, she'd clearly been first in line when they were handing out figures.

The squatter girl next to her was obviously Candy. She hadn't changed much in looks or shape. Mrs Sweet was right about it being incriminating. Candy had her arms outstretched towards an unbalanced Foxy.

It looked as though Candy was shoving her into the sea.

65

Ashley passed the photograph to Hector, then looked at Mrs Sweet.

'Where did you find that?'

'Candy's boyfriend, Elliott, begged me to help clear out her stuff. He wanted to get it done, but was struggling. It was a horrible job, but, to be fair to him, he'd started and was just checking if I wanted anything.'

Mrs Sweet glanced down at Timmy. Her head and chin wobbled. Ashley noticed she had odd socks on, and there were stains down her dress.

'Can we talk in the kitchen?' asked Ashley

'Of course.'

'Carry on,' said Ashley after following Mrs Sweet into the next room.

'Candy had so little, you know? For a whole life, she had so few things. It was a squandered existence. She never functioned properly after that sodding party. Makes my blood boil when I think about it.'

Ashley looked down at the photo. She didn't want to say that maybe Candy was so consumed by guilt that she was unable to function.

'Was it in a drawer or hidden somewhere?'

Mrs Sweet glanced up, eyes sharp.

'It looks bad, but she could also be reaching out to try to save Foxy. Or they could be playing.'

'I suppose,' said Hector. 'So where was it?'

'At the bottom of her wardrobe. The funny thing is, it's the identical picture as the one I told you she received years ago, but in colour. I don't know where either came from. She was always staring at the photo that arrived not long after the party. She went mad when she found out I'd ripped it up. Elliott said Candy seemed obsessed by this one as well.'

'You don't know who took it?'

'No, Candy had a camera, but she didn't use it much. I don't remember any other pictures of that night.'

'But this photo turned up fairly recently?'

'I've no idea when exactly, but it could be why she'd been upset. I guess seeing it might have caused her to kill herself.'

'That makes sense. Does her partner know anything about it?'

'No, she would never talk about what happened.'

Mrs Sweet frowned. She swallowed and grimaced as though she'd eaten something nasty.

'The photo was one of the reasons I moved us out of Cromer so quickly. It looks so incriminating.' Her eyes narrowed, as though she'd said too much. 'Sorry, but you'll have to leave. I promised little Timmy that we'd go to McDonald's.'

'Happy Meal!' shouted Timmy from the next room.

'One last thing, Mrs Sweet. Do you remember a boy called Kenneth Markham?'

Mrs Sweet's expression didn't change.

'No, should I?'

'We understand he was a close friend of Candy's at school.'

'No, it's not ringing a bell. She only had a few mates, so I knew them all.'

'Oh, okay. That's odd. Do you recall anyone who

hung around with them who had unusually big teeth?'

Mrs Sweet's face changed instantly.

'Not Kenneth Markham,' she snarled. 'It's Keith Morecambe. And yes, I know that little cretin very well.'

66

Ashley had a sinking feeling which, judging by his face, Hector was also experiencing.

'Keith Morecambe,' whispered Ashley, as though it pained her to say it. 'We were told by the old head-teacher, Mrs Lythgoe, that his name was Kenneth Markham.'

'Is she still alive?' asked Mrs Sweet. 'I saw her a while back and she didn't even recognise me. She was very frail, so she was probably confused. It's easily done after thirty years, even without dementia.'

'Yes, but I repeated the name to Keith himself and he didn't correct me.'

'That's doesn't surprise me. He was a real bad egg, even back then. He's done time and everything.'

'He's done what?' asked Ashley.

'Yes, he moved away, but I visited his mother every now and again. We were friends for years while the kids were pally. She was so generous. Her husband had a big plot at the allotments and gave us loads of free veg. They were good people, even if their son was a little shit. Anyway, it all changed when he and Foxy progressed to further education and my Candy, Bob, and poor old Eddy got left behind.'

'What was Keith in prison for?' asked Ashley.

'Drug dealing. He got a big stretch last time because it wasn't his first offence. He was up north somewhere, maybe Manchester. His mum was upset about it, but she should have been used to it by then. He was always up to no good at school.'

'Was he dealing drugs there?' asked Hector.

'Well, I think so. I reckon it was him that got them on it. A few spliffs here and there aren't so bad, but he got that Bob on heroin, the rest on pills, and Eddy had mental health problems. He shouldn't have been taking anything. It's no wonder he went mad.'

'Could Keith have been dealing LSD?'

'He was into everything. He was devious and cunning, and he'd encourage the others to get up to stuff as well, and Bob, Candy and Eddy were all easily influenced. Keith revelled in other people's misery. But you can't choose your kid's friends. Candy was a pretty horrible teen, so any interfering in her life was only going to cause more friction. I hoped she'd grow out of it. I suppose they did because they began to detach themselves from him.'

'What about Foxy?'

Mrs Sweet paused for a moment.

'What about her?'

'Did Keith get her on drugs?'

'No, Foxy didn't need any encouragement. She was as wild and naughty as him, but she had a good heart.'

'Sorry, you said they detached themselves. Did Foxy stop being friends with Keith?'

'Foxy went to the sixth form with Keith, but she started hanging around with those posh boys. Keith didn't like it, got all jealous. As if he'd ever have had a chance with her. Because of that, Foxy stopped seeing him as much, but she kept in touch with my Candy. She was loyal, you see.'

'Yes, you said. I was wondering if Keith got angry about not being invited to that party.'

'I've no idea, but I'd say he would've been royally miffed if he'd found out that he wasn't invited. Although I suspect it was usually him who they bought their drugs off, so I'm not sure what they'd have told him if they'd still bought them from him. I always believed they'd got the LSD from the hippies that night.'

'Is it possible Ron and Ruby were just a pair of potheads?'

'They certainly did that because they often stank the beach out with it.'

Mrs Sweet wasn't daft. She pointed her finger at Ashley.

'People my age associate LSD with hippies, so maybe I jumped to the wrong conclusion. You reckon Keith did it, don't you?'

'Did what?'

'The killings. I wouldn't put it past the snidey toad. He'll blame it on someone else though.'

Ashley almost chuckled at her phrase.

'I doubt he's in good enough health to be running around on the beach and burying people,' she said.

'Why? What's wrong with him?'

'He's got a wheelchair for a start.'

Mrs Sweet leaned forward in her seat and laughed. Ashley saw her teeth move. When she looked back at Ashley, she wasn't laughing, though. She was livid.

'You fools. He lied to you. It's what he does. That chair was his mum's. I saw him pushing her up the promenade in it once. Yes, uphill.'

'What about his fibromyalgia?'

'I'll bet he doesn't have that. I chased after him with a broom once when he was young and he was soon away on his toes. Idleness was his problem. He was bloody smart, but always looking for a shortcut. He's your man. Either he murdered my Candy, or he sent that photo to her and as good as murdered her. You better lock him up or I'll kill him.'

'I don't suppose his mother's the type who'd dish the dirt on her son?'

'No, probably not, but it wouldn't matter, anyway. I went to Vicky's funeral a little while back.'

Ashly choked back a comment to let the woman continue.

'I bet his inheritance was why Keith came back. She'd been terminal for a while. He'd see it as easy money. Vicky and her husband owned and ran the guest house next to their property until he died, so I assume that's his now.'

'When did Keith's dad pass away?'

'They found him dead in his allotment about eighteen months ago. Some kind of embolism. Fit bloke, he was. He ran the guest house with his wife and a manager, but Keith's mother went rapidly downhill after he died.'

Ashley and Hector thanked Mrs Sweet for her

time and said they'd be in touch shortly. She was one of the few witnesses from that period who was alive and sane. Mrs Sweet called Timmy through to say goodbye and he passed Ashley his drawing at the door.

'Here. It's for you,' he said.

Ashley looked down at the picture. The tank was on fire.

67

Ashley waited until she was sitting back in the car with Hector before she swore.

'That oily little git has had us for mugs.'

'Possibly a murdering little git.'

'Yes, look, I need a few moments to get my head around all this. Ring Sal at the office and ask him to do a background check on Keith Morecambe.'

Ashley rubbed her temples. It made sense for it to have been Keith. They'd been struggling for motive all the way through, but maybe it was just good old-fashioned jealousy that had been simmering on the stove for over thirty years. Perhaps it was fortuitous timing that Keith came back for his mum at the same time that Eddy was released. Not fortuitous for Eddy, obviously.

The Bob angle was odd, though. How was he involved?

Ashley let her mind wander until Hector finished talking on the phone, then announced what she'd been thinking.

'Right,' she said. 'Bob, Eddy and Candy were all easily influenced by Keith. That's what Candy's mother said. Bob returned to hard drugs about a year ago. Detective training isn't necessary to work out who was responsible for that.'

Hector was up to speed straight away.

'A heavy heroin habit is expensive, so Bob would have started needing more than he could afford. Who knows what he was forced to do to get his fix? Same as Eddy and Candy. Keith might have talked them into doing various things with ease. Maybe by giving them drugs. He could easily have persuaded Candy to visit the beach with him, then killed her. Or perhaps he got her so off her face that she drowned.'

'Perhaps Keith provided the drugs for the beach party knowing he wasn't invited, then sneakily went anyway. None of them could remember anything, so he might have deliberately overdosed them.'

Ashley recalled Michelle's comments about too much LSD. More madness and worse flashbacks.

'The thing,' said Hector, 'is proving it. If he got others to do his dirty work, then his hands might be clean. Mrs Sweet more or less said he was too smart for his own good. We might need Eddy or Bob on the stand pointing at Keith, and neither of them will make strong witnesses.'

'Keith lives close to the seafront as well. If he'd wanted to, he could have just walked down the white steps to the beach, then strolled along to the place where the killings occurred. There'd be no CCTV.' She paused, remembering the point of the phone call. 'Sorry, what was Keith's previous? Let me guess. He has a long record.'

'It's not too bad. Possession of class A and B, low-level dealing, but then he got stung for eighteen years. Looks like he was caught with a significant amount.'

'Wow, eighteen years, so he'd have served nine in-side with a further nine on licence. Is he still under supervision now?'

'No, it finished a year ago. Maybe he stayed up north to finish his licence, then came back when he had a clean slate.'

'Yes, he probably didn't know his mum was ill.

Cheeky sod. He gave us the impression she was in the house.'

'There's something else. There was a fire in the early hours of this morning. One of the beach huts got burned out.'

'Was it the one Eddy hired out? Or, as I'm now thinking, Keith made Eddy hire out.'

'No, it was four beach huts up from that. Sal checked the register. It was privately owned. It belonged to a Victoria Morecambe.'

'Oh, no. That's where I saw that name. Great.'

'Yes, Sal realised straight away when I mentioned Keith Morecambe.'

'There goes the evidence, and it's worse than that.'

'In what way?'

'Keith had the foresight to hire the second hut in Eddy's name. Clever Keith must have suspected we'd look into who owned them. Eddy's was a decoy. No wonder there was nothing inside Eddy's one. Keith used his mother's and when he saw us searching Eddy's hut, he torched the evidence.'

'Dylan Crabb rang in as well. He checked the serial number of the wheelchair which was at the step-down place. It matches the one that was next to Brad in the sea.'

'That makes me think Keith asked Eddy to take it,

which means Keith lied about how often he saw Eddy.'

'Right, we'd better visit Keith. Do we call for support?'

Ashley's phone rang.

'Detective Sergeant Knight speaking.'

'It's Keith Morecambe!'

Ashley almost dropped the phone at the hissed voice. Instead, she put it on loudspeaker. It registered that he'd used his real name. She could hear Keith hyperventilating.

'Yes, Keith, calm down.'

'It's Peter Ibson and Eddy.'

'What is?'

'They're here. Eddy's been staying at mine for a few days. Peter came around about ten minutes ago wanting to speak to him. I told him that Eddy wasn't very well. He's not been taking his medicine. Peter pushed past me, and they started screaming at each other. Then it got violent.'

'What happened? Is anyone hurt?'

'Yes, Peter's been knocked out. Eddy's gone completely insane. Keeps bellowing about there having to be seven, whatever that means. He sparked out Peter, then crouched next to him and shouted that Peter has to return to the sea. I think he's going to drown him.'

'Where is he now?'

'Hang on. I'll peek around the door. They were in the kitchen.' The line went quiet for three seconds, before a breathless Keith returned. 'Eddy's lifted Peter onto my wheelchair. He's taken Peter's shoes off and removed his shoelaces. Wait. He's tying Peter's wrists to the chair. Shit. He's seen me.'

There was another couple of seconds of silence.

'No, don't, Eddy. Stop. I didn't do anything.'

An inhuman wail rent the air, then a scream of pain, followed by the smash of breaking glass. Loud, steady breathing came onto the line. A burst of static blared out of the phone.

Then the line went dead.

68

Hector shoved the car into gear and was about to screech away.

'Hold your horses,' said Ashley. 'Uniform are going to have to sort this. It's unlikely we'll get the armed response unit here in time, so it'll have to be a Taser team from Norwich.'

'I suppose he's heading to the section of the beach where the other murders took place. It's lucky it's overcast, or the sands would be packed.'

Hector licked his lips.

'What do we do?' he asked.

'Calm down, for a start.'

Ashley pulled out her phone and rang Emma.

'Hi. Are you and Jan still in town?'

'Yes.'

'Then head down to the area of the beach where Ron, Ruby and Candy died. With extreme caution. It's probably Eddy's on his way there. Ring Control for the latest just before you arrive.'

She cut the call.

'You may proceed,' she said to Hector.

Hector smiled, put the car into gear again and moved swiftly away.

Ashley called Control and gave them a quick update.

'All received, Sergeant. Anything else?'

'I need the closest Taser team to attend Keith Morecambe's property. Barry Hooper is also in town. Ask him to meet us there, too.'

'How long for backup?' asked Hector when she'd hung up.

'We're in luck. There's a Taser unit just finished at Bacton. A traffic cop on his motorbike is floating around this side of Norwich, too, so maybe twenty minutes for both. We need someone in PPE in case this is some kind of ploy. Who knows what's at the scene? Eddy might still be there.'

Ashley knew that as soon as the news hit the air-waves, any uniforms within thirty miles would head straight for Cromer. That was the way it had always been, but at least uniform would have stab vests, PAVA spray and batons. All Ashley had to protect her was choice language, and she wasn't sure Hector even had that.

Fifteen minutes later, they rounded the corner for Morrisons' petrol station and drove along the road next to the promenade. She half expected to see screaming holidaymakers fleeing the beach, but, apart from two strolling dog walkers and an elderly couple with linked arms, it was postcard still.

'I just realised,' said Ashley. 'I've been thinking this madness started with Eddy's release, but all of this coincides with Keith's return. He's been like a virus steadily infecting everyone. Maybe Peter got a photo like Candy did, which drove both of them off the rails. That's the thing Peter accused Brad of sending.'

'Wouldn't they have known it was Keith who sent it?'

'No, I don't think so. Remember, Peter didn't have a clue what went on at the beach, and he was still confused with events when we spoke to him, but our conversation dislodged something, and that's why he came to see Keith. The whole county's been looking for Eddy. I bet Keith's had him in his spare room.'

Hector was parking up outside Keith's house when Ashley's phone rang. It was Control.

'DS Knight.'

'Hi, ringing to inform you we've had a member of the public contact us after seeing a man pushing a wheelchair with a person in it who was bleeding profusely from the head.'

'Location?'

'Last sighted at the entrance to the pier.'

Ashley thought for a moment. Was Eddy on the way down to the beach? Then she recalled the sand. He hated it. Eddy was going to take Peter to the end of the pier and throw him off it.

'ETA for the first Taser team?'

'Eleven minutes. Traffic officer on bike to your location, four minutes. No Taser.'

'Okay, redirect the first unit to Cromer pier, sirens off. DC Fade and I are outside Keith Morecambe's property.' She gave the address again. 'We don't expect there to be any trouble, so we'll redirect the ambulance if it's not needed. If the situation is stable, we'll head to the pier. I will advise. DC Barry Hooper has just pulled up behind me.'

'Understood. Out.'

Ashley looked across at Hector.

'Ready?'

'Born ready.'

'Come on, then.'

They left the car and trotted up to the front of the house. Hector rang the bell, while Ashley had a sneaky look through the letter box.

'Keith's on the floor, motionless. Nobody else in sight,' she said.

She rested her hand on the door handle and slowly pushed down. It was unlocked. She eased the door open and stepped back so only her head was visible to anyone in the house. It looked as if Keith was on his own. There was a smashed picture frame on his stomach and a puddle of blood that would have come from the gash on the right side of his forehead. His eyes were closed.

She strode in and put two fingers on his wrist, quickly finding a strong pulse. Keith groaned.

'Mr Morecambe. Keith! Wake up.'

Ashley moved the frame off him. It was a picture of the book *Treasure Island*. At the bottom were the words, 'Fifteen men on a dead man's chest'.

Keith jerked himself up to a sitting position and Ashley supported his back.

'Take your time, Keith.'

'Has he gone?' he spluttered.

Barry checked the rear of the house, and Hector

glanced in the lounge. They both shook their heads at her. Ashley's eye was drawn to the other framed print on the lounge door, which had on it the words, 'What will we do with a drunken sailor?' She glanced down at Keith.

'Yes, it looks like it. Are you okay?'

'I think so. He hit me with that picture, tied Peter in the wheelchair, then shoved him into the street. He's going to the sea. You'd better get after him.'

'It's in hand.'

She glanced outside at the sound of a motorbike pulling up, then across at Barry.

'Got your cuffs?'

'Always.'

'Good, although I doubt you'll need them. Ring for an ambulance, but first arrest Keith Morecambe on suspicion of murder.'

69

Ashley and Hector left the house. She had a word with the officer outside to follow, then jumped back in their car. It was less than half a mile to the slip road down to the promenade. Ironically, it was the one Eddy had driven down and crashed all those years ago. There were far more people down there than she expected, but Hector cruised to the bottom with the motorbike's flashing lights in front of them, grabbing people's attention.

A police estate car appeared at the top of the slip road, then another. The cavalry was here, and they headed down to them.

'Park here, Hector, across the path,' she said, leaping from the car.

The motorcyclist dismounted.

'What do you want, Sarge?'

'No one goes past the car towards the pier. Okay? No one.'

'Understood.'

She knew Eddy had gone onto the pier when there was a high-pitched scream in the distance from that direction.

Ashley waited until the four uniformed officers had arrived and got out of their cars. It felt like a monster movie as she watched people on the pier fleeing towards the exit. Half the pier was featureless apart from two small pavilions halfway along for visitors to admire the view. At the end was a walkway around the theatre building. That was also the access to the lifeboat station, which had a ramp into the sea. Eddy had to be on the other side of the theatre because he was out of sight. She dreaded to think what had caused the scream.

'Okay, team. I'm DS Ashley Knight. Listen up.'

There were two young male officers whom she vaguely knew, but the Taser team had been in uniform for a long time. Jack must have been in twenty years and Sally not far off that. After a quick update, they all jogged to the pier.

The narrow entrance was between two domed

shops. She sent one of the non-Taser officers to the beach steps to stop anyone else approaching from that direction, but they didn't have to worry too much. Apart from the odd gawker, panic was spreading, and people were escaping. Ashley put the other younger PC on the entrance to make sure nobody came down the cliff steps to enter the pier.

She called Control and gave them a final update on what she was planning and suggested any further officers arriving should be sent to the end of the pier, where she expected to find Eddy, and hopefully Peter.

She ran up the steps with Hector and the two officers with Tasers. Massive fluffy clouds of grey and white were hurtling across the sky, so the sun shone down and lit them up as though under a spotlight, then plunged them into gloom. The sea seemed alive with long, frothy breakers dashing to the beach. Ashley glanced between the wooden planks at the turbulent water, which swirled dark and deadly, windblown and choppy below.

The pier was now empty except for a lone elderly man running surprisingly fast towards them.

'There's a psychopath back there. He's out of control.'

Ashley stopped in front of him and produced her warrant card.

'Police. Stop, please. Where is he?'

'He's at the far edge, behind the theatre. There's a man in a wheelchair, but he's tied to it and looks injured. The big guy's crazy. He's shouting at the water. I thought he was going to kill me.'

'Give your details to the officer at the entrance,' said Ashley.

The old guy scanned the officers one by one, shook his head, then ran to the exit.

'Four of us will have to be enough, but we'll need to split up,' said Ashley. 'Sally and Hector go around the theatre on the left-side footpath, Jack and I will take the right. If we wait for further backup, Peter will be in the drink. Taser officer leads,' she said for Hector's benefit. The other two would know their roles.

They strode towards the theatre, their footsteps echoing on the wooden boards. Through the gaps, Ashley could hear the waves slapping the support pilings. Sally and Hector peeled off to the left footpath, and she kept to the right behind Jack.

The eerie silence was broken by a raging and roaring voice. It had to be Eddy. The fury was brought clearly to them on the stiff breeze. Then it went quiet, as if even the seabirds knew to leave.

She thought of calling Dylan for his support, but

this was no place for a civilian, and it seemed they were out of time.

Jack edged around the side of the wooden theatre wall, Taser raised.

'Police!' he shouted. 'Kneel on the floor.'

Ashley heard Jack curse. She looked over his shoulder and realised why. Eddy was at the corner of the pier as it curved around to the entrance to the lifeboat station. He wore a big black anorak. Perhaps the one he'd been scrawling the graffiti in. The wheelchair was facing out to sea. Eddy had a hand on Peter's neck, but his other hand was pointing and prodding down at the waves. Peter was slumped forward.

'Eddy!' shouted Ashley.

Eddy stiffened. He swivelled around and looked first at Hector and Sally on one side of him, then at Ashley and Jack. Eddy's huge eyes were filled with horror, his mouth a cruel jagged line. The flies to his trousers were undone, as was one of his shoelaces. His free hand reached out like a claw, scratching the air. He blinked slowly, as though trying to clear his mind, but instead he released a mighty roar.

Ashley's options were limited. The Taser prongs wouldn't go through coat material that thick. Tasers could also be used as stun guns, but the basis of those was pain, not paralysis, because the point of impact was much narrower. Whatever was driving Eddy to act in this way, whether it be drugs or madness, would likely not be subdued by pain. It might even enrage him.

At least Eddy didn't seem to have a weapon.

Ashley glanced at Sally and Jack, who'd understood the situation quicker than she had. They'd holstered their Taser guns and grabbed their batons, which had been flicked to extend. They held them down by their legs to avoid instant escalation, but Eddy was beyond picking up on subtle signals. Even PAVA spray would be of no use. More would hit themselves with the onshore breeze.

'Calm down, Eddy. Let's talk,' shouted Ashley.

Eddy's head twitched twice to the right.

'No, it's too late,' he bellowed. 'I-I—'

Eddy wiped the back of his hand across his forehead. Ashley realised he was crying. His teeth clamped together in an ugly grimace. Wild eyes rolled while his neck strained. It was as if he was trying to escape himself.

Ashley glimpsed the scared boy who life had left behind. The young lad who stood no chance.

Eddy's head bent in her direction, and his eyes returned to focus. His cheeks raised in half a smile. He spoke slowly but clearly.

'I don't want to die.'

Ashley edged along the railing, which came up to just below her shoulder. Jack had crept forward, glued to the wall of the theatre. Sally and Hector closed in.

'You don't have to die,' said Ashley. 'I know this isn't you. It's okay to be scared. We'll get you safe and warm.'

Peter stirred in the chair, and his head moved in her direction.

'You don't want to hurt Peter, do you? He's your friend.'

At that moment, the sun shone down on Eddy, and for a second Ashley thought the peace that appeared on his face was him calming down, but the smile fell. The snarl returned. Eddy noticed how close they were.

His jabbing finger rose to taunt her. Words rumbled from deep within his chest.

'There must be seven.'

He reached down into Peter's lap and pulled out what appeared to be a gym weight. The same type that had secured Brad to the sand. Eddy leaned back,

ROSS GREENWOOD

then casually clubbed Peter around the head with it. Peter slumped to the side.

Jack moved forward, truncheon raised, at the same time as Sally. Eddy brought the hand that held the weight up behind his head.

Sally crouched lower with her truncheon poised behind her back.

Eddy twisted and flung the weight. Not at Sally, but at Jack, where it thudded into his nose. Blood sprayed from Jack's face, and he hit the floor.

'No-o-o!' roared Eddy, scratching his hair with both hands. 'He must die!'

He spun to the chair as Sally stepped forward. He opened his stance, squatted, then grabbed under the arms of the wheelchair and, with a mighty howl, lifted it up and rested the handles on the railing. Sally pounded his back with her baton, but it was as effective as hitting a steel drum.

Ashley watched in horror as Eddy began to upend the wheelchair, so it, and the man inside, would plunge into the waiting depths. Hector leapt forward and seized the handle of the chair closest to him. Ashley rushed over and grasped Eddy's arm, which was hard as iron, and tried to yank him away. Despite their efforts, the chair edged past its tipping point.

Out of the corner of her eye, she saw Sally bend

and hammer the baton into the back of one of Eddy's knees. He half collapsed with another roar and fell towards Ashley. Hector was straining with all of his might, but the chair was winning their battle. Sally grabbed the other side and halted its descent. Peter opened his eyes and cried out, looking like a crazed king, raised on a mad throne.

Eddy maintained his balance. He pulled Ashley into a lover's embrace. His hand gripped her throat. The gaze that burned into her was devoid of sense, absent of reason. There was no pity.

'The sea must have what she wants,' he roared into her face.

His teeth bared into what might have been a smile. He spat his words out.

'So the sea shall have you.'

70

Ashley brought her left fist across in a sweeping blow and clubbed Eddy above his ear. His hand released her throat, but he immediately wrapped both arms tight around her back, crushing her ribcage. She gasped as the air was forced from her chest. Her eyes widened as she realised what he was about to do.

Ashley shoved at his shoulders to make space to breathe. She inched upwards but his grip tightened further. Blood pounded in Ashley's head and her heart hammered.

She felt herself being lifted as he stepped onto the bottom rung of the railing. Then he rolled them both over the side.

Ashley snatched at the top rail as they were suspended for a second above the crashing waves, but she was powerless to stop the combined weight of their fall. Time slowed as she braced for impact. She hauled in a huge breath. Her brain reeled at the shock as they plunged down into the Devil's Throat.

They crashed into the surface horizontally and sank beneath the waves. Straight away, the violent tug and pull from the current embraced her as the swarming sea surged around the pillars that held up the pier. The crushing hug from Eddy remained.

They were buffeted onto a pillar. Ashley felt the jar as the impact went through Eddy's arms. She opened her eyes. The water seemed a murky green with visibility down to less than a metre, which meant all she could see was Eddy's blurred face. Determined eyes bored into hers. Ashley tried to wedge her fingernails into those dark pits, but he scrunched them shut.

She kicked her legs, but Eddy was frozen still, and they started to sink. She glanced up as the light dwindled, her chest tightening as her lungs complained. A wave washed overhead, but the turbulence and the sunlight, which lit up the frothing water, both struggled to penetrate the depths.

They bumped into another pillar. She grabbed the protruding end of a huge metal nail and tried to hang on, but it was greasy and slimy. Ashley remembered her penknife. She reached into her suit pocket and pulled it out, managing to open it between their faces as Eddy and she swirled in a crazed dance. The bubbles she'd been releasing from her mouth, which was a technique she'd learned from diving, were few now. Her lungs screamed as they descended towards the stony sea floor.

She yanked her arm back to drive the blunt knife into Eddy's throat. His eyes blinked open. They were human and seeing again, as though the cold and quiet down there had brought him round. The grasp around her slackened, and she felt his hands move to her armpits. She experienced his power for the final time as he shoved her upwards, causing him to vanish to the depths.

Ashley looked down once, as Eddy slid from sight. She kicked out again, but her strength had gone. The sunlight speckled the surface above, but down in her silent world, it seemed miles away. Her head felt as if it would explode. Her body craved air. She instinctively opened her mouth. The seawater gratefully rushed in.

She choked and thrashed. Her legs flexed again, but they were heavy now. A shoe came off. Her struggles began to slow.

Her eyes were glazing over, her worries fading, when a large object bombed into the water next to her. More rough arms grabbed her, but these dragged her up. She was propelled towards the light, taking another huge mouthful of sea, when they crashed through the surface. A wave smashed into her face.

Ashley felt a vice-like grip around her waist, then she was lifted above the waves. She vomited water out of her mouth. Spitting, gagging, crying, her throat burning, she spewed more liquid as another wave surged gleefully towards them. Hector was below her, holding her up. A lifebuoy landed next to them. She felt Hector kick as the wave arrived, which raised her higher. The wall of water swept past, consuming him, but he held her aloft, even as he was shunted against an upright.

Her arms stretched out as though crucified in mid-air.

The last thing Ashley heard was the sound of a powerful engine and the holler of a man as her exhausted mind and body failed her, and the world was snatched away.

71

Three days later, Ashley opened her eyes in her bed at home, looked around and blinked, then dropped her head back down on her pillow. She was much improved from when she'd woken on Monday evening in the hospital feeling as if she'd drunk half of the North Sea.

She stretched her body under the duvet and was relieved to find all the aches had diminished. Ashley knew it was the mental side of things that would take the longest to heal, but this time, she felt she wasn't alone.

Hector had wanted to stay with her at the hospital after the incident, but Bhavini and Emma had taken shifts so someone was there when she woke. Instead of that, Hector had returned to the station to start on the paperwork.

There were concerns around the amount of water she'd swallowed, so they kept her in for a second night. Secondary infections were common after experiences like the one she'd been through and there was also the risk of post-immersion syndrome, or what used to be called dry drowning. Ashley had never been so tired and fell in and out of sleep, only managing brief chats with whomever was beside the bed.

It was Bhavini who came in with Jan at ten the next morning to take her home. Ashley felt subdued in the car, only asking after everyone's health. She caught Bhavini giving her a concerned look.

They fussed over Ashley back at her house and got her cosy on the sofa. Ashley had given them a quick report the day before, but they wanted her to rest until the next day at the very least. She spent the afternoon making notes. Much of it had seemed like a dream. The news had reported that a police diver had recovered Eddy's body a few hours later from netting at the bottom of the pier. Ashley went to bed early and slept fitfully.

Ashley had been debating whether to go into work, when the doorbell rang. They'd said to take the rest of the week off, but she couldn't get the case out of her mind. She was surprised to see Emma and DCI Kettle at the doorstep.

'Hi,' she said.

'Morning,' said Kettle. 'I thought I'd take a statement from you here. Save you coming in today. You don't look too bad. They do say wild swimming's good for you.'

'Perhaps not that wild,' said Ashley with a grin.

She ushered them into the little dining room and filled the cafetière with boiling water. When the coffees were ready and on the table, she joined them.

'Okay, please tell me you've got enough to charge Keith.'

Kettle shook his head.

'No, we haven't. All we have is suspicion because the people who know the truth are dead, or, like Bob and Peter, keeping quiet.'

'What did Peter say?'

'To be fair to him, he was in with us all Tuesday afternoon. The hospital kept him and Keith in on Monday night, in case of concussion. They both came to the station on Tuesday, but Peter came of his own accord. He spoke more freely than he had in his previous interview, but I suspect he wasn't completely honest.'

'You reckon he was keeping something back?'

'Definitely. He told us about Foxy's death and the terrible guilt he felt afterwards. He repeated that he never got close to anyone ever again. Peter believes that apart from his police work, he's wasted his years.'

'What about his relationship with Eddy?'

'You mean how come Eddy ended up trying to lob him off the pier?'

'Yes, and how did Peter know where he was, and why didn't he tell us?'

'He said he wasn't certain but guessed at where Eddy would be. Peter received a photograph through the post with him and Foxy on it shortly after her death all that time ago, and another a few months back.'

'Does he still have it?'

'He reckoned not, but I think he does. It isn't in his house, though, because we've searched there. It seems he's another victim in all of this.'

'Did he describe the photograph?'

'Yes, it was similar to Candy's, but instead of her with hands on Foxy, it was him. Peter said it looked like he could have been pulling Foxy out of the sea or pushing her in. He only knew Keith was back recently because Eddy told him. Eddy had gradually been losing control for months, but Peter doesn't reckon it was anyone else's fault.'

'Why did he think Eddy was at Keith's house?'

'He'd suspected it was Ron and Ruby who sent the photo at first, or maybe even Brad. He'd seen loads of photographs at Keith's house and after his talk with you it suddenly clicked that it was more likely to have been Keith. Peter headed to Keith's on Monday to challenge him face to face. He also wanted to find Eddy and protect him.'

Ashley's mind was struggling to keep up.

'But how did Keith get the photos if he wasn't there? He wasn't one of the seven.'

'Peter doesn't know, and nor do we. It's a weak link in an already weak arrest. Keith said he knows nothing about any photographs. We've got an expert looking at his PC now, but so far there's nothing on it. Although the lack of much on it is suspicious in itself. Peter wondered whether Bob knew anything about the photos. There are so many tangled lines of investigation that it's difficult to unravel.'

Kettle gave Ashley a moment to absorb all the information.

'What do you now think has gone on here?'

Ashley took a deep breath.

'I believe Keith was in love with Foxy too, and he became angry when she spent more time with Peter and Brad. His jealousy meant he got ejected from the group completely. I suspect that when Foxy died, he blamed Peter and the others for her death. Maybe he heard about the beach party, or was asked to provide drugs and spied on them.'

'Yes! That makes sense. The photos had been taken from a distance.'

'Exactly. Perhaps he also deliberately spiked everyone's drugs. Nobody remembered a thing afterwards. Keith has a long history of drug-related criminality behind him.'

Emma, who'd been quiet, tutted loudly.

'So, in effect, Keith killed Foxy. People drown in a couple of inches of bathwater when they're intoxicated.'

'Right,' said Ashley. 'But I doubt he'd connect the dots to himself. He'd blame the others. I've been thinking about the pictures and photos at Keith's as well. He's obviously interested in the beach and sea shanties and photography, so maybe he began to scare Eddy after Foxy's death. I reckon it's Keith who's writing this stuff on the wall. Eddy's mental health was probably destroyed by the LSD and the loss of his only good friend, Foxy. A young woman he worshipped. Keith's rhyme probably pushed him to his failed suicide attempt.'

'Why did Keith start now, all this time later?' asked Kettle.

'Okay, this is where my theory suffers, but back then, Eddy crashed his car and got sectioned. The hippy couple vanished. Brad escaped to university, and Peter went travelling. Candy moved to Felbrigg. Meaning, apart from Bob, who wasn't invited to the party either, there was nobody left in Cromer. Keith headed off to university, so life carried on. Now he's back. Peter and Brad have seemingly lived charmed existences compared to Keith's, so he decided it was time for revenge.'

'Yeah, but I don't get the Bob thing,' said Emma.

'Hector told us you think the blood was squirted on his clothes,' said Kettle.

'Yes, Bob was in no fit state to commit those crimes,' said Ashley.

'But nor was Eddy,' said Emma. 'Despite all this evidence pointing at him, and the fact he also tried to kill you, Peter and Keith. He was clearly mentally unstable.'

'Did Keith say Eddy was responsible for all the crimes?'

'That's what Keith's saying. That he was friends with Eddy, let him stay, then he went crazy. Apparently, he'd already threatened to kill Keith before

Peter turned up. Keith's story that Eddy did all this is slightly more convincing than our view that Keith did it because Keith has physical limitations.'

'This is crazy. What about Keith giving us the wrong name and lying about his mother?'

'He said he must have misheard you.'

Ashley wrung her hands. It was true that Keith had given his correct name when he'd rung up and reported Eddy's assault.

'What about the searches at his property or the guest house next door? I think he was selling or giving drugs to Bob and Eddy.'

'If he was, he didn't keep them at his home. His phone is clean. No suspicious clothes, paint or tools. I suppose they could have been in the beach hut before he torched it. Although, considering the condition he's in, we have serious doubts that he's even responsible for that burning down. There's no strong CCTV evidence of him moving around in town. We've caught his mum's car on ANPR camera up north at the time of one of the incidents. The driver has a dark coat on with a hat or hood. It could be anyone, but a court would see it as Keith unless we can give them someone else.'

'Damn!' shouted Ashley, throwing her arms in the

air. 'We've got nothing.' She put her head in her hands. 'Keith's going to get away with it.'

'I understand your frustration,' said Kettle. 'Incitement to violence is always difficult to prove under these circumstances. Eddy most likely killed Ron and Ruby, Brad and Candy, perhaps even Foxy, because he tried to kill Peter and you. That's what the Crown Prosecution Service would have been interested in. Proving Keith told him to do so would have been hard, even if Eddy was still alive.'

Emma smiled at her.

'CPS have said they need more to charge Keith with anything. DNA will be back tomorrow morning, as will tox reports on Eddy, but they're unlikely to help because we can't find any drugs at Keith's or Eddy's homes. They've also picked up Bob's fingerprints in the guest house. No doubt his DNA will be in there, too.'

'Are Bob and Keith friends, or dealer and customer?'

'Who knows? There's other odd stuff. Very little money has been going through Keith's bank account. His mobile phone has been pinged in the town centre, but not at the times we think the graffiti was done, which actually helps him.'

'That proves he can move around unaided, though.'

'Yes, unless someone pushed him in the wheelchair. His phone hasn't been tracked to the beach either, like Eddy's has.'

'Was Eddy's phone on the beach when the murders took place?'

'No, at other times, but we already knew he was shouting over the cliff edge. My guess is that Keith got inside Eddy's head and convinced him to commit these crimes. I assume he probably helped him with some of them, but he was smart enough to hide his involvement. Even if we could connect him to one of the scenes with DNA, he only needs to mention that Eddy went around his house regularly, and it contaminates that link.'

'Damn!'

'I also spoke to Keith's GP, whose contact details Keith gladly gave me.'

'His illness is real,' stated Ashley.

'Yes. The way he's been in the interview room, I would say there's not too much wrong with him at the moment, but these conditions can come and go. My niece has fibromyalgia, and she's in a desperate state for months on end, but is then reasonably okay for a while. Getting any help or even sympathy is hard because it doesn't have an obvious clinical diagnosis.'

'When will the decision be made on Keith?'

'We'll give it until tomorrow lunchtime to get the last reports in and finish the searches. We've uncovered an address up north through Keith's GP records. He lived there after leaving prison, so we're checking that out. If there's nothing incriminating, Keith will be a free man.'

72

The next morning, Ashley showered, dressed, ate, and got straight in her car. She'd told Kettle the day before she felt fine and could come in and work, but he'd insisted she took another day off. Ashley had pleaded to be able to interview Keith Morecambe, but Kettle declined her request.

Ashley's plan was to spend the day in the incident room, trawling through the entire case from start to end. There had to be something they'd missed.

There was a subdued mood in the office. Two women had vanished near the Suffolk border and Sal and Emma were investigating. Bhavini was at a wedding, which left Hector, Barry, Jan and her. Only Jan had beaten her in.

'Have we got anything?' she asked him, hopefully.

'No, although I keep thinking there's no way this Eddy guy could have done it. Then I reckon it has to be him, because if Keith was involved, surely we'd have found evidence of that by now.'

'Maybe Keith's simply been too clever.'

'Perhaps. The station's moving on. It's just as well because this case is driving us crazy. We can't solve them all.'

'But is it finished? Perhaps Keith won't stop until there are seven.'

'Which brings us back to Peter. If he's involved, at least it would explain our struggles because he'd know how to hide the evidence.'

Ashley frowned. Her instincts had served her well in her career, but this conclusion didn't fit. She needed to flip her instincts. Peter and Geoffrey were decent people, but decent people sometimes did bad things. Then there was Bob. She'd have put him in the same category as Peter and Geoffrey, despite his addictions. But she also knew desperate addicts would do almost anything to satisfy their drug lust. Regret would come later, but the damage would have been done.

Ashley drew a diagram with each person's name

on it and lines to indicate connections. It ended up looking like a spaghetti junction, so she threw it away.

At nine o'clock, she called the prison.

'Hi, this is DS Ashley Knight. Can I speak to the prison's Police Liaison Officer?'

'Sure, putting you through now.'

There were a few seconds of silence before the line rang. It was swiftly answered.

'Sam Jakes speaking.'

'Hi, Sam, it's Ash.'

'Hey, Ash. Long time. I've not seen you in town lately.'

Sam was another who frequented the pubs in Cromer. His wife used to let him out on a Sunday teatime, and he'd let off steam playing pool and darts with whomever was about, then usually finish off with a meal in his favourite Indian restaurant, Masala Twist. He'd introduced Ashley to the Masala Twist Special, an amazing sizzling meat dish, which made Sam responsible for at least one of her love handles.

'I've been hibernating, but I'm emerging now.'

'Great to hear. Are you ringing for a thrashing at pool or business?'

'Business. Robert Redding. Can you visit him in his cell for me?'

'No worries. I was sad to see him back. He was in a weary way at arrival, but he looked chipper when I saw him yesterday. Told me he was going to bite me when his false teeth arrived.'

'Nice. I want to speak to him, but there's no point in me booking an appointment and coming in if he's unlikely to leave the wing and see me. He must have seen the news.'

'Yeah, we all have. There's a lot of gossip in here about it. I read Keith Morecambe had been nicked for questioning. One of the officers here transferred from Strangeways. Said he knew Keith up there and he was an irritating, lying, devious prick. When can we expect him?'

'That's the thing. We don't have enough to charge him, so we've got to let him go. Obviously, you can't tell Bob that, but perhaps you could test the water a bit. Tell him I want to come in and see him. Today if he likes.'

'What about Bob? Is his case still going to court?'

'We have a CPS meeting this afternoon. With all the ambiguity, it makes any prosecution against Bob weak too.' Ashley paused for a moment. 'Tell Bob I believe him. Say I know he's a good person. Bob was scared. The others were, too, apart from Peter Ibson, and they all had a right to be because people were dying. Ask him what he wants in exchange for the truth.'

'No problem. I'll catch him when they're doing methadone in an hour. I'll ring you later.'

Ashley was putting the phone down when Kettle came into the room with a glum face. She raised an eyebrow at him.

'There's a tiny amount of Keith's DNA on the coat that Eddy died in,' he said. 'I'd put good money on it being Keith's coat, but it's been washed recently.'

'Just like Bob's trainers were before Keith squirted blood on them.'

'Yes, but all he has to say is that Eddy's been in his house. We can't connect the trainers to Keith, or Peter, for that matter.'

'Anything from the beach huts? The clothes? How about CCTV? Did the weight that hit Jack match Peter's gym weights?'

Kettle chuckled ruefully.

'There's nothing salvageable from the burned-out beach hut, but Eddy's DNA is on the clothes found in the hut he rented. Eddy's bank card was used to pay for it, but the call wasn't recorded. The weight used was the same type as the one used to secure Brad, not the much newer type that Peter has in his gym. Hector found something interesting yesterday, but it's not enough.'

'Go on.'

'There was a leg brace in Keith's house. The kind you wear after knee surgery.'

'So?'

'Remember the limp. A brace would give you a straight leg limp, not Eddy's collapsing one.'

'God, yes.'

'There's more. We think we can see a speck of black paint on it. We've sent it for testing.'

'That's great.'

'Kind of. Keith's doctor confirmed his health issues, which would probably stop him from killing people on the beach, but it wouldn't prevent him from writing his rhymes in town. He'd also be capable of driving Eddy around.'

'Did you ask his GP whether he had any leg issues?'

'Yes, he said there was nothing on his record. We asked Keith, who said it was his mum's brace. Cocky git said she got it from a friend.'

Ashley frowned as she considered what that revelation meant for the case.

'Prosecuting Keith for criminal damage won't get the press off our backs,' she said.

'No, and a successful conviction wouldn't be a given. I even had a handwriting expert check the graffiti to see if it matched Keith's, but apparently we don't generally write the same as we paint. Eddy might end up being the only one to get a black mark against his name in this whole saga. We got his bloods back and they're compelling. He had almost every drug going in his system, apart from the ones he was prescribed.'

'I suppose it's not surprising he was psychotic if he wasn't taking his anti-psychotics.'

'Precisely.'

'I don't suppose Lorna Garrett said anything to Scott while he was with her.'

'No, she's devastated. She's blaming herself for not knowing about Brad's struggles.'

'What about the other team who were chasing up retired officers who were in the force at the time of Foxy's death? Did any of them have a different theory?'

Kettle shook his head, then closed his eyes for a moment. When he opened them, he seemed exhausted.

'We're going to look like fools,' he said.

Ashley spent the morning poring over the computer files of the case and kept returning to the same infuriating question. Where was Keith or Eddy's equipment? Where was the paint? She looked through Keith's bank statements. There was nothing unusual about them at all. In fact, they were sparse, so he hadn't been buying things with his bank card, and he hadn't been withdrawing cash either. Where was his money coming from?

Hector joined her to see how she was getting on.

'There was a nice bicycle at Keith's house,' she said. 'So I've asked Williamson's team to find him riding it near the relevant times on the masses of CCTV, seeing as it might have been easier for him to get around on that than on foot.'

'Wow. That's a monstrous task.'

'Yes, they were overjoyed. All the teams are checking thousands of minutes of CCTV, various banks accounts, phone records, driving records, with more bodies knocking on houses and taking statements. Nothing's sticking. We've got ninety-six hours maximum to hold Keith, but keeping him that long isn't an option if we're just fishing.'

'Any new angles popping up?'

'I think Keith's got another storage place. He must have. A detective from Manchester constabulary visited the address that he'd been at under probation, but there was nobody home. Maybe it's worth a trip up there.'

'I'd say so. The fire report came back from the beach huts. It was hard to say what was inside the ruined one. The investigator suspected it had burned at a very high temp because of the speed it disintegrated. That indicated an accelerant was present. Perhaps that was where the paint had been stored, and any white spirit would have helped with the blaze.'

'Yes, but so would petrol.'

She rang Kettle and gave her thoughts.

'That's good,' he replied, 'but my hopes for surveillance aren't great. If Keith torched his mum's shed, or got Eddy to do it for him, then it's likely Keith's disposed of any other evidence. He's known all along that we'd be interested in him. Even if there is a place, he won't leave here and go straight to wherever it is. He's been too smart so far.'

'Too smart for us. Too smart for Eddy. Too smart for Peter.'

'Yep. That's a good point about his bank account having few transactions.'

'Of course he isn't paying for things. He'll be skint. His mum's only been dead six weeks. I bet he hasn't notified her bank, so it will all be coming out of her account.'

'Sneaky.'

'Yes, and, whilst illegal, it's not enough to hold him longer.'

'No, I guess not, but it's worth checking out. Perhaps there's a regular payment or bill that could give us something new. He could have rented another beach hut.'

Ashley clicked her fingers. 'His dad had an allotment. It might have a shed.'

'That sounds promising.'

'Although,' she said, 'there are loads of allotments around here. I'll get Sal on the bank account in case it's paid monthly, and Emma can call her contact at the council.'

'Great. Barry and Bhavini have been doing the interviewing with Keith, but they haven't made any progress. I've asked Jan to replace Bhavini for a final interview in a few minutes, in case Keith has a hang-up about women. I'd like you to watch.'

Ashley put down the phone, grabbed Hector, and went to a room where they could view the conversation via a live stream. Kettle joined them.

'Okay,' he said. 'Short of Keith confessing now, we'll release him on police bail, to report here at midday tomorrow, then every second day at the same time. His solicitor will get him to agree to that.

We've been declined full team surveillance at this point.'

'How come?' asked Ashley.

'As far as the super is concerned, the killer, Eddy, is dead. Even if we knew Eddy was the gun and Keith was squeezing the trigger, we can't prove it at this point beyond reasonable doubt.'

Ashley frowned.

'Surely, we're still working the case.'

'Yes, visit Manchester tomorrow and snoop around. Take whoever can stay overnight.'

'Will the press know that Keith's being released?' asked Hector.

'Yes, as you know it's standard procedure to let the public hear the investigation is still live.'

'Someone should ring Peter Ibson,' said Ashley. 'He's the last person standing.'

'He called me this morning. Zara offered him medical retirement, which he's just accepted. He has a good pension, so he'll be fine.'

Ashley and Hector exchanged a glance. Peter, a man who lived to work, no longer had a job. Ashley suspected he'd be a long way from fine.

'Is he coming in to say goodbye?' she asked.

'No, not under the circumstances.'

'That's piss-poor after nearly thirty years. He's

been put through the wringer, not to mention nearly being thrown off the pier. We need to mark his service and commitment. I'll clear his desk for him and take it around on my way home. Wish him the best. Hector can start a collection.'

Kettle winced. 'What if he is involved?'

'Are you worried he might be in danger, or that the public is at risk from him?'

'Zara spoke to him about being number seven. He said he's not bothered. Peter believes it was Eddy who killed everyone, sent mad by trying to cope with real life. He thinks Bob helped him. Maybe in Eddy's mind, he could have used Bob as the seventh victim instead of himself, which was why Bob was so scared.'

'What about Peter's thoughts on Keith sending those photographs?'

'I'm not sure. Zara had the impression Peter considered the matter closed. Eddy's dead and Bob's in jail. He doesn't believe Keith's a killer, even if he did send those pictures. If he's right, then who else is there to hurt him?'

They didn't have time to debate it any longer. Barry and Jan's interviewee had arrived for questioning. Ashley and Hector watched as they tried to grill Keith for the final time but Keith blanked them.

When they told him he was going to be released on police bail, he laughed.

Ashley stared, mesmerised, at the screen. Keith's eyes squinted upwards, while his nostrils flared. The big teeth became more prominent. Ashley wondered, as she listened to the chilling sound of his cackle, if he could be described as evil.

73

Ashley returned to her desk and was tutting at the impromptu update that her computer had started when the phone rang. She snatched it up. It was the PLO from the prison, Sam Jakes.

'Hey, Ash. I've been to see Bob.'

'Excellent. Is he happy for me to visit?'

'No, he's paranoid now Eddy's dead. He accepts he can trust you, but he doesn't want to be released until it's finished.'

Ashley frowned. Why wouldn't Bob think it was already over?

'Bob knows that's not how it works,' she replied. 'Is he worried about being homeless when he's free? That's assuming he gets out.'

'Maybe that's part of it. He asked if you could find him accommodation for when he returns. Something with a bidet.'

'Cheeky git.'

'Yes, he did laugh at that. He was in excellent form. His methadone dose is controlling him. He isn't acting like he's guilty of anything, but he reiterated that he is involved. He wants you to keep looking.'

'Where?'

'He refused to say any more. He won't leave his cell if you come to the prison.'

Ashley cursed, but knew they wouldn't allow her on his wing. She finished the call and carried on reading through the files until they released Keith Morecambe at one o'clock. Ashley made sure she was down at the custody suite as they brought him out of his cell. She expected more crowing, but he looked downcast. Even so, he couldn't resist a few taunts.

'You lot don't know your arses from your elbows. Fancy trying to pin all this on an innocent man. I should sue you. Just because I've got previous. The bloody killer is in your mortuary.'

There was no strength in his words. His eyes blinked rapidly, and he swallowed deeply as Ashley watched him leave the building. The doctor had seen him and given him the all-clear, but Ashley thought he looked frail and unsteady on his feet. Maybe he was ill, after all.

Sal and Emma still weren't back from the missing women's case, so Hector and Ashley researched local allotments. It was Norfolk, so they were everywhere. There was a small patch in Cromer and bigger ones at East Runton, Overstrand and Sheringham. Ashley needed fresh air, so she told the team she and Hector would have a snoop around. While they were in Overstrand, they'd drop in on the now retired Peter.

It was a rare, completely still day on the coast. Hector drove with the windows down, which filled the car with the floral scent of spring. Ashley felt as if she needed a holiday. She glanced at Hector, who was checking back on her with a serious expression.

'Are you all right?' he asked.

'Yes, you?'

'Yep. You know, you really aren't what I expected.'

'Neither are you.'

'Do you want to talk about when you said you couldn't have a baby?'

'Nope. Do you want to talk about your sex life, or lack of one?'

He returned his gaze to the road, but his cheek twitched.

'Yes, but perhaps not today.'

They'd passed the sign for Overstrand and were pulling into Peter's driveway when her phone rang.

'DS Knight.'

'Hi, it's Elliott.'

'Elliott who?'

'Candy's boyfriend.'

'Oh, sorry. How can I help?'

'I'm ringing about Candy's mum. She heard on the radio you've released the man you were holding for the murders on the beach.'

'That's right.'

'She went mad. Said she was going to talk to him.'

Ashley realised Elliott could be referring to Keith or Peter.

'Does she mean Keith?'

'I don't know.'

'Talk to him by phone?'

'No, face to face.'

'Okay, don't let her leave. We'll come now.'

'No, that's why I'm ringing. She's gone already. Screeched away about five minutes ago. It took me that long to find the card you left.'

'Okay, that's fine. Don't worry. I think I know where she's going. We'll go down there and make sure she doesn't do anything daft. I'll ring you soon. Is your son safe?'

'Timmy's with Grandpa.'

Ashley cut the call. Mrs Sweet was probably driving to Keith's, but it was possible she was coming to see Peter. Ashley noticed Peter's car was on the driveway. Hector was already at the front door. She suddenly thought of Peter's brand spanking new gym. What had he done with his old weights? Her stomach gurgled as Hector knocked on the door. She got out and shouted to him.

'Be careful.'

He gave her an odd look, but stepped back from the doorstep while he waited.

She called Control and informed them they were heading to Keith's home. The nearest response vehicle was ten minutes away. Hector returned to the car.

'No movement. Rear gate is open. Want to look?'

'Okay, we'd better.'

They peeked through the window into the kitchen. There was a note left on the table next to an envelope and a set of keys at the side of it. Ashley had left her glasses in the car.

Hector turned to face her, looking alarmed.

'What is it?' she asked.

'It looks like your name is on the envelope.'

'Christ.'

'Shall we break in?'

'Have you got anything to break in with?'

Ashley told him about Elliott's call so instead they rushed back to their vehicle. Cromer was a mile away. They were at the outskirts in less than a minute. There was plenty of traffic in town, with tourists wandering everywhere because of the mild weather, but four minutes later they were passing Morrisons' petrol station and were almost at Keith's house.

'What do you think?' asked Hector. His grip was white around the steering wheel.

'A furious Mrs Sweet, who already hated Keith, might already be at the property. For all we know, Peter could have come here as well. The nearest response team is—' she checked her watch '—still five minutes away. We're police. Lives are at risk. We have to go in.'

There was a car parked haphazardly across the parking spaces of the guest house next door. Ashley had seen it at Mrs Sweet's house. Hector stopped on the other side of the road. They were leaving their vehicle when a figure came staggering out of Keith's house. It was Mrs Sweet. She had a hand clutched to her mouth. She shook her head, looked as if she was about to be sick, then lurched to her car and got in.

Hector and Ashley ignored the woman, even as

they heard her vehicle's engine fire into life. They reached Keith's front door as it was slowly swinging shut. Hector pushed it back with his foot.

'Peter, Keith, we're coming in. It's the police. Do not move!'

They crept inside and looked down the hallway.

A pained sob echoed from the end of the house.

There was an umbrella stand so Hector picked the lone brolly out of it. Ashley stopped moving when Peter appeared at the kitchen door. He was in the same dark grey suit trousers he'd worn often in the office. White shirt, no tie, brown loafers. He grimaced.

Then he smiled coldly. Sweat dripped from his chin.

He stepped closer, fist raised at them. There were red splatters on his face and speckles on his shirt. A small but solid-looking serrated knife was in the hand at his side. He raised it to show them. Ashley heard the front door click shut behind her.

With three quick strides, he was next to them. His face a mask of hate.

'In the kitchen, now,' he growled.

They edged past him, then strode as fast as they could to the kitchen. Keith was slumped on the floor, legs spread, leaning back against the corner of the units. He glanced up, as if still surprised by what had happened to him, and let out a laugh. His eyes drew up, nose flattened, and the teeth stood out, but the sound that came out was a poor imitation of the mad titter that he'd made at the station. This one tailed off into a whimper.

Ashley looked at the blood-splattered Peter, then back to Keith. There were three distinct separate cuts in Keith's cream T-shirt. Two in his stomach, and one under his heart. Tears poured from Keith's eyes as his face twisted with pain. He lifted his hand and jabbed a finger at Peter. Blood oozed from the corners of his mouth.

'P-Peter. Peter...'

Sirens sounded in the distance. Peter pointed his knife at them, then ran for the front door. Ashley took a second to make up her mind. She shouted at Hector.

'Stop the bleeding. Make sure Control have sent an ambulance.'

Then, despite the obvious danger, she raced after Peter.

74

When Ashley reached the front of the house, Mrs Sweet had thankfully left. Ashley spotted Peter running towards the promenade and his hands appeared empty. She sprinted after him, knowing he would head to the fifty or so white steps which gave access to the beach. Peter crossed the road and trotted down them. Ashley pounded after him.

Then Peter veered right, went over some steps over a high groyne, then picked up his pace and headed for the pier. One of Ashley's slip-ons came off in the sand, so she kicked the other one away and left them behind. In just her socks, she gained on him as his shoes filled with loose sand. The gap widened again as he reached the harder surface under the pier, and he was soon lit up by a burst of sunshine on the other side.

Peter had always kept himself trim and fit. She recalled his gym at home. He regularly cycled to work. She cursed. They'd found a bike at Keith's. She suspected it was Peter's, not Keith's, and that was one of the ways he'd been getting around.

Ashley tensed her jaw, attempted to control her breathing, and tried to keep up. As she passed under the pier, she saw in black letters on the wall of the entrance structure a painted number six. Poor Eddy. She pushed the thoughts away and drove herself after number seven.

As they headed towards the fishing boats, Ashley realised it was already too late to use her mobile due to the weak signal. Geoffrey was unlikely to still be around, but would she want him trying to stop an armed Peter if he was?

The beach was busy. There was a surf school staring disappointedly at the minuscule waves. They first gawped at Peter as he galloped past, then laughed at her as she lumbered by.

'I think that's a no, darling,' one of them shouted.

'Ring the fucking police,' she bellowed as she went by.

She began to boil in her suit, and she almost

tripped. She dragged off her jacket and threw it into the arms of a couple holding hands as she splashed through the wet sand. Her breath was laboured now, her stitch stabbing. Peter pulled away.

She guessed either he was going to run all the way along the shore to Overstrand, or he would go up the wooden steps near where the murders had taken place. She'd lose him with the latter, but if he continued on and she climbed the cliff steps herself, she could get a signal at the top and have officers pick him up in Overstrand. If Peter got off the beach and into the woods, they might never find him.

A big wet poodle jumped up at her as she skirted the rock pools, almost knocking her down, but as she slowed to a fast walk, she noticed Peter had stopped. It was the spot where the Jerrods were killed, where Candy drowned, and where Foxy had perished all those years ago. Brad as good as died here, and Eddy had breathed his last not far away. They were the six.

Gasping, she walked the final hundred metres, leaning to the left, hand resting on the side of her stomach. She was gratified to see Peter was breathing hard, too, but then he did still have his suit jacket and shoes on. He stood at the water's edge, staring out to sea, the water circling around his feet. She stopped ten metres from him. All her senses were on fire.

This far from the pier, there was only one family with a toddler playing in the sand about fifty metres away and a few dog walkers past the next breakwater.

'It's beautiful here,' he said, gazing up at the blue sky and cotton-wool clouds.

'Yes,' she replied, glancing back up the beach before returning her stare to him. 'It is.'

'Did you know I found a photo album?' he asked.

'No. Where was it?'

'In Bob's shed.'

Ashley guessed straight away.

'Keith had hidden it there.'

'Yes.'

'We should have known he liked taking photographs, and then sending them.'

'He paid the price today.'

Peter closed his eyes. Up close, Ashley could tell that he hadn't shaved. She didn't think she'd seen him with stubble before.

'Why did you do it, Peter? Why? You could have retired. You were free to do whatever you wanted.'

Peter's head dropped down, then twisted to his left. His right eye squinted to keep out the sun. His nostrils flared.

'I've never been free.'

Ashley sighed.

'You won't ever be free now.'

'Oh, sorry. You mean why did I kill Keith?'

'No. Why did you murder them all?'

75

A smile crept onto Peter's face.

'Don't you think Eddy killed them?' he asked.

'Not now. This is beyond anything Eddy could have organised. We've known that for a long time.'

'Not Keith, or Bob, or maybe Brad?'

'No, Bob and Brad were terrified. Not of what they'd done, but of someone else. When I looked at Keith bleeding out on that cheap lino, I saw a sad, tired, ill man. Would Keith really know how to cover his tracks to this extent? We were looking for evidence that didn't exist, because you'd done it. Where are your old gym weights? I bet you got Eddy to hire the beach hut out. You were his friend. How could you?'

'It's funny how things turn out. I hadn't planned to kill Keith today. His life is torture enough, but I wanted a favour. Did you know the sea shanty was his idea all along?'

'We'd guessed that, but why kill him last if he started all this off? He sent the photographs. He drove you all mad.'

Peter laughed. It was a sinister sound that gave her goosebumps despite the pleasant sunshine.

'You don't understand. Yes, his photographs started all this. I went to ask him if he was responsible, but he said he thought it was Ron and Ruby who took the pictures. When I visited them, they denied it. I went back to Keith's to accuse him again but Keith told me Brad and Candy had been pushing Foxy into the sea that night. I later searched Bob's shed and found the album. He said Ron and Ruby gave it to him.'

'That's ridiculous. Ron or Bob wouldn't have lugged an album around for all these years. And why would Candy or Brad hurt Foxy?'

'Perhaps.' Peter's face curled into a frown. 'You'll understand my torment if you ever see the photograph that I received a few days after Foxy died, which I now know Keith sent.'

Peter smiled, but it lacked warmth.

'It brought back memories. Foxy told me that night of the party she was going to go out with Brad instead of me.'

'No!'

'Yes. Ron and Ruby had already left. Eddy and Candy were off their faces, laughing in the shallows. Foxy told me with a smile, then cheered as my best friend and I fought over her. My memory disappears at that point. When I woke up, I thought Brad had killed her. It was a month later, when I next went to a beach abroad, that I had my first flashback of what I might have done. Just glimpses of me and Brad drug-fuelled fighting. I knocked him out, then turned to her. I remember thinking, if I couldn't have Foxy, then nobody would.'

Ashley felt like slumping to the ground. Who could live for all this time with that pressing on their conscience?

'So, was the graffiti some kind of distraction?'

'No, that was Keith's bit of fun all those years ago, but in a way, I liked it. I went to see Ron and Ruby a month back, believing it was their drugs which drove us insane. They denied it and I didn't believe them. But if Keith took the pictures, then I guess the LSD was his.'

'You've killed innocent people.'

'Ron and Ruby, Eddy and Candy, and Keith. They were wastes of space.'

'Even if that were true, you aren't God.'

Peter pointed at her again. The knife was back in his hand. He spoke calmly.

'None of them were innocent. They were all complicit in one way or another.'

'And Brad?'

'He shouldn't have stolen my girl.'

Ashley could make out the sound of rapidly approaching sirens.

'I don't think he did.'

'What?'

'I reckon she was just having fun. Playing you off against each other. Brad never so much as kissed her.'

A shadow passed over Peter's face. He shook his head.

'That's not true,' he snarled. 'You know, I visited Eddy for years, part with worry he'd remember what went on that night, and part with hope, that my torment could end. Part of me still doesn't believe I killed her, but I don't know what's real any more. And now I never will.'

'Why did Eddy try to kill you?'

'It was cunning, clever Keith. He must have guessed I was responsible, but he also knew that I could pin the blame on him. So he had Eddy move into his place, then filled his head with lies so he'd protect him.'

'Then Keith convinced a befuddled Eddy that you had to die.'

'Yes. I'd planned to leave one of my old gym weights in Keith's house, to incriminate him if necessary. Ironic that Eddy then used it on me. He attacked me the moment I arrived. Maybe he did see me drown Foxy and finally remembered it, or perhaps he just guessed I was responsible, but I bet Keith told Eddy that I'd killed her, because he knew that, in his unmedicated state, Eddy would be guaranteed to punish me.'

Peter's eyes blazed.

'Is that why you stabbed Keith today?' whispered Ashley.

'I only went today to ask Keith to continue writing the shanty on the walls after I'd gone. He could keep the legend alive. In that way, the world will know that I, us, the seven were here.'

'Keith's painting days are done.'

'It's your story to tell now,' he shouted.

Ashley bit her lip from saying what she thought as she took a step away from him.

The world will have a pretty good idea that you existed, you evil fucker.

The sirens were loud now. Peter's gaze left her face and looked behind her. She glanced back and saw a multitude of police vehicles streaming their way.

'It's finished, Peter. You're going to die in prison just because a girl said no.'

'Ah, but you never met Foxy. Perhaps if you had, you'd understand. I felt like I was in heaven when I was with her. Anything less has been hell.'

Peter stared at the knife in his hand. It was a simple tool that you could find in any home, but deadly in the wrong hands. Its blade was dulled by dried blood. Ashley took another two steps back. She thought of the little penknife in her pocket, then remembered losing it when Eddy died. She wouldn't have fancied her chances, anyway.

Peter focused on the approaching police. His face twisted with rage, then sorrow.

'Peter, you've created a nightmare here,' she said, quietly. 'The people in the town have been living in fear.'

'I've done good things, too, although I doubt anyone will remember that.'

'Peter! You were supposed to help your community. You lied to us. You lied to me.'

His gaze dropped on her, heavy as an anchor.

'Yes, I did, and I lied to myself. When it was obvious Eddy couldn't cope with real life, I decided that enough was enough. I'd failed again. It was time.'

Staring into his eyes was like falling into a deep, dark pit. Peter spoke through bared teeth.

'A growing part of me wants me to kill them all.'

'Who do you mean?'

'All the criminals and no-hopers.' Peter took a step closer to her. 'I thought I'd feel terrible after Ron and Ruby, but I didn't. Something hidden inside me resurfaced. I liked it. They deserved punishment. It was time for real justice.'

The look he gave her made her knees tremble. It was a stare of pure, unadulterated hate and fury, which twisted his face into a vision of absolute terror.

Ashley had found her monster.

76

Peter let out a sound that sounded like a scream ripped from the bowels of the earth. He bellowed again, then flung his knife at her.

She expected to feel it sticking in her throat, but it flew well wide and hit its intended target, the windshield of the first police 4x4, which skidded to a halt in the sand.

Peter turned to her. He removed a bigger, more deadly blade from an inner pocket. It glinted in the sun as he raised it aloft, then he threw it into the sand at her feet.

Peter turned to the water and strode forward, stepping over the waves, which were little more than ripples. He lifted his feet high as he stepped like a giant through a flat lake. The sea didn't rise and crash, it undulated, up and down, as though it were a beast that was sleeping.

Ashley raised her hand to keep out the sun and stared as the water reached Peter's waist and then his chest. He leaned forward, falling into a shallow dive, then began a steady crawl as he headed further out. His face glinted and flashed in a moment of sunlight as he rolled onto his back, seemingly looking at her. He waved, wide and slow, then, as another cloud came over, he turned and powered on.

Peter became smaller and smaller as the sun broke out once more. It shone down on the twinkling surface as though millions of diamonds had chosen that moment to rise from the depths. A slight swell lifted the moving figure.

Then Peter disappeared, and the sea welcomed him home.

77

Ashley couldn't sleep that night. She lay in bed thinking of Peter. He was further proof that it was the quiet ones you needed to watch out for. Over the years, she'd investigated numerous people who led calm lives, but under a seemingly tranquil surface, uncontrollable currents raged.

As the police officers had left their vehicles the previous day and stood next to her on the sand, Ashley had realised she was still unclear on the full story.

It was hard to think of those young people, laughing and dancing on Cromer beach over thirty years ago with their lives ahead of them. Completely unaware of what fate had planned for them. It wasn't just Foxy who died that night; it was all of their hopes and dreams. Time hadn't eased Peter's guilt and anger. Instead, unchecked and unchallenged, it had warped and grown, until the horrifying events of the past few weeks had occurred.

Ashley finally dropped off at five and woke late, so she didn't have time for a jog. She made a promise that she'd go the next day. After two slices of toast and jam but no butter, she showered and waited in the lounge until a car beeped its horn. Hector was waiting when she got outside.

'Morning, did you sleep okay?' she asked as she got in.

'Nope, you?'

'Nope.'

'Come on, then, let's head off. I bet it's been a while since Bob had anyone waiting for him when he left prison.'

The jail had been falling apart, so a new category B block was built in the 1980s, but it was still a daunting and eerie building to approach. Ashley imagined many a mouth had dried as they were driven up towards the imposing gates for the first time.

Bob had been notified of his release late the previous afternoon, but Ashley had rung the liaison officer and explained that she wanted to speak to the council to see if they could find Bob a place to sleep. Bob had agreed to stay the night in prison. After what Ashley had read the previous night, Bob was going to be okay.

She knew that the prison didn't usually chuck anyone out until nine o'clock, but if charges were dropped, they could leave as soon as they were processed. Ashley had agreed with Sam Jakes that they'd be outside at nine and not to release Bob until then to make sure he didn't wander off.

It was a cool morning with a stiff breeze, but they left the car and leaned against the bonnet as they waited. She told Hector about her theory that if society let people drift to the margins and they became isolated, it was no wonder they ended up snapping.

'That's true,' he replied. 'People have breakdowns and lose control all the time. I'm sure many could be prevented with earlier intervention.'

'Instead, we pick up the pieces.'

'Do you know what I struggled with last night in bed?'

'The loneliness.'

He turned to her and grinned. 'It was, actually. Keith and Peter lived their lives isolated. Eddy spent his life incarcerated. Even Candy and Brad seemed to have been stuck within their minds.'

'They say the strongest bars are in your head.'

'I suppose Bob was different.'

'He chose to spend life out of his mind.'

Hector chuckled. 'Yes, but it goes full circle. You know what Johann Hari said.'

'No.'

'The opposite of addiction is not sobriety, it's human connection.'

Ashley considered the words, then smiled. She didn't say anything, but maybe Bhavini was right. Hector was the chosen one.

At nine thirty, the gates opened. Four men edged out of the darkness just as it spotted rain. Two were young and their parents were there to meet them. They hugged and laughed, then left, grinning. An older gentleman, clutching a brown, battered suitcase, shuffled forward and was met by whom Ashley assumed was his wife. They didn't hug. She stared at him for a few seconds, then shrugged, as if to say, come on.

Bob was left on his own, blinking in the daylight. A plastic bag of clothes in one hand, and a slip of paper in the other. That would be a one-way train ticket to somewhere. But Bob had nowhere.

Or so he thought. Ashley strolled towards him. 'Bob, fancy a lift?'

He raised an eyebrow. 'I can cope with a walk to the railway station.'

'No, back to Overstrand.'

'Why would I want to go there?'

'You've won the lottery.'

'I don't do the lottery.'

'Someone did it for you.'

Bob smiled. 'It had better be more than a tenner.'

The detectives got back in the car, and Bob slipped onto a rear seat. He buckled himself in and ran his fingers across the trim and seat covers.

'Been a long time since I was in a new car,' he said.

'You were driven to the station in a patrol estate vehicle when you were arrested.'

'I don't recall much of that ride.'

Ashley grinned. 'I suppose not. You've seen the news?'

'About Peter? Yes, it's all over the jail. He nicked a lot of them at one time or another, so they weren't sure what to make of it all. I bet you found investigating all of this confusing.'

'We did.'

'Who were you blaming instead of Peter? The homeless guy, the sick bloke, or the crazy one?'

'Which were you?' asked Hector.

Bob frowned but couldn't help himself and giggled.

'Fair enough. All of them, I suppose.'

Ashley had to be careful talking to Bob about the case, but she wanted to hear the truth about Peter. She hoped Bob would feel the urge to fill the silence that had settled in the car. They pulled away and left the stark building behind them.

'I'm sorry I didn't come clean about what I knew,' he finally said.

'We don't know what you knew,' said Hector.

'To be honest with you, I wasn't certain of anything. It's a bit of a shock that Peter did all that. He used to help me out. I'd often find food where I was sleeping or outside my shed when I settled there.'

Ashley exchanged a look with Hector.

'But he also left Ron's blood on your T-shirt and some trainers.'

'I only own one pair of trainers, and I was wearing them.'

Ashley sighed.

'That information would have helped earlier.'

'As I said, I'm sorry. But I was scared. Keith got me

back on the heroin when he returned to Cromer. I saw him in town, and he gave me some for free later. It was so stupid, after having been off it for so long.'

'I don't understand why you'd start again,' said Hector.

'That's a surprise, considering your job, so this lesson is free. Heroin's amazing. When you're on it, you're happy, wherever you are. All the pain, the shivers, the running nose and eyes, the aches, they all go away. You'd be on it if wasn't so deadly.'

'I'm not so sure about that,' said Hector.

'And Keith knew you'd need to see him for more,' said Ashley.

'Yes, but I think he was just lonely. His mum was really ill, and he had nobody else. He was angry at life. It was him that sent the photographs to the others. He kept a photo album of our lives when we were young.'

'We heard about the photos, but we haven't found any.'

'The beach party was where it finished. It's a nice album apart from that section. He always took a good picture.'

'Bob, I really need you to come to the station and make a full statement. None of this is admissible at the coroner's inquest if it isn't done properly.'

'No, you can hear it now, or not at all. Why are we stopping at Peter's house?'

Hector had pulled up outside the property. There were two small CSI vans and another van with a trailer. Ashley unclicked her seat belt and turned to Bob.

'Peter left half this house to charity, and the other half to you.'

'What?'

'Yep. We came back here last night and entered the house to make sure there weren't any more surprises. Peter left me a copy of his will. His old partner's widow gets his money, which was quite substantial, but you got half this place.'

'Bugger me. I'll take the bottom half. Can I sit in it now?'

Ashley chuckled. 'No, the crime scene guys are still inside. I assume you'll have to wait for probate to be sorted and it to be sold, but I've walked around inside myself. There's virtually nothing in there and it's spotless. It's as though he'd already moved out.'

'I liked Peter,' said Bob. 'In a way, it was Keith's fault.'

'I'm not sure a jury would have seen it like that.'

'Maybe they would, you see, Keith and me, we went to the beach party. When we turned up, Foxy wanted Keith's drugs, but insisted we weren't invited. Keith told them the LSD was weak, and they'd need a lot of it. Then we hid in the trees halfway up the cliff and watched. Keith laughed and took photos from there with a zoom when they started acting weird. He had all the gear. He said he was going to post the pictures anonymously to mess with their heads.'

'Did you watch Peter kill Foxy?'

'No, I took off. Keith stayed, but I felt like a massive loser. We'd both been left behind. They were my only friends, and they didn't want me with them.'

Ashley stayed quiet to let him continue.

'When I heard Foxy had died, I was sad. But I was also angry that nobody looked after her. I would have done. She was special. I didn't know at the time that Keith had overdosed them so badly. It was also his idea to make that poem up and write it in town.'

'Do you think Keith watched Foxy drown?'

Bob loosened his lips.

'I wouldn't put it past him.'

'What happened to Eddy?'

'Eddy had been losing his marbles for months, maybe longer. We all knew it, but we kind of helped him along. Foxy's death pushed him over the edge. He ended up crashing his car and getting committed. Keith did feel a little guilty about that, so he stopped the graffiti. He moved to uni. Everyone left, apart from me.' Bob shook his head. 'I don't know where all the years have gone. At times, it's like it all just happened a few days ago.'

Bob shrugged.

'In a way, I'm to blame as well. I'd see Keith to score most days after he came back last year. He still had contacts up north. It was me who told him Peter and Brad were local. I'd also learned that Candy lived in Felbrigg. I told him that, too. Keith said he was going to send them the photos again. He'd festered over their treatment of him. I was there when Peter came to accuse him of sending the photos, but Keith blamed Ron.'

'Were you scared of Peter then?'

'Yes, very. He came back and said Ron and Ruby denied knowing about the LSD that night. They told Peter that it was us who provided the drugs. He threatened to prosecute us for the manslaughter of Foxy. He reckoned with both of our previous records we'd get life.'

'What stopped him?'

'I don't think he knew what to believe, but then Keith lied to him. He explained that he saw all the commotion on the beach. Keith told him that Brad and Candy had tried to drown Foxy. Peter gave us a funny look. He took Keith into a different room and talked to him there. I dealt with it the only way I know how and got off my face.'

'So, Keith didn't know Ron and Ruby were going to be murdered?'

'No. I was at his house getting high when he found out. He thought it was amusing. Keith loves all those sea shanties and stuff. Eddy had been coming over by then. It was as if Keith wanted the old gang back. Eddy wasn't making much sense by that point. Keith had been quoting the rhyme to him again. Told him that the sea would win in the end, and they all had to die. He convinced Eddy the rhyme was real. Eddy began to rant about there being seven.'

At Ashley's disgusted tut, Bob frowned.

'I know, but I've often had no friends at all. No one who'd let me in their house, anyway. For a while, I felt like I belonged somewhere.'

Hector took over.

'We haven't located the paint.'

'It's probably in the big shed at Keith's dad's old allotment, along with his stash of drugs. Keith let Eddy store some of Peter's old gym weights inside it. Keith kept a big fisherman's raincoat in there. He said he occasionally walked through town wearing it when the nights were dark and misty. Keith was always a bit twisted. It didn't seem as obvious when we were kids, but he basically had no morals. He was scared, though, whenever Peter came to visit. I was too. I've never seen anyone so on the edge as him. What's that phrase? Having a face like murder. Well, he sure did.'

'Where's the allotment?' asked Ashley.

'Sheringham.'

'What else do you know?' asked Hector.

'Jesus. I wish I'd walked home now. I'll tell you one last thing if you drop me at my old place.'

'We can do that, although I'm not certain you'll be able to get in.'

Hector put the car in gear. Ashley watched Bob turn around and stare back at the house in the rear-view window as they pulled away. He slumped back in his seat with a confused expression.

'Am I really going to be rich?'

'Yep. Now, what's that one last thing?'

'I think Peter was genuine about helping people. I reckon he worked hard to be a good policeman, as if it would right the wrongs he did as a teenager. He visited Eddy, you know?'

'Yes, but mostly because he was worried Eddy would remember what happened at the party,' said Ashley.

'No, they liked each other. I saw Eddy in town after he got out, and he said Peter's visits kept him going. It was great to see his progress when he first arrived, but I also saw him begin to struggle. He became obsessive about working out. I'd find him doing press-ups in the garden of the place where I slept. Peter also had a gym that he let him use. He even bought new equipment, but Eddy was steadily getting confused about who he was and what he was doing here.'

Bob was clearly dragging something from the recesses of his memory.

'What is it, Bob?' she asked.

'I remember bumping into Peter and Eddy together at the cliff edge not far from my shed. Eddy was yelling at the sea and Peter was shouting at him, pleading for him to calm down. I like to think that Peter thought if he could have saved Eddy, he could have saved himself. But he couldn't.'

Bob undid his seat belt and leaned forward between the two front seats.

'Here will do.'

Hector pulled into a parking space next to the cricket pitch.

'Bob,' said Ashley. 'Please come in and do a recorded statement. We need it all on file.'

'When do I get my inheritance?'

'God knows. The solicitor dealing with it is Hansells in town. I'm sure they'll be happy to advise you.'

Bob dropped back into his seat. He gave them a black-toothed smile.

'Maybe they'll give me an advance and I'll buy a nice little caravan at the seafront. I'll give you a statement there. My new teeth will have arrived from the prison by then. I'll put the kettle on.'

Ashley and Hector couldn't help smiling as Bob left the car.

He walked down the road, then punched the air.

78

Hector indicated right and pulled out into the traffic.

'Back to base? I'll let you tell Bob's story to Kettle,' said Ashley.

'Very kind.'

'Do you believe what he said?'

'It's plausible and a better explanation than the sea wanting them back. You know what's hard to believe?'

'What?'

'How the hell couldn't we find a madman running around town when there were so many of them?'

Ashley chuckled.

'Strange how Bob still thinks of Peter in friendly terms when he's killed all those people.'

'Yep, but Peter kind of looked out for them all this time, and he helped that guy's widow. Sal rang her. She said Peter often visited on his bicycle. Makes me wonder if he visited Candy as well.'

'Her mum or Elliott would probably know.'

Ashley slid her phone out of her pocket, then returned it.

'Actually, let's drive over. It's only ten minutes. I like to see the whites of their eyes!'

The traffic was heavy with holidaymakers, so it was twenty minutes later when they arrived at the house. Ashley went to knock, but nobody came to the door. She got back into the car. Hector was about to pull away when his phone rang. His lip curled when he pulled it out and saw the incoming number.

'Mother!' he said, although he still answered it with a cheery hello.

Ashley glanced out of the windscreen and spotted Mrs Sweet walking up the road with her grandson. Timmy was chattering animatedly, and Ashley could see the evident love and pride on his grandmother's face as she looked down at him.

Mrs Sweet had come in for a statement, but all she gave them was that she went there to shout at Keith. When she arrived, Keith had just been stabbed by Peter. She panicked and ran away. That was when

Ashley and Hector arrived. With all the goings on yesterday, nobody had chance to question her in further detail.

Ashley waited until they were close to the car before she got out. When she did, the boy noticed her straight away and waved but Mrs Sweet's face was very different. For half a second, it was as though Keith's ghost had appeared in front of her. Mrs Sweet recovered fast. She gave Timmy the door key and shooed him towards the house.

Mrs Sweet waited until he was inside before she turned back to Ashley. She opened her mouth, then closed it. She wrung her hands.

'I've just been speaking to Robert Redding,' said Ashley. 'AKA Homeless Bob. We've released him.'

'Oh.'

'No comment on what a bad person he is?'

She shook her head. 'Perhaps everyone deserves a second chance.'

Mrs Sweet smiled, but it was more of a grimace.

'Did you know if Candy ever met with a Peter Ibson over the years?'

'The name doesn't ring a bell.'

Ashley stared at Mrs Sweet. Ashley knew when she was being lied to. After all, Peter's name had been in the news about the case recently.

Mrs Sweet had also chosen to keep that damning photo of Foxy and Candy to herself all those years ago. If the police had seen it, they might have been more suspicious about Foxy's death.

The front door opened, and Timmy came running out of the house. He handed Ashley a sheet of paper.

'I drew this for you. It's a cop car.'

'That's excellent,' said Ashley. 'And it's not on fire.'

The lad beamed at her. Mrs Sweet put her arm around his shoulder and hugged him in close. Her eyes pleaded with Ashley.

Ashley pursed her lips.

'Cherish this young man.'

'With all my heart.'

Ashley held eye contact with her, then nodded and returned to the car. Hector had finished his call.

'All good?' he asked.

Ashley took a deep breath.

'Yes, I think so.'

Mrs Sweet and Timmy watched them as they drove away. Only the boy was still waving as they disappeared.

Ashley was pretty certain that if she went into Mrs Sweet's house and checked her kitchen drawer, she would be missing a serrated knife.

79

The next morning, Ashley pulled on her trainers and did a few stretches in the lounge. She opened the front door and stepped out into the chilly air. Dawn was coming, but it was still dark. She had time to see the sunrise.

Ashley began with a slow jog, but lifted her pace at the chalet park. She was up the hill in seconds and still breathing steadily. She felt good, which reassured her she'd made the right decision regarding Mrs Sweet. Maybe her suspicion had been wrong, but she doubted it. After all, Mrs Sweet said herself she'd kill him.

She ran past the house that for her would always be Bob's place, even though he only ever slept in the garden. She wondered if he was in there now, but there was a new door with a modern combination lock.

When she reached the bronze bust of the great Cromer coxswain, Henry Blogg, in front of the old watch-house, she stopped and rubbed his nose for luck. The nose was shiny, where thousands had done the same thing.

She jogged by the sunken garden and the white house, which, now CSI had finished gathering their evidence, had been returned to its former blank canvas. After shortening her stride down the gangway to the beach, she met Geoffrey on his way to his boat.

'Morning,' she said, stopping, but jogging on the spot. 'Are you okay?'

'Yes, have they found him yet?'

'Peter?'

'Who else?'

'Yes, the tide left him behind on Overstrand beach yesterday evening. Strange thing, though.'

'What?'

'His head had been eaten.'

Geoffrey's face fell. Then he gave her a gentle shove. 'Idiot.'

'I'm glad it's all over,' she said, chuckling.

'Me too, but it might do some good.'

'In what way?'

'People who come to Cromer will hear of the seven and that all hands were lost. They'll walk down the white steps, wander under the pier, and think of Eddy. They'll follow your pursuit of Peter past the beach huts and through the rock pools. They will gaze out across the waves where the others met their end and they'll remember.'

Geoffrey gave her a big grin.

'Then they'll go into town and buy my crab.'

Ashley laughed. 'It's a haunting tale. Perhaps the story will spread.'

'Aye. People should never underestimate the sea.'

Ashley nodded as she watched the gentle waves roll in. 'It's hard to imagine what happened down here on a calm day like today.'

'It's the way of things. It's the life we lead. The sea has always been a cruel mistress.' He walked past, then shouted back at her.

'And, eventually, she always gets what she wants.'

Ashley stopped jogging, but Geoffrey's long strides had taken him away down the beach. She looked to the horizon and saw the first edge of orange appear, so she raced along the promenade and entered Cromer pier. Her footsteps rattled on the boards as she headed to where Eddy had rolled her in.

She peered down from the railings. The sea had quietened, seemingly at peace. Ashley tried not to think that was because she had what she wanted.

When Ashley glanced back up, the sun was erupting like a volcano from the depths of the ocean. It rose into the sky. A hazy, shimmering ball of fire.

Ashley felt the first rays of heat on her face and raised her chin. There was comfort in knowing that some things in life were constant. With a nod to the memory of those who perished, she turned to go home.

Ashley strolled between the white pavilions at the centre of the pier, stopping to admire the magnificent and imposing façade of the Hotel de Paris, which dominated the skyline. The medieval tower of the church of St Peter and St Paul soared behind it. Invigorated, she raced out of the pier entrance and along the promenade to the gangway, past the RNLI museum and the path down from North Park.

At the beach huts, her muscles burned, but it was a good pain. As she reached the hut that was a charred ruin, she considered the man responsible. Yes, Peter probably killed Foxy, but he was out of his mind on an overdose that Keith had given him.

It seemed Peter convicted himself of the murder anyway, then spent his life trying to do the impos-

ROSS GREENWOOD

sible and make up for it, until he couldn't take it any more.

Perhaps he was an unlucky man, whom fate turned bad. As a police officer, he served the public well for thirty years. He even took the blame for Keith's death. But nobody would remember him for that. Peter would get his wish. He was part of the legend, but only for the evil monster he became.

He would be forever infamous, for death on Cromer beach.

Ashley dropped onto the stones and glanced across at the Banksy artwork. She slid to a stop on the shingle, her eyes wide. A seagull floated in the gentle breeze above as though it were a final witness to the tragic events that had occurred. It released a plaintive cry, then soared away to the heavens.

Next to the drawings on the sea wall, huge in black, was written the number seven.

The paint was still dripping wet.

AUTHOR'S NOTE

Thanks for reading *Death on Cromer Beach*. I'd written a detective series set in Peterborough and found myself coming to a natural end after six novels, so I spent a few days at my parents' chalet on the Kings Chalet Park in Cromer wondering what to do next. I'd just finished a prison novel, so I decided to do another detective book.

DI Barton is the main man in the other books and he's remarkable in the genre for being unremarkable. He is a decent married man who likes a joke, looks after his team, makes mistakes and struggles with work-life balance. The drama, tension and excitement are around the murders.

I fancied doing something almost the opposite,

but I wanted to keep it realistic. Ashley doesn't have the support many of us have within our family units or friendship circles, but she's not alone. Many people come home to quiet houses after work and find themselves at loose ends during the weekends, so I wanted to focus on that in the background. Hopefully Ashley and the others in the story will be able to pull themselves out of their ruts as the series progresses.

Cromer is a brilliant place to set a story like this. I've been on holiday in the area for forty years. I find the town incredibly peaceful and the people friendly. The sunrises, vista and architecture are so stunning they can make professional photographers out of all of us, even if you're only using the camera on your phone.

For me, every street holds memories. Hopefully you'll pay Cromer a visit and see what it's all about. Maybe you can get an ice cream at Windows and wander down to the pier and see the guys at the museum. Perhaps you can try one of Geoffrey's crabs.

You can pre-order the next in the series, *Death in Paradise*, and follow Ashley and team to Hunstanton where it's not just the sunsets that are killers.

ACKNOWLEDGMENTS

As always, it takes a lot of people to get a book to market, and each layer adds more gloss. This was a complicated old plot, set over many years, so it's been a real labour of love for all involved. So thank you to my editors, Sarah and Sue, and to my proofreader, Shirley. Well done.

My beta team and early reviewers also do a wonderful job, so a big shout out to them as well. And of course, you readers, whose kind reviews keep me going.

Finally, a round of applause to the companies who were so supportive of my idea and enthusiastically gave me permission to mention them by name. Hopefully, when you next go to the area, you'll drop into those businesses and say hello.

Perhaps it's time for another visit, so Cromer can welcome you home.

MORE FROM ROSS GREENWOOD

We hope you enjoyed reading *Death On Cromer Beach*. If you did, please leave a review.

If you'd like to gift a copy, this book is also available as an ebook, large print, hardback, digital audio download and audiobook CD.

Explore the bestselling DI Barton series another exciting series from Ross Greenwood.

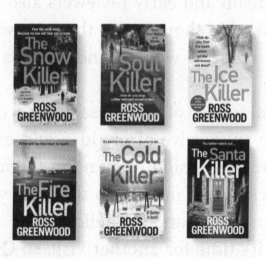

ABOUT THE AUTHOR

Ross Greenwood is the bestselling author of over ten crime thrillers. Before becoming a full-time writer he was most recently a prison officer and so worked everyday with murderers, rapists and thieves for four years. He lives in Peterborough.

Follow Ross on social media:

twitter.com/greenwoodross

facebook.com/RossGreenwoodAuthor

bookbub.com/authors/ross-greenwood

instagram.com/rossg555

THE *Murder* LIST

THE MURDER LIST IS A NEWSLETTER DEDICATED TO ALL THINGS CRIME AND THRILLER FICTION!

SIGN UP TO MAKE SURE YOU'RE ON OUR HIT LIST FOR GRIPPING PAGE-TURNERS AND HEARTSTOPPING READS.

SIGN UP TO OUR NEWSLETTER

BIT.LY/THEMURDERLISTNEWS

Boldw**oo**d

Boldwood Books is an award-winning fiction publishing company seeking out the best stories from around the world.

Find out more at www.boldwoodbooks.com

Join our reader community for brilliant books, competitions and offers!

**Follow us
@BoldwoodBooks
@BookandTonic**

Sign up to our weekly deals newsletter

https://bit.ly/BoldwoodBNewsletter